I0641587

THE MASKED RIDER ARCHIVES
VOLUME 2

MASKED RIDER

ARCHIVES VOLUME 2

RIDER

FEATURING
EL VIBORITO
BY JAY J. KALEZ
PLUS
BAD MEN OF THE CAYUGAS
BY GEORGE A. STARBIRD
AND
THE VALLEY OF CRUCIFIXION
BY LINCOLN HOFFMAN

ALTUS PRESS • 2015

© 2015 Altus Press • First Edition—2015

EDITED AND DESIGNED BY
Matthew Moring

PUBLISHING HISTORY
"El Viborito" originally appeared in the November 1934 issue of *The Masked Rider Western Magazine* (Volume 1, Number 4).

"Bad Men of the Cayugas" originally appeared in the February 1935 issue of *The Masked Rider Western Magazine* (Volume 2, Number 1).

"The Valley of Crucifixion" originally appeared in the January 1936 issue of *The Masked Rider Western Magazine* (Volume 2, Number 2).

THANKS TO
Tom Johnson, Ray Riethmeier and Randy Vanderbeek

ALL RIGHTS RESERVED
No part of this book may be reproduced or utilized in any form or by any means, electronic or mechanical, without permission in writing from the publisher.

This edition has been marked via subtle changes, so anyone who reprints from this collection is committing a violation of copyright.

Visit altuspress.com for more books like this.

Printed in the United States of America.

TABLE OF

CONTENTS

* "The Valley of Crucifixion" was credited to "Orrin Hollmer,"
but this was actually written by Lincoln Hoffman.

EL VIBORITO

JAY J. KALEZ

THE LONE RIDER

T HE GOLDEN GLOW of a desert sunset was rapidly dulling with the creeping stain of night. Solemn and stately, towering pinnacles of rugged rock poked up from the desert floor to hover above the shallow arroyos that marked the badlands' border, foreboding and threateningly. Faintly, the distant bawl of milling cattle echoed up over the rim of a deep, wide coulee that slashed the desert's smoothness like an ugly scar. All else was still. The hush of the desert night was descending.

Suddenly, a shapeless mass in against a clumsy outcropping of scab-rock upon the coulee rim, took form. A lone rider urged his horse a step nearer the coulee edge. Horse and rider stared down. Down into the coulee bottom from whence came the echoing moan that alone marred the desert quiet.

A weird figure, this lone rider that poised atop a matchless stallion, black as the night itself. A startling figure. A black *mantilla* flowed from his straight shoulders to drape about his tall form from throat to toes. A black sombrero sat atop his head with beneath it, marred only by two gaping eye-slits, a black hood, long and flowing, to meet the wrap of the *mantilla* about his shoulders.

Now, as the black-masked rider stared down, his eyes seemed to smolder and suddenly blaze behind the gaping eye-slits of his shielding hood. It was all as Blue Hawk had said. Greed had maddened the cattlemen of the desert border. Across the border to his mountain retreat, Blue Hawk had brought him word of the sudden havoc the hand of man had stirred amid the badland brakes, where, as a youngster, he had first scrumbled to the captivating spell of the desert's grandeur. Now he was seeing it with his own eyes. Had been seeing it since first his trail swung into the badland's border. Dying cattle, thousands of them. Thirst-maddened critters, milling until they dropped. Milling helplessly, bawling piteously, with ever before them the torture of brimming waterholes. Waterholes, secure and impossible behind crude barricades of brush and rock. It was as the Mexican Indian, Blue Hawk had said, the devil had whispered into the ears of white men of the desert border.

For minutes The Masked Rider stood surveying the gruesome

scene below. Then suddenly, he seemed to lean forward in his saddle. His one hand raised to hood his eyes as he peered down. Below him a single rider had appeared as if from nowhere and

was now worming his mount through the milling herd. The Masked Rider marked his course. It led straight towards the barricaded waterhole in the center of the coulee bottom.

As The Masked Rider watched, a faint smile toyed at his hood-covered lips. Below, the lone rider had dismounted and was now tearing the barricade of brush and rock from about the glistening pool of the waterhole. The smile widened to a grin. The Masked Rider saw the man in the coulee bottom below had no intention of replacing the barrier once he had watered his own mount. The grin deepened to a low chuckle.

FOR HOURS HE had been trailing that single rider below. Trailing him as an enemy. Now, he was glad he had read the trail signs wrong. Here was a man after his own heart. A man who loved the desert badland for itself. People might brand The Masked Rider for an outlaw and place a price upon his head, dead or alive. They might speak of him as a myth, a ghoul of the night. They might call him a killer, merciless, fearless. But, never could they brand his deeds those of greed. Justice was his creed. A queer, man-spoken justice, but justice. It alone was dictator to The Masked Rider's conscience. It alone urged him on, just as sight of those suffering cattle below was urging the lone man in the coulee bottom to defy the rights of fence and ownership.

The Masked Rider eased back in his saddle. Hours before, he had sent his faithful Mexican Indian liegeman, Blue Hawk, on along the trail to the border town of Los Comino so that he might follow alone the tracks of the single rider who had traveled from waterhole to waterhole as if his purpose was a count of the bloated carcasses that bore silent witness to their impregnable barricade. Now, he realized some other purpose must be behind the strange cross-range trail of the man below. Some purpose, humane as the act he had now performed.

The Masked Rider lifted one hand as if to raise the black hood from about his face. The hand lashed down with the invisible speed of a snake's strike. It gripped the ivory butt of a six-gun at his hip. From somewhere across the coulee rim a shot had echoed. Now, the echo rumbled, identifying it as a rifle shot.

The Masked Rider searched the opposite rim. A faint puff of smoke spurted out from amongst the rocks almost straight across the rim from him. It pointed down. The Masked Rider dropped his stare to the coulee bottom. He stiffened. There, alongside the waterhole in the coulee bottom, the lone rider of a minute before was staggering weakly towards his mount. Now, with the second shot, he dropped and lay still.

A protesting rage flamed within The Masked Rider. His eyes blazed as he glared across to the coulee's opposite rim. A head and shoulder was just lifting above a scab-rock ledge. Before they had lifted hip-high, The Masked Rider had jerked his rifle from its saddle scabbard and flung it to his shoulder. The rifle roared once. Across the coulee, the head and shoulders above the scab-rock ledge swayed an instant, then toppled forward.

With the dying echo of his shot, The Masked Rider touched spurs to his anxious stallion and went plunging down the steep, narrow trail that led to the coulee bottom. Like a black falcon of the desert he descended. The black folds of his *mantilla* whipped out from his shoulders, wing-like. The rumbling clatter of trail rocks seemed to chant a warning to his passing. Justice; in that instant he had dealt it out as he had seen fit. Now to succor the one for whom he had judged. Across the coulee bottom towards the waterhole, horse and rider raced.

Already, the thirst-crazed cattle were surging through the barricade break and crowding about the waterhole. Immune from their danger, The Masked Rider pushed through their center to the spot just inside the barricade where, beside his horse, lay the sprawled body of the man he had witnessed shot down a minute before.

THE MAN LAY face down. Dismounting, The Masked Rider hurriedly knelt alongside him. Gently, he turned him upon his back. A curse breathed past The Masked Rider's lips as he stared down at the blood-covered face. Evidently, the first bullet of the killer upon the opposite coulee rim had spattered upon the rocks about the waterhole and rained lead into the face of the man drinking there. Blood from a dozen face-wounds blinded his eyes. It was the second shot, however, that had taken toll. A great, awkward smear of blood was staining the wounded one's shirt front. Each breath wheezed through his throat like the rattle of buckshot upon canvas. The man was dying. Dying, yet realizing in death that the hand now gently raising him was the hand of a friend.

The Masked Rider raised the dying man's shoulders even higher. Bubbles of blood formed at his lips as he attempted to speak. The Masked Rider allowed his arm to circle the dying man's shoulder the more. His fingers touched something cold and metallic, pinned beneath the blood-soaked vest. He glanced down. Understanding of the strange trail the dying man had led him upon that day leaped to the phantom in black. The dying man wore the badge of a Texas Ranger.

"Thanks, stranger," the blood-painted lips mumbled as The Masked Rider eased the dying man's head forward. He made no effort to open his closed eyes. "Reckon… reckon those bawlin' critters 'll be a might more peaceful-like now. You… you from these parts?"

The dying man's voice was fading. The Masked Rider bent low to hear. "No, ranger," The Black Caballero answered, an unbelievable kindness in his voice. " 'Spect, stranger suits me best for these parts."

The Masked Rider felt the head pillowed against his arm attempt to nod in understanding. The ranger was struggling to force more words from his throat. "If… if you happen to pass Los Comino way," the dying man managed, "I'd be obliged if you'd… you'd see Judge Mann there and… and jest… jest tell

him facts. Reckon… reckon that sign yonder 'll explain. Me…
me… I'm… I'm…."

The dying ranger jerked in a sudden convulsion. His face
twisted with pain. He seemed to grip himself to say more.
"Tell… tell the judge," he forced through his pressed lips. "Tell
the judge that… that… El Viborito is… is…."

The ranger's head dropped limply back against The Masked
Rider's supporting arm. His chest sank. The Masked Rider
pressed his face close for one more possible word. It never came.
The ranger was dead.

Gently, the figure in black lay the body back upon the sand.
The gasping words of the dying man still hummed in his ears.
Judge Mann… El Viborito… what had the dying ranger been
struggling to say?

The Masked Rider straightened to his feet. He glanced away
from the waterhole to where the ranger had ripped aside the
barricading fence of rock and brush. A weathered piece of board
caught his eye. A protruding nail showed where it had once
been made fast to the barricade's side. But a single mark appeared upon its surface. The mark of a running iron traced across
the center of the board in a wavy line.

THE MASKED RIDER walked to the barricade and picked the
board up from the ground. It must be the sign the dead ranger
had mentioned as capable of explaining. The Masked Rider
puzzled as he stared. What could that burned brand upon the
piece of weathered board explain? What could that wavy line
mean? Like something out of the past, a dim voice within The
Masked Rider called the answer. Called it in the same droning
chant he had heard a thousand times about the loading chutes.
El Viborito… the Little Snake… that is the way that brand
would have been called by a brand inspector. That wavy line
was the brand of the man that had thrown that barricade about
the waterhole. He remembered now having seen it at other
similar barricades. El Viborito was a person. A living person.

The ranger had struggled to name his identity when death had sealed his lips.

In a surge of anger, The Masked Rider hurled the crude sign back into the barricade. His sudden vent of rage was as an urge of fate. With the bend of his body forward, something whined past his ear. A milling steer, ten feet beyond, bellowed once and dropped to its knees. In the wake of that bellow, a rifle cracked, high up on the coulee rim. Another barked. Then another. Their lead hissed as The Masked Rider dropped behind the barricade.

For a minute the firing from above ceased. The night's shadows were already thickening fast in the coulee bottom. High up on the coulee rim, however, the sky still held the ghastly paleness of the dying day. The Masked Rider squirmed a dozen feet along the barricade and cautiously peered up. Outlined against the sky above the coulee rim, at the very spot where he himself had halted to stare down upon the milling herd below, stood three horsemen. Now, as The Masked Rider still failed to show himself again, they wheeled their mounts and started down the steep trail leading to the coulee bottom.

From behind the barricade, the black-draped figure watched. There was no fear in his steady stare. It was a flash of anxiety that caused him to glance towards the spot where his black stallion, head high, ears pointed, watched the three horsemen start their descent into the coulee bottom. Perhaps those three men were friends of the dead ranger lying behind him. Perhaps they had heard those shots from the rim and riding forward on his trail, had viewed the dying man in his arms as a victim of his own gun. The Masked Rider did not make war upon the innocent. His guns, he had vowed, were only for those of proven guilt. On the trio descending into the coulee he could not pass judgment—yet.

The Masked Rider made his decision quickly. A low whistle from his lips and his stallion dragged the reins of its bridle to his finger tips. Still crouched behind the barricade, The Black Caballero waited until the trio upon the coulee trail had reached the most treacherous point. Then, leaping from the ground, he swung into the saddle and wheeling his mount, sent it racing through the opening in the barricade.

The black stallion seemed to fly through the gathering gloom. The black *mantilla* about The Masked Rider's shoulders blended man and horse as one. Straight across, towards the opposite coulee wall, The Masked Rider headed. From his stand upon the rim minutes before, he had sighted the steep trail ascending the coulee side to the opposite rim.

The cloaked rider was well away from the waterhole barricade before the trio of riders descending into the bottom sighted him. Instantly their lead began to sing about The Masked Rider's head. He did not answer the fire. Bending low in his saddle as he raced across the bottom, he only searched the black wall ahead for the ascending trail. Suddenly, it loomed in a sharp twist about a screening wing of rock. The black stallion no longer needed a guilding rein.

WITH A PLUNGE behind the wing of rock, the firing across the coulee bottom ceased. The Masked Rider swung up the steep ascending trail. A minute and the bottom loomed dimly through the curtain of dusk. The three riders had halted at the waterhole. One had dismounted and now crouched above the sprawled body of the ranger. When again he climbed to his horse, The Masked Rider was almost at the coulee rim. A glance told him the riders below were not abandoning his trail. His black *mantilla* making himself and mount invisible against the black shadows of the coulee wall, The Masked Rider drew reins and waited until the trailing trio were almost at the entrance of the ascending trail. Then, screened from view by the tall wing of rock, he touched spurs and urged his mount to the rim.

At the coulee edge the trail leveled off to twist crazily along its edge. A dozen paces and the black stallion suddenly snorted and leaped to the side. The Masked Rider's gun hand dropped.

His body bent forward. In the trail ahead stood a lone, riderless horse.

For only an instant did The Masked Rider poise alert. Even in the thick dust about the rock-fenced trail, The Black Caballero's eyes had swept about for sight of an ambusher's gun. The sprawled form across a shelf of rock twenty feet away answered for the riderless horse alongside the trail. The animal was the mount of the man his own rifle had accounted for from the opposite coulee rim—the man who had shot down the ranger as he hurled back the barricade about the waterhole.

There was no time for even a glance for the identity of the dead man upon the rock shelf. Already the scraping dig of climbing horse hoofs sounded on the trail below him. The trio below were pushing their mounts hard. A minute and they would be at the rim. The dead man upon the rock shelf and the riderless horse alongside the trail would undoubtedly delay them for a time. The Masked Rider intended making the most of that delay.

As he swung by the riderless horse the animal turned to follow. For an instant a sprawled brand upon its hip showed plain even in the fog-like dusk. A sprawled "S" tilted and flared at the peak. The brand printed itself in The Masked Rider's mind. He had picked up his second trail-sign of who his badland enemies might be. The first was the brand of The Little Snake. The second a Lazy S brand, not unlike the first, save that it stood erect. Both marked killers; one of dumb cattle, one of men.

The black stallion beneath the outlaw rider had been dancing nervously, impatiently. He gave the animal its head. In place of a lunge forward, the animal still danced. The Masked Rider caught the anxious point of its ears. They pointed ahead. Somewhere before them was danger. The understanding animal beneath him sensed it.

An instant The Masked Rider listened. Suddenly, faintly above the clatter of rolling trail-rock from below him, he caught the protesting snort of a horse against its binding saddle cinch. It came from somewhere beyond the blinding screen of rock ahead. Now, he caught the clatter of hoofs upon hard-packed earth. Many hoofs. It was more than one horseman swinging up the winding trail along the coulee rim.

With a touch of spurs The Masked Rider wheeled his mount at right angles to the trail. The black stallion leaped ahead, picking its path with the sure-footedness of a mountain cat. In through the tangle of pinnacle rocks it pushed. The blackness of the hooding shadows swallowed both horse and rider. Swallowed, but not with distance. Behind him, The Masked Rider heard plainly the shouts of riders as the trio from the coulee bottom met the advancing party of riders from up the trail, almost at the spot where he had turned off.

FOR A MOMENT, the fugitive thought himself safe from pursuit. A blast of signaling shots from the riders at the coulee edge told him different. More of the party must be scattered about. They were signaling to each other. As he halted for an instant he could even hear the sound of riders close behind him. They were fanning out in a netlike fashion to close in about him. The Masked Rider smiled beneath his hood as gently he patted the neck of the animal beneath him. In pursuit he had no fear. No horse had yet matched the speed and trail-sureness of the black stallion he rode.

The Masked Rider touched spurs. The stallion bounded ahead. The Masked Rider allowed the animal to choose its own course. Twisting, leaping, lunging, the stallion plunged through the now thick darkness. Time passed. The sounds of pursuit from behind him faded. The rough, broken trail of the badlands grew smooth. The towering shafts of rugged scab-rock grew fewer. He was breaking out upon the mesa which, like a huge elevated platform of earth, stretched from the badlands to the border.

Suddenly the stallion slowed its pace. The Masked Rider peered into the blackness. He had come to the flaring mouth of a shallow canyon. The badlands seemed to halt at its entrance. A rolling lift of land stretched in the opposite direction.

The Masked Rider halted. His head lifted to stare up at the star-spangled skies above. A round full moon was just poking its crest up over the distant hills. The rider grasped his directions. The rolling lift of land led towards the Rio Grande and the Mexican border. It could not be many miles away. The canyon ran west and north. West and north was the direction of Los Comino. He had learned much in the past hour. Perhaps at Los Comino he would learn more. Perhaps the Judge Mann the dying ranger had mentioned could tell him more. Could tell him who this El Viborito was that signed himself with The Little Snake brand. Could tell him what outfit the Lazy S was that stationed its killers about the coulee rims. In Los Comino he might learn towards whom he must direct his hand of man-justice. Blue Hawk should have gathered in some information as well. He had already seen enough to know the Mexican Indian had spoken only truth. The devil had whispered into the ears of the white cattlemen of the badlands. The swift man-justice of The Masked Rider's gun hand was needed. He had not traveled the desert in vain.

CHAPTER II

THE SIGN OF EL VIBORITO

THE MASKED RIDER had paused close in against the canyon wall while he mused with his thoughts and allowed his stallion to gather its wind. Now, suddenly, he became conscious of a crimson glow creeping high in the sky, somewhere beyond the canyon rim. As he watched, he appraised the cause of the flickering sky-sign. Leaping flame tongues… somewhere a few miles up the canyon and to the west a heated fire of some sort was painting the night in a silent alarm.

The Masked Rider gathered his reins and stirred in his saddle. An ominous sign—that sky glow. It came from the direction of Los Comino. Could something have happened? In the little cowtown huddled amid the desert dryness? The thought commanded attention. The Masked Rider lifted his spurs, held them poised. He sat motionless in his saddle, body slightly bent. From somewhere far down the canyon came a symphony of pounding hoofs. Riders, many of them, racing with all the speed of the mounts beneath them. The Masked Rider backed deeper into the impregnable blackness against the canyon wall as he listened to the galloping rumble mount to a roar.

A hundred yards from where he stood, the canyon trail swung sharply to the right and on up the sloping rise beyond. There, it seemed to dissolve in the yellow glow of the full-faced moon just vaulting the false horizon. The crescendo of pounding hoofs now thundered. The band of racing horsemen were almost at the swing in the trail. The Masked Rider appraised their number. There must be twenty riders in the band at least, he figured.

Suddenly, in mass, the band swung into the trail-turn. The yellow moonlight flooded across them. The features of The Masked Rider hardened beneath his black hood as he caught sight of the sea of wide-rimmed sombreros and flying *mantillas*. Mexicans... the entire band seemed to be made up of picturesquely clad vaqueros from across the border. Drift of their urging shouts made him certain.

The outlaw watched the band dash up the sloping trail. His mind groped for an answer to their purpose. Why should this band of Mexican riders even be across the line? Why were they racing their mounts at so killing a speed back for their protective boundary? That ominous flame-glow in the sky far up their back-trail, seemed to scream with an answering suspicion.

The Masked Rider had barely grasped of that suspicion when involuntarily he stiffened in his saddle. The racing band had swung full into the trail-turn and now for a moment rode parallel to the sloping rise beyond. Their forms shaped leaping silhouettes against the moonlight. A single rider led the band. A slim, straight-shouldered rider who rode with the grace of one born to the saddle. Not that grace alone had caught The Masked Rider's eye. It was the whipping toss of flying hair, fanning out over poised shoulders that held him. The leader of that band was a girl. A young girl. The proud tilt of her head bespoke youth and courage.

A QUEER WONDERING puzzled The Masked Rider. From his invisible shelter against the canyon shadows, he watched the band of riders top the crest of the slope beyond and disappear. Sight of the flame-glow painting the skies to the west seemed still to accuse. Allowing a few minutes to make sure there was no one in pursuit of the band, he touched spurs and headed up the black canyon. Ahead, the dancing sky glow was his beacon.

The canyon trail was easy to follow. Easy also, the tracks of the band that had just traveled it. The black stallion pounded out distance with the speed of the wind. One mile… two miles… suddenly the trail turned and shot across the canyon. At the canyon wall it seemed to push into a narrow gulch that sloped up towards the rim above. The Masked Rider paused a moment to make sure the band he tracked had taken the trail-turn. Satisfied, he urged his mount up the sloping gulch. Above, the sky glow was brightening.

The black stallion had traveled the best part of a mile when abruptly the trail broke out over the canyon rim. The Masked Rider drew reins. He knew now his suspicions of that sky glow had been right. But a few hundred yards beyond him flamed the cause, the smoldering ruins of a ranch house and corrals. Beyond it, still licking at the night with its lashing red tongues, were two burning haystacks. An outfit had been burned out completely.

The Masked Rider cursed beneath his breath as in the flame-light of the burning stacks he read plainly the tracks that swung down from the rim into the canyon below. That band of Mexicans, led by a slip of a girl, had traveled this way. Had passed this spot. Why had they not halted to offer aid? Why had they been racing away instead of towards this scene of havoc? The Masked Rider was not one to guess at reason. He passed judgment only on facts.

Silently, The Black Caballero advanced through an open gate into the yard before the smoldering ruins of what had once been a fair-sized ranch house. The flames of the burning hay stacks painted the night plain. There was not a sign of life about. Not a sign of man or animal. It was as if destruction had swept clean.

Suddenly the black stallion snorted and shied to the side. A shapeless heap lay alongside what had once been the base of a windmill. The Masked Rider leaned forward in his saddle and peered down. It was a body. The body of a woman, clothed in a dark dress. Alongside her, lay two other still forms. The bodies of two men.

The Masked Rider swung from his horse and stepped across the scattered ruins to examine closer. Something inside him seemed to gnaw, then burst as he peered down. Blood smeared the clothing of the dead trio, even the woman. They had been shot to death. Murdered. The gruesome evidence about the ruins was too plain to even question. The killers had made no effort to cover their deed.

For minutes The Masked Rider stood straight and silent, benumbed by the scene of death and destruction. Within him a strange voice kept shouting a denial to the accusing scream of the evidence before his eyes. This could not be the work of the girl-led band of Mexicans whose trail swung down the gulch beyond. No girl, girl or woman, could have been guilty of such cold-blooded murder. The dead victims had been given no chance to defend themselves. Had made no effort to fight.

The signs about showed they had been huddled against the windmill base and there slaughtered. Slaughtered like....

The Masked Rider paused in the rage of his thoughts. A sudden tongue of flame had leaped high. Against the piled rock at the windmill base a piece of board had loomed for an instant. The Masked Rider stepped close. He picked up the square of wood and raised it to the flame glow from beyond. His fingers clenched as his eyes fastened upon the marking across the face of the board. A single, black, wavy line. The brand of The Little Snake. It was identical to the sign he had picked up back at the canyon waterhole. El Viborito had left his mark. Signed for his deed. Boasted of his fiendish slaughter.

His HANDS TREMBLING with the scorching rage within him, The Masked Rider turned towards his mount. A step and he stopped short. A six-gun appeared in his hand as if by magic. He half crouched. Even in the flame-light, the black *mantilla* about his shoulders dissolved him into a nothingness against the ground.

For a minute The Masked Rider crouched so. Then slowly he straightened erect. That sound his alert ears had grasped above the flame crackle... it had come from somewhere beyond. Somewhere past the gruesome pile of bodies about the windmill base. It had spun him to action but now he knew it had been no warning. That sound had been a choking sob. A frightened sob. A plea.

Slowly The Black Caballero advanced. The flame-light outlined the ruins of a building ahead. Between it and the windmill base was a low watering trough. The Masked Rider was almost alongside it before his ears again caught the choking gasp. He halted and whirled. The sound came from the watering trough. He stepped closer. A wet, shaggy head appeared above the trough rim. The head of a wide-eyed, shivering child. A youngster. A sobbing bit of a girl of four or five.

At sight of The Masked Rider the child again began to sob

in hysterical fright. The outlaw became conscious of his hooded face and black-garbed body. An instant he thought of unmasking. The sobbing babble of the child held him. With her mince of words he caught the name, El Viborito, spoken in choking horror. He understood. To unmask was useless. The child believed him to be the killer, El Viborito.

"I'm not El Viborito. Don't be afraid of me, little girl," The Masked Rider said, a plea of kindness in his voice. "I've come to take you on to town. I'm not going to hurt you."

The child still cringed and sobbed as she crouched inside the watering trough. The Masked Rider swallowed at the choke in his throat.

"Look, little girl," he suddenly managed to continue. "If my horse isn't afraid of me, you don't have to be afraid of me, do you? Watch now."

The Masked Rider gave a low whistle. Instantly, the black stallion still beside the windmill ruins, tossed his head and dragging the reins of his bridle, advanced to the watering trough's very edge. The mask of fear seemed to leave the child's face. Her sob went silent. The stallion pushed its nose out to the edge of the watering trough. The Masked Rider watched confidence creep into the little girl's eyes.

"See. He's not afraid of me," The Masked Rider coaxed. "Now you let me take you in my arms and we'll get up on my horse and ride to town. Will you?"

A moment the child only stared. "Will... will you take me to Uncle Joe's when... when we get there?" the child finally spoke. "Will mamma come... come with us?"

The Masked Rider swallowed the lump in his throat. "Mamma may come later," he answered slowly. "We'll go right straight to Uncle Joe's though, fast as we can ride."

The child lifted itself weakly from the watering trough. Its body shivered with the chill of its wet clothing. The Masked Rider gathered the shaking form in his arms and folded his black *mantilla* tightly about it. With the child thus wrapped snugly, he mounted the black stallion. He dared not look back as he swung the animal through the open gate. Something far worse than hate now burned within him. But one purpose consumed him. Not the devil had visited the badlands' border. A fiend had descended there. A fiend that tortured helpless cattle. That supported ruthless killers. That murdered helpless ranchers. That made war on children. That fiend was the slinking coward that signed himself with the brand of The Little Snake. El Viborito… God pity him when his hand of justice descended. He hoped the girl leader of that Mexican band from across the border was not a member of the ravaging killers.

THE AVENGING RAGE within the masked outlaw mounted even higher as with the warmth of his *mantilla,* the fear of the child in his arms thawed to confidence. From those innocent lips he learned the truth of what had happened at that ravaged ranch house. Learned how a band of masked horsemen had ridden through the ranch yard gate, herded the child's mother, father, and one hired hand into the open and there ruthlessly slaughtered them. With the echo of their murdering guns still in the air, they had then applied a torch to the buildings and haystacks. Learned how the little child, unseen by the killers as she made mud-pies alongside the watering trough, had escaped the slaughter. In the gathering dusk, the instinct of fear had saved her. With the charge of the raiding killers, she had hid behind the trough. With the scorching heat of the flames about, she had crawled into the trough for protection. She alone bore witness to El Viborito's deeds. Only of the deeds alone could she speak. No hopeful clue could she offer as to El Viborito himself. On through the hour's ride to Los Comino, The Masked Rider questioned in vain. The child could offer nothing, save with her growing confidence in The Masked Rider, to fan his avenging purpose the higher.

With sight of the lights of Los Comino, The Masked Rider

cautiously circled the town and approached from the rear of the double line of buildings that fenced its single street. The child had described her uncle's house well. Cherry trees in the back yard was her babyish landmark. Few trees marked any house in Los Comino. The outlaw rider was able to locate the place without risking a ride through the single street. The child identified the rear of the house at which he halted. Behind a shed inside the unfenced yard, the cloaked outlaw dismounted and, leaving the stallion well concealed amid the shed's shadows, crossed the yard to the back porch. A light burned inside.

Cautioning the child to remain quiet, The Masked Rider worked his way to one of the rear windows and peered in. A stern-faced man, his hair and beard tinged with gray, sat in a chair beside a kitchen stove. At a table opposite, a woman busied herself with a pan of dishes. Satisfied the two were the only ones in the house, The Masked Rider crossed to the door and knocked. He had swung his *mantilla* from about the child so she might be seen. With the swinging open of the door, The Masked Rider was inside and had clapped the door closed behind him before the two occupants of the room could recover from their startled amazement.

The Masked Rider's eyes focused on the gray-bearded man before the stove. His one hand rested upon the butt of the six-gun at his hip as a bid for peace in case the man in the chair should decide differently. The man in the chair only stared, his lips unconsciously curling into a sneer.

The child in The Masked Rider's arms had begun to squirm to be put down. Slowly, the outlaw lowered her to the floor. With open arms she ran to the seated man and began babbling her tale of horror. The eyes of the seated man seemed to flame as the childish lips mentioned the name, El Viborito. They lifted to blaze at The Masked Rider.

"What... what is Mary trying to tell me?" the seated man finally spoke, his voice cold and toneless. "Are you El Viborito?"

"IF I WERE El Viborito would I be coming to you with this child?" The Masked Rider snapped back, a scarred challenge in his voice. "Who I am makes no difference. What I am is for my own purpose. The child is trying to tell you her mother and father have been murdered, their home burned, their stock driven off, all by someone that calls himself El Viborito. I'm not El Viborito. I don't even know who El Viborito is, except that he's a killin' fiend that signs himself with the brand of The Little Snake. I came here to bring the child where she might have care and where I might learn more about this El Viborito. You can give me that information, or not give it to me. That's up to you. You can believe this though. Before I ride off this range, the snake signing himself by that brand, will be known. Known and made to pay for his killings or I never expect to see the sun top the rim of the badlands again. I've seen enough tonight to wish there'd never be another sunrise until I've satisfied my conscience."

The gray-haired man holding the child leaned slightly forward. "If you're here to trail down El Viborito, what are you doing masked?" he queried suspiciously. "Only El Viborito and his likes go masked in these parts."

The Masked Rider steeled himself for patience with the older man. "I'm asking questions, not answering them," he announced bluntly. "Who is this El Viborito?"

"I wish to God I knew," the gray-haired man before the stove ground out. "I'm not a cattleman. I run a blacksmith shop here in town. But I know what the cattlemen of this range have been through. A few more months of this and there won't be an outfit left this side of the Sawtooth Basin. El Viborito will have burned out or killed off every rancher and head of stock on it. This range is doomed."

"Doesn't anyone even suspect who he is?" the outlaw quizzed on. "Hasn't a posse ever taken to his trail?"

"No one has ever seen El Viborito or his band, except from a distance, and lived to tell about it," the man before the stove answered. "Some say he rides masked and alone. Some say he rides with a band. All I know is that for the past year almost, he has raided and killed on this range until, aside from Mel Craig's big spread over in the basin, there isn't a half-dozen independent outfits left on this range. Folks have their suspicions, yes. But their talk doesn't fit in with the man they mention. Jed Rawlins might have skipped across the border and tied up with a bunch of Mexicans after the law put its mark on him in these parts, but he'd never do a thing like... like you claimed you witnessed when you found little Mary, here. Jed was a hot-headed young fool, but... but he was no woman killer."

"And who is Jed Rawlins?" The Masked Rider shot at the sober-eyed man before him.

The gray-haired man lifted the little girl in his arms tighter. A minute he eyed the masked man before him. A trace of suspicion again mounted into his eyes. His bristled jaws set tight.

"Reckon you'd better talk to old Judge Mann about that," he spoke slowly. "I ain't sayin' I believe what you've told me or I don't believe things aren't none too healthy around here for people that talk too much. Judge Mann's one person that hasn't made any bones about declarin' himself. Reckon he can tell you all you want to know about Jed Rawlins, good and bad."

With mention of Judge Mann's name, The Masked Rider's mind flashed back to the dying ranger alongside the coulee waterhole. Judge Mann was the very person to whom the dying ranger had requested him to report the happenings in the coulee bottom. With a curt inquiry as to where the judge might be found, The Masked Rider prepared to leave. The man before the stove watched his every move as he backed to the door. Until now, the woman at the kitchen table had only stared in silence. Her eyes followed the outlaw on through the few steps of his retreat towards the door. A queer fire seemed to burn behind them. Then, as The Masked Rider opened the door at his back, the little girl in the arms of the man before the stove squirmed to the floor.

"GOOD-BYE, MISTER MAN," she called politely. "Thank you for bringing me to Uncle Joe's."

The Masked Rider waved a hip-high hand as he backed through the door and closed it before him. He did not see the sudden, sweeping change in the stare of the woman beside the table. Did not see her as she stepped before the gray-haired man and blocked his reach for a rifle hung from the kitchen wall. Did not hear her scolding voice as she continued to block the gray-haired one's path to the rifle.

"Leave him go, Joe," the woman before the gray-haired man commanded. "He might've fooled you and me with his talk but he couldn't've fooled little Mary. She saw it all and she trusts him. Reckon if she can do that, we can do as much till he proves he isn't worth trusting."

In the center of the kitchen, little Mary still stood, waving a limp hand towards the closed kitchen door through which The Masked Rider had just disappeared. From outside came a muffled clatter of prancing horse hoofs. Little Mary's face sobered.

"He was a nice man, wasn't he, Aunty Kate?" she spoke with childlike sincerity. "He won't let El Viborito hurt us, will he?"

CHAPTER III

THE MAN WITH THE SCARRED FACE

OLD JOE STRENTSTROM, the town's blacksmith at whose home The Masked Rider had left little Mary, had mentioned the Sun-dance Saloon as the most likely place to locate

Judge Mann at that time of evening. The Masked Rider had no intention of riding boldly to the saloon in his hood-garb to look for the judge. There were several things he wished to do before he met the judge. First, he wished to locate Blue Hawk and find out what information, if any, the Mexican Indian had picked up about town. Blue Hawk left him at sun-up that morning and should have had at least the whole day to wander about town with his ears open. Second, he wished to identify Judge Mann first so that he would make no mistake when he approached him as The Masked Rider and passed on the message given him by the dying ranger at the waterhole.

Riding a short distance back from town, The Masked Rider therefore halted, and dismounted, shed himself of his black *mantilla* and hood. These he folded neatly and, uncinching his saddle, placed them beneath the folds of his saddle blanket. This done, he again mounted and, circling the town wide, boldly entered Los Comino's single street. It was as Wayne Morgan, a drifting cowhand, that he leisurely walked his stallion into the entrance of the Star Stable. Ordering the animal fed and bedded for the night, he uncinched his own saddle and tossed it with his saddle blanket into a stall of straw, with the request he be allowed to return later and bed himself down in the hay loft above.

The request quickly granted, Wayne Morgan walked down the street, eyes alert for a sign of Blue Hawk. He had not far to go. A few doors past the stable, a bronze-faced, tall, straight-backed Indian, his tattered cotton clothes as ancient as the silver studded belt about his middle, stood in the shadows between two buildings. The soft chirp of a cricket had made his presence there no surprise to Wayne Morgan. Stooping over as if to straighten the roll of his trouser legs about his boots, he halted a few paces back from where Blue Hawk stood.

"What have you learned, *amigo?*" Wayne spoke, a glance about showing him there was no one within possible earshot.

"But little of proven truth, *señor,*" the Mexican Indian answered from the shadows. "I have walked with lifted ears like the feeding rabbit but those about me seem to fear for what their tongues may speak."

Wayne Morgan nodded in understanding. "Have you heard of one that does not hold such fear?" he asked. "A man who calls himself Judge Mann?"

"*Si, señor,* Blue Hawk answered quickly. "It is he alone that speaks his thoughts unafraid. You will find him at this moment in the place-of-food but a few steps away from where the white man fills his thirst. He now talks to a man that within this hour has ridden into town from the west. A man with the mark of a knife upon his cheek."

"Good, *amigo,*" Wayne answered. "Remain close to me but do not speak. You have told me right. The devil has whispered much in these parts."

"*Si, señor,*" the Indian answered. "I have heard as much again this day. This devil is called El Viborito."

Wayne straightened from his fumble with the boot top and proceeded on down the street. He was well away from the black opening between the two buildings before Blue Hawk emerged and followed.

THE SOUND OF boisterous shouting quickly located for Wayne the Sun-dance Saloon. Passing its crowded hitching post, Wayne paused at the entrance of the small restaurant a few doors farther on and peered in. The several customers in the place gave him the assurance he wished, not to be conspicuous. He entered the place and taking a table at the far end of the restaurant so that he might see all about him, he began looking over the bill-of-fare. Over the top of the bill-of-fare he allowed his eyes to search about. Two tables away, a broad-shouldered, thick-necked man with his back towards him was talking earnestly to a heavy jowled man facing him. Glimpse of a huge scar that ran from ear to mouth upon the heavy jowled one made Wayne sure the man with his back towards him was Judge Mann.

Wayne gave his order to the waitress and under pretext of reading the paper offered him, kept his eyes upon the pair. The Judge was doing most of the talking. The man with the scarred face seemed to be gathering in every word. They had long finished eating. Wayne himself was almost through with his meal when the scarfaced man arose and left the table. A minute later, Judge Mann followed. As he paid his check, Wayne had a good look at the judge's face. It was a stern, heavy-lined face with features that bespoke a man not afraid to declare himself.

Wayne watched the judge disappear through the door and then turned back to his meal. It was not until he arose to pay his check that he became aware of the sudden commotion that had arisen a few doors down the street. Men hurried by the restaurant door towards the Sun-dance Saloon. Going outside, Wayne saw that a great crowd was gathering at the hitching rack in front of the place. He hurried down the street with the others.

Moving in with the crowd, Wayne saw that the man commanding the crowd to stand back wore the badge of a sheriff. On the ground at his feet was a blanket-covered body. A second, similarly wrapped body, was just being unloaded from the back of a horse the sheriff steadied. Side by side, the two still forms were laid out upon the walk in front of the hitching rack.

Suddenly from down the street came a group of six trotting horsemen. A stocky, giant of a man was in their lead. He rode a mammoth dark bay horse that seemed to push its way through the scatter of animals at the hitching rack as if it had long been ridden by one that commanded. Without a word, the stocky man dropped his reins across the hitching rack rail and without waiting for the rest to dismount shouldered his way through the crowd.

"I just got your word, Sheriff," the stocky man bellowed in a voice that carried well beyond the crowd. "One of your men caught me down at the corrals. What's up?"

"El Viborito and his band been on another raid, Mr. Craig,"

the sheriff announced respectfully. "They wiped out old Steve Stentstrom's outfit just before sundown. Murdered everybody on the place. We got a sight of them hightailin' it for the border over in Smoke Coulee. About ten or fifteen in his band."

"Too bad," the man addressed as Craig offered seriously. "Steve was a good cattleman. Is that what you wanted of me?"

"No, reckon we got some bad news for you, too, Mr. Craig," the sheriff went on. "Somebody'd fenced off the big waterhole down in the coulee. Two deputies and myself were ridin' the south rim trail when we sighted the herd around the hole. They were in pretty bad shape but we seen a couple of hands in at the hole tearing down the barricade and figured they'd be all right. Just then, El Viborito and his band swung down the coulee and well... so far El Viborito has sorta left your outfit alone, Mr. Craig. Reckon the basin was a little too far out of his line of travel. Tonight, I'm thinkin' you've been elected. One of them two hands we saw shot down was a ridin' a horse with your brand. I was wantin' you to identify him before we do them the honors."

A CURSE BLASTED from the lips of the man Craig. "I sent two men scouting for strays over Smoke Coulee way this morning," he roared. "If that skunk, El Viborito...."

The big man had taken a position alongside the two blanket covered bodies. Now he chewed at his words as he whirled on the sheriff. "You saw them killed, Sheriff?" he demanded. "You had a look at this El Viborito?"

"A good look," the sheriff answered. "We was out of gun range but one of my deputies had a pair of field glasses with him. El Viborito was wearin' a Mexican outfit like the rest of his band but I'm thinkin' I can call his brand."

"You mean it was Jed Rawlins leading that band of killers?" Craig bellowed. "Rawlins killed my men for trying to open that coulee waterhole?"

"I'm not sayin' yes nor no, Mr. Craig," the sheriff answered meaningly. "But I'm aimin' to find out right soon. What I want to know first though is, were these two poor devils workin' your brand?" The sheriff nodded his head towards the two bodies stretched out on the sidewalk.

Pushing his way casually towards the center of the crowd, Wayne's mind flashed back to the scene at the burning ranch house where, as The Masked Rider, he had made the same gruesome discovery as the sheriff now announced. Evidently, he had ridden out of the ranch yard only a few minutes ahead of the sheriff and his men. A strange foreboding gripped him with the thought. Could the band of Mexican horsemen the sheriff claimed to have witnessed trailing the alleged El Viborito be the same band that had passed him in the canyon? Wayne was unfamiliar with the name, Smoke Coulee. That could have been the name of the canyon he had ridden up but he had sighted no cattle or waterhole along the trail.

The man Craig had stepped between the two bodies on the sidewalk. The sheriff bent down and prepared to lift the covering blankets from off their bodies.

"They were both dead when we got to them," the sheriff was saying. "We threw what lead we could at El Viborito and his band but they were too well mounted. We only chased them to the coulee rim, then doubled back to pick these two up."

The sheriff had lifted the blankets covering the two bodies well back. The yellow reflected light from the windows of the Sun-dance Saloon flooded across the ghastly features of the pair. Craig stooped over.

"They're both my men all right," he announced. "Two new hands I took on a month or so ago. One's name is Hank Hall and the other one calls himself Scaldy Jones. Both damn good hands."

A strange quietness settled over the street. Still in the middle of the crowd, Wayne began working his way forward for a look at the bodies. Now, as several men turned and started back towards the entrance of the Sun-dance, Craig's voice boomed again.

"Listen to me, all you men," Craig roared. "Up till now, this El Viborito has left my outfit pretty much alone. I've been satisfied to let it go at that. But now I'm calling my colors along with the rest of you. I'm asking the sheriff to bear me witness. I'll pay a thousand dollars to the man or men that brings in this El Viborito, dead or alive. The Lazy S declares war on his yellow hide along with the rest of you."

A howl of approval went up from the crowd. Wayne Morgan did not seem to hear it. With mention of the Lazy S brand he had stiffened. Lazy S… that was the brand upon the hip of the killer's horse whose body he had left lying across the shelf of rock upon the coulee rim. Was that killer in the employ of the man Craig? Was Craig responsible for the guard placed above that fenced waterhole?

WAYNE PUSHED BOLDLY through the crowd to where the two bodies lay upon the sidewalk. An instant he stared down. His fists clenched. His eyes narrowed. One of the dead men, he had never set eyes on before. The other…. Wayne's lips were moving in a mumble. The other body was that of the ranger that had died in his arms alongside the waterhole in the coulee bottom.

For a minute Wayne stood staring down at the ranger's body. A tangle of thoughts raced through his brain. A tangle of questions. Of possible answers. One fact screamed above it all. The sheriff's story of witnessing the killing of two Lazy S hands by El Viborito and his band as they swept down the coulee after their raid upon the Stentstrom ranch was a bold lie from beginning to end. Craig, the owner of the Lazy S had collaborated that lie. Why?

Wayne racked his mind for cold facts to smother his kindling rage. He must be positive before, as The Masked Rider, he dealt out his vengeful code of justice. Those two bodies stretched upon the sidewalk had been brought from the coulee where they had died. If the sheriff had seen with his own eyes the ruins of the Stentstrom ranch, he must have followed Wayne's own trail up the canyon and on into Los Comino. What, then, had become of the band of horsemen that had been moving along the rim trail when he had turned off for his dash towards the canyon? The sheriff had spoken only of himself and his two deputies. Who, then, were the riders that had fired the signaling shots after the sheriff met them in the trail beside the dead gunman upon the coulee rim? Why had Craig been so quick to name Jed Rawlins as El Viborito? Even Joe Stentstrom, the man who had first mentioned Rawlins' name to him, had spoken of suspicions, but refused even to connect Rawlins with the murderer of his brother's family. Craig had voiced his suspicion loudly. Could Rawlins be the key to it all? One man should know. That person was Judge Mann.

CHAPTER IV

THE SHOT FROM THE DARK

WAYNE MORGAN MOVED away from the scattering of men still about the bodies upon the sidewalk and sauntered slowly towards the stable where he had left his stallion and belongings. As he walked he whistled a strange tune through his teeth. The chirp of a cricket was soon his answer. Wayne stepped into the black shadows between the two buildings and waited. A few seconds and Blue Hawk was at his side.

"You wish me, *señor*," the Mexican Indian asked, humbly.

"Yes, *amigo*," Wayne answered. "It is time I speak to the man they call Judge Mann. You know where he lives?"

"*Si, señor,*" Blue Hawk answered quickly. "It is but a few paces beyond where the white man fills his thirst. A stairs leads up where he enters."

"That is good," Wayne answered, remembering the entrance to the two story frame building he had passed in reaching the restaurant where he had first seen the judge. "Remember now what I shall tell you. I shall visit the judge masked but it is better that I do not remove my stallion from his stall. Should danger trap me, I trust you to pick for me the fastest horse at the rack before the place of drink. I shall watch for the signal of where you shall be. You understand, *amigo?*"

"*Si, señor,*" Blue Hawk answered. A touch of Wayne's hand and he had vanished deeper into the darkness while Wayne continued on down the street.

At the stables, Wayne made sure the stable-hand on duty saw him take his blanket roll and climb into the straw loft above the horse stalls below as if to turn in for the night. A few minutes to assure himself he was not watched and Wayne had removed his black *mantilla* and hood from the blanket's folds and was silently sliding down the straw chutes at the rear of the stable. Another minute and in the darkness he was shaking the folds from his *mantilla* and hood. A black, phantom shadow suddenly moved through the darkness toward the upstairs rooms of Judge Mann. The Masked Rider again prowled.

SILENT AND INVISIBLE as a bat in the night, The Masked Rider carefully appraised the lay of the land about the rear of the building where the judge lived. The frail outline of a stairway showed along the rear of the structure, leading up to a porch-like platform at the second floor. A lighted window showed at the porch end. Careful to avoid its rays, The Masked Rider crouched low as he crossed the black space to the stairs and quickly ascended. A few quick steps and he was at the lighted window. He peered through. Inside, a man sat bent over a table. The Masked Rider needed but a glance to identify the occupant of the lighted room. It was Judge Mann.

Quickly, the black phantom found the rear entrance and moved into a narrow hall. A door was but a few feet ahead. Stepping to it, he knocked sharply. Steps sounded from inside. The Masked Rider poised ready. With click of the opening lock he sprang against the door and forced it wide. Before the startled judge could gather his senses, The Masked Rider had closed the door behind him and stood facing the judge, his gun hand poised.

"Who... who are you?" the judge demanded, his voice startled but firm. "What do you want?"

"To talk to you, Judge Mann," The Masked Rider caught up. "To talk to you of the one they call El Viborito."

A frown knitted the judge's brow. "Are you El Viborito?" he spoke, a note of scorn in his voice. "Are...?"

"I will ask the questions, Judge." The Masked Rider interrupted. "I was told by one I have already visited tonight that you could tell me of Jed Rawlins. I wish to know of him first."

"Who sent you to me for that information?" the judge demanded, a queer set to his jaw. "And why do you come masked?"

The Masked Rider allowed his hand to drop slowly away from the holstered gun at his hip. "I have heard that you were the one man in town that was not afraid to declare himself," he taunted. "Perhaps the blacksmith they call Joe, was wrong."

Judge Mann's features seemed to twist. His tenseness seemed to relax for an instant.

"Joe Stentstrom sent you to me, eh?" the judge offered slowly. "I just saw Joe down the street. They... they were getting ready to send a rig out to his brother's ranch and bring in the bodies. He... he mentioned nothing to me of... of...."

"He had nothing to mention," The Masked Rider cut in. "I only questioned him as I am questioning you. I have seen the workings of this fiend that brands himself El Viborito. I am here to wipe him from this range. Do you care to help me or don't you?"

"What is it you wish to know?" the judge spoke after a moment. "You can not expect me to trust you at your mere word. How do I know but what this is one of Craig's tricks?"

The eyes of The Masked Rider widened behind his hood. "Craig, the owner of the Lazy S?" the outlaw quizzed. "You do not trust him?"

The judge snorted. "Craig would give plenty to lay his hands on Jed Rawlins," he dragged out bitterly. "He knows Jed has one possible chance. One fighting chance. Why do you suppose he has been in town these last two days? He is afraid Jed may take that chance. He's here to prevent it."

"You still haven't told me who Jed Rawlins is," The Masked Rider spoke up. "I only know he has been outlawed from this range. Why, I have not heard."

A moment the judge eyed The Masked Rider suspiciously. "Jed Rawlins once owned the Tipped T outfit," the judge began, "the largest spread along the badlands' open range. He killed Snap Harris, Craig's foreman, in a quarrel over some cattle. Snap accused Jed of rustling Lazy S stock and selling them across the border. Jed shot his way out of jail just ahead of a lynching party Craig was leading. He made it across the border and has been there ever since. That was three years ago."

THE MASKED RIDER nodded his head thoughtfully. "Three years ago, he repeated wonderingly. "What became of his outfit?"

"Hank Parker's outfit, the Pitchfork, is alongside the Tipped T," the judge began again. "Hank's daughter Tess was supposed to marry Jed just about the time the killing happened. The girl tried to hold Jed's place together until something could be done but old man Parker died and tryin' to run two places was too much for the girl. Jed's outfit went for taxes last year. Craig bought it. It gives him open range from the Sawtooth Basin to the badlands."

"And now?" The Masked Rider encouraged as the judge grew quiet. "Craig suspects Rawlins of all these range crimes as a sort of vengeance against him and the rest of the ranchers? Suspects him of being El Viborito?"

The judge's face seemed to flush with anger. His huge hands doubled into fists.

"Craig's planted that suspicion," the judge ground out bitterly. "Jed is across the border trying to get another start. If it wasn't for that suspicion and Craig, Jed would come back here tomorrow and stand trial for that killing. Craig is afraid that's just what he may do. Come back here with enough money to redeem his outfit before the year's grace of the tax sale expires. I've known Jed Rawlins from youngster to man. Knew his father. It isn't in that boy's blood to do the things this El Viborito has done on this range. I don't know who this El Viborito is, but I soon expect to know. When I do...."

Judge Mann's head shook with emotion. The Masked Rider's mind flashed back to the message the dying ranger at the waterhole in the coulee bottom had given him. He saw a meaning behind the judge's hope.

"There was someone besides you working to prove who El Viborito really is?" The Masked Rider asked. "Someone whom Craig could not question?"

"I can't answer you that," the judge snapped back abruptly. "If I knew I could trust you, I might. I will, though, tell you what Mel Craig already knows. He knows I have gotten to the governor with Jed Rawlins' case. Knows other law besides that represented by our sheriff here, is well aware of El Viborito and his crimes on this range. Knows that proof may be presented any minute to clear Jed Rawlins of all suspicion. When that proof comes…."

Judge Mann became silent. His deep-set eyes blazed fire. The Masked Rider felt a wave of pity grip him at the thought of the words he must now speak. The ranger that had died in his arms at the waterhole was the man in whom the judge was trusting all the hope that now consumed him. The ranger whose dying breath had failed before he could speak the name that would have branded El Viborito for his true self. Now, The Masked Rider must tell the judge that man was dead, his information sealed between breathless lips.

The Masked Rider steeled himself for the disagreeable task. The judge had taken a step back. In the dead silence of the room the quick breathing his emotion of the moment had caused sounded plain. The Masked Rider opened his mouth to speak.

"You have told me only things I know already, Judge," he began. "Now I must tell you things you do not know. That person you expect to bring you this information as to who El Viborito really is, that ranger that your plea to the governor had caused to be sent to this range. He… he…."

THE WORDS SMOTHERED behind The Masked Rider's lips. The crash of glass sounded from almost beside him. In that instant the room went black. The yellow flame of the lamp that had been upon the table before the window vanished in nothingness. Then, above the tinkling of glass came the echoing roar of a rifle. A shot had shattered the window and blasted to nothing the light that had been upon the table before it.

The Masked Rider dropped into a crouch. That rifle shot had come from somewhere outside. Somewhere in line with the window at the rear porch. For an instant The Masked Rider's mind flashed to the thought of an ambusher. The sudden mounting howl of shouts from the night beyond told him otherwise. Men were calling to one another somewhere below the porch steps. Feet were pounding in the outer hall. Voices were closing in from all sides. He had stepped into a trap. That, or his presence in the judge's rooms had been discovered and an alarm given.

With only an instant's hesitation to map a possible avenue of escape, The Masked Rider leaped across the room toward the rear window. His gun was in his hand. With quick sweeps of its barrel he cleared the jagged splinters of already broken glass from the frame. A step through and he was out upon the rear porch. From below came the babble of shouts. Men were rushing up the porch stairs from the darkness below.

"Come on. He's still in there," some one shouted as their feet pounded upon the stairs. "We got 'em trapped. The sheriff'll hold him the front way."

The Masked Rider did not need the warning to know men were already swarming into the hallway before the entrance to the judge's rooms. Swarming in the street in front. Swarming in through the blackness below the porch. The place was surrounded.

The outlaw in black cast a swift glance about. The narrow porch ran the full length of the building. At the end nearest him, the roof of an adjoining building loomed a few feet below.

The Masked Rider whirled and ran towards the porch end. His heels clicked to his steps. He reached the end and peered down. An alley-like space separated the porch from the adjoining building. He could hear the hard breathing of men below, pushing from the street through the alleyway to the rear of the building.

"It's El Viborito. They got 'im trapped up in Judge Mann's room." The babbling chatter sounded up from below. "That scarface *hombre* that was with the judge tonight, went up to the judge's rooms and spotted El Viborito through the window. That shot must have been the end of the judge."

The Masked Rider poised at the rail edge. The scarfaced man the judge had been eating dinner with. It was he that had sighted him and spread the alarm. Perhaps he had heard the voices in the room and stepped to the window before knocking. Regardless, he was trapped. That rifle shot had been a warning, not an ambusher's shot. Without it they might have sneaked up on him and had him surrounded. Who could have fired that warning shot?

There was no time to court the thought. A head had popped above the level of the stairway. "There he is," a voice blasted. "El Viborito." A gun roared. With its stab of flame The Masked Rider leaped to the porch rail and hurled himself out. A wild leap. A desperate leap. The Masked Rider's toes and fingers barely caught upon the roof of the building adjoining. From behind him came the excited warning of his escape.

"Scatter! Scatter!" went the cry. "He's jumped to the next roof. Holler at the fellows in front. He's going over the roof tops. Watch out! Don't let him get away!"

LEAD SANG ABOUT The Masked Rider's racing form. He did not attempt to return the fire. At the front of the building across which he ran, a glance down disclosed men still pouring from the doors of the Sun-dance. The alarm had been spread all over town. People were racing from every direction. "El Viborito," was the cry on every lip. "Get him on sight!

The trap had already closed about him.

Then suddenly as The Masked Rider stared down, a queer cry rent the night. It sounded sharp and piercing above the wild shouting about. The shrill scream of a horse that had been kicked or given a painful jab. It came from some place beyond the hitching rack before the Sun-dance Saloon. The Masked Rider recognized the cry. Blue Hawk... he had not failed him. Somewhere beyond the Sun-dance entrance Blue Hawk waited with a ready horse. That signaling cry was from his lips. If only he could reach the spot.

The men upon the porch edge were now pouring lead in the outlaw's direction. His black hood and *mantilla*, melting him against the night, offered too poor a target. The Masked Rider did not risk returning the fire lest his flaming six-gun give them a better sight. Crouching low as he ran, he raced the width of the roof. A second roof was beyond. It was a bare step across. The Masked Rider leaped the distance and rushed on. He was atop the roof of the restaurant a few doors from the Sun-dance, he reasoned. At the end of this roof was the open street.

The hooded outlaw did not pause. To the roof end, then he peered down. The side street was empty. The crowd in the street before the building where the judge lived had not as yet been warned of his direction of escape. On the main street everybody still rushed that way.

Like some huge, crawling spider, the black form of The Masked Rider flattened against the edge of the roof and seemed to roll over its side. In reality, The Masked Rider lowered himself at arm's length from the roof edge and dropped. He landed with a jarring jolt upon the soft dirt below. Hardly had his feet touched, when again the shrill cry of a pain-stabbed horse caught his ears. Blue Hawk was somewhere close. He had seen him drop from the roof of the low building.

The sound of firing still rattled from above. The men who

had closed in on him at the porch end were still aiming at where his shadow had last traced itself against the roof edge. The Masked Rider threw a swift glance about. No one in the main street had seen him in his drop. He had a second. A second, and the alarm of his direction of escape would be in the street. He was still far from clear of the trap's jaws.

Suddenly, a crouching form slunk across the narrow street opening in which he stood, moving down the main street in a direction opposite to the hurrying scatter of men. An instant and the form disappeared into the darkness. Then again, sharp and shrill, came that cry of a prodded horse. The Masked Rider spotted its position in the black shadows somewhere up the street. An instant he wondered. Only an instant. Into the street in the wake of the shadow, a horse appeared. It jerked its head nervously, as would a frightened animal that had just pulled its reins free from the hitching rack. That jerking head told The Masked Rider a far different tale. The animal was being led along by the slow drawing in of a slack rope. Somewhere in the darkness beyond, Blue Hawk was the slow dragger of that unseen line.

HUGGING THE BLACKNESS of the building wall, The Masked Rider took a dozen steps towards the street. The shouts and cries from beyond were now a meaningless tumult. All attention was centered down the street. The Masked Rider glanced at the horse in the street, still stubbornly prancing and tugging against its invisible lead-line. He felt a thrill of satisfaction as he recognized the animal. Blue Hawk had done well in picking the animal for his escape. He need fear none of the horses now at the hitching rack overhauling him. Blue Hawk had picked the sturdy bay for his mount. The proud animal Mel Craig had ridden to the rack when he had answered the sheriff's summons before the Sun-dance saloon.

The Masked Rider poised ready. Then bending low he leaped from the black shadows against the building wall and raced towards the ready mount in the street. His hand was upon the animal's bridle before horse or man had sighted him. With a jerk, The Masked Rider freed the slip-knot of a lariat end and caught in the animal's bit. He was in the saddle as the first spit of flame from across the street announced his discovery. Firing as he forked leather, The Masked Rider dug spurs. The anxious bay sprang ahead. With a hail of lead singing about him, horse and rider flew down the street. From behind came the chaos of shouts and commands as the street mob scattered for horses.

The Masked Rider chuckled to himself as he felt the powerful swing of the animal beneath him. He was headed towards the same end of town, where he had first circled with the little girl from the destroyed Stentstrom's ranch. Ahead must be Joe Stentstrom's home. The Masked Rider glanced that way. The gun in his hand leaped ready. Along the deep shadows of the walk he made out the form of a man walking in a direction away from all the shouting and disorder down the street. The man carried a rifle in the crook of his arm.

As the hooded outlaw dashed even, the man in the street glanced up. The rifle in his arm did not move. The Masked Rider, alert eyes sighted over his ready gun, blinked as he recognized the walking man with the rifle. It was Joe Stentstrom, himself. Now his free hand raised in a guarded salute. The Masked Rider wondered. Could Joe Stentstrom be the one who fired that warning shot through the window of Judge Mann's room? If so, Joe Strentstrom had done his purpose well. The pursuing mob before the Sun-dance saloon were just getting under way.

The sing of lead from those still firing wildly down the street faded as The Masked Rider flashed past the edge of town and into the black, true night of the open trail. The sturdy bay beneath him seemed to know the trail. It raced along with the sure-footedness of The Masked Rider's own stallion. The outlaw found himself wondering at what the results would be in a fair race between the two horses. Little did he think that one day soon his own life as well as the lives of those he hoped to save would depend on just such a race. He rode a prize in horse flesh. A prize in reckless spirit that seemed to match even his own stallion. However, not a prize in heart. The Masked Rider had yet to learn that.

CHAPTER V

THE RIVER TRAP

THE RUMBLING OF horse hoofs from behind him told the hooded phantom that the posse taking his trail was taking it in earnest. It sounded as if every man in town who could lay hands on a mount had hit leather. He might have swung suddenly off the trail and taken a chance on the posse's passing him, then double back into town and steal up to the hay loft above the Star stable. But at the moment that risk was too great. There would still be Mel Craig's horse to account for. For his purpose, the people of Los Comino must believe The Masked Rider was somewhere far out on the range. There was yet much that he, as Wayne Morgan, wished to accomplish in Los Comino before, as The Masked Rider, he would call a show-down. Wayne Morgan and the black stallion must remain without a breath of suspicion upon them.

Giving his mount its head, The Masked Rider therefore trusted to the speed of the sturdy bay to make distance his point of safety. The animal was fast proving that possible. The trail they traveled was a well worn one and the footing sure. The Masked Rider urged the animal on.

Suddenly, as the trail swung down into a long narrow canyon, The Masked Rider realized why the route he traveled seemed so familiar. He was racing down the same trail he had traveled in bringing little Mary from the ravaged Stentstrom ranch into Los Comino. He remembered this long canyon. It ran for about a mile then twisted its way up over broken land to the mesa. The Masked Rider added a touch of spurs as he urged his mount for an extra burst of speed through the canyon bottom. On the mesa beyond he would do his back-tracking and lose the posse. Back in Los Comino, he would locate Blue Hawk and have him ride the bay out across the range in the opposite direction from town while he sneaked back up into the stable loft to resume his role of Wayne Morgan.

However, with that plan still flashing through his mind, The Masked Rider suddenly drew rein. From down the canyon trail ahead came a queer rattling noise. Faintly it sounded above the pound of the bay's hoofs. The Masked Rider slowed the horse to a trot. He listened. The rattling noise from ahead sounded plainly. The sound painted a mental picture in the black-garbed outlaw's brain. Ahead, several mounted horsemen with a light wagon were traveling the canyon trail in the same direction he was going. The Masked Rider suddenly remembered the statement Judge Mann had made when he questioned him back in his rooms. A rig was being sent to the Stentstrom ranch to bring the bodies of the murdered rancher and his wife back to town. He had overtaken that rig and its escorting party.

The Masked Rider glanced anxiously back down the blackness of the trail he traveled. It was too late to turn back. Already he could hear the distant thunder of hoofs as the pursuing posse plunged down into the canyon. The canyon was too narrow at this point to hope to sneak past the rig ahead and its escort of riders, unseen. He was between two fires. Two creeping fires. Of the two, the one ahead seemed to beckon. There the element of surprise would be with him.

For a minute The Masked Rider allowed his horse to hold its easy trot in the hope that a possible flare in the canyon's bottom might give him an added advantage. The mounting thunder of the posse as it drew closer shrieked the danger. Suddenly that danger crystallized. The rig and its escorting party ahead had caught the sound of the approaching posse. They had halted. It was now or never.

Bending low in his saddle, The Masked Rider touched spurs. The bay leaped ahead. Swinging over as near the black canyon walls as possible, The Masked Rider allowed his mount to pick its own trail. He was upon the rig and its escorting party before they had even sighted him sweeping along the canyon wall's blackness like a phantom shadow.

A STARTLED CRY went up from the half-dozen riders trailing the light wagon and team. A warning cry, "El Viborito, get 'im!" A shot stabbed the night. Another. Then another. The canyon walls roared with their blasting echo. In the flame flashes The Masked Rider's bent form, black *mantilla* spread wide in its flare across horse and rider, loomed plain. The escorting horse-men behind the light wagon, swung in pursuit. The lead spattered against the canyon walls beyond The Masked Rider. The plung-ing bay was only a dozen leaps in their lead. The pursuit was hot.

The hooded outlaw did not answer the spattering lead that poured after him. He had long ago learned that a muzzle flash is too perfect a target in the darkness for an expert gun-hand. Crouching low in his saddle, he swept the bay around the rig and back into the canyon trail. At least he was past the block-ade. Now, again, he trusted to the speed of the bay as his ally.

The racing horse seemed to understand the urging touch of The Black Caballero's spurs. It gave its all. However, the trailing horsemen behind seemed to cling close to him. The Masked Rider began to understand. The bay was straining every muscle to hold its pace. Those behind, while dropping slowly back, were losing distance because of caution for the canyon trail in the darkness, not because of speed. Those behind evidently rode fresh horses. The bay was now showing signs of already having been ridden far and hard that day.

Safely out of gun range, The Masked Rider attempted to

ease his mount's lunging pace. The bay refused to yield to the draw of its reins. It gripped its bit and held its head defiantly. The Masked Rider understood. The animal had long been trained to pursuit. Stubbornly, it now fought to run the race as it had been taught. It seemed to know every turn, every rock in the trail. The Masked Rider finally yielded to its struggle for a free rein. The bay took its head understandingly. Of its own accord it gradually slowed its pace as if satisfied to merely hold the pursuing hoof-pounds behind at the distance from which they now thundered.

A few minutes, and they broke from the canyon to swing out upon the open mesa. The Masked Rider now merely held the bay's reins, allowing the sensitive horse to pick its own trail and speed. The mesa lay a flooded sea of moonlight. The Masked Rider cast an uneasy glance back over his shoulder. In this moonlight he dare not risk allowing the posse to creep too close. Even with the protection of his black *mantilla,* he offered too perfect a target. With a grunt of satisfaction he noted the distance of the first band of horsemen that popped up out of the canyon. He rode with a good quarter of a mile lead. Now, if the bay could only hold that lead until he reached the shelter of the black shadows of the badlands ahead, he was safe. Moonlight or no moonlight, no rider could be trailed through the badlands with speed.

Suddenly, the bay swung sharply from the mesa trail. The Masked Rider attempted to turn the animal back. It fought for its head. The outlaw yielded. The animal seemed to know where it was going. Its general direction was still towards the rugged rim of blackness ahead, that marked the badlands. The Masked Rider began to wonder. Could the understanding horse beneath him be struggling to take him towards some hidden rendezvous wherein it knew safety from pursuit lay? He had marked the horse's actions when Mel Craig had first ridden the animal to the hitching rack before the Sun-dance Saloon. Marked it for an animal that had been trained in more than range tricks.

Could this he one of its special trained tricks. Throughout the chase the animal had acted as if leading away from close pursuit was no new experience to it. It had not as much as shied to the sing of lead about it. Had Mel Craig trained the animal to that as well?

THE BAY HAD now picked a low rolling bit of ridge for its trail. The ridge footing was perfect. The bay, without increasing its pace, gradually increased the distance between it and the double posse still clinging to their trail a half mile behind. Steadily that distance increased the more. Miles rolled beneath the bay's steady pace. The badlands shadows were almost upon them.

Then abruptly, so abruptly The Masked Rider pressed stirrups for balance, the bay wheeled at right angles to its trail. Down into the black shadows of a deep coulee, invisible until that moment, the horse plunged. Its pace slowed. Its head held low. Cautiously it picked its way through the treacherous scatter of scab-rock. Deeper, and deeper they descended until the coulee seemed to take the form of a deep canyon. A light, cool breeze seemed to shift up from the blackness ahead. The Masked Rider sniffed it wonderingly. It was a cool, damp, river breeze. Was the Rio ahead? Was this canyon some cross-range short-cut to the border waters of the Rio Grande? With every step of the bay, The Masked Rider became more positive that was the answer.

For a half hour the bay held to its slow cautious descent. Now and then an ugly stench mingled with the damp breeze. The Masked Rider attributed it to the decaying carcass of some dead critter that had died within the canyon. Then suddenly the canyon bottom leveled out. From ahead came a low, swishing purr. A blue glaze, streaked with yellow moonlight, blocked the trail ahead. The Rio… he had guessed right. Mel Craig's bay had led him down to the river. Ahead was a wide easy ford where the river swung into a graceful bend between high banks. Across was Mexico. Of its own accord, the bay halted and drew in its breath deep. It seemed ready now to respond to the guide of its reins.

For minutes The Masked Rider only sat silently in his saddle, staring out across the water. Why had Mel Craig's horse, under pressure of a chase, guided him so stubbornly to this point? What use could Mel Craig be making of this little known route to the border? Cattle had been driven down this route. Thousands of cattle. The signs and tracks showed plain in the moonlight along the river bank. The smelling carcasses in the canyon marked the drive as recent. Why had they been brought to the border this way? There was only one answer. Only rustled cattle were driven across the Rio at points such as this ford offered. Rustled or wet cattle, they could have come from either direction, the bandlands range or Mexico.

The Masked Rider's silent musing was suddenly interrupted by the sound of shouts from somewhere far back up the canyon. He listened. Faintly he heard signaling shouts echoing back and forth. A queer uneasiness gripped him. Had the posse been able to hold to his trail even into the unseen canyon entrance? Even the bay had turned itself around and now, with pointed ears, peered suspiciously back up into the blackness.

The shouting grew closer. Now and then the clatter of shod-hoofs against rock rang through the stillness of the river edge. The Masked Rider gauged the distance of the sound. It was as he feared. The posse had held to his trail. Now slowly and cautiously they were descending the canyon.

The Masked Rider glanced about him. He had no desire to ford the river and cross the boundary into Mexico. His task was to get back into Los Comino before daylight, get rid of Mel Craig's horse and sneak back up into that hay loft to resume his role of Wayne Morgan in the morning. To cross into Mexico might make that impossible.

THE STEEP CANYON walls guarded one side of the ford. Downstream, in the opposite direction, the rough-rocked bank of the river was passable for a distance until the high cliff seemed gradually to push into the water to form a perpendicular boundary. Hopefully, The Masked Rider urged his mount towards the screening wing of the cliff. The rocky shore line might continue on past the blocking wing of rock extending into the stream. If so, there was a chance of following on downstream and working out of the canyon without crossing the ford.

Willingly, the bay trotted to the blocking wing of rock. Then, without an urge from The Masked Rider, it waded belly-deep into the stream, rounded the blocking wing of the cliff and was ascending a fairly wide trail along the cliff wall, formed by a shelf-like formation of the rock.

The Masked Rider allowed the animal to proceed. It seemed to know where it was going just as it seemed to know of the hidden trail behind the screening wing of rock it had waded belly-deep to circle. The shelf-like trail climbed slowly along the perpendicular cliff. Below, the waters of the river seemed to gather force as the throw of the current sent them hissing in against the cliff base that formed its perpendicular bank. For a hundred yards the trail continued. Then abruptly, blankly, it ended flush with a second outward jut of the cliff.

The Masked Rider cursed to himself. The bay had led him into a blind trail. The cliff ahead was impassable. The waters of the river were a good twenty-five feet straight below. He was blocked completely. His only hope was to turn back and make the ford. To remain here meant being trapped if one of the posse should chance to investigate past the wing of rock that seemed to bound the ford.

The bay beneath The Masked Rider had halted. An instant the outlaw listened. His body set in a queer stiffness. From up the river voices drifted. Many voices. It was too late to turn back. Already men were at the ford. He could hear them shouting as the downstream draft of the air carried their voices plainly.

Suddenly, The Masked Rider's grip on the bay's reins tightened. From up-river came the splash of a horse's feet entering the stream. Someone was approaching the wing of rock to investigate beyond. He was trapped. His only hope, other than a fight, was to freeze against the cliff wall that blocked the trail end and trust to the darkness and his black *mantilla* to conceal him from any searching eye that might advance up the trail.

With a jerk of his reins, The Masked Rider attempted to pull the bay back close against the cliff. Instead of responding, the animal turned broadside in the trail and began prancing nervously. Its head faced out towards the river. The Masked Rider drew his reins together as he attempted to steady the prancing beast. His spurs accidentally touched. Abruptly, without the sign of a warning, the animal leaped ahead. Straight out over the trail edge it lunged. Far out, directly into the swirling sweep of the river's water, twenty-five feet below.

The Masked Rider grabbed leather as he felt himself and horse fall. Down… down… they sailed to land with a deafening splash in the current. The Masked Rider clung to his saddle-horn. The current gripped him and swung him clear of the saddle. Still clinging to the saddle-horn he felt the rhythmic beat of the bay's feet as it began swimming with the current. Already, the inky blackness of the cliffs had closed about them. The current was sweeping them downstream with the speed of a mill-race.

THE MASKED RIDER managed to cling to his grip upon the saddle-horn. The swimming bay beneath him seemed to show no sign of panic or fright from its plunge. It swam steadily and surely on downstream, a mere snort now and then to clear its nostrils of water, the only sound of its efforts. Managing to gain a glance upward, The Masked Rider saw the perpendicular cliff seemed to continue on down the river even as it straightened from its bend. The swing of the current still held them close in against the cliff's side. Their only hope was to ride the current until the cliff fell away or the current released them to make swimming towards the opposite shore possible.

Suddenly, The Masked Rider felt a new swing in the current. Its pull seemed to lessen. Beside him, the bay seemed to turn its head in towards the cliff and to double its efforts. The current seemed to release them. The bay was swimming with ease. The Masked Rider's wondering was short. Abruptly, his body swung against some floating object in the stream, hard and secure. It did not yield an inch to the sweep of the current or his own weight. The bay was following along its edge. A touch of his hand and The Masked Rider identified the object. A boom of anchored logs jutted at an angle out into the current to form a sort of current-break and scooping guide to whatever might come down the river. The boom seemed to have its base in a narrow passageway in the cliff's side, that in the darkness, loomed like the black mouth of a tunnel.

The side of the boom half supporting them and guiding them against the current towards shore, the outlaw suddenly felt the bay's feet touch bottom. Slowly the now puffing horse began climbing from the water. The tunnel-like patch of blackness in the cliff's side took form. The bay pushed boldly into it. There, high and dry upon a smooth sand bottom, it paused to catch its wind.

Standing alongside the puffing animal The Masked Rider stared out into the river. He was beginning to understand the actions of the hard-breathing horse, beginning to understand the purpose of that blind trail along the cliff side. Of the log boom swinging out into the river. Ten minutes later, as cautiously working the bay up the narrow passageway from the river, the trail suddenly flared out into a huge, pocket-like canyon, he understood more. Even in the darkness, the frightened snorts and nervous bellows that greeted his approach at the pocket opening, told him what was beyond. Cattle… a herd of them.

The high-walled canyon acted as a natural corral. It could be nothing else but a rustler retreat. A perfect one. All signs would lead to the river ford and point to a swing across the border. The Masked Rider's knowledge at the moment spoke differently. Driven around that wing of rock into the hidden trail along the cliff's side, the river was the trail into this hidden retreat, with the log boom, the water fence to guide them. A perfect rustlers' retreat. Whose? The familiar steps of the bay horse beneath him, now skirting the edge of the herd, seemed to speak the answer. Mel Craig's mount had been to this spot before, been, by the same watery route they had just traveled together. Many times before.

CHAPTER VI

TESS PARKER

MEL CRAIG'S BAY seemed more than faintly familiar with the pocket-like canyon in which it now circled with The Masked Rider. Around the herd, and the animal began working its way over towards the steep walls. As if its vision were perfect even in the inky blackness of the canyon bottom, it suddenly swung onto a trail that seemed to slowly work into an opening that ascended the canyon's wall.

Suddenly, the animal pulled to a halt before a barring pole gate. Cautiously, The Masked Rider dismounted. Beyond the gate he made out the crude outline of a low cabin built up against the canyon wall. He did not care to investigate as to whether or not it was occupied. His ammunition and six-gun were still dripping from their watery bath as well as his clothing. Quietly opening the gate he led the bay through and then urged it at a walk on past the cabin and up the trail.

The animal seemed reluctant to ascend the trail at first but once well beyond the gate, it again demanded its head and followed the trail willingly. While leading up slowly as it twisted through the walls of rock, the trail seemed to be following the river's course. Several times The Masked Rider halted to listen for some sign or sound of his being followed. There was none. Evidently, the posse at the ford had assumed he had crossed the border or had failed to discover or search for him beyond the wing of rock that protected the blind trail. If there was anyone at the cabin beside the pocketed herd in the canyon, he had passed them unseen. His problem now was once more to gain the mesa and ride hard for Los Comino to protect his identity there as Wayne Morgan.

As the bay held to the easy pace of its climbing ascent, The Masked Rider puzzled over the breaks of the chase. Surely, Mel Craig had obtained a horse somewhere and joined the chase for him across the mesa. If Craig was with that posse when they reached the ford, why had he not investigated the hidden blind trail. Perhaps he had, The Masked Rider reasoned with himself, and finding no one there, assumed no one not knowing the boom below would ever risk the current, therefore took it for granted The Masked Rider had crossed the border. That part was easier to understand than how the alarm of his presence in Judge Mann's rooms had been spread to quickly to start the chase. The scarfaced man had worked fast in surrounding the place. Could Joe Stentstrom, the blacksmith at whose home he had left the little Stentstrom girl have talked with someone and mentioned his visit? Mentioned his inquiry as to Judge Mann? That seemed hardly possible, if it was Joe Stentstrom that had fired that warning shot through the judge's window. Yet, the scarfaced man who had spread the alarm of his presence at the judge's must have known of his intended visit. He had only been in the judge's rooms a few minutes. The scarfaced man could not have gathered the town together as he seemed to have done in that short length of time.

The Masked Rider still mulled his thoughts as the bay beneath him suddenly broke from the canyon into a stretch of badland. He searched about for some landmark to establish his direction.

The moon had dipped behind the horizon and only the deep indigo of the star-speckled; sky offered him a hope. From it he gathered that the river was off to the right of him. He decided to swing towards it and ride the river trail until he reached some point where he would pick up a familiar trail leading back towards Los Comino.

AT A WALK, he guided the bay in and out of the towering pinnacles of scab-rock that dotted the badlands like set bowling pins. Blacker and blacker the night about him closed in as he pushed deeper into the badland's ruggedness. Then suddenly, the animal beneath him seemed to start. It snorted loudly. They had just ridden past a wall-like break in a shallow coulee bottom. Ahead stretched a pocket of blackness. From it came the answering snort of a horse. The Masked Rider jerked reins. The bay stopped still. There was someone in the blackness of that open space ahead. A rider. Several of them. He could hear the clink of spurs. Now they clinked louder. Horse hoofs trotted with muffled beats towards him. The Masked Rider froze still. Two riders were pushing out of the blackness towards him.

"That is you, *Señor* Pittnor?" a voice called in sputtering Spanish from the darkness. *"Diablo!* You come upon one like a walking ghost. We have waited for you since sundown."

The Masked Rider's muscles tensed as he poised ready for fight or flight. The voice speaking to him in the guttural sputter of a vaquero showed no sign of doubt as to his being other than the *Señor* Pittnor he expected. The Masked Rider's brain worked fast. There must be a dozen men at least, waiting in the darkness beyond. To declare himself now might mean disaster, considering that he had no way of telling whether or not the shells in his gun and belt had been damaged by their soaking in the river. As long as the Mexican addressing him believed him someone else, in the darkness there was a chance of carrying on the deception until at least he learned what was expected of him.

The Masked Rider mumbled a greeting of the night in Spanish and waited.

"*Bueno, señor,*" the Mexican called in answer to his greeting. "Maybeso, it is better you do not come on time, *hé!* The night is short for those bitten with love, *hé.*" The man in the dark laughed coarsely. "Come, *señor. Vamos.* I shall tell them you are here. The trail is yonder.

The Masked Rider puzzled at the Mexican's words even as he heard him wheel his horse and push on into the blackness. A sudden new thumping of trotting horse hoofs held The Masked Rider to the spot. An instant and almost beside him, a horse and rider pushed past. The Masked Rider caught a mumbling whisper, almost a sob, that called for him to follow. The clatter of many hoofs in the darkness beyond told him most of those standing in the darkness had touched spurs and were racing away in a direction opposite to that in which the trotting rider had commanded him to follow. He was alone with the single rider that seemed at the moment barely able to speak above a whisper. The Masked Rider made his decision quickly. He would follow the single rider. Follow at least until the sound of the band of horsemen with their Mexican spokesman had faded.

For several moments the outlaw allowed the bay merely to trail the horse ahead. In the darkness no word was spoken. The single rider in the lead seemed to have found a fair trail and to be following it without effort. The Masked Rider was willing to accept as much. For ten minutes they trotted their horses along, swinging in and out of the jagged pinnacles of rock that forced the turns. Suddenly, the rider ahead slowed her mount to a walk. The Masked Rider allowed the bay to come almost even. His gun hand was ready. He was playing cautious.

"I'm... I'm sorry, Mr. Pittnor," the rider ahead spoke. "I... I didn't want you to see me crying. It... it was so good of you to come this way. Jed and I have been talking and... and—"

The Masked Rider barely heard the words. Beneath his hood

his chin dropped in astonishment. Now, as for an instant a rise in the trail outlined the rider ahead against the star-speckled skyline, it dropped the more. The voice of the rider ahead was the voice of a woman. The outline against the sky was that of a woman. A young woman riding straight and graceful, with hair hanging loosely about her shoulders. A girl. The same girl he had witnessed leading the band of Mexicans down the canyon hours before, when he had halted in his escape from the riders of the coulee rim. Beneath his hood, the outlaw's eyes widened, questioningly.

WITH NO ANSWER from The Masked Rider, the girl turned in her saddle and glanced back. The grotesque form of The Masked Rider, with his flowing *mantilla* and high sombrero, shaped a silhouette against the star-spattered skyline beyond. The girl gave a startled cry and attempted to spur her mount into a dash. The Masked Rider was too quick. A touch of his own spurs and the bay was alongside. The Masked Rider crowded the girl's mount into a blocking shelf of rock.

"Don't be afraid, miss," he spoke, "I'm not going to hurt you."

"Who... who are you?" the girl demanded in a frightened stammer. "How did you get here? Where is Mr. Pittnor?"

"One question at a time, miss," The Masked Rider interrupted. "You do not need to be afraid of me. Who I am is of no importance. Enough that I do not make war on women. As to where I came from, I rode into your waiting party and passed myself off as Pittnor to protect myself. I know nothing of this man you call Pittnor."

An instant the girl stared. "You lie," she finally spat at him. "You are El Viborito. You have murdered Mr. Pittnor. You trailed me and my vaqueros here in the hope that you might find Jed Rawlins and murder him as well. You... you...."

With mention of the name Jed Rawlins an understanding light suddenly burst upon The Masked Rider. He remembered what Judge Mann had told him about the outlawed cattleman and his sweetheart, Tess Parker. Also, he remembered the words of the Mexican vaquero who had ridden through the darkness to meet him. It stood to reason that Jed Rawlins and his sweetheart must have some secret rendezvous. "The night is short for those bitten with love," the Mexico vaquero had spoken. He must have referred to Jed Rawlins and the girl beside him.

"You are Tess Parker?" The Masked Rider risked. "Judge Mann is your friend?"

The girl only stared. "How did you know that was my name?" she finally asked. "Did... did the judge send you?"

"The judge told me of both you and Jed Rawlins," The Black Caballero answered. "He did not send me. Our meeting is a chance one. My purpose is to find the man you accuse me of being. I am searching for this fiend that calls himself El Viborito."

The girl still stared. "Why do you go masked then?" she spoke after a moment. "No one that is out to get El Viborito need fear the people of this range."

"Perhaps I mask for the same reason you ride the badlands trail with your Mexican band," The Masked Rider snapped in answer. "I have followed your trail already tonight. Why did you and your band ride from the direction of the burning ranch house upon the mesa tonight?"

The girl stiffened. She drew back in her saddle.

"Now I know you are El Viborito," she spoke scornfully. "It was you and your band we chased into the badlands tonight. It was you that committed those murders at the Stentstrom ranch."

"It was I who discovered them, perhaps just as you discovered them," The Masked Rider answered, beginning to understand now why the trail of the Mexican band the girl led had caused for a time to suspect even her. "If I were El Viborito would I be without my men now? Would I have known of you and Jed Rawlins from Judge Mann?

For a moment the girl did not answer. She seemed struggling with herself. "How do I know Mel Craig has not told you all that?" she finally blurted out. "How do I know Mel Craig has not sent you here to waylay Mr. Pittnor and... and maybe murder him?"

"Who is this Mr. Pittnor?" The Masked Rider asked. "Judge Mann did not speak of him."

MR. PITTNOR IS the man I was waiting here to meet," the girl answered. Suddenly she seemed to grasp a new thought. She leaned forward in her saddle. "You say you are a friend of Judge Mann," she shot at The Masked Rider. "You can prove that easily. Prove it in a way the judge will be more than willing to repay you."

"How?" The Masked Rider snapped.

"By helping me find Mr. Pittnor," the girl answered. "Something has happened to him I am sure. He was to meet us here on the river trail between sundown and midnight. We… we did not wish Mel Craig to know he was coming to Los Comino. If Mel Craig knew that he might… might…."

"But who is this Pittnor?" The Masked Rider cut in patiently. "I can not help unless I know whom I am looking for."

The girl seemed to lapse into a hopeless despair. She suddenly seemed to realize that for the moment she had no one else to turn to but The Masked Rider. If The Masked Rider was not what he claimed, a friend of Judge Mann, she had already lost all chance of accomplishing her purpose. On the other hand, if he was what he claimed, there was still a hope.

"Mr. Pittnor is a cattle buyer from Laredo," the girl began willingly, a tremble in her voice. "The Mexican vaqueros you saw me with tonight were all friends of Jed Rawlins and have been across the border these past two days helping me and my men make a quick roundup of every head of cattle I own, for shipping. Today we completed the roundup and are holding the herd at my ranch. Mr. Pittnor was to look at them in the morning. His money, the money he paid me for my cattle, was the money Judge Mann was going to… to redeem Jed Rawlins' holdings before the year's grace of their sale for taxes expired. Jed was to give himself up tomorrow and… and risk standing trial. If… if Mr. Pittnor…. If Mel Craig has found out of this…."

The girl seemed unable to go on. To The Masked Rider the picture was now dawning clear. Jed Rawlins' Mexican friends had furnished the extra hands for the secret roundup on the Parker ranch. It was they the outlaw had seen the girl leading back to the border. From further patient questioning he learned more. The girl and her Mexican band had ridden past the Stentstrom ranch but a few moments after the murderous raid upon the place. They had halted only a moment to investigate but finding all dead and the buildings in flames beyond possible fighting, had given chase. In the canyon where the girl and her band had passed The Masked Rider, they had lost the trail of the killers. Fearing for their appointment to meet the cattle buyer on the trail, the girl had led the band to the border where they had been waiting in vain since shortly after The Masked Rider saw them disappear over the rolling slope at the canyon end.

"This cattle buyer, Pittnor," The Masked Rider asked, "he carried the money with which to buy your herd with him? He—"

"That is why he was coming by the river trail," the girl spoke quickly. "He carried the money in cash. No one knew of his leaving Laredo but Judge Mann, Jed and myself. It seemed the safest way. We did not want Mel Craig to suspect what Jed intended doing. If he did he might... might...."

The girl broke into a soft sobbing. They had turned back into the trail and were now walking their horses slowly along. The Masked Rider allowed the girl to have her moment's weeping. A clearer picture was beginning to paint itself in his mind. From what he had heard Judge Mann speak in the few minutes he was with him and what the girl told him as they twisted their way on through the badlands' rugged trail, he was beginning to understand much of the man Mel Craig.

MEL CRAIG'S OUTFIT in the Sawtooth Basin was the largest spread in those parts. However, in the basin range, Craig had been having trouble getting water. Several times he had attempted to buy Jed Rawlins out when the young cattleman still operated, and thereby give himself an outlet to the badlands' grass and waterholes. Jed Rawlins had refused each time to sell.

Only a year back, Craig had succeeded in accomplishing what he had long desired by purchasing the Rawlins holdings at a sheriff's sale for taxes. There was only one sticker in the purchase. By law, Jed Rawlins had one year's grace in which to redeem his holdings by paying to the county the full amount of Craig's purchase price. If he failed to do that within one year, the final deed was Craig's. That year's grace, for Jed Rawlins, would be up at midnight the next day. There was yet but some forty-eight hours in which Rawlins' sweetheart, Tess Parker, hoped to raise the redeeming tax money by a sale of her cattle, and reclaim the land for Rawlins while he himself returned to stand trial for the killing of Mel Craig's foreman and at the same time, be present to demand his tax redemption rights.

The Masked Rider and Tess Parker had been riding slowly along while the girl continued to relate to the outlaw how a year back, the fiend El Viborito, had first appeared on the range. At first his work had been simple rustling raids in which the smaller cattlemen of the district had been stripped of their herds. Then, with most of the small ranch owners forced to leave the country, El Viborito had taken to the fencing of waterholes. This had almost forced the few large land holders left to herd their stock day and night and keep them within their own range. Towards the last had come El Viborito's murderous raids. The Stentstrom ranch was not his first. Bolder and bolder he was becoming.

Only Mel Craig, some distance away in the basin, had missed El Viborito's scourging hand. Because Craig's outfit was well away from the badlands, this fact had caused no suspicion. Craig however had created a suspicion of his own as to who the fiend, El Viborito really was. He had branded the raids, rustlings, and waterhole fencing as the work of Jed Rawlins, seeking revenge on the people of the badlands' border for the loss of his land and his outlawing. Jed Rawlins with his Mexican friends, Mel Craig, openly declared, was the only man that knew the badlands well enough to accomplish the deeds El Viborito admitted by his brand signature, left at the scene of each crime.

The Masked Rider had been about to ask the girl something about the band she and her Mexicans had pursued from the

Stentstrom ranch to lose on the canyon trail, when suddenly, he drew reins. The girl halted beside him. Ahead, a tiny glow of red was painting the sky above a huge pinnacle of rock. The Masked Rider stared. Somewhere behind the screen of rock ahead, a tiny fire was burning. A small fire of greasewood, such as a cowhand would use to fry a bit of bacon or heat a running iron. The Masked Rider wondered. Who could be using a fire for either purpose at this time of night?

As they stood in the mocking silence of the badlands a sudden, faint moan drifted through the night. The Masked Rider straightened. The girl wheeled her horse closer.

"Wait here," The Masked Rider whispered low. "I'm going to see what it is. Don't follow me unless I call."

The girl did not answer. Cautiously the outlaw worked his mount in through the treacherous scab-rock towards the signaling glow beyond. Suddenly as he rounded a pinnacle of rock, the blackness about him dissolved. Ahead, in a pocket between two towering shafts of rock, burned a tiny fire. A man crouched over it. For a moment the outlaw thought him alone. Some drifting puncher warming himself, he reasoned. As the man before the fire straightened, however, The Masked Rider saw something else. Lying flat on his back a short distance from the fire, was a second man.

As The Masked Rider watched he saw the prone man squirm as if struggling to rise. The man who had turned from the fire crossed over to him. In his hand he carried what for the instant appeared to The Masked Rider to be but a burning brand from the fire. The standing figure bent over.

The Masked Rider saw more clearly. That glowing shaft in the hand of the standing man was a heated running iron. The man was holding it threateningly above the prone one's head.

SILENTLY, THE OUTLAW slid from his horse. The animal never moved. Hugging close to the rocks, his *mantilla* high as a shield to the white of his face, the hooded shadow crept closer. Faintly, a sneering voice drifted from the direction of the fire.

"I guess this'll make you talk, mister," the sneering voice spoke. "I'm givin' you one more chance now. Where you carryin' that money? C'mon. Spill it."

The crouching man thrust down the glowing iron point. A cry of pain sounded from the man on the ground. For the first time, The Masked Rider saw that the man on the ground was bound, hand and foot. The man with the running iron was touching its heated point to the helpless one's ears. Now, he drew it across the bound man's forehead.

The Masked Rider's blood boiled. His six-gun was in his hand as he cautiously and quietly crept closer. He was almost at the fire. The man with the heated running iron, his sneering curses drowning the soft patter of The Masked Rider's footsteps, still hurled down his threats. The Masked Rider was almost beside him. Then suddenly, a horse-hoof clicked against rock behind him. The standing bay had moved to follow.

Beside the fire, the man with the branding iron whirled.

"Stick 'em up," The Masked Rider ordered.

The answer of the man with the heated iron, was to hurl straight at the phantom-like shadow that crouched alongside the fire. The Masked Rider leaped to the side to dodge. He saw the hand that had just hurled the iron dive for the gun at his hip. Saw more, the face of the man that hurled the iron was masked.

The cloaked caballero's teeth bared in a snarl as he pressed the trigger of the gun in his hand. Only a dull click answered the hammer snap. Some sand from his swim in the Rio had jammed the cylinder in his gun. The weapon was useless. Across, a gun muzzle was lifting to bear down at him.

Like a leaping panther, The Masked Rider hurled himself forward. With the move, he flung the useless gun in his hand straight at the muzzle of the weapon lifting to meet him. A

shot roared in the night. Another. The flame stab singed
the cloth of The Masked
Rider's hood. The lead hissed
by his ear. His hurled weapon
had thrown the aim of the
torturer to one side. That frac-
tion of an instant off balance

was all The Masked Rider
needed. Like some charging
beast he closed in. Together
the two battling men went to
the ground. The Masked
Rider's fists lashed out like
plunging ramrods.

However, the man beneath
The Masked Rider was no
weakling. He met The Masked
Rider's charge, blow for blow.
Over and over they rolled.
Once a scream of pain blasted from the man beneath him
as the cloaked man clutched
for a throat grip and pushed
the hand of his victim against
the still glowing branding iron
that had bounced back into the center of the struggle from the
rocks about.

The Masked Rider had succeeded in forcing the man beneath
him to release his grip on the gun in his hand. Now, with the

battle fist to fist, man to man, The Masked Rider half straightened as he snatched down to rip the mask from about the face of the man he struggled with. That move was fate. The man beneath him seemed to double one foot underneath him and lash it out like the spring of a striking snake. It caught The Masked Rider full on the hip and hurled him backward. Before The Masked Rider could again scramble to his feet, the man with whom he struggled had whirled and leaping across the fire, dashed to where his horse stood a dozen paces away.

THE MASKED RIDER leaped to follow. He saw he was too late. His victim had gained his saddle and wheeled his mount. The Masked Rider clawed about for the gun he had forced from his grip. Even as he lifted it to fire, the mounted man twisted his horse past a screen of rock. On foot, The Masked Rider raced to follow. By the side of the bay he halted, crouched low. A second horse had wheeled past the screen of rock. The Masked Rider held fire. In the glow from the fire he saw it was the girl he had left back at the trail. She pushed hurriedly in to where The Masked Rider crouched.

"Quick," she called excitedly. "That shot; they heard it somewhere down the trail. I heard men shouting. They are coming this way. A band of men."

The Masked Rider stood alongside his horse. "What of that poor devil!" he barked. "That fiend was torturing him with a hot running iron. Trying to make him tell where he had his money hid."

"I'll take care of him," the girl snapped back. "You'd better ride. I'll wait here. It's the sheriff and his men coming. I heard someone shout for him."

The Masked Rider swung into his saddle. The posse from the river, he reasoned. They were returning by the river trail. The girl would be safe with them. The hoof pounds were already plain.

A startled cry as he made to wheel his horse past the screen of rocks whirled The Masked Rider in his saddle. The girl was bending over the bound man on the ground. "What's the matter?" The Masked Rider called.

"Why... why," came the choking answer. "It's Mr. Pittnor. And look. El Viborito's snake brand, it's... it's been burned across his forehead. El Viborito's branded him."

The Masked Rider wheeled his horse into the blackness and touched spurs. He himself had caught a beckoning shout for the sheriff, sounding from some place down the trail. His breath blasted a curse as the bay leaped ahead. Pittnor... El Viborito had lain in wait for the cattle buyer from Laredo. Had traced his snake brand across the helpless cattle buyer's forehead. El Viborito himself; and his hand of justice had failed. The pound of the racing bay seemed to scream a taunt. The whip of the breeze soothed him. He would see El Viborito again. Again soon. And he would know him.

The outlaw bent low in his saddle, urging his mount toward Los Comino. His mind reeled with the new developments, and in his heart he vowed that El Viborito would not escape again.

CHAPTER VII

WAYNE MORGAN
GOES CALLING

IT WAS A low chuckling that awoke Wayne Morgan next morning from his bed in the straw loft above the stalls at the Star stables. He opened his eyes to stare up at a grinning face standing above him. His brain flashed clear as he forced an answer to the grin. It was as he had planned.

Riding from the badlands, hours before, he had cautiously worked his way back towards Los Comino. There, he had cautiously circled about until his imitated signal of a coyote's cry had brought Blue Hawk. Sending the Mexican Indian to get his own horse, staked at the edge of town, he had then ordered Blue Hawk to take Craig's bay and turn it loose somewhere out on the edge of the badlands. With that he had sneaked back into the loft of the Star stable where, concealing his black hood and *mantilla* in the folds of his blanket roll, he had bedded himself down in the straw of the loft for a much needed sleep. Now, the grinning stable-hand was discovering him so.

"Be Jabbers, I've heard of them that can sleep through hell and high-water but I never believed it," the round, wrinkled face of the stable-hand cracked to speak as he raked his pitchfork into the straw. "What mind of man be ye, cowboy! Ye mean ye slept through all that rumpus last night with never a roll over?"

Wayne Morgan grinned the wider as he studied the homely, Irish face above him. "Reckon maybe I just ain't used to peaceful quiet," Wayne offered, sensing the meaning of the stable-hand's words.

"Well, you certainly didn't have it last night," the stable-hand spoke up. "I ain't seen such excitement since the reservation opened."

"What happened?" Wayne quizzed, innocently.

"What happened?" the stable-hand puffed. "Well, first of all, nobody but that skunk what calls himself El Viborito paid the town a visit in person. At least the sheriff says it was El Viborito. Judge Mann, the fellah that was honored with the visit, says it was an *hombre* what's known around other parts as The Masked Rider. Who or which don't make no difference, he sure kicked the light of day into this town. The town boys 've been stringing in here since daylight. Last I heard, they'd found Mel Craig's horse that this El Viborito stole to make his get-away, clear down in Smoke Coulee. Old Pete Pittnor, the cattle buyer from Laredo, is in town with his ears all done up like they was frost bitten and nobody ain't got nothin' to show for anything, but a lot of excuses. The El Viborito *hombre* trail-tricked 'em proper. Mel Craig's sorer than a wet settin' hen."

"Was Craig with the posse that set out from town?" Wayne asked easily, a hopeful suspicion behind his question.

"Didn't have no horse to get out of town on," the stable-hand answered. "He sat around the Sun-dance waitin' for word all night and when this morning the sheriff came riding in with Pete Pittnor and that Parker girl, I thought he'd throw a fit. Told the sheriff he couldn't catch cold in a draft. Mad… huh!"

The stable-hand set about tossing down his straw. Wayne crawled from his straw bed and folding his blankets climbed down from the loft. As he walked down the street towards the little restaurant beyond the Sun-dance, one doubtful hope was removed from his mind. Mel Craig could not have been the man that had waylaid the cattle buyer from Laredo. Since he had ridden from that little fire in the badlands he had courted the suspicion that Craig might have been the man that had escaped him. Now, the stable-hand's words assured him differently. Craig had remained in Los Comino during the chase.

WAYNE ATE BREAKFAST at the little restaurant and then wandered into the Sun-dance. The first person he sighted at the bar was a small, gray-haired man with forehead and ears wrapped in clumsy bandages. He did not need to wonder who the little man was. Talking to him was the man with the scarred face, whom Judge Mann had eaten dinner with the night before. The scarfaced man was grinning as he talked. Wayne could not help but overhear his words as he stepped to the end of the bar and ordered a drink.

"Well, you sure had a narrow escape, Mr. Pittnor," the scarfaced man was saying. "Lucky for you the sheriff came along when he did. El Viborito would have done more than just run his brand on you."

"Lucky that fightin' cuss they call The Masked Rider came along, you mean," the cattle buyer Pittnor interrupted in a wheezing voice. "I've heard of that fellow along the border a dozen times but always figured he was just bunk-house talk. Now I know different."

"Are you sure *he* wasn't El Viborito, and the fellow that stuck you up just some gun-hand laying low in the badlands?" the man with the scarred face questioned. "Somebody usin' El Viborito's reputation."

"Darn right I'm sure," the little cattle buyer replied. "This fellow that stuck me up knew who I was and that I was carryin' that Parker cattle money, just like somebody'd told him. Lucky I had my cash all hid inside the secret saddle pocket or Tess Parker would go whistlin' on sellin' her herd to...."

The little cattle buyer muffled his words with his lips. He glanced cautiously along the bar. Wayne was in the act of downing his drink. "Plumb forgot," the man Pittnor, censored himself. "Judge Mann says we're not to go talkin' about that around town. Sorry. Have a drink."

The scarfaced man nodded his head solemnly. He drank with the little man and together they talked on in low voices until finally the cattle buyer left. Wayne wandered over to a chair and began reading a paper. The scarfaced man remained at the bar.

Wayne had remained in his chair reading the paper. Glancing up he saw Mel Craig swing in through the Sun-dance's doors and cross to the bar. Craig nodded curtly to the scarfaced man at the end of the bar and with a show of naturalness at his conversation, invited him to a drink.

"You sure let a thousand dollars slip through your fingers last night," Craig called in a friendly chiding to the scarfaced one. "You know I've posted a thousand dollars reward for that snake El Viborito, dead or alive."

"We'd have had him one way or the other if somebody hadn't fired that signaling shot through the judge's window," the scarfaced man answered. "He got out just a half minute too soon. Another half minute and we'd had the place surrounded."

"Too bad, too bad," Craig mumbled. "Any idea who fired that shot?"

The scarfaced man shook his head. "It came from some place well back. A lookout, I suppose. Judge Mann thinks it might have been meant for him. He was near the window."

"Who'd want to kill that old fool?" Craig snorted. "I've heard around town he doesn't even believe it was El Viborito. Thinks you should have given him a chance to speak his piece before you closed in."

"Yes, he thinks that more than ever since that cattle buyer Pittnor and that Parker girl talked to him this morning. Seems right glad the sheriff and his posse didn't catch up with the masked devil."

WAYNE HAD BEEN watching cautiously over the top of his newspaper, drinking in every word. Now suddenly he saw Mel Craig do a curious thing. He saw him step close to the scarfaced man and under the pretext of pouring a drink for him, whisper a few hasty words from the side of his mouth. The scarfaced man nodded his head understandingly. Craig then downed his drink and left the saloon. A minute later the scarfaced man followed. Wayne waited until the scarfaced man had cleared the door and then wandered outside himself. Craig was walking down the street in the direction of the Star stable. The scarfaced man was just entering the stairway that led up to Judge Mann's rooms and office.

It was only a few minutes until Craig came riding down the street on his bay. Shouting to a passerby on the street that he intended riding on out to the home ranch to see how things were going, he passed the Sun-dance and continued on out of town. A half hour later the scarfaced man came from the direction of Judge Mann's office and passing Wayne as he still loitered at the hitching rack, hurried on to the Star stable. A few minutes and the scarfaced man rode by the Sun-dance headed along the same trail Mel Craig had taken.

Wayne did not care to risk suspicion by taking the trail of either Craig or the scarfaced man in the daylight. Moving down the street he quickly located Blue Hawk.

"The man that calls himself Craig and the man with the knife cut upon his cheek have both ridden towards the north, *amigo*," Wayne spoke as under the pretext of lighting a cigarette he paused a moment beside where the Mexican Indian lounged against a building wall. "It might be best if we learn when and where they meet. I shall wait here for your return."

Minutes later Wayne saw Blue Hawk urging his sleepy pony down the street, unhurried, as if time and distance were of no consequence.

The day passed slowly for Wayne. He learned but little of value aside from the fact that the scarfaced man was a stranger in town and called himself Jim Eddy. The cattle buyer, Pittnor, had left town about noon with Judge Mann and the Parker girl, to look at and appraise the herd the girl was holding at her ranch. The funeral of Steve Strentstrom, the murdered father and mother of little Mary, was held that afternoon and Wayne attended with the rest of the folks about town. There he saw Mary and Joe Stentstrom, the dead man's brother. Joe's stern, set face did not conceal his true grief. There was a vengeance written in the narrow squint of Joe Stentstrom's eyes.

Wayne had taken his black stallion out of the stable to attend the funeral, and after it was over he returned to the Sun-dance saloon. Hardly had he hitched the black to the rack when he caught sight of Blue Hawk, moving in from the opposite side of the rack as if to mount his own pony, hitched close to where Wayne had drawn up.

"He of the scarred face and the man that calls himself Craig are together at the ranch of the Lazy S," Blue Hawk spoke quickly. "All is not well, *señor*. I traveled the trail past the ranch house. Many men are gathering there, *señor*. It is as if every man is being drawn in from the range."

"You heard nothing?" Wayne asked quickly.

"Nothing, *señor,*" Blue Hawk answered. "Save what my senses tell me. Tonight something shall happen.

Wayne frowned nervously. What had been that whispered message Mel Craig had spoken to the scarfaced man called Jim Eddy? Why had Eddy left immediately for the rooms of Judge Mann? Why was the action at Craig's main ranch in the basin such as to create suspicion even to the Mexican Indian, Blue Hawk?

It was now late afternoon. Already the sun was beginning to dip. It would soon be dusk. Wayne Morgan resolved to answer his own questions. Mounting the black stallion he rode out of town in the direction of Mel Craig's ranch. Well clear of town he turned off the trail and headed for the shadows of a distant cliff. From beyond the cliff it was The Masked Rider that dashed from behind the sheltering rock and like a fleeting shadow in the night, gave his stallion its head towards the main ranch of the Lazy S.

CHAPTER VIII

THE RAID OF THE PITCHFORK HERD

IT WAS BLACK night when The Masked Rider topped the low rim that surrounded the Sawtooth Basin and started down at the flickering lights of the Lazy S main ranch below. Carefully he mapped the lay of the ground. Then swinging wide he circled the place and drew near the main ranch house by way of a brush-fenced creek that crossed the ranch yard.

Leaving his horse well concealed in the brush The Masked Rider proceeded on foot. The Lazy S ranch yard seemed alive with men. At the horse corrals they were busy at the task of roping and saddling. A strained buzz seemed in the air. The

Masked Rider crawled closer. His flowing black *mantilla* blended him into the blackness of the ground. Nearer and nearer he approached the house.

Suddenly, The Masked Rider dropped flat. A flood of yellow light cut the blackness from a door that had opened beyond a low porch along one side of the house. A man stood in the doorway.

"Griz. Kip." The man in the doorway shouted. "Come on in here a minute. I want to talk to you before you start out."

Two men detached themselves from the group at the corrals and crossed the ranch yard toward the house. Their spurs clicked across the plank porch. The door closed shutting off the flow of light. From within the walls of the ranch house came the muffled hum of voices.

Quickly, The Masked Rider crawled in close to the house wall. A window with a tightly drawn shade was just ahead. He moved beneath it. Plainly the voices now sounded. It was Mel Craig who was speaking.

"All right, now get this, you two," Craig was saying, a commanding slur to his voice. "For certain reasons, Jim or I can't ride with you tonight. Things are getting ticklish around town with this masked devil running loose. You boys will have to run this show alone."

An instant the room went silent. There was the rustle of paper.

"All right, look at his map, you two," Mel Craig's voice began again. "We've got a pretty good idea from what Judge Mann told Jim here, that those Pitchford cattle are being held down in that dry canyon about a mile north of the Parker ranch. That's a hard place to get into without settin' off an alarm, but with those cattle starting on a trail drive for the loading chutes at Rawhide tomorrow, every spare hand on the Pitchfork is going to be rolled in his blanket if possible. Griz, you come in from the lower end of the canyon. Kip, you drop down the side trail. You know what to do then. Head 'em for the river and keep 'em going fast. Don't slow them up till you're over the ford trail and got 'em in the river pocket. Then scatter your men and let them drift back to the ranch slow. We'll work the brands on the herd when we get around to it. Savvy that, you two?"

There was a mumbling answer from within the room. Crouched beneath the window, The Masked Rider clenched and unclenched his fists. Blue Hawk had been right. All was not well at the Lazy S. Mel Craig was planning a bold raid on the herd of shipping stock Tess Parker was holding in the hidden canyon beyond her ranch. The Masked Rider's blood began to boil. Judge Mann had betrayed the location of that hidden herd. Betrayed it to someone Craig called Jim. That person could be no one but the scarfaced man he had seen the judge with about Los Comino. The man Jim Eddy was the go-between of the judge and Craig. The Parker girl was the victim. Mel Craig was going to halt the sale of the Parker herd at any price. He must know that without the herd money which the cattle buyer Pittnor would turn over once the cattle were safe in the corrals at the shipping point, Jed Rawlins' hope of redeeming his holdings was impossible. In twenty-four hours a final deed to the Rawlins ranch and range would be Craig's, his hold would be complete.

THE MASKED RIDER found himself subconsciously refusing to believe the very words he had just heard regarding Judge Mann. Now, as evidently Craig's two top hands Griz and Kip, left the room, he heard Craig's voice again. "You're sure the judge is not holding anything back?" Craig was saying.

"Why should he?" said a nasal voice The Masked Rider now recognized for sure to be that of the scarfaced Jim Eddy's. "I've worked with him hand in glove haven't I?"

"Yes, but this fellow, The Masked Rider," Craig went on. "I've heard some of the boys talking. He's nobody to play with. They say farther up the border they swear by him."

Somebody chuckled nervously. "Well forget him. He's across

the border some place now. I ought to know shouldn't I? I saw him last."

Alongside the ranch house The Masked Rider strained his ears for more. There was the sound of someone walking across the room. The voices faded. A moment and the yellow shaft of light from the open door cut the darkness. Craig and the tall man The Masked Rider placed for Jim Eddy crossed the yard towards the corrals. A minute and they had mounted up. Together they started down the trail.

The Masked Rider squirmed nervously in his crouch in the darkness. He must work fast if he was to save the Parker girl's herd. First, though, he must know where Craig and Jim Eddy were headed for. To trail them might mean a swing away from the direction of the Parker ranch. For a moment he crouched undecided in the darkness. The rage within him mounted at the precious seconds he was losing. An instant he allowed his caution to drop as he moved nearer to the men at the corrals. That instant was nearly his undoing. A hurrying form rounded the corner of the Lazy S ranch house and fell in a sprawl over The Masked Rider's crouched body.

The Masked Rider whirled and leaped like a startled cat. His hands were clutched into the throat of the sprawled man before the falling one could even attempt to scramble to his feet. He crushed the man down with his body. There was no attempt at an outcry from the throat into which he buried his relentless fingers. Instead, a grip like the closing jaws of a clamping vise wrapped about his wrists. Fingers like steel claws ripped into the flesh. The Masked Rider felt his grip on the man's throat being torn free. Still no sound of an outcry came from the man beneath him.

The Masked Rider called on all his strength. He was battling a man with muscles that seemed, at a command, to bulge free of his very grip. He attempted to bring his knee up and crash down. A pair of claw-like legs wrapped about his hips and squeezed with a pressure that was torture. In desperation, The

Masked Rider released one hand from its clutch on the man's throat and snatched at the gun in his holster. The move was timely. At that instant the man beneath him gave a mighty squirm and twisted his body to grip The Masked Rider between his legs in a killing scissors hold. Every nerve within the outlaw seemed to paralyze. Calling on every ounce of strength within him, The Masked Rider lifted the heavy gun in his hand and lashed down. It hit with a sickening thud across the skull of the man atop him.

Weakly, The Masked Rider rolled free as the crushing wrap of legs about his middle relaxed. Gun in hand, he still crouched ready. Had sound of his struggle reached the ears of the men at the corrals? With a flush of relief, the outlaw caught the sudden new commotion about the corrals. The men of the Lazy S were mounting up. At least twenty horses and riders were milling about the corrals. The Masked Rider still held his pose. Would the unconscious man on the ground beside him be missed?

"ALL RIGHT, MEN," a voice suddenly bellowed from the center of the milling band alongside the corrals. "Take it easy and save your horses. We don't want to hit that canyon below till midnight. Be plenty of time to burn up horse flesh after that. C'mon."

Crouched low to the ground, his black *mantilla* tossed in a concealing fold across the still unconscious man sprawled beside him, The Masked Rider waited as the band of Lazy S riders went dashing away from the corral. Mentally his brain groped to gauge the time. Midnight… it could be no more than two hours away. He had no choice now. He dare not attempt to follow Craig and the scarfaced, Jim Eddy. He must beat that band of Lazy S riders to the Parker ranch and warn Tess Parker.

The Masked Rider listened a minute to make sure there was no one left about the place. Not a sound came from the house or direction of the corrals. The light within the house had been left burning. A thin streak of yellow painted the black earth a few paces ahead of him. Across it The Masked Rider saw the trace of a strand of baling wire. The man on the ground beside him was just beginning to stir from his unconsciousness.

Grabbing the unconscious man roughly by the collar, The Masked Rider dragged him to the thin seep of light from beneath the drawn window shade. Snatching up the strand of bailing wire he grabbed the wrists of the fast reviving man with whom he had struggled a moment before and began twisting the strand into a binding wrap. Suddenly, he halted in his work. Behind his hood, the eyes of The Masked Rider opened wide as he stared down into the face of the man beneath him. The man whose wrists he now bound was Joe Stentstrom, the blacksmith from Los Comino.

An instant The Masked Rider stared undecided. What was the uncle of little Mary doing here at the Lazy S? How long had he been here? The Masked Rider understood now why the fingers that gripped over his own had been like steel. That understanding brought a hope. Perhaps Joe Stentstrom had overheard more than he. The unconscious man was now stirring weakly. Perhaps Joe could tell him what he wished to know, where Craig and Jim Eddy were headed for.

The Masked Rider tossed the wrap of wire free of Stentstrom's wrists. He began shaking the blacksmith's husky shoulders.

"Stentstrom," he hissed in the limp man's ear. "Stentstrom, come to."

In the streak of light from the window, Joe Stentstrom opened his eyes weakly. A moment they held their blank stare. Then suddenly, with a sign of the grotesque outline of the man above him, they popped wide. Stentstrom's senses flashed clear.

"That... that was you I... fought with?" Stentstrom stammered.

"Yes. I didn't know it was you until just now," The Masked Rider snapped back. "Quick, tell me. How long have you been here? Craig's men have just left for a rustling raid on the Parker ranch. Craig and that scarfaced man that was with Judge Mann in town left first. Do you know where they're headed for?"

Joe Stentstrom was now himself. His wide eyes narrowed as he stared at The Masked Rider. He seemed groping for a thrust to his answer.

"Craig and that Eddy *hombre* are headed back to town so they will have a perfect alibi when the raid's pulled off," Joe Stentstrom finally spoke. "I heard them plan the whole thing. I didn't see Craig or this fellah Jim Eddy at Steve's funeral and I got to thinkin' about a few things. I came out to make sure."

"Sure of what?" The Masked Rider shot at Joe.

"SURE JUDGE MANN was really in with this bunch of skunks," Joe ground out. "That night you brought me little Mary and I told you Judge Mann could tell you more of Jed Rawlins. I met the judge on the street when… when they brought them two bodies in. I told him he might expect a caller that would ask him something about Rawlins. A masked caller. A minute later I saw the judge talk to this scarfaced fellah Eddy. Right after that Eddy talked to Craig. They all looked kind of scared. Craig started gettin' the boys together. He said El Viborito was going to pay the judge a visit. It was me fired that shot through the window. I was waitin'. If it had been El Viborito I'd have aimed a little different. When I saw it was you I began to understand a lot of things. After Steve's funeral I rode out this way to make sure of a few of them."

Joe Stentstrom's iron-like jaw set. He stared with narrow eyes at The Masked Rider, "Reckon that's talkin' enough," Joe finally growled. "Whatcha aimin' to do, mister?"

The Masked Rider was thinking fast. "We've got to warn Tess Parker of this raid," he snapped. "Got to get to her ranch before those Lazy S riders."

"Tess Parker's outfit won't have a chance against that band that just left here," Joe Stentstrom mumbled. "I heard Craig talkin' about it. Tess hasn't a dozen hands all told on the place.

Craig isn't a-figurin' on leavin' signs around that herd that might point his way, either. I heard him say that. Them words was all that kept me from blastin' daylight through him right there. Craig said if they left no signs, El Viborito would get the blame for the job. That's what I came here hopin' for. I was wrong. Mel Craig's not El Viborito."

The Masked Rider barely heard. His mind was flashing a vision of twenty ambushing riders charging down on a sleepy handful of surprised men. A vision of Tess Parker's useless sacrifice to regain her sweetheart's land. A curse muttered past his lips. It was lost in the flash of a sudden hope. There was a chance of beating those rustlers at their game. A desperate chance. A chance that only he himself could execute or hope to complete. A chance that even made him grin beneath his masking hood at the thrill it might offer.

"Listen, Stentstrom," The Masked Rider hurled at the man before him. "Mount up and ride straight for Tess Parker's. Craig's men are circling. You should beat them there. Tell her to turn out her men. There will be plenty of help on the way by the time Craig's men near the canyon. Get going, man. Every minute counts."

An instant Joe Stentstrom searched the black hooded form before him as if seeking assurance to The Masked Rider's words. Then, without speaking, he whirled and went hurrying off into the darkness. The Masked Rider was already running towards the creek. A sharp whistle as he cleared the creek brush and the black stallion came plowing its way through. The Masked Rider was in the saddle and away like a phantom streak in the night before Joe Stentstrom had reached the Lazy S ranch yard gate. He saw only the flash of a flying shadow of blackness sweep by him with only the thunder of racing hoofs as an assurance that his eyes had seen true.

BACK TOWARDS LOS COMINO, The Masked Rider gave the black stallion its head. The animal responded as if joying in the chance of unlimbering its stride. The ground flew beneath it. Miles reeled by to the rhythmic tabor of its hoof-beats. A half hour later, the lights of Los Comino twinkled ahead. The Masked Rider never slowed his pace. Straight for town he held the stallion's head. Straight for the single dust-paved street. Straight for the yellow lighted entrance of the Sun-dance Saloon.

A few stragglers in the street halted, glanced once at the black caped rider dashing down the street, then dived for the blacker shadows. To the Sun-dance hitching rack and The Masked Rider swung the stallion between the rack and the walls of the Sun-dance. The sound of loud laughter reached his ears. Glasses were clinking. The Sun-dance was crowded. Still The Masked Rider never paused. Straight to the swinging doors of the place he urged the black stallion. Then as the door parted to reveal horse and black-robed rider, framed in the doorway, The Masked Rider jerked his six-gun from his holster. A wild, weird cry blasted from his lips. A challenging cry. It was drowned in the roar of the six-gun in his hand as from the hip, The Masked Rider sprayed lead into the mirror and stacks of bottles atop the Sun-dance's back bar.

With the click of his gun-hammer upon the last shell, The Masked Rider whirled his black stallion. Around the hitching rack he circled it. An angry howl sounded from within the saloon. The Masked Rider turned the stallion a hundred yards down the street and then again swung the animal to send blasting in the air the load of his second gun. The challenge was accepted. Out of the Sun-dance poured its reveling crowd. Flame-stabs lashed out at The Masked Rider. Curses drifted with the roar of gunfire. Men lashed at the tied reins along the hitching-rack as they forked leather. The Masked Rider waited tauntingly until the first horse broke from the rack. Then whirling the stallion he sent it racing back down the single street of Los Comino. Back on the trail that led to the Parker ranch. The chase was on.

CHAPTER IX

THE AMBUSH

H OLDING THE STALLION only to a pace sufficient to keep his lead over the racing posse at his back, The Masked Rider swung out across the range for the Parker Ranch. The posse held to his trail firing wildly now and then as some fleeting shadow ahead offered a possible target for the masked devil that had challenged them. Quickly they swung up on to the mesa. Tonight, banks of heavy clouds masked the moon. However the trail towards the Parker outfit was plain. Far beyond it loomed the horizon of the badlands.

Suddenly, in the hooded light from behind the clouds, a single towering pinnacle of rock loomed ahead. In his day about town as Wayne Morgan, the outlaw had picked up enough idle talk to know that lonesome pinnacle of rock marked the boundary line between the Parker ranch and the old Jed Rawlins place. He was close. The hidden canyon Mel Craig had mention must be just a mile or so beyond.

The Masked Rider glanced back to see how close the posse trailed. They were not a quarter of a mile behind him. Now, deliberately, he halted the stallion and taunted the trailing band closer. As he waited, the night was suddenly split by the distant rumbling echo of a shot. Another followed. Then another. They came from ahead. Had Craig's men already started their raid? Was he too late? Those shots must be from the hidden canyon.

The Masked Rider touched spurs and urged his mount on. Behind him, the posse, too, seemed to have heard the shots. They were holding their fire, despite The Masked Rider's nearness as if trying to place the direction from which they came.

The ground rolled beneath the stallion's flying hoofs. Abruptly, the trail seemed to dive into a mass of rugged rocks. It pitched steeply down. From below it came a chaos of bawling cattle. Milling cattle. The shots must have come from within the canyon. The bawling herd below screamed it.

Like an answer to his doubt, guns began flashing in the blackness of the canyon. Up they roared to the rim. The Masked Rider now skirted. The Black Phantom did not hesitate. Over the steep rim edge he urged the stallion. The brave animal felt an instant for its footing, then gamely started its descent. The Masked Rider was a hundred feet down the steep canyon's sides when he heard the trailing posse thunder by him on the rim above. They were holding to the rim trail that would dip down into the canyon a half-mile farther on.

In the canyon bottom the firing was now scattered from a dozen places about the blackness. Shouts echoed with the bellow of terror-mad cattle. The Pitchfork men had a double battle on their hands. A battle to keep the frightened herd from stampeding as well as keeping the raiding band from gaining a position to force the stampede.

The Masked Rider was almost into the canyon bottom. Now a new rumble of shots began to thunder. The Masked Rider grinned beneath his hood. The posse had jumped the raiding band poised to drop down into the canyon once the cattle had been started on the move. The crack of rifle and pistol echoed and roared from every side. The canyon became a pit of confusion. Then like a gathering roar of thunder, above it came a loud rumbling. Quickly it mounted. A terrifying sound. The beat of maddened hoofs. The canyon herd had stampeded. Down the canyon, away from the chaos of noise, they were racing. Racing madly, blindly. Blindly to destruction.

THE STALLION WAS at the level ground of the canyon bottom. Above towered the walls, like the sides of a deep basin. The Masked Rider paused, cursing in his hopelessness. No one could guess where the trail of that stampeding herd might lead. No one could guess its fate. If those shouting riders in the bottom already riding the edge of the herd were Pitchfork men, there was a chance. If they were others… who could tell what the dawn might reveal as the results of the raid?

The Masked Rider knew it was useless for him to attempt to aid in checking the stampede. The canyon began to take on a hollow stillness as past its fencing walls the echo of herd and men faded. The Masked Rider crossed the canyon bottom to avoid the danger of meeting some straggling rider, and following the far wall, worked his way towards the canyon mouth. He was almost to the point in the canyon where the walls suddenly flared wide to fan out and gradually disappear, when a nervous snort of the stallion beneath him warned him to added caution.

Quickly, The Masked Rider swung the stallion in against the black shadows of the rocks and listened. Faintly, voices drifted through the darkness. Whispering voices. They came from somewhere across the open stretch away from the canyon walls. The Masked Rider peered into the darkness, but could see nothing. Then suddenly, his ears caught the name, El Viborito. Twice it was repeated. The rest of the words were but a mumble.

The Masked Rider slipped from his saddle. The black *mantilla* billowing above his head as he moved like a wave of blackness through the night. The Black Caballero was worming his way towards the open space. The voices grew plainer. They were not twenty feet away but even in the canyon's new stillness their whisper was barely audible.

The Masked Rider had approached as near as he dared without certain discovery. The open space ahead offered no sheltering shadows even in the blackness. Dropping flat to the ground, he strained his ears. The whispering mumble began to take form. The Masked Rider cupped his hand to an ear as he still strained to gather the words from beyond.

"It's the only way I tell you," a heavy voice was speaking. "Suspicion is bound to point our way now. We've got to clear it up. If it wasn't for those cattle stampeding, they'd have got our men flat footed. Our luck is that Griz and his men took to the other side of the canyon. If he's only got sense enough now to make for the rim trail on Smoke coulee and scatter his men like he always has, we're safe there. With a dead El Viborito here to take the blame, this raid and every other one, will be laid to him. Even if they start tracking, they lose the trail where they always do, along the rim-rocks above Smoke coulee. It'll be El Viborito's doings, first and last."

THE ANSWERING WHISPER was too low for even The Masked Rider's strained ears to gather. Evidently, the second man in the darkness beyond was asking instructions.

"As soon as you find out from the judge where his hiding spot is, get going," the heavy-whispering voice, which the outlaw was now beginning to recognize as Mel Craig's, was saying. "Tell him for his own safety, he's to ride in here masked. Bring him in an hour or so after dark. I'll have Griz take about ten men and start burning things, that'll be your signal. Then I'll ride up with the sheriff. We'll have Tess Parker herself for a witness that it's El Viborito we shot down. It'll wash us clean of every suspicion anybody may have. Get going."

There was the clink of spurs. In the darkness ahead the two riders drifted on down the canyon. Behind them, still crouched beneath his black *mantilla*, The Masked Rider did not move. A jumble of thoughts was milling through his brain.

Had he heard the voice he was positive was that of Mel Craig's for their true words? Was Mel Craig planning to decoy El Viborito into a death trap of the sheriff and his own men? A trap wherein El Viborito would be caught red-handed raiding and burning the Parker ranch, with Tess Parker a witness? From the words he had just overheard, Judge Mann was the one person that knew the real hiding place of El Viborito. Who was Craig sending to the judge as the decoy?

Beneath the hooded mask, the outlaw's features hardened. From the talk about town that day he knew Judge Mann and the cattle buyer Pittnor were leaving that morning for Rawhide to receive the Parker herd, which would be delivered that day. The judge must be the one the girl was trusting to bring back the cattle money. What manner of man was this Judge Mann that he would so deceive a girl willing to make the sacrifice Tess Parker was making to try to save the name and land of her sweetheart? What sort of plan could Judge Mann be hoping to execute once the cattle money was in his hands? Somehow, despite the evidence his own eyes and ears had gathered, The Masked Rider's mental impression of Judge Mann refused to coincide with the villainous wretch the evidence painted him to be. One thing was certain, Tess Parker must be warned of Judge Mann and his connection with Mel Craig through the scarfaced Jim Eddy.

Cautiously crossing the canyon, The Masked Rider turned his mount up the trail to the canyon rim. At the rim he held to the shadows of the rougher ground and gradually worked his way on a circular course towards the Parker ranch house. Within sight of the corrals he moved the stallion into a narrow alley of blackness alongside a shed and dismounting started for the ranch house.

AT THE RANCH house all was dark. The Masked Rider made sure the house was entirely empty, then returning to where he had left his stallion, he decided to wait until Tess Parker arrived. It was to be a longer wait than the hooded outlaw expected. It was within an hour of dawn before a lone rider approached the ranch house and swung in towards the corral. The Masked Rider muttered in disappointment as he saw the rider was a man. That disappointment vanished as he suddenly recognized the stocky form of Joe Stentstrom.

Joe Stentstrom had dismounted and was about to enter the ranch house when The Masked Rider stepped out of the darkness alongside of him. Joe started back as his hand went for his gun.

"Hold it," The Masked Rider snapped, his own gun coming up in self protection on the chance that something unforeseen had changed the blacksmith's friendly attitude.

Joe Stentstrom's gun was already sliding back into its holster. "Didn't expect you about," he offered sheepishly. "Thought that posse was still on your tail."

"What happened to the herd?" The Masked Rider asked anxiously.

"Reckon luck was with us there," Joe Stentstrom answered. "When they pulled out they headed straight for the cross-desert trail to Rawhide. Most of the boys that was trailin' you, swung after them and just sort of let them run themselves out across the sand. Reckon they didn't lose a head."

"Where's Miss Parker?" The Masked Rider continued quickly. "I must see her at once."

"Reckon you'll have to go on in to Rawhide to do that," Joe Stentstrom answered, matter-of-fact-like. "I got here just in time to turn her and her trail crew out for the canyon when they make the first try at running 'em. When the posse mixed with that second band on the rim, they all took for the badlands. Miss Parker's taking no chances as long as she's got half the drifters in town willin' to stick with the drive. She's gone on in with the herd. They're drivin' them right on for the corrals at Rawhide."

The Masked Rider shifted weight impatiently. "But Judge Mann will be there with that cattle buyer too. I learned in town they were leaving at daylight. Did you tell her what you suspected of the judge? That he was in with Craig and dealing with him through the fellah Jim Eddy?"

Joe Stentstrom grinned queerly, "Reckon you and I were both wrong about the judge and that scarface fellah," Joe finally spoke. "I'm supposed to keep this under my hat but reckon you rate in on part of this. That scarfaced fellow's just about the *hombre* that's goin' to put a knot in Mel Craig's tail. He's a Texas ranger. One the judge sent clear to Austin for to do some private investigating on this range. Ain't no one knows it but the judge and Miss Parker... and now you and myself."

BEHIND HIS HOOD The Masked Rider's eyes held a far away look. His mind was flashing a vision of two still bodies laid out upon the sidewalk before the Sun-dance Saloon in Los Comino. His ears were buzzing with a queer possibility to the words he had overheard down in the canyon bottom a few hours before.

The scarfaced Jim Eddy a ranger... the thought screamed with doubt. A vague understanding began to dawn upon The Masked Rider. An understanding that carried him back to the Texas ranger dying in his arms alongside the barricaded waterhole in the coulee bottom. It was possible. So possible. He knew now why the sheriff had lied about how he had discovered the two bodies alongside the waterhole in smoke canyon. Knew now why Mel Craig had been so quick to identify them as his Lazy S riders. Knew the purpose of that reward Mel Craig had offered. Jim Eddy was no ranger. He never thought of being a ranger. Never, until that ranger badge had been discovered upon the dead man lying alongside the waterhole. The dead man whom Craig's own killer had downed. Then, as Craig's raiding party was hurrying to lose their trail in the rim rocks after Tess Parker and her band of Mexicans had jumped them clearing out of the ravaged Steve Stentstrom ranch, Craig had decided upon this bold stroke of passing one of his own men off as the dead ranger.

The Masked Rider cursed beneath his breath at the thought. That was how Craig knew every move Judge Mann made. The judge confided in the man he believed to be a person of the law and that person in turn passed the information on to Craig. That was how they had almost trapped him in the judge's rooms. How they knew of the secret roundup at the Parker ranch. How they knew of the cattle buyer coming from Laredo. How they knew his proposed trail and where El Viborito might best waylay him and rob him of the cattle money. Mel Craig was not the fiend, El Viborito. No. But Mel Craig directed the working of that fiend. Directed it just as he had overheard him direct the trap that would end the life of El Viborito, a few hours before. But it would *not* be the real El Viborito. The Black Caballero now guessed that more trickery was afoot.

The Masked Rider had leaped into the darkness and was running towards the spot where he had left the stallion. Joe Stentstrom stood watching. Even through the black hood of The Masked Rider, Joe recognized the urge behind the hunted man's haste.

"Which way headin', mister?" Joe Stenstrom called. "Be needin' a hand?"

"Wait here," The Masked Rider shouted back as he swung into his saddle. "When Miss Parker comes back warn her not to trust the scarfaced Jim Eddy. He's no ranger. He's Craig's undercover man. I'm headin' for Los Comino to try and catch the judge before he leaves town. Craig's planning to plant a fake El Viborito on this range tonight. Lead him and plant him. That El Viborito is somebody the judge is tryin' to protect. Jed Rawlins' the name, is my guess."

A clink of spurs and The Masked Rider was away. Behind in the darkness, Joe Stenstrom mumbled to himself. Mel Craig was framing Jed Rawlins to be branded as the fiend El Viborito. Why? Fear always had a reason. Joe's hand was unconsciously stroking the butt of the six-gun at his hip.

CHAPTER X

THE AVENGING RIDER

THE MASKED RIDER spared the black stallion no hazard as he sent the willing beast flying wildly over the trail for Los Comino. The lights of the little cowtown still twinkled lonesomely in the gathering glow of the slate-gray skies as the outlaw drew in sight. Once he halted, and throwing his head back, emitted the weird wailing cry of a coyote. A minute and it was answered from the edge of town. The Masked Rider headed towards the sound. Blue Hawk advanced to meet him.

"The fellow, Judge Mann," The Masked Rider demanded hurriedly of the Mexican Indian. "You have kept an eye for him, *amigo?* He is still in town?"

"No, *señor*," the Mexican Indian answered. "The moon still lit the sky when he and the man with the bandaged face left towards the north."

The Masked Rider cursed beneath his breath. Judge Mann and Pittnor the cattle buyer must have received word that Tess Parker had decided to drive her herd directly on into Rawhide, and they had left at least an hour or more before the time planned.

"Tell me, *amigo*," The Masked Rider questioned on. "The man with the scarred face. He has been to town? You have seen him?"

"*Si, señor*," Blue Hawk answered quickly. "It was he that brought the word that sent the judge on his way. The man with the scarred face still remains. But this moment I saw him before the place of drink."

The Masked Rider thought fast. Jim Eddy was still in town. There was little chance of overhauling the judge before he reached Rawhide. His best hope was to wait here in Los Comino until the judge returned. As long as Jim Eddy remained in town nothing was likely to happen. It was not until night that the trap he had overheard being set in the darkness of the lonesome canyon was scheduled to be sprung. Judge Mann should be back in town by then.

The horizon was already taking on the blaze of dawn. The Masked Rider gave a thought to his own safety. If he remained in town it was best he did so as Wayne Morgan. Therefore, quickly slipping from his black hood and *mantilla*, he uncinched his saddle and secured his disguise safely in the folds of his blanket. Again he circled town to approach the Star stable from the direction of the trail leading towards the Parker ranch.

Riding boldly into town, Wayne Morgan had his mount stabled, and having instructed Blue Hawk to warn him should Jim Eddy attempt to leave town, Wayne crawled once more into the straw loft for a bit of much needed rest. The stable-hand assuming he had been one of the party that had joined the chase from town on the heels of The Masked Rider that had shot up the Sun-dance, offered him the privilege of the loft willingly.

WAYNE AWOKE WITH the sound of voices in his ears. From the angle of the streaming sunbeams through the cracks in the loft's wall, he judged it was well past noon. A dozen men were just unsaddling their horses and having them stabled in the line of stalls below.

"Old Judge Mann seemed as glad to see that Pitchfork herd hit them corrals at Rawhide as that Parker girl, eh?" someone spoke from within a stall. "Reckon he's taken kind of a chance, though, staying out to that Parker ranch with all that cattle money and El Viborito still riding loose on this range."

"Joe Stentstrom's there with them," a second voice called back. "Saw him over at the barn when we pulled out. Reckon there's not much danger, long's it's daylight."

Wayne Morgan waited to hear no more. Remaining in the loft only until the men below had cleared out he quickly saddled up the stallion and not waiting to locate Blue Hawk and inform him of his intention, hit the trail again for the Parker ranch.

It was still early afternoon when he approached the place. There was not a sign of life about the ranch yard though a faint wisp of smoke arose from the chimney at the end of the ranch barn. Riding up a shallow arroyo, Wayne managed to work the stallion unseen into a bunch of cotton woods directly below the house. There, he quickly removed his hood and *mantilla* from beneath his saddle, and creeping into the barn made a quick search about. There was no one around and the three horses in the stalls made him sure that Joe Stentstrom and the judge were still there with Tess Parker.

Taking a block of wood he found on the barn floor, The Masked Rider began beating it against the side of a stall to imitate a wild kicking horse. The noisy commotion brought a quick reward. It was Judge Mann himself who came hurrying from the ranch house to investigate the commotion amongst the stabled animals.

The Masked Rider allowed the judge to enter the barn before he stepped from the shadows against the wall. The judge drew back with a start. Sight of the hooded man before him making no move towards the gun at his hip seemed to give him confidence. "You… you are The Masked Rider?" the judge quizzed.

"The same that visited you in your rooms at Los Comino," The Masked Rider answered quickly. "I came to warn you of this man Jim Eddy. The man you believe to be a ranger. I—"

"Yes… yes… Joe Stentstrom had been telling me," the judge cut in anxiously. "I am positive Eddy is a ranger. He showed me his papers. Even showed me a confidential letter in answer to the one I wrote to the governor. You must be mistaken."

"When did this Eddy first show you his papers?" The Masked Rider demanded coolly. "When did you first meet him face to face?"

"Why… why… the same night you visited me in my rooms," the judge answered. "Just a few hours before you visited me. Just before the sheriff—"

"Just before the sheriff brought in the body of the real Jim Eddy along with one of Mel Craig's killers," The Masked Rider cut in. "The real Jim Eddy died in my arms. That scarfaced man posing as Jim Eddy is one of Craig's men masquerading as a ranger."

THE JUDGE SEEMED to stiffen erect. His lips chewed for words. "Then… then… this scarfaced man… he is leading Jed Rawlins into a trap. I… I… have sent Jed to…."

The Masked Rider caught the remorseful terror in the judge's voice. "You have what?" he shot at the judge. "What does this fake ranger know?"

"He knows where Jed Rawlins is hiding across the border," the judge answered weakly. "I sent him with a letter instructing Jed to return with the man I supposed to be a ranger. This... this man I supposed to be Eddy was to bring Jed into town after dark so that Jed might claim his tax redemption rights. I had it all arranged with the court clerk. This supposed ranger was then to arrest Jed and take him to Rawhide for trial. I... I...."

The bait of Craig's clever trap as revealed in his words spoken in the darkness of the canyon beyond the Parker ranch, now flashed clear to The Masked Rider. He had been right. Jed Rawlins was to be led into a slaughtering ambush where Craig and his men, lying in wait with the sheriff, would plant on him the evidence that would leave no doubt but that Jed Rawlins was the fiend who had terrorized the badland's borders. The scarfaced man posing as Jim Eddy was leading him into that trap. After the murder of Jed Rawlins, the masquerading ranger would drop from sight leaving no witness to prove Jed's innocence or deny the positive evidence Craig and his men intended planting.

"Quick, man!" The Masked Rider barked. "We must warn Jed Rawlins before he steps into this trap. Where is his hiding spot?"

"At the deserted sheep camp a mile or so across the border at the Big Sand Ford," the judge gasped in answer. "But... but, you will be too late. This... this Eddy was to leave for there shortly after noon. It is now...."

The Masked Rider cursed to himself. The masquerading Jim Eddy had undoubtedly been in town when he had left or Blue Hawk would have warned him. There was only one hope. The speed of his stallion. The Masked Rider dashed from the barn and plunged into the cottonwood thicket. With only a shout at the wide eyed judge to remain at the Parker ranch until he heard from him, the outlaw gave the stallion its head. The animal seemed to understand. Out across the mesa trail the beast raced. There was no need of urging spurs. Like a sweeping bat lashing through the sunlight, The Black Caballero headed south.

He knew well the location of the Big Sand Ford. An hour's riding and he was pushing the stallion belly-deep into the Rio. Hopefully he glanced up at the sun. It was dipping fast. A foreboding dread gripped him. If Jed Rawlins and the masquerading Jim Eddy were to reach the Parker ranch at dusk, they must be well along the trail by now. His only hope was of meeting them.

With this in mind The Masked Rider sacrificed time and speed to the chance of a meeting. He did as much in vain. At the abandoned sheep camp, after having doffed his disguise, he quickly learned from the few Mexicans about that Jed Rawlins and an unknown man had left a good hour before. Left about the time he himself had started from the Parker ranch.

THAT FACT MULLED its way through Wayne Morgan's brain. Why had he not run into Rawlins and the scarfaced man on the trail? A sudden light leaped to Morgan. The masquerading ranger would not dare ride the open trail to the Parker ranch in the daylight. He could undoubtedly skirt the badlands and lie near their edge, as close to the Parker ranch as possible, until dusk. If he could pick up their trail beyond the ford....

Morgan was away and headed back for the border with all the stallion's speed. Back at the ford, he slowed the stallion's pace as he began searching the trail for signs. They showed plain. Two riders had crossed the ford not an hour before and headed to the north. Two riders, traveling side by side. Wayne Morgan donned his hood and cloak.

For a mile The Masked Rider worked his way slowly along, always holding the trail of those two riders in sight. Suddenly he jerked the stallion to a halt. A queer sinking gripped him.

The trail had turned sharply to the right. To the badlands. Hopefully The Masked Rider followed. The sinking within his middle repeated. The trail swung into the scab-rock. Already it was disappearing. No man could follow even a track as fresh as the one that had led him here, through the badlands' rocky stretches.

With that very vanishing of hope, a new tenseness seemed to grip The Masked Rider. His eyes had caught another marking upon the trail. A strange marking. A third horse had here swung as from nowhere to follow in the wake of the two riders. The Masked Rider's lips cracked into a grin as he studied that third track. A shoeless horse.... Blue Hawk. The faithful Mexican Indian, finding The Masked Rider had disappeared from the stable loft, had resorted to what he believed The Masked Rider would wish of him. He had trailed the masquerading Jim Eddy from Los Comino.

For a few minutes The Masked Rider rode deeper into the badlands until he had gained a shallow coulee rim. Then lifting his hood, he threw his head back and with all the power of his lungs emitted the weird, lonesome howl of a coyote. Out across the coulee rim the howl echoed... re-echoed... faded. Dead silence settled. Then, faintly but clear, came an answering howl. Blue Hawk had caught his signal.

Twice The Masked Rider repeated the call. Twice it was answered. Gray shadows were already beginning to drop across the badlands. Dusk was not far away. On The Masked Rider urged his stallion. Then suddenly from out of the gloom barely past the trail edge, came the sharp chirp of a cricket. The Masked Rider jerked reins. Blue Hawk stepped out of the shadows.

"They are just ahead, *señor*," the Mexican Indian whispered in a guarded voice. "He of the scarred face and a man whose face is strange. They rest among the rocks."

Together The Masked Rider and Blue Hawk worked their horses along the trail that zig-zagged back and forth through the screening pinnacles of rock. Suddenly, Blue Hawk hissed.

The Masked Rider turned. Blue Hawk pointed. A shielding wing of rock protruded just ahead. From behind it came voices.

"WE BETTER BE starting soon," someone spoke from behind the shielding rock. "You say the judge told you to have me there right after dark."

"It won't be dark for an hour yet on the mesa," a second voice, The Masked Rider instantly recognized for the masquerading Jim Eddy answered. "We want it almost dark when we ride into the Parker ranch. They're setting off a couple of cocks of hay for a signal. When we see a sky glow we'll start."

The Masked Rider listened to no more. Quickly he drew Blue Hawk towards him.

"Ride like the wind, *amigo*," he whispered into the ear of the Mexican Indian, as the desperate plan that had been toying in his brain since he took the trail to the ford, suddenly took form. "Ride to the town of Los Comino. Speak so all may hear, *amigo*, and say you have heard spoken that El Viborito raids the ranch of Tess Parker at dusk. Ride swift, *amigo*. There will be need of much help at the ranch of Tess Parker within the hour."

The Indian was away like a vanishing shadow. The Masked Rider crept closer to the rock edge. His gun was in his hand. Around the rock the two men still talked. The Masked Rider waited for his moment. Then leaping ahead he raced a dozen strides to round the shielding wing of rock like some demon popping from nowhere.

"Stick 'em up!" The Masked Rider's voice rasped from beneath his hood. "Hold it, Rawlins. I'm not after you."

Two startled men froze motionless in their squat against the rock at their back. The eyes of The Masked Rider never left the face of the scarfaced masquerading ranger.

"This man was walking you into a trap, Rawlins," The Masked Rider began speaking as he still kept the two men before him covered. "He passed himself off to Judge Mann as the Texas ranger one of Mel Craig's killers murdered across the badlands.

Tonight he was leading you into a trap Craig has set for you that would have ended with you being ambushed and evidence planted to show you were El Viborito. Is that enough to prove to you my gun's not hunting your trail?"

A tall, square-jawed young man arose slowly to his feet. His hands remained shoulder high.

"But... but, this *hombre* said Judge Mann and Tess were waiting for us at Tess's place," young Rawlins managed in a puzzled drawl. "If Mel Craig's tryin' something there, how—?"

"Mel Craig's trying plenty there," The Masked Rider cut in. "That sky glow signal you're waiting for was to be no few hay cocks. It was to be the Parker ranch house. But don't worry. I've already sent that information on into Los Comino. There should be plenty of men on hand to greet Craig's outfit if they start anything."

"Reckon I'm convinced," Jed Rawlins mumbled. "I... I savvy now why this *hombre* insisted on me ridin' into Tess's masked. I... was to be...."

The masquerading Jim Eddy had attempted to move a step back. "Hold it, Mister Scarface," The Masked Rider grated threateningly. "I ain't aiming to kill you less I have to. You'll do some nice talkin' I'm thinking when you meet up with Mel Craig face to face."

THE SCARFACED MAN did not stir. The Masked Rider risked a glance to the two standing horses a few paces beyond. Recognition flashed to him of the sturdy bay nearest him. It was Mel Craig's horse, the same animal he had ridden in his escape from the trap at the judge's rooms. Evidently, Mel Craig had seen to it the masquerading Jim Eddy was mounted upon the fastest piece of horse flesh his outfit had to offer to insure his get-away in case of a chase, once the trap at the Parker ranch had been sprung.

Jed Rawlins had moved a pace away from the scarfaced man.

"I don't know who you are stranger," Rawlins spoke, "but I'm backin' your play. What now?"

"We're mounting up and riding for the Parker ranch," The Masked Rider snapped in answer. "This *hombre's* going with us. We'll wait there until the folks from town ride in to be ready for Mel Craig's surprise party. Maybe by the time they get there, we can drag a few words out of this skunk that will make Craig sing a different tune when he rides up. Start movin', we want to get there before dark. Craig will be closin' in after that."

The man with the scarred face still held his hands shoulder high. At The Masked Rider's command, he turned and started to his horse. Jed Rawlins was already beside his mount. The Masked Rider followed a pace behind the scarfaced one.

At the standing bay, the scarfaced man reached slowly out and gathered in the reins of the bay. His hands lifted to the horn of the bay's saddle. The Masked Rider watched those hands. Now he stepped close to reach out and flip the scarfaced one's gun from his hip holster. With hand almost at the holster tip, The Masked Rider froze. His eyes glue to the back of the hand now upon the horn of the bay's saddle. Something seemed to be shrieking through his brain. Pounding through. On the back of that hand, a long ugly burn crossed from little finger to thumb base. A burn such as would have been made by a glowing branding iron. A pressed branding iron.

The Masked Rider's brain flashed a vision of the crouched man he had sneaked up on, back at the tiny grease-wood fire amid the badlands' brakes the night before. The man that had traced the wavy, snake-like brand of El Viborito upon the forehead of the helplessly bound cattle buyer Pittnor. The man with whom he had struggled. Fought... and in fighting heard utter that cry of pain as his thrashing hand came down upon and pressed against the still glowing iron upon the ground. That man would have had a fresh scabbed burn across the back of his hand such as the hand now placed upon the bay's saddle horn fronted before him. That man had branded himself. Branded himself for the fiendish killer of the badlands, El….

The Masked Rider had remained frozen in the thrill of his racing thoughts. Now, so suddenly the upward jerk of the scarfaced one's boot was invisible in the shadows, the man with his hand upon the bay's saddle whirled. His leg kicked out. It caught The Masked Rider upon the knee. Not that alone sent The Masked Rider bowling backward. With the jerk of weight to its saddle, the bay whirled as well. Its rump forced The Masked Rider off balance. Before he could catch himself, the bay had sprung past the mounting Jed Rawlins. On the ground, The Masked Rider was forced to hold fire. Jed Rawlins blocked his aim. Blocked even sight of the leaping bay as it sprang ahead and rounded a shelf of rock with the scarfaced man still fighting to gain the saddle.

"Don't fire," The Masked Rider shouted as he saw Jed Rawlins' gun come up. "Hold it. I want him alive."

A whistle blasted from The Masked Rider's lips. An instant and the black stallion came racing around the shelf of rock. "Quick, Rawlins, get going!" The Masked Rider hurled at Jed Rawlins. "Judge Mann and Tess are at the ranch. Tell them to wait for me at Joe Stentstrom's house in Los Comino. I'm bringing back El Viborito. The real El Viborito… the snake of the badlands. Get going."

The Masked Rider's instep had touched. The stallion lunged forward like a lashing whip tongue. Around the wing of rock it dashed. A shallow arroyo loomed ahead. Hoof pounds thundered from it. A low crouching form upon the back of a flying flash of horseflesh was just clearing the arroyo three hundred yards ahead. The stallion swung into pursuit. The Masked Rider did not attempt to draw down with the gun in his hand. Instead he stuffed the gun into its holster as he bent low in his saddle. This was to be a test of beast against beast. Dumb courage against dumb courage. He wanted El Viborito alive. The Masked

Rider's avenging hand of outlaw justice would descend—but not until its stroke dealt righteousness to all.

CHAPTER XI

EL VIBORITO, THE SNAKE

IN THROUGH THE twisting alleys of the badlands' rock-walled passages, The Masked Rider tore in pursuit of El Viborito and his racing bay. Now he sighted the lunging bay for an instant. Now only its thundering hoofs guided him in the chase. Gradually they began working towards the high lands. El Viborito was not heading back towards the Parker ranch. Instead he was twisting and turning his mount through the broken ground in a general direction of the borderlands. The smooth land of the mesa seemed his goal.

Suddenly the badlands seemed to fade away. The broad mesa, smooth and stretching endlessly into the gathering dusk, swept beneath them. The Masked Rider peered ahead. El Viborito still bent low as he urged the bay on. The Masked Rider gauged the distance. The black stallion seemed not to have gained an inch. El Viborito still raced with a good three hundred yards' lead between him and the lunging stallion that now, with sight of his quarry, seemed to gather in a new burst of speed.

The Masked Rider gave the eager beast its head. The stallion seemed to understand. Ears back, eyes wide, nostrils dilated, it gave its all without the prod of spurs or lash of quirt. Ahead, the sturdy bay seemed to sense the added burst in the thunder of hoofs. It too, seemed to give its all.

Mile after mile reeled off beneath the two racing beasts. The black stallion seemed not to have gained an inch. The bay still held its lead. Dusk was thickening about them, making the trail footing less sure. Still the two horses and riders plunged on.

On across the mesa to where, now fast growing closer, a black horizon marked the opposite bounding border of the badlands.

The Masked Rider began to sense a familiarity in the trail he rode. That horizon ahead had appeared before him once before within the past few days since he had crossed the desert. He was riding straight south towards the Rio and the Mexican border he knew. That alone did not map his course. Once before that bay, now setting the pace, had led him toward a horizon similar to that ahead.

The Masked Rider remembered. The long canyon to the Rio ford where two nights before he had ridden the bay on to the blind river trail. Ahead was the entrance to that canyon. The bay knew only one avenue of escape in a chase. Either the horse or the hand that held its reins would choose that avenue. The bay was again headed for the Rio ford with its hidden blind trail that led to the secret rendezvous between the canyon cliffs.

Even as The Masked Rider recognized the trail, ahead, the bay seemed to leap through a frame of blackness and disappear. The last mile the black stallion had been gaining fast. Not a hundred and fifty yards separated the two beasts. Now out of the frame of blackness ahead came a shower of flame spurts. Lead whistled about The Masked Rider. The black stallion never slowed its pace. On into the very face of the firing it pushed. The canyon's blackness swallowed them.

THE MASKED RIDER still gave the stallion its head. Recklessly the brave beast plunged through the blackness, seeming to miss rock and trail hole as if some hidden sense guided it. The pace had been a grueling one, The Masked Rider knew. The stallion was tiring, he knew. So too must the bay ahead be feeling the pace. However, the stallion made no offer to slow up. Down... down through the inky blackness of the rough canyon it raced on. Only the hoof clatters ahead seemed its goal, its urge.

Suddenly the glazed sweep of the river loomed ahead. At its

edge the bay was just plunging into the water to round the cliff's wing. The Masked Rider was not a hundred yards back.

The stallion too had sighted the disappearing bay. Without the touch of reins he headed straight for the wing of rock. To the water's edge, and he waded deep. Around the wing of rock all showed black within the canyon. Ahead a hoof clicked against rock. The stallion needed no more. Its feet found the shelf-like trail. On to it the horse climbed. Once it snorted as from ahead came a loud, resounding splash. The Masked Rider understood. The stallion only raised its ears, raced to the trail end and then as if suddenly realizing where the only avenue of escape lay, whirled to face out toward the swirling waters below.

The Masked Rider touched spurs. The stallion leaped out. Down… down… down, horse and rider plunged. The Masked Rider held to his saddle-horn. He knew this time. Gently he spoke to the stallion as the beast began using all its remaining strength in a vain effort to swim towards the shore.

Down the stream the current swept them. The Masked Rider only waited, crooning soft words of courage to the stallion. Then abruptly, the sweep of the current changed. The black cliff moved closer. They were at the boom. For the first time The Masked Rider spoke an urging word. The stallion pawed for shore. Not twenty yards ahead was the bay, barely visible in the gloom, struggling to gain the shore.

From the shore line came a spurt of flame. The click of a hammer upon a dead shell sounded above the fading roar of a shot. The stallion, too was now climbing the shore. The Masked Rider still held his fire. Twenty-five yards ahead, the bay whirled and went plunging across the dusk-draped opening toward where a single lighted window showed against the cliff. The stallion sprang in pursuit. Stride for stride they raced. Stride for stride, the black gained. Twenty yards. Ten yards. Five…. The bay seemed to cave and go down on its knees. A pitiful moan sounded through the night. As the noble horse sank the man upon its back slipped from the saddle and made a wild dash for the door of the cabin against the cliff. A cry was upon his lips. A cry for help.

The cabin door swung open. A man with gun in hand stood poised. "Kip, it's me," the man racing for the cabin door screamed. "Get him. The Masked Rider."

The Masked Rider's gun spoke first. The man in the door slumped. As he sank down, the barrel of The Masked Rider's gun lashed across the skull of the man he had chased. He too sank. For a moment The Masked Rider waited ready for what more might come. A foreboding stillness clamped down over the little hidden canyon. Only the wheezing moan of the bay marred the quiet. The bay that had given its all in vain. The black stallion stood by, the conqueror. The bay's head dropped to the ground.

THE MASKED RIDER peered inside the single room of the cabin. A candle burned upon a shelf at the far wall. A piece of baling wire hung beneath it.

The man upon the floor had stirred. The Masked Rider picked him up bodily, and sat him in the heavy chair. A minute and with the baling wire he had the unconscious man's arms bound securely to the legs of the chair. Not until then did his ears catch the queer buzzing sound coming from a box in one corner, covered by the finely barred grate from the wreck of a stove nearby.

The Masked Rider stepped across the cabin and peered down into the box. He straightened with a jerk. A huge rattlesnake lay a prisoner in the box. Evidently, the man he had killed in the doorway had captured it and was holding it a prisoner to exhibit to those that would doubt its size.

The bound man in the chair had opened his eyes. He cursed The Masked Rider as he came to his full senses. The Masked Rider did not speak. A strange twist curled the lips beneath his hood. Now he searched the room until he discovered a tablet and pencil upon a shelf. These he lay on the table before the scarfaced masquerader for Jim Eddy. The eyes behind the black hood gleamed. The scarfaced man was watching every action. Only when The Masked Rider lifted the wooden box from the corner of the cabin and brought it before the scarfaced one that he might see what it contained, did the sneer leave the lips of the bound man. Only then did the hooded outlaw speak.

"You call yourself *El Viborito*," The Masked Rider said, his voice hollow as an echo. "In Spanish that means The Little Snake. You've earned your name. You've earned something else. I'm giving you one chance to redeem what you have earned. There is pencil and paper. I'll give you one minute. If in one minute you haven't started writing a confession, naming your deeds and who is responsible for them, you will learn the true meaning of El Viborito. Make your decision quick."

The bound man in the chair attempted to work a sneer to his lips.

"You think I'm a fool," he snorted. "You're trapped here. Craig and his men will be riding this way as soon as they get that fool Rawlins you sent walking into their trap. Then I'll do the talking. I won't write or sign anything."

The Masked Rider did not answer. Cautiously he lifted the box containing the mammoth rattlesnake from the table. As cautiously he set it upon the floor at the back of the bound man's chair. In his fingers he held a bit of the baling wire bent in a hook like a hair pin. Now he began untying one of the bound man's arms.

"What are you going to do?" the killer El Viborito half gasped, a catch in his voice as he struggled to see behind him. "What are you going to do with that damn snake?"

The bound El Viborito's one arm was free. The Masked Rider forced the arm back and down until El Viborito's hand touched the outside of the box. "I gave you your chance," The Black Caballero ground out. "You call yourself The Snake. Then The Snake you are. Snake meet snake."

WITH HIS WORDS The Masked Rider took the bent piece of wire between his fingers and brought it across the back of El Viborito's hand in a quick digging scratch. A scream sounded from El Viborito's lips. The Masked Rider only kicked the box across the floor to allow it to dump its maddened prisoner before El Viborito's eyes. The big rattlesnake coiled an instant and then began a quick retreat through the open cabin door. In his chair El Viborito sucked for words as he lifted his hand before his eyes and stared in terror at the two blood red scratches across it.

"It's bit me. I'm bit," El Viborito jabbered. "Quick, do something. Get me a knife. Let me slash the bite."

"Plenty of time. Hours of time," The Masked Rider taunted, his lips grinning beneath the hood at the assurance that El Viborito believed the wire scratch to be the fang marks of the rattlesnake that was disappearing through the door. "There's pencil and paper there. You might start writing before your arm swells so you can't write. A confession is all I ask. A confession of El Viborito and those that rode with him."

El Viborito stared wildly about. The scar across his face was blue against the paleness of his cheek. His eyes seemed fastened on the two red scratches across the back of his hand.

"I'll sign. I'll tell," El Viborito husked. "Only do something quick. I can feel the poison working already. Man or devil, whoever you are, you wouldn't stand by and see anyone die like this. You wouldn't...."

"Start writing," The Masked Rider only chanted. "You're the one wasting the time."

El Viborito grabbed up the pencil. "I'll sign it. I'll tell everything," he jabbered on. "I'm El Viborito. I've been signing his brand across the range ever since Mel Craig first started rustling the badland cattle and bringing them to this hideout to run their brand before he drove them to his own range. I was in on the raid on the Stentstrom ranch. I did some of the killing but

I wasn't alone. Craig's whole outfit are hired killers. Craig ordered it. Craig—"

"Write it," The Masked Rider only spoke. "Then sign it. You can talk later."

El Viborito began scrabbling across the paper. Cold sweat dripped from his brow. His lips twitched. His eyes turned constantly from the paper to the twin scratches upon the back of his writing hand. Fear was written in every line of his face. Not the fear of death. The fear of the torture that would come first. The fear of slow death.

"There it is, every line signed," El Viborito suddenly cried. "Now do something. Something quick." He extended his right hand.

Behind his masking hood, The Black Caballero toyed with the smile upon his lips. El Viborito had been tricked completely. Fear was consuming him, to bring out the true cowardly heart of the killer. Those twin scratches upon the back of his hand seemed to have him hypnotized. El Viborito even believed he could feel the poison of a rattlesnake's fangs working through his system. It was best he continue to feel it. There was still much to be done in Los Comino. A signed confession might be doubted as some trick but not a spoken confession. The Masked Rider thought fast.

"I'll get you into Los Comino as fast as we can ride." The Masked Rider spoke as he snatched at a piece of leather saddle lacing upon the wall. "Here, this will help until the doctor at Los Comino can get to you.

The Masked Rider grabbed the string of leather and began wrapping it in a tight bind about El Viborito's arm just above the elbow. El Viborito now moaned and babbled like a terror-stricken child. "Cut it and make it bleed, burn it with a hot iron," he pleaded. "I'll never live to get to Los Comino if you don't."

"You'll live to get more than to Los Comino," The Masked Rider spoke meaningly as he loosened the bonds of the man in the chair. "C'mon. Mount up. We'll be in Los Comino inside an hour."

The Masked Rider pushed the babbling El Viborito out of the cabin. Mel Craig's bay still lay upon the ground where it had dropped. Its wheezing moan had stopped. The sturdy horse lay still. Deathly still. The Masked Rider felt a wave of admiration and pity sweep him. The bay had given its all. Raced its heart out. It had dropped to breathe its last. It had the speed, the courage, but not the heart of the black steed that still stood alongside of it.

The saddled mount of the dead man in the doorway stood hitched at the edge of the cabin. The Masked Rider, still covering El Viborito with his gun, saw El Viborito into the saddle of the horse. The drawn gun was but a sham now. El Viborito babbled and pleaded in a cowardly frenzy that swept The Masked Rider with a feeling of revolting disgust. This killer that knew no mercy for man or woman, now pleading for mercy. The Masked Rider stuffed the confession the pleading man had written into a pocket and mounted the stallion. Up the steep canyon trail they started.

For an hour almost, The Masked Rider listened to the moaning jabber of El Viborito. The wrapped leather about his arm had stopped the circulation. El Viborito believed that pain to be the working of the poison in his arm. Fear had the killer completely. With the lights of Los Comino in sight, he pleaded with The Masked Rider to allow him to ride straight into town for the home of the doctor. The Masked Rider had other plans. Carefully he circled the town. Then approaching from the rear he halted within the black shadows behind Joe Stenstrom's house. The house was lighted.

Cautioning El Viborito to silence, The Masked Rider forced El Viborito on to the rear porch of Joe Stentstrom's house. He glanced through the window. Judge Mann and Joe were in the kitchen. Boldly, The Masked Rider hurled the door open and pushed El Viborito in ahead of him.

"Here's your man, Judge," The Masked Rider spoke as both the judge and Joe stared in mute surprise. "Here's his confession. Better see if it covers everything."

Without a word the judge picked up the paper The Masked Rider had tossed upon the table and began reading. His face began to flush as he read, then drain white. El Viborito had confessed fully. Confessed to the range rustling. The range killing. The barricading of the waterholes to force out the small cattlemen. Craig had planned the entire badland range for himself. Planned to freeze out every independent along the border by killing or rustling their stock so that he might claim the range. El Viborito told all. Named all concerned, even to the sheriff and the latter's tie-up with Mel Craig. Mel Craig was responsible for all.

"This is your confession?" the judge finally spoke, as he turned his burning eyes upon the scarfaced man. "You admit it all? Admit this is your signature?"

"Yes… yes, it's mine. I admit it," El Viborito gritted. "I'll admit anything, only for God's sake do something for me. Look at my arm. It's blue to the elbow. I'm dying by inches. Do something."

"You're not dying, you killing louse," The Masked Rider cut in, as the judge called Joe Stentstrom to witness the confession with himself. "You only think you're dying. You were never bitten by a rattlesnake. I only scratched your hand with a piece of wire. Here."

THE MASKED RIDER jerked free the wrap of leather about the scarfaced man's arm. El Viborito stood as in a daze. His features twisted and contorted as he rubbed his arm and stared unbelievingly at his hand, which with release of the tourniquet above the elbow, was beginning to lose its swollen blueness. A new look of terror crept into his face. A look that spread as from somewhere outside a low babbling of many voices drifted into the room.

The Masked Rider, too, had caught that angry babble. Beneath his mask his face sobered. He recognized the sound. Outside somewhere, many men were moving closer. Moving down the street, shouting and cursing as they came. The Masked Rider swept his glance to the puzzled stare of the judge and Joe Stenstrom.

Suddenly running feet sounded upon the front porch. A door opened and slammed. The Masked Rider took a step back, gun ready. Someone was rushing through the house. Then into the lighted kitchen burst Tess Parker. Her face was a deadly white. Her eyes wide. She ran to the judge to grab his arm.

"Judge. Judge. Come quick," she gasped as she pulled Judge Mann's arm. "They've all gone crazy. They're moving in on the jail. Mel Craig has the men in town believing that Jed killed Sheriff Cook before Jed rode into his crowd and the men at the ranch found them. They're moving on the jail now to… to lynch Jed."

The Masked Rider stiffened. "Lynch Jed Rawlins?" he blasted. "Why? What happened?"

The judge was already on his feet. "Jed rode right into Craig's men when he tried to reach Tess's ranch," the judge spoke. "The crowd from town closed in about the same time. Craig had two of the sheriff's deputies with him and claimed he, too, had been warned of the intended raid on the Parker place and had turned his men out with the sheriff to try and capture El Viborito."

"Certainly, that was his plan," The Masked Rider snapped. "But what of the sheriff?

"Someone had shot him in the back a little ways from the ranch," the judge answered. "The deputies arrested Jed for the shooting. He… he was being…."

The Masked Rider waited for no more. "Joe," he snapped at Joe Stentstrom, "Here, take this skunk along as your prisoner.

Judge, get down to the jail with him. Read that confession to the mob. Craig probably killed the sheriff himself. Was probably afraid the sheriff might talk when it came to a show-down. Get to the jail. I'll be backing your play."

Joe Stentstrom needed no second command. His gun in the small of the scarfaced man's back, he pushed him forward. Judge Mann grabbed up the signed and witnessed confession of El Viborito and started for the front of the house. Tess Parker paused an instant, then whirled to where The Masked Rider still stood before the kitchen door.

"You won't let them lynch him, will you?" she pleaded. "They can't lynch him. Everything is set so perfect for Jed to come home. The cattle money is with the court clerk and the papers all arranged for Jed to sign. He didn't kill Sheriff Cook. He couldn't have killed him. Why… why…?"

The Masked Rider extended a soothing hand. "They won't lynch him," he spoke kindly. "Not when the judge reads that confession. Hurry. Go with them."

Tess Parker stared an instant at the hood-covered face. A new wave of confidence seemed to sweep over her. She turned and hurried after the judge. The Masked Rider backed slowly through the kitchen door. A minute and he was back to where he had left the stallion. The animal pranced nervously as the wild shouting mob farther down the street now burst out with new howls. In the saddle, The Masked Rider skirted the blackness that bordered the street. His goal was the howling mob a block away.

A HUNDRED SHOUTING and cursing men milled about the tiny Los Comino jail as The Masked Rider rode to the end of the milling crowd. Helpless for the moment, The Masked Rider watched them batter down the jail front and stream in. A minute and they poured out of the place, a helpless prisoner in their midst. A hay and feed store adjoined the jail. On the loading platform of the feed store the helpless prisoner was hoisted. A rope sailed through the air. A dozen hands dropped it about the prisoner's neck. Still The Masked Rider waited. Then suddenly as he caught sight of Judge Mann and Joe Stentstrom, struggling to pierce the crowd, his spurs touched the stallion's flanks. The animal leaped ahead. Into the very midst of the mob, The Masked Rider plowed. In at the very point where the judge and Joe Stentstrom struggled to enter with their prisoner.

The black stallion, head high, chest forward, feet barely lifting, plowed through the crowd. Men were bowled right and left. Bowled a second time as with wild swings of his rump, the understanding stallion cleared a path twice the width of its body. In the saddle, a six-gun in either hand, The Masked Rider rode straight. His eyes were for but one man. Now as he sighted him, his insteps touched again. The stallion leaped. To the front of the crowd, Mel Craig suddenly felt himself jerked bodily from the ground, to be hoisted by leg and arm breast high with The Masked Rider atop the black stallion. A booming voice howled above the crowd's roar.

"Hold it, you loco fools," the voice of The Masked Rider bellowed. "Hold everything. You may get me but I'll blast hell into twelve of you fools before I go down. The first will be this skunk. Hold it."

The bellowing voice of Judge Mann caught up The Masked Rider's words. So quick had been The Masked Rider's assault that for an instant the mob stood stunned. The Masked Rider kept the stallion twisting. Mel Craig's body, held by one wrapped arm about the throat in a strangle hold and one knee caught in his crotch, squirmed helplessly. His body shielded the hooded outlaw from those that might have chosen gun play. The judge's bellowing voice held the others. The howling shouts died to a puzzled muttering. The judge still commanded to be listened to. On the platform beside him stood Joe Stentstrom, his gun in the back of the scarfaced El Viborito. Jed Rawlins, a rope still about his neck, stood alongside. Now as Tess Parker rushed forward to toss clear the rope and throw her arms about her sweetheart, the mob seemed to come to its senses. An awkward quiet settled, with only the voice of the judge to be heard.

"You've been tricked, fooled, men, from first to last," the judge howled at the crowd. "You're about to hang an innocent man. Here is El Viborito. This man standing before you. Here is his confession. Are you going to listen to it?"

The crowd stood dumbfounded. Every eye turned to the scarfaced man upon the feed store loading platform. The Masked Rider, realizing his position, seized the moment. The crowd was too stunned by Judge Mann's words to move to action. Slowly, The Masked Rider began backing the stallion along the edge of the platform. The animal seemed to understand. The Masked Rider's arm began to cramp from holding the weight of the squirming Mel Craig, sputtering to speak through the choking wrap of the strangling arm about his throat. The Masked Rider struggled to hold on.

"THIS MAN HAS confessed to every deed of El Viborito," the judge roared out over the crowd. "He posed to me as a ranger I had asked to be sent to this range to investigate El Viborito's crimes, after the real ranger had been murdered. He admits fencing off the waterholes. Admits rustling your cattle. Admits the raid on the Stentstrom ranch. Admits every crime was planned to throw the blame on Jed Rawlins, the man you were about to hang. Now do you want to hear more?"

A howl of consent went up from the crowd. The Masked Rider felt his arm weakening to the pull of Mel Craig's weight. He could hold the man no longer. The stallion was now flush with the loading platform edge. With one last effort, The Masked Rider swung the animal and pushing out with arm and knee sent Mel Craig sprawling on the platform edge. Before Craig could rise to his feet, The Masked Rider had kicked his gun from his hand and slipped from the stallion's saddle to crouch alongside Craig. With his one gun in Craig's back, he commanded the cattleman to straighten to his feet.

An arm's reach away Judge Mann still howled out the confessed crimes of the scarfaced man, staring wide-eyed out over the crowd. The muzzle of Joe Stentstrom's gun still pressed in his back. Another step away Tess Parker stood with her arms about Jed Rawlins.

Judge Mann had the crowd now. He was shouting to them the solutions of the mysteries that had puzzled the borderland cattlemen for months. The crowd listened with open mouths. The Masked Rider seemed forgotten in the solemn setting of the faces below to stern reasoning. They were hearing the truth now.

His gun in the back of Mel Craig, The Masked Rider, however, still crouched ready for escape or fight as the case might me. The black stallion had remained close to the platform edge. Its saddle was flush with the platform. The Masked Rider's plan of retreat, should the crowd suddenly turn its anger on him, was complete. A leap to the back of the stallion and the open trail was but a lunge away.

"This man here is guilty of every crime he admits. There will be proof enough when you go to that hidden canyon on the river and find perhaps cattle of all of your outfits represented here, shedding your brand for the scabbed brand of another outfit. But I'm going to give you more proof. You'll hear it from this man's own lips. Here is the name of the man that hired him. The man that made fools of us all. Robbed us all. Murdered, while he walked amongst us as a friend. El Viborito himself will speak that name. Then you men can judge."

Joe Stenstrom pushed his gun deep into the back of the quaking El Viborito as Judge Mann turned towards him. A buzzing hum went up from the crowd. They began to mill. Joe Strentstrom, by force of the weapon in his hand, pushed El Viborito a step forward. The fear stricken killer opened his mouth to speak. He chewed for words. Words that were never to pass his lips.

Like a leaping cat, Mel Craig suddenly sprang forward. His

heavy hand fell upon the gun Joe Stentstrom pushed into El Viborito's back. His fingers clenched. There was a muffled roar. El Viborito seemed to lunge forward. Before he even caved to the slug of lead from Joe's gun that had cut his spine, Mel Craig had whirled and kicked back. The Masked Rider saw the boot coming and leaped. The gun in his hand could have spoken but there were yet things to be proved. Jed Rawlins must be cleared beyond a doubt.

The Masked Rider held his fire and attempted to swing his gun barrel down across Mel Craig's skull. He missed as Craig ducked and with a mighty lunge swung past The Masked Rider to leap to the back of the black stallion standing at the platform edge. The stallion gave a lunge past the edge of the crowd. Craig was beating his arm across the animal's rump for speed. The stallion gave two leaps. The Masked Rider made no effort to sight the gun in his hand. Instead, his lips emitted a shrill sharp whistle. The stallion whirled with the sound. Whirled but whirled too late. From alongside The Masked Rider came the roar of a gun. Mel Craig stiffened in the saddle, pawed air an instant, then toppled forward to slide to the ground. Beside The Masked Rider stood Joe Stentstrom, his eye still sighting down the barrel of his Forty-five.

THE MOB BEFORE the feed store platform now seemed to break and go wild. They rushed towards the fallen Craig. The Masked Rider seized the moment. The stallion had returned to the platform edge. Quickly, The Masked Rider slipped into his saddle. A wheel about and he was past the crowd's edge. A touch and he was into the darkness. There he waited. Waited while beyond the crowd milled, thinned, started drifting, then vanished.

An hour later the light in Joe Stentstrom's kitchen still burned. The Masked Rider rode close, then dismounted to creep to the lighted window. Inside he saw Judge Mann, a wide grin upon his face, busy sorting a mess of papers. Across from him, arms about each other's shoulders, stood Jed Rawlins and Tess Parker. Their faces were wrapped in smiles. Before the kitchen stove rocked Joe Stentstrom. His face, too, seemed to have lost its haunting sternness. Now and then he glanced toward the bedroom door away from the kitchen. That glance in itself was expressive. In there slept little Mary.

The lips of those about the kitchen moved as they talked. The Masked Rider barely heard the words. The sight of the smiling faces moved him. He felt they were his reward. Justice had been dealt by his outlaw hand. Silently he moved away from the window. Minutes later the weird, lonesome cry of a coyote drifted through the night. Its answer seemed to come from the edge of town. The Masked Rider turned the stallion that way.

At the edge of town a straight-backed rider pushed his horse from the shadows alongside the trail. Silently he rode abreast the black stallion.

"It has happened well, *señor*," the Mexican Indian, Blue Hawk, spoke as the true blackness of the trail closed about them. "The man Craig with his last breath branded himself for the truth. It was he that killed the man for whom the people of town sought vengeance. With his dying breath he told all."

The Masked Rider nodded. "He feared the sheriff would be as weak of will as the man he killed with his own hand, before all," The Masked Rider offered. "Those that kill from the back have not the courage to face a like death. Cruelty is a coward's most handy weapon. He craves to see the courage he has not."

For an hour the two men upon the mesa trail rode in silence. The black shadows of the badlands suddenly closed about them. The outlaw urged the stallion to a faster pace along the badlands' trail. Suddenly his lips began humming a song. A strange Mexican love song.

The Mexican Indian at his side peered wonderingly through the darkness. "Why do you sing, *señor*? It is a happy song on your lips."

"It is a song I learned in your country, Hawk," the Black Caballero spoke. "If Rawlins knew it, he would sing it now, I think. The girl—"

The Mexican Indian nodded his head solemnly.

"*Si, señor,*" he mumbled. "*Si,* but it is for *Señor* Rawlins, that song. Not for you. There is no more a price of gold upon his head. There is on yours," he cautioned. "And maybe there are friends of Craig in the badlands who would like very much to collect. They have sharp ears, *señor,* the friends of Craig and El Viborito!"

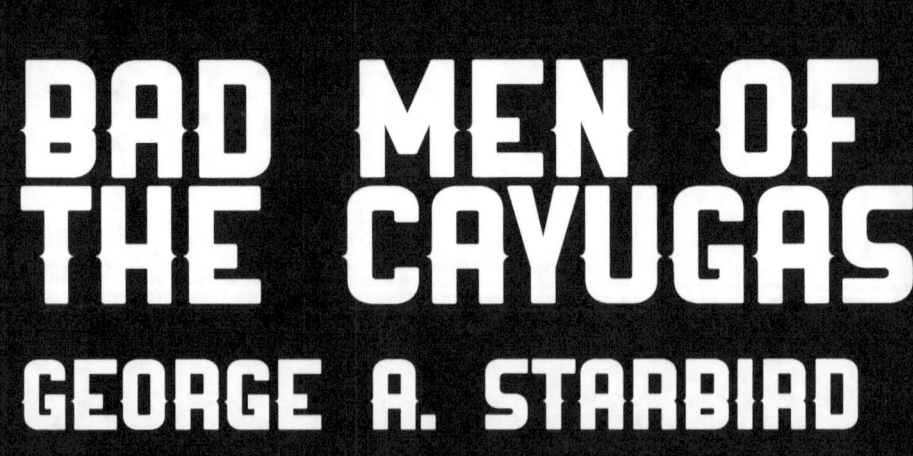

BAD MEN OF THE CAYUGAS

GEORGE A. STARBIRD

CHAPTER I

MIDNIGHT RIDERS

T HE PONY RIPPED wild-eyed through the night wind.
Against the hard-packed surface of the mesa land, its
hoofs beat a thunderous tattoo. Now and then it swerved away
from the patches of shadowy mesquite that dotted the silver
pool of moonlight. Its eyes were saucer-round with fright.

The rider seemed as unconscious of the passing brush as the
pony. He clung to the saddle-horn with both hands. Pain and
horror were written on his youngish, pale features. He was
hatted, yet the soft glow of the moon suddenly caught his face,
and in it the staring eyes were unlifelike, glazing. The man
swayed in the saddle and with great effort managed to graze
his spurs along the pony's heaving flanks.

The horse snorted in terror; its gait broke into an aimless,
pain-racked flight. The rider weaved in his seat, then hunched
precipitously forward as the pony reached a rise in the mesa
land and bolted into the dim black shades of the mesquite and
greasewood beyond the rise.

ON THE FLOOR of a nearby brush-lined barranca, hidden from
the mesa land above. Wayne Morgan had pulled up his black
stallion. It was he who had first caught the distant thunder of
the headlong flight above them. With almost instinctive caution
he had paused, awaited the approach.

But now, as the rapid clatter of hoofs on hard-pan died into
silence, he turned to the shadowy figure on the sorrel behind
him. Except for the high quick jingle of their ponies' bridle-

irons, the noiselessness of the dark barranca was complete and eerie as death. For a short moment, the two riders sat in pregnant silence.

The voice of the man on the sorrel broke that silence first. It was a guttural voice, soft yet with accents plainly from south of the Rio Grande. The rider chuckled.

"Loco drunk," he said. "I think at first it is a posse of sixty men. That perhaps the *señor alcalde* of Claxton and his men

sprouted wings those two hundred miles behind and find us."
He chuckled again. "Now, *señor*, hear only one pony. *Si*, and I
feel sorry for his—what you call them—*costillas*, ribs!"

Morgan had wheeled the stallion out of the shadow of the
overhanging brush so that the soft sheen of the rising moon

cast full on the tanned and trail-hardened features beneath his wide, jet-black rabbit Stetson.

Some would say it, was a hard face, not young, but youthful. In it the eyes were dark and unwavering. Nor were the lines about the thin-lipped mouth a record of many smiles. Those lines told of trails hard-ridden; of winds of fate that dealt hard blows with small favors; of hard living in a hard land. And in the angular cast of the jaw, in the thin tightness of his lips again were written tokens of the man's past.

He looked up at the lip of the barranca which had hidden them from the rider above.

"Loco drunk or hurt," he said, half to the other and half to himself. "We'd better go up, Hawk. Even a drunk man knows better than to ride a pony at that pace at night. That cayuse was scared—judging from the uneven running. Scared ponies and drunk riders make a bad combination."

The stallion heaved and snorted at the steep climb, but mounted to the barranca lip like a great agile cat. The sorrel followed.

Once outside of the barranca shades, Morgan paused. In the dark blobs of mesquite and greasewood obscuring the mesa land, it would be impossible to follow the rider. Morgan's first reaction had been to throw to the winds the caution that had made them travel in the barranca bottom. There was undoubtedly an injured or drunk man riding the pony they had heard. They should follow him, find him. It was the code of the range.

The second rider seemed to sense Morgan's thought with disapproval. He said: "Loco drunk or hurt. *Quién sabe?* I think it is better we let him ride." He pointed in the direction the hoof-beats had disappeared. "Over there, Red Rocks. He will get help."

In the wan glow suffusing the mesa land, the rider's face showed bronzed, high-cheeked and sombre, a Mexican's. But, the straightforward flash of his dark eyes, the upright seat on his sorrel pony, came from forebears far more noble. Save for his round-crowned black hat, he might well have been mistaken for an Aztec chieftain. Such was Blue Hawk, son of the border.

"He will get help," said Blue Hawk. "Come, *señor*, we ride again?"

The broad-shouldered young man on the black shrugged. In spite of the vague premonitions that sobered him inwardly, he grinned at Blue Hawk.

"I'd like to find out 'how come,' Hawk. Maybe you're right— he'll find help or get sober. 'Cording lo our horoscope if there's a sheriff within fifty miles of this barranca, we'd like as not ride square into him, trying to save a poor lost soul from the evils of bad liquor."

"*Si, señor?*" asked Blue Hawk. "But certainly you do not mind these sheriffs now?"

MORGAN LAUGHED, WHEELED the black stallion. The sorrel shuffled itself about. In that second both riders were brought to ramrod-stiff attention.

Far to their right, in the opposite direction from which the first rider had disappeared, came a new tattoo of pony's hoofs. At first it was like the patter of far-off rain. But with the same rising intensity, it beat against their waiting ears.

Blue Hawk nudged his pony into the low shade of a pin-oak.

"One pony this time, too," he muttered.

Muffled by the mesa's brush, the hoof-beats had seemed far off. Now suddenly they became nearby thunder, were yards away. Morgan saw the rider first.

Out of the dusk a weaving, dark blob of man and pony abruptly took shape. It was coming straight for them. The man's hat was off; he swayed drunkenly in the saddle. Even at some distance they could see the bulging whites of a terror-stricken pony's eyes; the red of its tortured nostrils.

Morgan neck-reined the black stallion about, out of the

shadows. With express-train speed, the horse and rider came bounding for him.

Then, when not twenty yards away, the racing pony saw the two shapes materialize out of the shadows. It shied unguided, away from the stallion, ran in a circling course away from the barranca lip. It had not gone fifty yards into the mesquite when the dark shape on its back flopped sideways and out of the saddle. The pony ran a few steps and trotted to a halt.

Before the rider was out of his saddle, Morgan had kneed the stallion to a gallop, pulled it up stiff legged beside the prostrate form. Even then he could see the knife in the man's back.

A second later, Morgan had rolled the man over on his side. He was still alive; his lips muttered, mouthed at words.

Morgan turned, bit out one word: "Water."

He took Blue Hawk's canteen, sloshed water across the man's mouth and wet the graying long hair over the forehead.

The man's eyes fluttered, then opened bright and hard on Morgan.

He had a high forehead, square jaw and heavy crinkles beneath his eyes. It was a distinguished face, almost aristocratic. Morgan thought, sixty five. The man was chesty, ox like, and long armed. His vest was of mottled calf-hide; long black trousers were tucked in his boots. But Morgan's second guess was that he was not a cowman. The hands were loo light skinned, though bony and strong.

"You might have picked a softer spot to spill," said Morgan, grinning. "A little more water, mister, and lie still a moment. We'll start to get this pigsticker out of you."

Though he grinned, the angle at which the long-handled stiletto jutted violently out from above the shoulder blade, told Morgan that his hopes were useless. It would be only a matter of time before the man must die. That knife had been fatal.

Even now driblets of blood specked the man's thin, hard lips. Morgan swallowed hard.

The heavy eyes closed, then opened. The eyes that caught Morgan's were hard, unyielding.

"Who—who are you?" the man muttered. "I'll never tell where it is—no matter who you are or what you do!"

Morgan swallowed again. "I don't want to know anything, mister. Can you drink some of this?"

The wounded man stared, opened his mouth to the water-bag. But something was wrong with his throat. The knife had done that. He tried to swallow. The water dribbled helplessly out of his mouth, down his white shirt front.

MORGAN PULLED THE water-bag away. Something felt hard and awkward in his throat. He had seen men die, quickly, violently; nothing like this. For a second pity made him wince.

The man's eyes closed again. Something crashed off to Morgan's right. It was the man's pony. Down and done for; run dead. Its quivering legs had simply folded in under it.

"Señor," said Blue Hawk's voice. "Perhaps the knife should stay where it is. Pull it out and the man will bleed to death in seconds."

"I was thinking of that," said Morgan. "Yank the hull off that pony and we'll brace up his head."

The man's eyes were still closed when Blue Hawk brought back the dead pony's saddle, placed it gently beneath the gray-haired head. Morgan splashed more water across the man's forehead. His eyes opened.

"What's the name?" asked Morgan quietly.

"You don't... don't know me then?" the man asked, doubtfully. "I didn't realize... John Harris... Red Rocks... the bank. Someone got me with this knife...." The voice dribbled off into silence.

Morgan turned to Blue Hawk, his eyes hard and questioning. Blue Hawk's head shook. He had never heard the name.

The man, Harris, had closed his eyes again. He was going fast, Morgan knew now. Morgan's own eyes became cold, flint-like.

"Never tell where what is, Mr. Harris?" he asked. "Maybe if you'll say who got you—?"

The eyes fluttered open. Morgan had expected them to be glazed, but they weren't. They were bright, unyielding as ever. His voice seemed stronger; but Morgan knew hopelessly that it was the last burst of strength before the end.

"I'm going to die," Harris muttered. "...going to die with a secret. I have a daughter, Leona. In Red Rocks... tell her I didn't know who got me... tell her I died with my boots on... with a secret. Maybe she'll understand.... But find Stimson. Stimson, y'understand... tell her... *find Stimson!*"

"Take it easy," said Morgan, quietly. "Talk slower, Harris. Was that Stimson in front of you?"

The wounded man sighed; he reached aimlessly for the water-bag again. They held it up to him, and watched the un-drunk water dribble again and again out of the man's mouth. Morgan cursed beneath his breath. Man wasn't made to suffer torture like that.

"Can't drink," murmured Harris. "That... that knife doesn't hurt at all. Funny... I'd tell you the secret—what that murdering rat wanted to know. How do I know you wouldn't double-cross me—or my daughter? *I don't know!*"

"Trusting us is up to you," said Morgan, quietly.

"I never trust strangers—in the cattle country," said Harris. "Men without a brand usually have a reason for it."

His head rolled weakly, but still those dark eyes pinioned Morgan's.

Wayne Morgan nodded. Something in the fine old man's face told him there was no half-way. He would never give a stranger his secret. He would die with it—as much as he wanted to tell it to some trustworthy person.

Morgan squatted on his heels, surveying the granite hard, fine face of the wounded man. How did he know how important the secret might be? What relation did it have to Leona, the daughter? Would this Stimson himself reach Red Rocks alive? Was that Stimson who rode past first?

A hundred answers to such questions were hidden behind the pale tortured face before him. Morgan bent forward suddenly.

"Listen," he said quietly, "it's said The Masked Rider has shown up in these parts. Think he ever had any part of that knife in his hand?"

The question seemed to take effect. Harris' dark eyes shifted, scanned Morgan quizzically.

"I never met the man… often said I'd like to. For some men he's a cutthroat and a coward. Others say no straighter man is living. Me—I'm one of those who'll vote twice for him!"

HARRIS' CHIN DROPPED, and he sighed hard, deeply, as though the speech had taxed him badly.

Wayne Morgan hesitated. He, himself was now taking a long chance. If by some remote miracle Harris lived, Morgan might have cause to deeply regret his rashness. Morgan's angled jaw lightened.

"Yes," he said slowly, "this *hombre,* The Masked Rider, has a record as long as your arm. But in spite of that you'd like to meet him. I gather, Harris, that under some circumstance you might unload your troubles to him. Even if you wouldn't to us. Is that so?"

The face of the old man lolled back; the jaw loosened unsteadily. But still his glittering eyes were held unwavering. His speech, though weak, was meaningful.

"That man, son, is sky-high straight…. Finding a man in a tight place, that *hombre'd*…."

Harris' mouth wouldn't make speech that his will and mind were demanding. His voice trailed off. There was no doubt, he would be dead in minutes.

Wayne Morgan stood up. His step was purposeful as he walked away from the dying man. The black stallion had wandered towards the barranca lip and was pulling the leaves off a stunted alder. At the shrill whistle from Morgan, the stallion dipped its head, trotted towards the figure of its master. Then it snorted when the *cincha* straps were being loosened.

HOWEVER, MORGAN'S WHISTLE had carried farther than he would have wished. Over a rise in the mesa-land, a quarter of a mile away, a rider pulled up his pony. He let the animal walk a moment, while he studied the direction of that whistle. Purpose seemed suddenly to come into his actions, for he reached into the *alforja* behind his saddle, brought out a black bandanna.

This he tied swiftly about his face so that only his eyes were revealed. Then with sure movements he pushed his pony in the direction of the whistle, feelings again as he did in that same *alforja*. The second object he brought forth twinkled briefly in the moonlight. It was a stiletto.

CHAPTER II

TWO KNIVES IN THE DARK

FOR TWENTY-FIVE YEARS John Harris had been president of the Cattlemen's Trust at Red Rocks. He was a man liked by most people, feared by some. In his long career he had seen many acts of violence, had seen death strike sudden and sure. Now he knew death had at last pointed its icy finger at him. Many things should be told before he died, but grimly he clamped his teeth. Never would he tell unless he had a hearer he could trust.

For that reason, even with his last breaths, his eyes widened in surprise at the apparition that stalked grimly out of the shades towards him.

It was a man, dressed entirely in black from head to foot. A great flowing black cloak enshrouded him at once in mystery. And underneath the Stetson an even blacker hood covered the figure's entire head and shoulders.

"The Masked Rider," Harris breathed.

The cloaked figure approached, bent forward to Harris' side.

"Yes," the masked man said. "So I'm called. Does that help, sir?" And the voice that spoke, muffled by the heavy cloak, was Wayne Morgan's.

"Son," the old man's voice quavered high and uncertain, but with conviction. "...son... maybe I'm the only banker in th' country that'd... that'd be glad to see the man that rides under that brand. But I am...."

"You'll talk then?" asked the man in black.

"I'm Harris of the Cattlemen's Trust... in Red Rocks. My daughter, Leona's gonna marry a devil-may-care redhead cow-poke owns a piece of ranch hereabouts. A good kid—I like him—Jimmie Weeder. I have a little fortune to put in her name. Took it out of the bank... for them. Some rat found it out. Followed me...."

The strain was too much. Harris' head fell back, relaxed. For a moment the man in black thought he was gone for good. Blue Hawk handed down the water-bag again. The masked one sloshed it over Harris' features.

"Talk," he said, soothingly. "You got to get it out, Mr. Harris."

Harris' eyes opened. "You're right," he went on, weakly. "Dry-gulched me and Stimson, my man, between Gila and Red Rocks... in a gully about four miles from Gila. I already hid Leona's nest-egg... cachéd it in a cave. I had a map... gave it to Stimson. He doesn't know what it is about—but he'll find out. Ask Stimson… tell Leona to ask *Stimson*. I gave Stimson the map right after I got this knife."

Harris' lips closed, his eyelids drooped. The man in the black cloak swallowed hard. No, he hadn't heard half enough. Harris must suspect who knifed him. Stimson might get away. If there was money, Harris should tell where it was. He had to!

"Brace up, Harris. You got to get it out. Hawk, more water!"

The Masked Rider turned to Blue Hawk. The tall Mexican-Indian rose to walk back to where a second water-bag had been laid aside.

In those few seconds, like the quick clicks of a watch, death struck out with sure aim.

The hooded man had wheeled away from the dying Harris, facing a slight rise in the mesa. And as he did, a figure rose to full height out of the mesquite that dotted the knoll.

Its hand shifted up, back; then shot forward. It happened so quickly that the man in the black *serape* scarcely shifted his feet. But when the intruder's arm had poised in its upright position, the moon's light caught and twinkled revealingly on the bared blade of a stiletto.

In that second The Masked Rider saw too that the target was the broad back of Blue Hawk just bending over the water-bag. The man with the knife was a scarce sixty feet away when he threw.

IT WAS AT a mere flash of light, the flight of a deadly cold-white flame through the air at which the outlaw in black shot. Later, he wondered why he hadn't shot the man. Instinctively, one ordinarily would have—unless, as in him, the instinct to preserve life was deeper and more basically ingrained than that to kill.

When his gun roared, the flash of flame blotted out the streaking bit of white light.

Blue Hawk wheeled like a cat, saw the moving blob of light, and he shot too. But before either his or the masked man's second bullet went screaming after the intruder, the black outline against the farther stars had ducked to safety.

Blue Hawk ran in soft moccasins. It was he who reached the rise in the mesa first. Poised there, scanning the dark, neither he nor the man in the black *serape* could distinguish the slightest movement in the brush about them. Their assailant had vanished as quickly, as easily as he had come.

A second later, far to their right sounded the quick beats of a pony's hoofs.

"Gone, *señor,*" said Blue Hawk. "It was a knife, no?"

"Yes, a knife."

"And you shot it, *señor.*"

The man in the black cloak turned slowly and stalked back towards the prostrate form of Harris. Behind him Blue Hawk trod, erect, silent. His comrade in the *serape* had shot a thrown knife. That knife would have buried itself in his back, even as one had plunged hilt-deep into this Harris man. Blue Hawk would remember that many years, along with other memories—memories of a similar occasion which had originally attached him to this mystery among men, The Masked Rider.

"*Señor,* who do you think it was?"

The hooded head shook. The cloaked figure was bending over Harris, touching the face, the closed, heavy-lidded eyes.

"Who knows, Hawk? It makes little difference. He is dead."

"Dead, *señor?* But only a minute ago—!"

The figure in the black cloak rose from the dead man. His lips were stretched tight, his jaw clenched and rocky.

"Finished, Hawk. And he took his secret with him. If this—?"

He paused and strode a few yards from the dead man, stooped, picked up an object half-buried in the hard-pan. It was a stiletto.

He brought it back. For a second both he and Blue Hawk bent, comparing it with the hilt that jutted venomously from Harris' shoulder blades.

The man in the black cape arose, hefting the weapon. It was long, a full sixteen inches, yet with a peculiarly shaped light thin blade. Holding it balanced it the palm, the hilt weighed more than the blade, thus making an ideal throwing weapon.

More strange was the character of that hilt. It was neither Mexican nor American. The metal was blued, and heavily carved. But the handle was neither covered with pig-skin like those below the border, nor was it the wood or bone from north of the Rio. For some peculiar reason its maker had covered the haft with heavy blue cloth of the character of plush.

However, what now struck the hooded man with vicious import was the fact that this knife, thrown at Blue Hawk, and that jutting from the back of the dead. Harris were identical.

"Our friend," drawled the man in black, "was sure unduly anxious that we didn't go any farther with our little talk. I suppose he had another of these playthings for me. That is, Hawk, if he'd got you."

THE EYES GLITTERING through the slits of the heavy cape turned to Blue Hawk. "For two *centimos* we'd ride after that rat, trail him from hell to breakfast until we put the sign on him. I'd lay twenty silver dollars we'd pin him, too, within two hours. But if we do, Hawk, in the meantime—what?

"First, this little girl Leona Harris doesn't find out soon enough that her father was knifed to death. Second, this man he talked about—Stimson—will probably fade out of sight soon as he can. And third, the mystery of this cave where he had hidden gold only gets deeper and deeper. I say to take the body into Red Rocks. But Hawk, you say ride after that yellow polecat and—"

Blue Hawk's high-cheeked, bronzed features writhed into a smile. "*Señor*, it is my honor to kill the gentleman of the knife. He was attempt my life. *Madre de Dios, señor, I* shall kill him! Not in two hours, *señor*, in one!"

The hooded head nodded. The man in the cape knew full

well that Blue Hawk's promise was anything but idle. Half a lifetime on the desert had left the Indian with the trailing instincts of his own native coyote.

"Yes," he drawled. "But that leaves me to lug the body into Red Rocks. The 'gentleman of the knife' will have to wait. *You're* taking the body into Red Rocks. Have you ever heard of Gila—this ghost-town? She lies eight or ten miles south and is a sure enough hangout for thieves and killers from either side of the border. Not likely to find an honest man around there these days."

"I know, *señor*. But do you think *Señor* Harris was there?"

"Yes and no," said the man in the black cape. "But if it's true—the town would stand looking over. Figure I'll do that. You take the body into Red Rocks. Tell them nothing except that you found him. Harris was already dead. Maybe things will work best that way. I'll meet you at this ghost-town, *amigo*. There's a girl up in this Red Rocks had a father killed by a sure-enough dirty viper. Hawk, you and I are going to help her a little."

"*Si, señor*," replied the Indian, and added, "although I like very much to kill this knife thrower."

The man in the dark hood wheeled. From his lips shrilled a whistle that brought the black stallion on the lope. The man rose to the saddle.

"In Gila then."

Blue Hawk nodded. Though his face showed little, his heart was heavy. Even less than the prospect of taking a dead man home did he like being separated from the man in the dark *serape*.

And as he lifted the sagging, dead body across his saddle bows, Blue Hawk swore that his search for the murderer would end only with his own bone-handled knife buried to its hilt—in the killer's heart.

CHAPTER III

THE GHOST-TOWN

A MAN CALLED Hunter named the town of Gila. He built and owned the store that was the town for many years, so he considered it his right. The town, or store, lay on the edge of the great Tule, the shadows of the high desert behind it and the long, spiny range, of the Cayugas dim in the distance. Later, a stage from Bisbee used to stop there carrying freight and passengers for the random cattle ranges that dotted the high desert and greener hills beyond.

Not long after the stage began stopping, a man named Mushy Clacks arrived with a burro and a pickax. He found yellow, interesting dirt right on the outskirts of town. At that time Gila numbered eight inhabitants. The next years, a full ten thousand people bellowed, fought, killed and sinned in Gila or tore the surrounding hillsides for more of that yellow stuff.

Gaining houses, with their due of thin-fingered, eye-shaded dealers; their hosts of hard-faced, shrill-voiced women; their booze and their killings lined the streets. Men lived, gambled and died in tents or beaver-board huts. Hunter was killed when roughnecks tried to rob his store. Mushy Clacks went crazy when his vein ran out.

AND SO TOO did the course of Gila run shallow and empty to its end. When the gold disappeared, so did the men in the gaming houses. When the prospectors came to Gila no longer, the women left. They left in a rush, as from a sinking ship.

Soon for each person that came to Gila, a hundred left. Finally, when even that one ceased coming, and the stage no longer ran into Gila, the last trailing remnants of humanity moved to other parts.

The town was left—an empty shell, a ghost; hollowed, littered shapes of false-fronted buildings; desolate, overgrown streets and crumbling boardwalks.

Then, while Gila gasped its last breath, cowmen began running their cattle on nearby ranges. A town sprang up some miles to the north of Gila. They named it Red Rocks and thought of Gila no more.

People avoided the ghost city, believing it was in truth haunted. Through its borders an occasional horse-thief or outlaw sneaked for short sanctuary from the forces of the law. For years not one pair of honest eyes was laid on the whitening, dismal skeleton blistered by the hot Arizona sun....

IN THE WAN moonlight a signboard that still read "Main Street" in peeled paint sagged within reach. A big Mexican, Viego, pulled it out by its roots as a woman would a graying hair and carried it towards a great bonfire roaring in what had once been the street.

Flames and sparks flared and streamed upward when he dumped it on.

"An' dees, *señor*, makes the end of wan fine Main Street. No?"

He laughed uproariously, with a laugh that thundered back and forth between the bulging, crumbling walls about them. He was a huge man, with an arm as big and long as a railroad tie. He had a chest like a wine tun. When he moved, the silver *conchas* on his great peaked sombrero glittered and tinkled merrily.

"Don Viego make the bes' dam' fire in Arizona!" he boasted to the man seated across the blaze from him.

Three-finger Costigan, squatting in the dirt on the other side of the coals ran his eyes over the big Mex. There was something almost reprehensible in the looks of Costigan—unhealthy. He had cold gray eyes, a jaundiced complexion. His clothes might well have been worn since he had reached maturity, they were so grimy with filth. His pants were a beggar's.

But the twin .45s slouching in double holster at his sides

sparkled like polished icicles in the light. Costigan was a plain killer. One could read it in every line of his disreputable appearance; in the stare of those glasslike eyes. The two middle fingers of his left hand were gone. Strangely enough, a Jaurez *mulo* had bitten them off.

"In Chihuahua I waz, *señor,* two months ago. Dees time that Sonora *oficial* say, 'Viego, you have kill wan man by break th' back. Dees is all. Tamarrow you hang.' Ho—Ho! Come *noche* I break tree more backs an' run away! *Madre mia,* Viego does not die for break wan back of dat cheater at cards. *Señor,* no. So today I am here. Tamarrow. *Quién sabe?*"

Costigan eyed the faded green vest over the jutting chest. The Mex had on a dirty yellow shirt, a sickly blue *bolero.* His black pants were gray with alkali dust and split up the bulging calves.

The Mexican had been making the great bonfire when Costigan rode into Gila. Invited, he sidled up to the fire like a half-frozen reptile and stayed there silent. Costigan had good reasons to be in Gila. Right at that moment any one of full fifty men in Arizona would have shot him on sight—if he didn't drop them first.

"An' now, *señor,* when do we have eat?"

The great Mexican turned his huge grinning face to Costigan. In it a set of pearly teeth, big as a horse's, glittered. He rubbed his stomach mightily and grunted at its emptiness.

Costigan's eyes were uninterested. "I ain't got none," he said coldly.

Night had some time ago covered the shadows of the leaning buildings about them. Outside the immediate circle of the fire, the moon cast pale, cold pools of light in the eerie street.

Around the rickety corner of a leaning, false-fronted skeleton—in former days "Eddy's Billiard Hall and Amusement Pallor"—a figure leaned out and examined the two men seated at the fire. Behind it a burro, tied to a splintered hitchrack, pawed at the dust.

The figure turned, muttered something at the burro, then moved out into the street towards the bonfire.

When it came into the light, Viego's eyes opened wide. Only on second sight could one be sure it was a man. His gait was a shuffling, halting walk. A cap, tattered and grimy, was perched on the top of straggling, matted, filthy hair that was at one time both gray and dirt-colored.

Baggy, caked overalls, a sweater frayed and open at the elbows tucked inside them, completed the man's dress. Shoes he had none.

Beneath his cap, beard and hair joined as one. What was most striking was the man's eyes. They stared, half unbelieving, at the two men at the fire. And in them was a look both startled and wild.

"Ho, *amigo!*" roared the big Mex. "Mebbe you come join the party, *señor*. Mysel', *señor*, I am Viego, Don Viego, the bes' dam gun-*hombre* outta Chihuahua. An' dees ees my frien'."

THE MAN STARED first at the big Mex, then at the cold-eyed killer. He looked as though he were going to run; he jerked his head sideways to look behind him like a scared rabbit. Instead, he shuffled closer to the fire, stretching out a pair of scarecrow filthy hands to the blaze.

"My name's Fred. Some people call me Crazy Fred, kinda. But I'm not crazy—more'n you or him." He jerked a gnarled thumb at Costigan.

Costigan's eyes hadn't shifted from the stooped figure bending towards the fire. When he spoke his voice was cold, metallic.

"Where d'you live?" he asked.

Crazy Fred turned. Again he looked behind him for unseen enemies before he spoke. "Here," he quavered in his husky voice.

"I live here in Gila all the time. Allus has. Me'n my burro. Jest 'round th' corner there, kinda."

By that time the big Mex had observed that Crazy Fred's name was not entirely unjustified.

"Crazy Fred, mine *amigo*," he thundered in his big voice. "You have come jes' in time. Seet, *señor*. An' now my fine frien', you have mebbe somethin' to eat—*caldo, pescados, vocal, legumbres*—*señor?* Anytin' you say. Or mebbe, *señor*, you share with us your dinner of—mebbe what you call—pack-rats!"

The big Mex let loose a gust of laughter that rattled the boards in the crumbling sidewalks.

Crazy Fred eyed the giant Viego with round eyes.

Costigan's cold voice calmed the Mex to silence. "If you live here," he snapped, "you got food. Get it."

"I ain't got nothin'," the scatter-witted one quavered. "I ain't et myself since last night."

Costigan's eyes were gray glass beads. "I say, you have food. Get us some before I have to wring yore skinny neck."

Crazy Fred was squatted near him, not three feet away. Costigan's arm darted out like a striking copperhead. Clutched in a steel-trap grip, Crazy Fred let out a yowl of fright, then whimpered with pain when Costigan brought his arm back and up.

"Yo're lyin', you dirty old rat. You ate this morning. I can see what you left in yore filthy beard. Get some more!"

Crazy Fred whined with pain and terror. His voice, cracked and high came: "Yeah, I got some. I'll get it—I'll get it—"

None of the three men had seen the figure that stepped into the firelight to the right of the big Mex. Behind the figure was a huge black stallion. Everything about the man blended with the dark shadow behind him. Even the flowing jet-black cloak and hood that covered his head and shoulders. It was tilted at one corner where the ugly snout of a six-gun peeked out, the black hole centered full on Costigan. Suddenly three pairs of eyes were glued on it.

For a short second all three of them were speechless with surprise.

"Let him go," the apparition's voice was soft, composed.

Costigan's hand dropped. Crazy Fred scuttled aside, wild eyes pinned to the black-cloaked figure.

"Madre de Dios!" blurted the mountainous Mexican. "Th' Masked Rider. Dees man of a charmed life. Dees man wanted from Jaurez to thees Dakotas *Señor of la careta negra*. Ef you are dees man, I make you th' bow. *Muchas bienvenidas, señor!"*

So saying the huge Mex rose, bowed low, doffing the mountainous sombrero with a gay jingle of silvery *conchas*.

"Sit down," said the cool voice of the man in the black cape.

THE EYES THAT glittered through the twin slits in the cloak turned to Costigan. "I'm not asking you who you are, *hombre*. Only keep your hands to yourself for a moment, while I ask other questions."

The big Mexican's smile never faded; he sat down. Costigan's face was sneering. There was $5,000 gold in Waco on the head of a man who wore a black *serape* like this. Another thousand promised in gold in Roseville. More thousands in many more places. Costigan was thinking of that now; so was the giant Mex....

"So yo're claiming t'be Th' Masked Rider, mister," Costigan's cold voice sneered. "Ain't you afraid some day yo're gonna get tangled in something you can't handle with that rig? How come you don't act big and bold like yore stories? With yore brand, you shouldn't need a gun to talk behind."

"I'll talk the way I please—for the time being," answered the man in black. Nevertheless, Costigan's eyes widened a little when the six-gun peeping from beneath the cloak was holstered.

The man in black calmly squatted not eight feet from the giant Mex. Costigan's eyes were cold, waiting. He knew it would be a toss-up whether he'd come out alive if he went for his gun. Costigan was a gunman, a killer—but he wasn't a gambler. He preferred to wait his chances.

"And so what?" he sneered.

The lithe figure in the mask was silent. He looked at the poor scarecrow of a human seated by Costigan. Even as he looked he knew most of the tale that lay behind those eyes.

Costigan he covered at a glance. The killer's face was now vaguely familiar to him. Beneath the hood The Masked Rider's voice was low, drawling.

"You're Three-finger Costigan. And I can't say I'm glad to meet you."

One thing Costigan didn't like was to be called by name. Three notches might have been carved in his gun butts—if he catered to the habit—for men who died for doing only that. The glance he shot at the masked figure was meaningful, a reptile's.

"And you, *hombrecito?*" drawled the masked one.

The big Mexican's chest expanded. "Don Viego—" he started, "—wan fine man, *señor.* Mysel' I am wanted—"

The low voice butted in. "That's enough. I heard the rest already."

Through the twin slits the hooded eyes slowly surveyed the form of the giant Mex. For the moment he thought his visit to Gila had been well chosen. Undoubtedly the man was danger-ous, a desperado, an outlaw. Else why should he be in Gila? In the proper place, the big one could probably pin an ace of clubs at sixty paces—with a stiletto.

On the other hand, he probably couldn't read a map if he saw one. Nevertheless, the masked man grimly cursed the fact that poor light had obscured John Harris' killer's shape. The giant Mex's bulk would have told on him. If the Mexican made the least wrong move, however—

Cat-like the hooded man was up on his feet. Costigan had

leaped erect too, as had the Mex. The sudden thunder of a pony's hoofs shattered the night.

They trip-hammered over far-off hard-pan—then rattled noisily when the rider came to even harder ground that had been the town's streets. Off in the shades a bolting shape materialized.

CHAPTER IV

DYING CATTLE

C OSTIGAN WAS STOOPING, edging backward, his elbows close to his side, gray cold eyes on the single rider.

The Mex stood his ground, waiting. Crazy Fred cast one backward, terror-stricken glance at the coming pony and scuttled out of the rim of firelight.

The man in the black cape backed into the shades, watching not the rider, but Costigan.

His voice cut over the clatter of the pony's hoofs. "Keep your hands where they are, Costigan. Don't move, either of you."

Costigan stopped. He saw now that a twin pair of gun muzzles had made an almost magical appearance from beneath the inky cloak. Costigan's jaw hardened.

A second later the rider rattled in over ancient cobblestones, pulled his mount to a stiff-legged stop directly before the fire, and swung down near the giant Mex.

The pony's sides were wheezing bellows as it backed away from the flame.

The man in the mask, now sheltered by nearby shadows, had a good chance to look over the rider before he spoke. He had red hair, an upturned, stubborn nose, a fighter's jaw. A boss Stetson was shoved back on his scarlet thatch. His blue eyes were spitting fire at Costigan and the big Mex, for not yet had he spotted the man in the black cloak.

"I'm Jimmie Weeder," he snapped without formalities. "I'm looking fer a couple of cowpokes or roughnecks that don't care how honest the next dollar they make is. Figgered I'd like as not run intuh something like that hereabouts. I don't know who you are—an' care less. Anyhow, I got two twenty dollar gold pieces for every hand that rides back to th' Closed C with me an' does one night's work. Interested?"

He bit off the last question sharply, his hard blue eyes on the two men before him. Jimmie Weeder believed in being blunt, and he was.

Neither Costigan nor the big Mex said a word. There were two guns covering both them and the rider. They were awaiting what the voice over those guns might have to say.

"Well?" snapped Weeder. "How come? Yo're not tongue-tied!"

"In a way," drawled a voice in the far shadows. Steps grated on the stones. Out of those shadows walked the man in the black cloak, full into the light of the fire.

Jimmie Weeder was a guileless young man. For a short second the anger boiling within him was blanketed with honest surprise. His jaw sagged agape.

"Holy jumping cat-fish! The Rider!"

Costigan stirred uneasily. The big Mex began to grin.

"Yes," drawled the cloaked man. "Kind of looks, young fellow, you choose a powerful unhealthy atmosphere to pick your hands from. This *hombre*," the guns indicated Costigan, "is Three-finger Costigan who would gladly murder your grandfather for one twenty dollar gold piece. Mister Viego here would skin you alive looking for a mere gold eagle, if he thought you had it on you. And I—you probably already know me by reputation."

Weeder had recovered from his surprise. His voice rapped through the still air. "I don't care a hoot who you are—any of you! What I said stands. Two twenty dollar gold pieces go to any man who'll follow me tonight.

"I got two hundred head of prime beef standing up at Closed C water bellering their heads off for a drink. Been doing that for nigh on to forty-eight hours. All on account a bunch of thievin', crooked Sandells put sharpshooters on the one Closed C waterhole that ain't dry, and fenced our cattle out. I'm routing them Sandells out tonight—but I need guns, an' men to work behind them!"

He paused, face flushed, breathless.

DEEP SILENCE GREETED his explosion. The two outlaws were again waiting for the man beneath the cloak to talk.

"You talking about your own waterhole, or these—Sandells'?" the low voice asked.

"I ain't goin' intuh that now. That water was Closed C water since my Paw was fed nuthin' but milk. For forty-eight hours my cattle ain't had a drop to drink. We lost twenty head of cattle in fifteen minutes when they stempeded intuh a barb-wire fence. *After that water!*

"I tell you, I ain't slept for one of them forty-eight hours. But if I tried to, I couldn't for the nightmares I'd have seein' them cattle dying of thirst. An' over their bellering, all I can hear is that snaggle-toothed old rat, Jake Sandell, chucklin' to himself and taking pot-shots at my punchers!"

The face beneath the black *serape* was frowning. The Masked Rider knew now why he had snapped to attention when the redhead introduced himself. The masked man could still hear the burble of the dying John Harris' words. Yes, it was Jimmie Weeder, Harris had named. Something to do with marrying Leona Harris....

"Just what are you planning to do with all this help you're going to buy?" asked the hooded man.

"I'm not only buying help, I'm asking for it!" snapped the redhead. " 'Tain't a cowman in ten counties wouldn't help me rather than see cattle die of thirst, whatever the facts of the case might be. Only thing is they wouldn't hanker to shoot a few Sandells. With three more men, I'd bust that Sandell outfit wide-open and ram—"

The voice of the hooded man was terse, meaningful, when it broke in on Jimmie Weeder. "How about you, Costigan?"

"He can go to hell," the killer said slowly.

"Madre de Dios!" roared the big Mex. " 'He can go to hell' you say, Cos'gan? You let some pore cattle die of thirs' an' you stan' there? *Ohe!* For wan *centimo,* I tie you down and let you die of thirs' too! *Madre mia,* I am go with dees *hombre.* An' you, Cos'gan, I pull you by dees neck to halp!"

The big Mex's eyes were splitting flames of fire. He took two steps towards Costigan, who stooped, his eyes contracting like a cat's.

"Let him be, Viego, snapped the hooded figure.

The great Mexican paused.

The masked one turned to Costigan. "You're a bad man, a hard *hombre,* ready for anything." His voice was steely with sarcasm.

Costigan eyed the big Mexican, the man in the mask, then Jimmie Weeder.

"For four twenty dollar gold pieces and a grub-stake. Let me have yore word on it, Weeder, an I'll go."

"Dios!" quoth the Mexican. *"Ochenta!"*

"You're on," snapped Weeder. "Do you go with me?" He saw the masked head nod.

Costigan turned, went behind a crumbling corner crowded with shadows. A second later he reappeared with a pinto pony. The big Mexican called down the empty, littered street.

"Collila, mine pretty wan. *Aquí!"*

Out of the shadow came a neigh. A few moments later the big Mexican was astride a towering gray mare.

Without a word Weeder lifted himself aboard his pony and

trotted down the dismal street. Behind him went Viego and Costigan.

THE MAN IN the mask did not holster his guns until they were out of shooting range. When he whistled, the black stallion moved to his side.

At that moment, a scuttling, half-bent figure ran out from an awry, crumbling doorway and clutched at his elbow. It was Crazy Fred.

"You'll tell me, mister," he was blubbering. "You'll tell me what happens to Jimmie Weeder's cattle won't you?"

The eyes in the wild face were rolling, appealing. "I know I'm mebbe crazy. But you'll let an old man know, won't you? You helped me before." He scratched at the black cloth.

The rider nodded. "It may not be nice," he laughed tersely. "Sure, I'll tell you. You'll find out."

Crazy Fred let him swing up into the stallion's saddle, watched the hooded figure with fascinated, questioning eyes.

The stallion shied and would have reared save for the steady hand on the bridle. Near, yet somehow muffled, abruptly had risen the high-pitched deadly clatter of a rattlesnake.

The hooded head jerked about. Plainly it was nearby; the black stallion was fighting the bit in wild-eyed alarm.

Only Crazy Fred seemed unmoved by the venomous, lethal signal of a diamond-back about to strike.

"It's all right," he was rasping in a quavering voice. *"It's all right!"*

The hooded man stared just before he let the stallion's bridle loose. A second later the black horse was racing down the narrow street. But engraved on The Masked Rider's mind was a picture. It was of a tight-skinned triangular head with beady eyes and a flashing tongue. A diamond-back rattler's head.

He had seen it appearing over the dirty bib of Crazy Fred's

overalls. Just before Crazy Fred had made a fumbling grab to shove it out of sight!

CHAPTER V

GUNS ON THE LOCO MULE

I T LACKED ONLY a few moments of midnight when The Masked Rider crossed the rise of the Cayugas and on to Closed C land. The three riders before him—Weeder, Costigan, and the big Mexican—loped their ponies as rapidly as the narrow trail would permit.

The hooded outlaw's reason for lagging behind at Gila soon manifested itself. A mile out of Gila, he paused, well out of earshot of the three and cupped his gloved hands over his mouth. The cry that he gave, that of a marauding, lonesome mountain cat, floated out across the mesa on a down wind. There was no answer.

A mile farther on he gave the call again. The sharp clip of a pony's hoofs on gravel signaled the approach of Blue Hawk.

"*Señor,*" greeted the dark blob that detached itself from the gloom of nearby trees. "I hear you that first time. Why aren't you in Gila? *Amigo,* you take many long chances. Do you know there are three riders ahead? If they see you in this *serape*—"

The hooded man's soothing drawl quieted Blue Hawk's friendly alarm. A few moments later he learned that Blue Hawk had arrived safely in Red Rocks, leaving his dead burden with the sheriff—Beanpole Jackson. Jackson had questioned him briefly, then let him go.

A moment later Blue Hawk was nodding acquiescence to Morgan's requests. He, Blue Hawk, was to trail them. A repetition of the call would be the signal for a rapid and hard-hitting onslaught. The Masked Rider was taking few unnecessary chances.

There was the potent threat that Costigan or the big Mexican or even Weeder would turn on him, force his hand. Moreover, Weeder's errand contrasted strangely against the impression given of the boy by Harris. Why should Weeder be looking for gunmen to carry out the attack on these Sandells? There was law in Red Rocks whose job this should be....

Alone, the hooded man closed up the gap between himself and the other riders.

ON THE RIDGE, dotted sparsely with pin-oaks, Jimmie Weeder's arm shot up in signal to halt. With care, the hooded man pushed the stallion into a position that would least tempt a shot from any of the three.

The redhead's voice cut the thin mountain air like a knife.

"Y'hear them down there now. A-bawlin' and slobberin' through the dirt. Not a blade of grass a fly could light on it in that valley nowadays. Driest year since my paw was a pup."

Weeder's long arm made an arc through the air. "Y'see where th' Loco Mule takes that turn down there? 'Cordin' to our survey Closed C land touches that water, the only water in twenty miles. Two nights ago the Sandells rushed down an' strung a line o' double barbs 'tween us an' the water. When we drove our cattle up to water next day, there was Sandell's eight Bar-H brand punchers with Winchesters holdin' th' fence."

From below, there drifted up to the riders on the ridge, the lonesome frantic bawling of thirsty cattle. The man in the black cape could well imagine the scene in that valley. Dying, tortured cattle, their quivering legs staggering through the sultry dryness. Bawling for water; bawling for lost calves.

The drawl of the hooded rider turned Weeder's head.

"You haven't said yet, Weeder, just whose water runs in the Loco Mule. Being law-abiding citizens for the most part, maybe we wouldn't hanker ourselves to shooting stray Sandells, just to clip a few wire strands."

Weeder's temper flared. "Lissen," he snapped. "There's dying cattle down there an' water to save them. I wouldn't give a damn if we lost th' price of every one uh them. I jest can't sit around seein' cattle die on account of hell-souled rats like Sandells. Holy jumpin' cat-fish—I'll pay yuh!"

Weeder's voice was sincere. He meant what he said. The man in the black hood nodded. Yes, the boy had a hard blow coming. Obviously he didn't know of the death of Harris. He was in a bog of trouble already, without that. The Masked Rider sensed all was not law-abiding in Weeder's proposition. Nonetheless, he nodded grimly beneath his mantle.

Though the Sandells were evidently on the side of the law, ethically the redhead seemed to be in the right.

"If we're going to do something about these cattle, son, better get rolling. We'll take your explaining later."

Weeder didn't answer. He cast a searching glance at the hooded face, jammed spurs into his stout little roan, and hammered downtrail. The others strung out behind him.

Moments later, the floor of the valley below them gradually took shape. Far to their right in the moonlight, could be seen the moving blobs of cattle in a long line banked up almost to the edge of the silvery ribbon that was the Loco Mule.

Occasional horsemen rose through them, trying to force the cattle away from the barb-wire towards which the smell of water in their tortured nostrils had magnetized the cattle.

On the other side of the fence, between it and the Loco Mule, was an empty stretch of land, No Man's Land evidently. Not a soul was moving on it.

The Sandell Bar-H outfit was hidden in the cover of the few pin-oaks on the other side of the Loco Mule. Safely ensconced, they could pick and choose their pot-shots at whoever was foolhardy enough to meddle with the barbed strands.

A small camp fire glittered on the Weeder Closed C side of the river. Jimmie avoided that, rode cautiously upstream, well up the side of the hill, until the cattle were out of sight behind them.

HIS AIM WAS to cut across the creek behind the Sandell's, give the signal for an attack from both sides, and drive the Sandell's Bar-H outfit out of position. With wire-cutters, the rest would be simple.

Soon Weeder's arm shot out. He wheeled the roan at right angles to the trail. They descended through a maze of underbrush on to the floor of the valley.

Countless cloudbursts bad left sandy debris that muffled their ponies' hoofs. Weeder signalled to halt, bent over his pony's neck.

Short metallic clips, followed by musical twangs and the barb-wire fence before them was down. They loped across the valley-bottom, forded the muddy, nearly dry stream, and mounted the opposite valley wall. They had gone perhaps a mile along this bank towards the cattle when Weeder again signaled a halt.

He rode ahead alone. From the brush into which he disappeared issued a lonesome maverick's bawl. Three times, with a short grumbling bellow at the end of them.

He came back, his fighter's mouth twisted in an ironic grin.

"That's the signal," he admitted somewhat sheepishly. "Paw's idea. I can't do it without laughin'."

His face sobered abruptly. "They're down there, strung away from the fence, in the oaks. Paw's ready. Soon's we fire, he'll be backin' us up on his side."

Jimmie Weeder wheeled the stout roan, kneed it to a slow trot. The bawling of the cattle in the bottom was loud now, and nearby.

Costigan already had one of his guns out. The Mexican unlimbered an old Sharps rifle from his saddle scabbard.

Weeder hadn't led them one hundred paces when his roan

reared. To the right of the trail a rifle flared with a truculent bellow. The hidden man shot again. The flash of his gun, The Masked Rider saw, was in the trees a good seventy yards away.

This time Costigan's pinto grunted as its knees hinged under it. Costigan rolled out of the saddle, rose, both guns out, his bitter cold curses cutting the night.

A second later, the whole valley bottom was in an uproar. Weeder and the big Mexican had by this time broken for cover. The hooded rider behind them, disguised by shadows from the hidden gunman, waited watching.

He cursed ironically. Weeder should have known the Sandells would not leave themselves entirely uncovered. Fearing such attacks they had strung a couple of men up the hillside at right angles to the stream.

Weeder had blindly run into one of them. What would happen now was entirely up to the luck of the redhead. Below, the Sandells would already be warned, guns ready.

Grimly, the black cloaked figure clenched his teeth. Costigan, Viego and Weeder had hit for cover. As soon as they ferreted out the sharpshooter they could proceed. By that time—

The man in the hood wheeled his black. He was making a decision. Hours ago he had determined to help out a girl whose father had been murdered by some night-riding sidewinder. At that time his plan of action was undetermined. Mainly it had consisted of finding the girl, telling her her father's story.

Now he found himself embroiled in a bitter water-rights fight on the side of the redhead who was supposedly this girl's fiancé. Whether he was on the right side of the law or not, mattered little. His blood too, had boiled at the thought of those dying cattle in the creek bottom, retching for water inches from their tortured nostrils.

Under the dark hood of The Masked Rider he knew the danger to his life was tripled. Nonetheless, a plan had already formed in his mind.

Weeder's own plans had struck a stone wall. Bottled on the hillside, it was doubtful anything he could do would rout the Sandells below from their positions. If he, The Masked Rider, went on with the fight, it must be a lone-hand play.

He touched the stallion's flanks lightly with his spurs. Even Blue Hawk should be left out of this....

THE NIGHT WAS punctuated by an angry roar from the rifle when a form separated itself from the shadows. The bullet went wild.

Seconds later, the man in the hood swung out of the saddle well out of rifle range and disappeared in the brush lining the trail.

He reached the creek bottom before the twin .45s under his cape appeared in his hands. Crouched in the brush, he made his way, a tenuous shadow, towards the bend in the Loco Mule where he knew the Sandells were hidden.

When he slopped, his lips were in a tight, thin line, grim. Off in the shades he heard a high, crackling voice cursing. A moment later, the hooded man had outlined the forms of eight men and eight rifles at rest facing the bend in the creek and the solid bank of cattle lined up against the silvery strands. It was the Sandells.

The man turned noiselessly and retraced his steps. Up the hillside a rapid burst of firing told him Weeder had locked horns with the hidden gunman. Brush crackled; a man's voice yelled orders. Then all was silent.

The man in the hood paused. Grimly he took the commands of his conscience. When he whistled softly, a movement in the brush above heralded the approach of the black stallion. When it trotted out to the noiseless sand of the creek bottom, the cloaked figure swung up into the saddle. He looped the reins about his wrist. Both hands, now ungloved, held ready .45s.

CHAPTER VI

THE RIDER STRIKES FIRST

TWENTY FEET APART sat the Sandells and their Bar-H punchers. Old Jake Sandell, wiry, hawk-nosed and foul-mouthed was in the center. On his right in order he had placed his sons; Andy, Louie and the youngest, Sam. A bald-headed puncher, whose shiny pate reflected the moonlight, was on his left. Three more punchers, rifles ready, completed the defense.

Already Sandell had listened to the firing on the valley lip. He was not one to be caught napping. Four more men, he knew, were strung up the hillside, his watchful eyes told him the Weeder's Closed C outfit still numbered what they had an hour before. In the shots above he read the approach of one man, at the most two. He was not worried.

The Weeder's Closed C had his orders not to approach the wire strands by less than five feet. Two Closed C punchers already had flesh wounds to prove Jake Sandell didn't mince words. Poor aim was all that saved their lives.

In four more hours, the Weeders would have to admit defeat. The only water those cattle could have reached, leaving the day before, was many weary, hopeless miles away. This time, Jake Sandell knew, the Weeders were facing a stone wall. Grimly, yet with relish, he admitted that his friend Harold Gangling had been right. The law was on his side. That water was his to give away if he wished and to hold if he wanted.

Gangling had said, "Break the Closed C and the Sandell's Bar-H will rule the range." Dwelling on this, Jake Sandell's insides twitched with anticipation and glee. It was almost fantastic that the law, which he had for so many years regarded as a hindrance and a stumbling block to his fortunes, should now be protecting, sanctioning him.

Squatted in the brush, his lean body shook with laughter. High-pitched laughter that died in his throat with fright.

The Rider struck from the dark, heralded by naught save the low muffled thunder of the stallion's hoofs. He came out of the shadows of the dry alders that lined the sand, his guns speaking over the black's flattened ears.

The bald-headed puncher leaped first to his feet. His rifle roared. Shooting from the hip, he missed, then crashed backward into the brush, kicked a moment and was silent.

The man had shot before he even recognized the rider of the dark stallion. By instinct alone he had pulled the trigger on the thundering black bolting out of the shades at him. Firing first, he died first, by the hooded rider's bullet.

The hooded man had counted on striking before the gunmen could well unlimber their rifles. One important consideration he had not valued fully; the startling effect of the apparition of a man in a great flowing black cloak. For a second it left the Sandells and their punchers agape. An express train thundering out of the alders could not have paralyzed them more.

Old Jake Sandell yelled in dismay, then terror. The great stallion was almost on top of him. Andy Sandell, long-limbed and bony, whipped up his rifle and coolly pulled its trigger.

Five voices yelled at the same time. Men scurried, stumbled, ran out of the path of the black horse. The first sight of Jake Sandell leaping to his feet had given the cloaked rider his cue.

A long pair of drooping *mustachios* named the man instantly. A twitch of the stallion's reins and Jake Sandell was in front of the churning dark hoofs.

THE THREE SANDELL sous had stood their ground Andy had shot once, with no effect. Louie and Sam Sandell had their rifles full on the masked figure, too, when it disappeared from the great stallion's back.

Those rifles' triggers never were pulled back. With light-footed sureness, the stallion straightened its forelegs like steel braces, wheeled on its hind legs, backed slowly up the hillside.

Jake Sandell was wheezing in terror. "Don't kill me! Lissen—!"

In that short moment's pause in the stallion's course, three more guns had been whipped around to bear full on the black-cloaked figure.

The Sandells were first, but they hadn't shot. If they had, they would have drilled their father's thin, bony body. By almost magical means, old Jake Sandell's body had reappeared with that of The Masked Rider on the great stallion's back. Now he was astraddle the black's withers, whining like a whipped puppy.

"I know who you arc! I know yo're Th' Masked Rider. Let me down—let me down an' they won't fire 'nother shot!"

He clawed vainly at the steely arm clamped across his chest. An ugly snouted .45 faced the others over his shoulder.

The black stallion was standing motionless as a statue, ears alert, watching the men with the rifles. From the flowing hood a soft drawling voice fell on the ears of the Sandell boys.

"Better drop those guns. Like as not you'll get careless and pull a trigger at a plumb wrong time."

Andy Sandell, long, a little stooped, stepped forward, his dark eyes glittering like coals beneath his battered sombrero. He was the oldest. Louie next, and Sam, the youngest, all more or less the same build, backed him up.

"I ain't dropping this rifle fer nobody. Yo're Th' Masked Rider, eh? Wall, yuh drop that man *pronto.* We *still* got plenty uh target tuh shoot at!"

The man in the mask did not move. He knew the Sandells were bluffing now. None of them would dare so much as to lift a rifle, much less fire it. The hooded man was thinking of those several men strung up the hillside behind him.

"I told you for your own good." His voice was low, dangerous. "You do your own choosing."

Taking a stronger grip on the old man, the hooded rider kneed the stallion forward. Carefully he guided it around the half-circle of Sandell men. They were motionless, wallowing in helpless rage.

As the stallion moved off, towards the muddy banks of the Loco Mule, the captor half-turned in the saddle, the form of Old Jake Sandell wheezing in craven terror always between him and those rifles.

"Where yuh goin'? I ain't done nuthin'!" The curses that followed it were prompted more by fear than by rage.

Grimly Morgan's arm contracted, squeezed the wiry shape in front of him in silence.

The black stepped into the water, plopped through it and up on the opposite shallow bank. Ten feet away were the red-rimmed eyes, the drooling mouths of steers. Their wailing bellows hammered against the hooded man's ears with terrible insistence.

"Ought to feed you to them," said he dryly. "They deserve a good drink of somebody's blood—but yours would poison them!"

"You an' them Weeders are gonna cut them barbs, ain't you," the Sandell wailed. "You can't do that. That water's mine—it's agin th' law. Stop-p-p…!"

The Sandell boys and their punchers were still lined up, watching with bated breaths the progress of the stallion towards the fence. For all they wanted to, they couldn't raise a hand in their father's help. From the brush behind them came a crackle of gravel. Out of the shades strode three figures, arms high in the air. Behind them, guns low and ready, came a redheaded shape, grinning.

Their backs to the newcomer, the Sandells could do nothing but drop their rifles, raise their hands on command.

"Jumpin' kingfishers!" chortled the redhead. "Lookit what

he's doin'. Line up, you bloated egg-suckers, an watch somethin' that'll shore make yore blood boil!"

Up in the shades of the pin-oaks, the giant Viego solemnly holstered his guns.

"Dees *hombre!*" he exclaimed with admiring exaggeration, "with wan hand takes eleven men. Dees Masked Rider he makes plenty money for us tonight. *Madre de Dios*, I t'ink for a while I lose forty numbers in gold!"

Costigan, standing beside him, eyed the scene below coldly. His voice was low, meaningful when he spoke.

"More than fifteen thousand dollars," was all he said. "For a black *serape!*"

CHAPTER VII

BARB-WIRE

PAW WEEDER, JIMMIE'S father, had been across the river waiting when the prearranged signal floated to him. His wrinkled, indulgent eyes, red-rimmed with riding herd for hopeless days without sleep, Paw Weeder could hardly believe his ears. Plainly it meant that Jimmie had got help of some sort.

Not a moment later Paw Weeder had aroused his relaxing punchers, handed rifles around—five of them.

A wide grin spread beneath his big white mustaches. The best pair of walrus whiskers in Arizona. His voice crackled hopefully.

"Yes sir. That boy o' mine'll be the death of them Sandells yet! Hear him up there! He's gonna plumb bust them wide open. An' I'll be damned if he don't get plenty of help from this side. Get goin' there, you lop-eared lobo," he urged a lagging, grinning cowpoke along with his sharp-toed cow-boot. "Remember now, I'm gonna cut that thar fence! If anyone's gonna be drug up tuh law, it's gonna be me!"

Mounted, his men spread out through the bawling cows and heifers. With the sound of the first shooting on the hillside, Paw Weeder swore in dismay. Things were going wrong. Soon, his heart was dragging along double bottom. Devoutly, he swore to kill every man in the Sandell's Bar-H outfit if anyone had harmed a single red hair up on the hill.

Then when silence persisted, Paw Weeder sadly ordered his men back to their stations. Moments later, he witnessed the great black stallion thundering into the thickets where he knew the Sandells were hiding out. He leaped to his feet....

Darkness obscured the goings-on at the opposite bank. Dimly he made out the form of a big horse and rider, all a queer-shaped blob of black, advancing towards the fence.

"Come on!" he grated. "If this *hombre* ain't on our side, we jest as well clean things up now as never."

Slowly he approached the fence. Still in gloom, the big dark horse trotted in close to the barbs. Its rider stooped; something detached itself from his shape. It was another man.

Paw Weeder swore and kicked his pony to a trot. But he was not soon enough. The great black wheeled, rose on its hind legs, and bolted.

When Paw Weeder reached the fence his eyes grew round with surprise. He swore, but not in the same tone as the form lying supine, tangled in the painful, jabbing steel spines.

"Jehovah gosh!" blurted Paw Weeder. "If it ain't Old Jake Sandell!" He leaped from his pony. "Yes, sir, I'm shore glad tuh help yuh outta that mess o' wire, Mister Sandell. Wait!" He grappled roughly at the shadowy form. "Here, whoa up a minnit, will yuh?"

Soon little clicks of steel punctuated with foul oaths from the other sounded. Wires dropped away like threads.

"Don't let 'em in too fast now, you thick-headed mutts," Paw

Weeder's triumphant voice rose above the din. "Remember, we gotta save a little *agua* fer that Bar-H outfit!"

Spitting like a cat, Jake Sandell stood up and looked into the dark muzzle of Paw Weeder's ancient colt. "You go court fer this, Weeder! You an' that long-legged coyote son of yores will go to jail long as I got a cent to my name!"

"We'll see," soothed Paw Weeder; "now jest keep quiet a moment. Hey, you redhead," he yowled gleefully. "Bring that band uh hootowls over this way. I got plenty other important work fer you tuh be doin'."

But Paw Weeder was so busy ordering his punchers and keeping the milling cattle from breaking through to water in one mad stampede, he didn't notice the silence that greeted his call.

GRIMLY, THE HOODED rider had wheeled the black about when he left Jake Sandell well wired in his own spiny barbs and made his roundabout way back to where he knew Jimmie Weeder should be.

Mounting the hillside on Sandall's Bar-H land, he paused. Softly from his hands rose the call of that companionless mountain cat.

He waited some moments in the same place. A pony trotted uptrail, rounded a turn and single-footed in close to the black.

Blue Hawk's voice was upbraiding. *"Señor,"* he said in his quiet tones, "once again now you have left me with guns in your hands. This time, if you failed—*quién sabe?* Maybe I see you alive no more. I am on the hillside, *amigo,* waiting for your call. It does not come. Next time I go to your help when you do not ask me!"

The hooded figure laughed low, somewhat bitterly. "Next time I call, Hawk, it will be for my own neck, I hope. We've been in this country only fifteen hours and already fifteen men know we're here. If it was my choice to risk my fool neck for a bunch of cows, why risk yours!"

For a moment the Indian was silent.

"Perhaps if I tie your arms, your neck will be safer," he said, finally, with a slow smile.

The outlaw grinned. "Afraid not," he muttered. "I have a small errand to be done in Gila, Hawk. Looks as though you're elected. You'll find a man named Crazy Fred there. Tell him this: 'The cows got their water.' He'll savvy. I'll meet you there tomorrow."

"But, *señor*. Tomorrow...!"

"Yes," said the hooded man slowly. "I'm taking a *pasear* back to where we found Harris. I got on idea this *hombre* Stimson might turn up. If he does, I want to be on hand. *Adiós!*"

With a wave, the masked man kneed the stallion into a lope. Sadly Blue Hawk turned his sorrel's head toward Gila. Nothing would he have liked better than to follow the man in the black cape after the almost mythical Stimson.

But first he must do a duty. It seemed as though there was always a duty to perform before one could enjoy. His sombre eyes lit up slightly. Relieved he dug soft heels into the sorrel's hide.

Was there a reason he couldn't visit the scene of their finding Harris too? Plenty of time remained to find this Crazy Fred.

Besides, On one of those rises out on the mesa land, there should be boot-tracks. The gentleman of the knife had left them, he was sure. They would he most interesting—in the daylight.

Blue Hawk bent forward and spoke a soft Indian word in the sorrel's ear. It quickened its pace to a trot, then a slow, easy lope....

CHAPTER VIII

ADVICE TO A REDHEAD

SUREFOOTED, THE BLACK made its way down the slope after the obvious tracks of Viego's big gray mare and Jimmie Weeder's roan. The hooded rider cut off to the left, avoiding the big Mexican and Costigan when their shapes loomed out against the white of the sands below. They didn't hear him pass.

Down on the flat, the redhead turned when the rider's low voice called to him. Weeder frowned, then barked up at the big Mexican to hold his prisoners until he returned. He tromped off into the brush in the direction of the voice. The big black he found in the shade of a pin-oak halfway up the hillside.

"I shore gotta thank you, *amigo*," said Weeder bluntly as he strode up. "Hadn't been fer you, we'd still be suckin' our thumbs up on that ridge. When you busted into them *hombres* below, it was easy as eating chocolate cake gettin' them lookouts up th' hill."

Beneath the hood, the masked man's face was tight-lipped and grim.

"I heard plenty of you b'fore—The Masked Rider," went on Weeder, somewhat annoyed by the silence of the other. "Heard of lot o' things yuh did back Texas way. Seems as though yuh get yoreself into good spots well as bad. I owe some gold pieces, don't I? Like as not it don't mean much to a man as took mebbe twenty thousand dollars off o' that train at Waco. Couldn't help but ask yuh to come anyhow. I was in a pinch. Here's yore forty. Always keep my word."

The hooded man's voice was terse. "So now I'm the one that did that Waco robbery—is that it? Like as not a week from now you'll hear that at this minute I was just finishing off a bank at Bisbee. Keep your money," the voice was tinged with bitterness, "you'll need that forty a lot worse than I will tomorrow."

"Meanin' what?"

Without answering, The Masked Rider went on. "Instead of shelling out, maybe you'll answer a few questions for me. Cutting down people's fences is against the law. I gather that the Loco Mule and land inside that fence belongs to Sandell's Bar-H. They don't have to let you use Bar-H water."

Weeder's words were close-clipped. "I'd rather pay you than answer, frankly. But you've been so dang helpful, I don't mind much. Fact is, Bar-H was always John Harris'—H stood for Harris. Three months ago, he sold out, lock, stock and cartridge-clip tuh these Sandells. In bad years we always watered stock on this side of the range on Bar-H water. It was all right by old man Harris."

His voice sobered, seemed to soften as if approaching a

painful, yet pleasant subject. "Well, yuh see, I'm gonna marry Leona Harris, sorta. John Harris' daughter. Think I am, anyhow. Harris don't exactly think I'm poison but he figgers his daughter ain't jest down my alley—she jest come back from an Eastern finishin' school last month. He can't see her hitching to a dry-dirt farmer, ner a cow-person either.

"When he sold out, guess he was thinking about other things—like he is sometimes—an' didn't say anything 'bout letting us water on Bar-H land in his deed. Our fault, I guess, cause we plumb missed it too an' he'd uh done it if we asked.

"Anyhow, come th' driest year we ever did see. 'Tain't a drop of water this side of South Pasture on Closed C land. We pushed our cows over this way like we always had and run into a plumb stone wall. No, sir, them Sandells would see us in hell first 'fore we'd git water—common range law be damned! We started a war and come to pass, *amigo,* you done hauled us outta th' bog by our eye-teeth!"

Weeder's open frank face was now grinning at the man in the shadows. When the hooded man spoke, however, his voice hadn't changed.

"Harris is your soon-to-be father-in-law, that it?" he mused softly. "How come you didn't go tell him of your troubles? You sure he wasn't up on Bar-H land, trying to reason with these Sandells?"

The grin before the masked man flicked away. The sharp blue eyes were questioning the shadowy form tersely.

"Meanin' what?"

The Masked Rider was silent. Weeder spoke up again, angrily. Without his knowing it his hand had drifted low, to the leather holster at his side.

"Mebbe he did," the redhead said impatiently. "But we sent Poke Andrews down to town last night to find Harris, jest tuh give him a hunch what mebbe we'd end up doin' tuh these Sandells. Wal, Poke come back sayin' Harris had ridden outta town with his man—Stimson. On business. Wal, I left things be. No sir, I wasn't gonna get him mixed up in this rattlesnake's nest. *What makes you think he was out here?*"

"Sort of wondering myself," said the hooded man slowly. "Let's forget it. Just the same, seems to me there's a certain *hombre* 'round these parts named Jimmie Weeder who ought to take dang good care of himself next couple of days. Might even ride down into Red Rocks and say hello to his fiancée. On another track," he went on without changing his tone, "I always like to think that when trouble comes in great big chunks, it usually comes from one place. Sometimes it helps figure out things. Remember that."

Tight-lipped the hooded man stopped himself from telling what he knew would send the redhead before him into a fighting, grief-filled frenzy. No, it was better that the boy find out for himself. He looked down at the hard-jawed, now completely mystified, young face before him. Jimmie Weeder's teeth were clenched, his voice tinged with steel.

"Lissen," he snapped. "You done me a good turn tonight, but that ain't enough. For all I know you could be bad as them Sandells. Mebbe I'm trustin' you too far. You know something I don't know, mister! *What is it?*"

The masked man's voice was calm. "Might be wise to sorta keep an icepack on that temper of yours, for one thing. Other is, learn better comparisons for strange people. Powerful healthy habit. Another is, take shorter steps for a while. These Sandells have got pinchers on you already. Law pinchers, and they hurt worst of all. Even though I would have done just what you did.

"That's three," he added them up lightly. "Last is, better visit Red Rocks *pronto. Adiós!*"

He swung up into the saddle, dodged a low-hanging pin-oak limb and was out of sight before Jimmie Weeder moved.

For a moment the redhead stood there, cursing doubtfully. Vague premonitions tore at him. The enigmatic man in the mask was an outlaw, wanted from Canada to the Rio. An outlaw and therefore not to be trusted. It was damn' funny—

He wheeled on his heel, jaw like a steel trap. Yes, sir, how'd he know this masked man wasn't working for a third party! Against both him and the Sandells. Look out, his mind said.

It was not until Jimmie had reached the bottom again that he remembered there was at least $15,000 on The Masked Rider's head. Then he cursed. There he had stood not five feet from $15,000—and talked! Yes, sir, if there was a dumb, loco, hot-headed calf…!

THE HOODED MAN touched his stallion's flanks lightly when he rose to the trail above the river. The black's pace rose to a quick lope, off in the general direction of Gila.

Behind him, farther back on the trail, a man came out of the brush. He was thin, rat-like. Coldly he cursed as he holstered the gun he had held for a full twenty minutes in hopes that the man on the stallion would ride his way.

Then he swung himself up on the pony borrowed from the Sandell Bar-H string he had found nearby, and pattered down-trail in what be concluded was the direction the black had taken. The man was the killer, Costigan.

CHAPTER IX

THE HOUSE
AT RED ROCKS

LEONA HARRIS HAD lived all but three of the years of her life in Red Rocks. When her mother died, John Harris sent her off to finishing school in the East. Her father's friends she knew well; and so, she thought, his enemies, too.

For that reason, even from the darkest reaches of her mind,

she could not summon courage or conviction to name who might have done her father to death.

In Leona's grief-burdened mind, unfruitful suspicions turned themselves over and over. Her father had been kindly, charitable. Not in his lifetime had a single man had cause to doubt John Harris' honesty. The bank had brought fortune to him; but so, too, had it brought relief and help to many a short-string cowman up against a financial wall.

On the outskirts of Red Rocks, cultivated acres of alfalfa and blue-joint hay behind it, John Harris had built his home. It was low, far-flung in the Spanish manner. Into his library Harris had put a small fortune. It was panelled with rich, heavy oak. The massive furniture, brought to Red Rocks at great expense and trouble, was heavily carved, fine mahogany. Great bookcases graced the walls. It was a room of quiet and peace.

Even now, with the morning sun bursting through the high arched windows, Leona Harris sat at the huge desk in that room, the peaceful atmosphere only adding to the torture of her aching soul.

She was tall, shapely-limbed. Her hair, rich and molasses-colored, was clipped short, curving to the outlines of her pretty head. Her chin, firm, almost stubborn, was held high. Her eyes, red-rimmed from one short hour's sleep the previous night, were nevertheless clear. She took her grief as a man would. A brief spasm of racking sobs and she was again in control of herself.

A short, squat Mexican peon, more of a toad than a man, brought in a small tray with coffee, left it before the girl. His great black eyes regarded her with an animal-like affection.

She said, "*Gracias,* Tollito," but did not touch the food.

The peon left as noiselessly as he had come. He, too, bore the burden of sadness.

Instinctively, she rose at the brief clatter of hoofs outside. Going to the window, she drew aside the great *cortinas,* looked out into the patio, open to the road. For a second her heart, woman-like, moved faster. For on the sweat-stained, weary roan pony that moved into the courtyard was a straight, redheaded figure with smiling blue eyes. Seeing her framed in the arched *ventana,* he lifted his hand in greeting.

Leona Harris' step was light when she left the window, but when she clicked open the lock of the huge oaken door, her heart was a river of sadness.

LATER, JIMMIE WEEDER sat on the big sofa in the library before the gaping black maw of an eight-foot fireplace. His honest, stained working garb contrasted strangely with the rich surroundings. Beside him the girl sat, too, staring into the fireplace.

Soon the stubborn line of Jimmie's mouth, his glittering eyes, showed that he could not be silent much longer. Haltingly, the girl had told him of Sheriff Jackson's visit of the night before, of the pitiful, limp burden he had brought. No, ma'am, I ain't got th' slightest idee, how it happened or who could uh done it. Like as not he had some money, showed it around and was murdered for it. No, they hadn't heard a word from Stimson, didn't know where he could be. The tall Indian who delivered the body told them where he'd found it. That was all. He didn't speak English very well, or he was a good actor. So had the sheriff spoken to her.

Jimmie's head whipped about.

"And what was he goin' to do about it?" he wanted to know.

The girl shook her head. "What can be done? Father's dead. Unless they get that Indian again to take them to the place Father was found, they'll probably never get a clue. Sheriff Jackson said something about a posse. But you know the type of man he is. In the first place, he should have held the Indian for questioning. I could make a better sheriff!"

Jimmie nodded. From the tone in her voice, he knew that his comforting had given her strength. Soon that stubborn chin she had inherited from her father, that had brought her back from the East to Jimmie against her parent's wishes, would give her new life.

Nonetheless, he boiled with righteous anger. He wanted to stride out to his horse, guns out and ready. Shoot, kill, fight like a caged beast. Anything to help allay the dull ache in his heart.

Suddenly his mind whirled to a halt. Teeth clenched, he blurted out one word, "Stimson!"

The girl wheeled, faced him. "I know what you're thinking," she said quickly. "Because they can't find Stimson, or rather he didn't come back, he and Father had some sort of fight, perhaps over money. No, Jimmie, you're wrong! Billie came from the East. Father took him as secretary several years ago because he was sick and because he could handle Father's business the way he wished. Billie was always grateful. He couldn't have done it. *He couldn't have!*"

In the tone of her voice, in the deep blue eyes that now turned, clouded, away from him, Jimmie read thoughts that belied the force in her words.

She didn't want to believe Stimson could have done the deed. But until they found him, or he showed up, there would always be that doubt.

Jimmie's face was on fire when he leaped to his feet.

"I'm goin' back to town," he gritted. "Beanpole Jackson's gonna show action doggone fast or I'll *know* th' reason why! Mebbe Stimson did or didn't have anything to do with this. But a posse'll find out a heap of things sittin' in town never will."

Slowly the girl rose to her feet. As the two stood there facing each other, sudden panic overtook the angry thoughts in Jimmie Weeder's mind. The girl was not thinking of his last words. There was something else in her mind; something at once frightening and unknown. Short hours before the mainstay of her life had been cut away. Now she floated on a blind, futile, dangerous sea alone.

Her glance shifted, down and away from his. Suddenly the stiff steel of her pride and reserve was gone. Blindly she reached out for him, crying as she did:

"Jimmie, *I'm afraid!*"

In pain that clutched Jimmie Weeder's vitals with icy grip, he winced and stepped forward to take her in his arms.

CHAPTER X

STOCKHOLDERS' NOTICE

R ANDSON BALBECK WAS assistant cashier of the Cattlemen's Trust of Red Rocks and had been for close to twenty years. He was a short, pudgy man whose blue eyes had a watery, myopic swimminess that gave the impression at a first meeting of a partially blind man.

Nevertheless, Balbeck saw clearly and usually farther than any of the horny-handed cowmen who taunted him behind his back. Only on courage was Randson Balbeck lacking, and, what he lacked in that, he made up in craftiness of a sort. For this reason, while Harold Gangling was still cashier of the Cattlemen's Trust, Balbeck had inched into his favor and confidence.

Thus it was that when Gangling wanted a message delivered, he called Balbeck into the high ceilinged Trustees' Room of the Cattlemen's Trust, and gave it to him.

With this message, though it was still only nine-thirty in the morning, Balbeck made his way slowly to the outskirts of Red Rocks towards the house of John Harris.

He knocked on the thick oak front door and was shown immediately into the library by Tollito.

What he saw there gave him momentary pause. Leona Harris

faced him with slightly cloudy eyes. A young man with red hair, who even as he looked flushed to the roots of his orange thatch, eyed him aggressively. Placing a random two and two together, Balbeck concluded that something soft and wistfully sweet had but recently clutched at the heart of each.

He cleared his throat briskly and fastened his watery, near-sighted gaze on Leona.

"Mister Gangling is at the bank now, Miss Harris. He wanted to know if it would be convenient for you to meet him there as soon as possible. He asked that you be told it is a matter of great importance to—the both of you."

Gangling had said, "—to her," but Balbeck knew better than to put it that baldly.

Leona Harris nodded, frowned. "Why, yes. I'll come."

"Good day," said Balbeck, and departed.

When he was gone, Jimmie Weeder wheeled.

"Since when does Gangling start telling you where to meet him?"

"Something to do with Father, undoubtedly," the girl said quietly.

Jimmie realized wistfully that the precious spell was broken. It didn't help his temper.

"I'm going, too!" he gritted. "Mebbe if—"

By a wave of her slim, strong hand Leona Harris silenced him.

"I must go alone. It wouldn't look right—you're coming along with me, though I certainly don't trust Gangling. But," she stopped at the door, her calm eyes turning now, taking in the redhead with evident disapproval, "Tollito was in town early this morning. He says that a Bar-H Sandell puncher was in with a long tale of woe for Sheriff Jackson. The Masked Rider is in the neighborhood. Somebody cut down a Bar-H fence on the Loco Mule and *muchas vacas* stampeded through it.

"Old Jake Sandell came home with a thousand scratches and

cuts. The Bar-H puncher was getting arnica. Also there was *mucha palabra* of a law-suit with the Closed C. Your trousers have mud on them this morning. Perhaps, Jimmie, you'll be more helpful staying right here in the house where the sheriff can't get at you!"

"But—" blurted the redhead frantically.

The word fell against a closed door. Disconsolately, Jimmie Weeder cursed—first Jake Sandell, then Tollito, Beanpole Jackson, Balbeck, Gangling, and even The Masked Rider. Later he sat, a thoroughly chastened young man, on the rich sofa, and mentally wrung his hands, unhappiness nailed to his soul.

THE SHERIFF'S OFFICE was next to the Cattlemen's Trust. When Leona Harris mounted the few stone steps of the bank which her father had laid with his own fond hands, she could see Beanpole Jackson over his desk, talking confidentially to a lolling, grim-faced cowhand.

The sheriff had mustaches and a straggling goatee that covered a weak chin. He was frowning and his chin whiskers were moving rapidly. Leona noted, too, before she disappeared through the open bank door, that the pony hitched outside the office bore the Sandells' Bar-H brand. Here, evidently, was the tale-bearer.

Nodding at Balbeck behind the cage, his pudgy shape now encased in an alpaca work-coat, she went rapidly inside. Harold Gangling, when he had become cashier under her father, had moved into the small apartment in the second story of the bank. No doubt he was there now.

She went straight to the high long-tabled Trustees' Room, and took a chair. Soon steps sounded on the hardwood floor at the door. Harold Gangling entered.

Gangling was tall, yet not thin, as his name naturally might have implied. His face was long, horsey, and marked with a pair of predatory dark eyes. Long black hair, straight as an Indian's, lay back from his forehead. When he greeted Leona, his voice was sharp, meaningful. Gangling seldom talked of that which he did not believe or mean.

For that reason he had soon attracted her father's confidence. Where he had originally come from doubtlessly only her father had known.

Leona watched him, head held high, as he pulled the door closed behind him. That was at ten o'clock.

At eleven o'clock the door of the Trustees' Room opened and Leona walked out. Gangling sat inside, watching her leave, his dark hard eyes intent. She did not bid him good-bye.

Balbeck, tacking a paper to the announcement board that stood between the bank and the Sheriff's Office and served the needs of both, lifted his weak eyes as she came out. He saw a face set hard in painful lines, eyes that stared straight ahead and seemed hardly conscious of their surroundings.

When she disappeared, Balbeck grunted and turned to the paper, in which there were already three tacks. He admired it, admired the pen-and-ink printing he had painfully fashioned out at his desk. Admired the wording, too, because he had written it.

The paper read:

NOTICE

IN ACCORDANCE WITH THE LAWS OF THE STATE OF ARIZONA THE MAJORITY OF THE STOCKHOLDERS OF THE CATTLEMEN'S TRUST OF RED ROCKS HAVE VOTED THE FOLLOWING CHANGES IN PERSONNEL DUE TO THE RECENT DEATH OF PRESIDENT JOHN HARRIS, TO WIT: HAROLD S. GANGLING, PRESIDENT; RANDSON BALBECK, VICE-PRESIDENT AND CASHIER.

(SIGNED)
HAROLD S. GANGLING.
MAJORITY STOCKHOLDER.

JIMMIE WEEDER HEARD the girl coming before she entered the door. He leaped to his feet, hopefully, waiting.. The message he read in her eyes was like a clap of doom about his ears. Something was terribly wrong.

"Tell me," he asked. "What happened? What did he want you for?"

Nervelessly the girl's hand rose to silence him. It seemed to him that she was not even aware of his presence when she sat down.

"Holy jumpin' cat-fish—!"

Leona Harris turned, eyes snapping like brittle icicles. "Just this," she said coldly: "Gangling now owns the Cattlemen's Trust."

"He—?"

"He bought out my father three days ago. For $65,000 cash. Bought fifty-five per cent of the stock of the Cattlemen's Trust. That gives him control. The rest is owned all up and down the valley."

"But wait!" the man blurted. "Then—"

The girl's eyes were still and cold. "Wait!" she asked. "That isn't nearly all. He showed me the books. Father took the money, deposited it to his account two days ago. Yesterday he drew out the money in thousand dollar bills and took it somewhere with him. He had Stimson along. When they brought him in last night, *there wasn't a cent on him!* That's why he was killed. Except for two or three thousand dollars in a savings account and this house, everything is gone!"

The redhead's mouth closed in a grim, crooked line. His eyes scanned the girl from head to foot, their expression lost.

"Why—why didn't your father tell you?"

"How could Father? He was leaving the bank. Without his being president there might have been a run on it. Father thought of other people's money. Gangling said he had warned

Father before he bought control. Now with Father dead there's nothing we can do."

Dismay, red anger, hatred, beat a crazy thunder in Jimmie Weeder's ears. He hardly saw the girl now standing tense before him. His tongue lashed out words he could hardly recognise as his.

"Gangling!" he snapped. *"Gangling!* I've always been suspicious of that rat! He did something to the books as soon as he heard your father was killed. And now you're— I'll see! He'll tell me what happened. He has to show me first how he bought that stock. I want to see it! He's in cahoots with Stimson, I tell you. They're robbin' yore father and you like the couple of yellow sidewinders they are. Balbeck, too. Gangling will talk when I get my hands around his skinny, slimy throat…!"

The redhead's battered Stetson was jammed down over his ears before Leona could move. Weakly she tried to tell him that Gangling had been right, that nothing they could do would help matters.

The great front door slammed. Jimmie was gone. He was wild, purposeless as a mad young bull. How could she stop him? So much had happened already.…. It hardly seemed worthwhile.

Dumb with pain, she sat motionless on the sofa, listening to the rapid hoofs of Jimmie's roan beat themselves into silence. When they did, she collapsed.

CHAPTER XI

THE TRAIL TO HELL

THE MASKED RIDER rode steadily towards the ghost town of Gila for the better part of what remained of night. When the full moon sank away, he moved the stallion off to his left in the high brush and divested himself of cloak and hood. Then he slept as a cowman would: on the black's saddle with the saddle blanket for a cover.

The tinkle of bridle irons and soft pad of a pony's hoofs coming downtrail awoke him, for he slept as a predatory animal, his subconscious mind attuned to all danger.

He rose, held the black's nose to keep it from snickering at the other man's mount. Soon, out of the shadows of the first flush of dawn rode a man groggy for sleep, his pony bearing a Sandell's Bar-H brand.

It was Costigan, eyes glued to the trail, though he had now lost trace of the great hoof prints that had assured him he was following The Masked Rider. Grimly, Costigan cursed the fact that the previous night he had been unable to see the animal the masked one rode.

Even now the outlines of that hood were eating into his memory, for he realized with the coming of morning that if he met the masked one face to face without his great cape, recognition would he impossible, his search fruitless.

Now he had lost even those hoof prints, but with clenched teeth he stuck to what he thought was the trail.

Morgan's lips tightened as the man approached. Morgan could have shot him, but let him pass unmolested into the cottonwoods and high mesquite. Now, added to the law's forces, was the constant threat of the killer, Costigan.

When Morgan finished a breakfast of dried foods from the small *alforja* of the stallion's rig, he re-saddled the black. The dark cloak and hood he fitted smoothly between the saddle and the mount's blanket.

His foot was in the *tapadera* when sounds of another rider coming along the trail stopped him.

When the oncoming pony came into sight, Morgan recognized the form of the big gray mare, surmounted by a man in a mountainous sombrero.

It was the Mexican, Virgo, swaying his huge body to the rolling walk of the mare and a soft tune:

*A donde ira veloz y fatigada la golondrina que de aquí se va
O, si en el viento....*

But for some reason the big smile that stretched across his features shone not in the hard black buttons of his eyes.

When he disappeared, Morgan mounted and turned the black's head at right angles to the trail. What the Mexican might be after, Morgan did not know. That Viega was on a man-hunt, too, he doubted. Still, that expression meant something. Was he returning to Gila, or simply taking Costigan's trail?

THE SUN WAS well over the ridge of the Cayugas when the instinctive bee-line Morgan made towards the spot at which he had found the dying Harris, finally led him over a rise in the mesa. He was then near the lip of that same barranca in which he and Blue Hawk had stopped not so many hours before.

The body of Harris' pony lay where it had fallen; Morgan's footprints and the soft impression of Blue Hawk's moccasins surrounded the bloody spot of ground near the pony's saddle. But now other footprints and marks of a new pony had joined his and the Indian's.

Wayne Morgan's angular tanned features frowned at these, though he had rather expected them.

So, too, when Morgan mounted the nearby rise, he found shifted gravel, many imprints of a man wearing a long-toed, heavy riding boot. There the murderer had stood. Morgan followed them in their weaving course through the brush, until they joined those of the pony again and led off to the west.

For moments Morgan stood in the mesquite. One principal question now made him frown. Had the man who had attacked him and Blue Hawk known about Stimson? If he had, why did he stop to attack them and not go on to find Stimson and get the map?

Morgan shook his head grimly and turned to the trail of that first night rider.

To THE EAST of the mesa on which he stood, Morgan could see the misty spiny reaches of the Cayugas. But to the west the scene was impressively different.

Miles away, in the shimmering first morning heat, stretched the great dun expanses of the Tule desert. Not far beyond him, the mesquite covered mesa dropped away to the great wide beds of rough and treacherous lava bordering the desert.

On this stretch of No Man's Land no vegetation or animal life lived. Even rattlers avoided this withered, hideous land, dotted with treacherous pot-holes and great masses of blue-black obsidian cast in fantastic shapes by the cooling of the holocaust ages before.

The barranca wound down and emptied out onto the dark lava flats below. Morgan followed along its lip.

Not far from the bloody saddle in the mesa he picked up the weaving hard prints of Stimson's frantic pony. As if spurred on by mad design, they led straight across the mesa, dropping as it did by degrees to lower levels. Then at last, moving down a treacherous incline, he saw deep, sliding marks where the pony had been pulled up.

Beyond stretched terrain that would reduce a man's boots to mere shreds in a few miles on foot. Even a pony's iron-clad hoofs could not last long on that spiny sea of terrible rock. And beyond that, shimmering away into obscuring distance, reached the parched, heat-dazed desert.

The hoof-marks of that night-ridden pony now led forward, straight into the lava in a wandering, meaningless trail. His lips and eyes grim, Wayne Morgan kneed the great black stallion after them.

CHAPTER XII

CRAZY FRED

THE MAN WHO built the Crossed Horn saloon in Gila, had for some wild notion conceived that it needed a cellar. Later, after it was abandoned, the saloon's roof fell in and the windows stared vacantly at sagging walls about it. But the cellar remained empty and dry and protected from the occasional sandstorms that swept with wild, angry gusts through the deserted streets.

In this cellar Crazy Fred had sought sanctuary. Lit only by the stray fingers of light that seeped through the rotten foundations, it was a gloomy, littered cave in which in solitary glory Crazy Fred slept, ate, and ministered to the needs of his burro, Lucile, who shared the dark hole with him.

Hidden thus from the ghost-haunted, wind-swept streets above, Crazy Fred sat this morning solemnly counting a greasy stack of cards over an upturned barrel.

This was his habit when he wanted to think. Forty-nine, fifty, fifty-one, fifty-two.... He gathered them up and began again. One, two, three— Years ago he found it had helped him to concentrate. And that was indeed what he wanted to do now.

Jimmie Weeder, he thought. Yes, he knew Jimmie Weeder. There was something about his cattle—? Yes, water. They were thirsty and needed water. Eight, nine, ten, eleven.... What happened to you when you didn't have water? You hurt inside, you dried up, the wind whipped you up and blew you away, away, away....

Twenty, twenty-one, twenty-two— The queen of hearts, a good card, he thought. Water, water everywhere, and not... a drop to drink....

FOR THREE-QUARTERS OF an hour Blue Hawk had patiently searched the bone-dry skeleton of the ghost-town for a sign of moving life. Morgan had said Crazy Fred would be in Gila. Wayne Morgan was seldom wrong.

Earlier that morning Blue Hawk, too, had visited the mesa and the bloody scene of the previous night. Already the black stallion and Morgan had passed, their tracks disappeared in the west. Blue Hawk had only paused to memorize the hoof-marks and the boot prints of the "gentleman of the knife." When he left the mesa those marks were engraved on his mind as with acid.

Never again in his life, if Blue Hawk saw them, would he fail to recognize them.

Solemnly now he searched the strewn alleys, the cobbled Main Street until he at last found recent traces of a burro. These led him finally to the Crossed Horns and the cellar below.

"Buenos días, señor."

Crazy Fred's head jerked erect. His startled, queer eyes scanned the newcomer from head to foot. Deciding he was not about to be scalped alive by the tall, erect form of the Indian above him, Crazy Fred swallowed hard, cleared his throat and gave vent to a husky "Hello." His voice sounded like the movement of a rusty gate.

Blue Hawk descended solemnly into the cellar, coolly avoiding the steel-spring hoof snapped out by the burro Lucile, chewing hay in a near corner of the dank cave.

"Señor," said Blue Hawk slowly, "I have been sent to tell you that the cattle of Jimmie Weeder got their water."

For a second Crazy Fred eyed him quizzically. The wheels of his mind ground slowly, but not for the life of him could he recall why it mattered that Jimmie Weeder's cattle got water. He had been peacefully counting his cards when this stranger descended on him.

Nevertheless, Crazy Fred nodded slowly and said, "Thanks." Then, "Who be you?"

Solemnly Blue Hawk answered. His sober eyes regarded the man before the overturned barrel, then ran quickly over the littered, dirty cellar. Finally they returned to question the other.

"*Señor*, my friend had called you Crazy Fred. Certainly that is not your name."

For a moment those shifting, queer eyes regarded his thoughtfully. The man seemed to swell out his sunken chest, raise the drooping shoulders. His eyes took on a new, almost rational light.

"Me?" he answered. "Me—didn't you ever hear of Frederick Colbone Harris? Frederick Colbone Harris. Yeah—that's—that's me! Once when I—I—"

A lost expression came into his face. Momentarily he groped for words, for memories that suddenly escaped him. His eyes were now vacant, lost. He shivered involuntarily; then turned to his cards once more.

When he heard the name Harris, Blue Hawk's eyes had pinned themselves to the half-witted man's face. Now he saw that the other, lost in the dark sea of the past, was unable to bring forth the memories Blue Hawk's question had momentarily stirred. Yet there was something about that half-witted face that now gripped him....

Blue Hawk lingered in the cellar for moments, waiting for Crazy Fred to turn his mind from his cards. But the other remained lost in his thoughts.

The Indian turned slowly, mounted the rough-hewn steps in the clay bank that turned down into the cellar. As he did so, behind him rose a deadly clatter.

Like a cat the Indian turned, hand on his gun. Out of a dark recess in the far corner of the cellar a hideous, blunt-nosed head crept into view.

Sinuously, the repulsive big diamond-back twined its shape

out to the cellar floor, its head several inches off the dirt, its horny tail a whipping blob of light from which issued the lethal warning of a rattler about to strike.

Blue Hawk remained statue-like on the rude steps. His hand had drifted down to his gun, but paused when he saw Crazy Fred rise slowly from his seat.

Then his eyes widened perceptibly when Crazy Fred stooped, lifted the big diamond-back in his hand caressingly, soothingly. When he turned to Blue Hawk smiling, his claw-like hands stroked the triangular, murderous little head. The malignant rattles stopped.

"Gits powerful nervous with strangers around," the bearded man said. "This's Dolly. Big, ain't she? Allus lets me know when she's hungry."

Stooping, Crazy Fred bent into the corner from which the venomous head had appeared. He hissed softly, soothingly. When he rose, another diamond-back, big as the first, was coiled about his arm.

"Yes, sir," Crazy Fred was saying. "Best friends man ever did have, them. Wouldn't bite *me,* either. Kinda seems like they knew how mad I'd be."

Blue Hawk didn't answer. Above he heard the rattle of a horse's hoofs on cobblestones. He bent, climbed from the cellar to investigate.

Solemn, almost emotionless as he was, Blue Hawk was glad to step outside into the clear light of the morning

WHEN HE HAD ridden into Gila that morning, Blue Hawk had taken caution to tie his sorrel pony well out of sight of any of the streets of the ghost-town. With careful eyes he had picked out a rickety lean-to well off the dead Main Street.

Of this he was glad when he stepped into the littered alleyway near Crazy Fred's cellar. From behind the corner of a leaning, whitened building, Blue Hawk observed the killer,

Costigan, ride down what was once the Main Street of the ghost-city, eyeing each vacant doorway, each littered side alley.

There was no doubt about it, Costigan was searching for someone. Who it might be, Blue Hawk did not know. The brand on the pony was familiar, Sandell's Bar-H. That was enough.

The Indian was relieved to see Costigan turn his pony's head and move out of town in the general direction of Red Rocks. After this, he put himself in an advantageous spot to meet Morgan when he returned.

Blue Hawk did not wait long. Out of the ruddy streaks of color in the west a big black horse soon appeared, bearing its rider at an easy distance-eating lope toward Gila. Spotting Morgan when he was still some miles away, Blue Hawk led out his sorrel, loped off to meet him.

When Morgan approached, the Indian saw that his lips were grim, the heavy cloth of his blouse and riding pants dirty with the gray alkali dust of the desert. Morgan's greeting was terse.

"Lost him!" he snapped. "I'd like to believe there never was a man named Stimson. If I'd kept on he'd probably have ruined my horse the way he must have his own."

"You found the trail then, *señor?*" Blue Hawk purred soothingly.

Morgan beat the alkali dust off of his shoulders and thighs. When he looked up at Blue Hawk, the cold gray of his eyes was relaxed, indulgent.

"Make a swell law-hound, now wouldn't I? You're going on that trail next, Blue Hawk. I can follow a walking pony when it leaves signs. But, after about three miles, that horse might just as well been a blue-jay for all the help it gave me. You're the only man I know that'll find a trail where there isn't one, Hawk. A deaf, dumb and blind beggar could do what I did."

Blue Hawk smiled briefly, "Sometimes, *amigo*, I have seen you find tracks old *Señor Lobo* himself would have missed," he said without emotion. "Into the desert they went, is that it, *señor?*"

Morgan nodded. Maybe and maybe not. He crossed into the *pomez* beds. A rock chipped here, a hoof print there—pretty soon even those gave out. "If he went into the desert at night, he'll probably never come out alive. But I don't think he did. I think he turned back—if he wasn't too badly wounded."

"Wounded, *señor?*"

Morgan's eyes were crinkled, enigmatic. "Yes. He got down off his pony once. I found blood."

"But, *señor,* if we don't find him—!"

"That's right," said Morgan, angrily now, "if we don't, this whole rumpus will never be cleared. That's why I want you to dust out there and do something I couldn't do, *amigo—find Stimson!*"

The Indian's face was sombre as he nodded. "Blue Hawk will," he said simply.

Morgan turned towards Gila thoughtfully. Blue Hawk waited before he spoke up again. *"Señor,* I have found something, too. It is the man, Crazy Fred. His name, *señor,* he says, is Harris. Fred Harris...."

Morgan's head whipped about. "Harris?" he repeated. *"Fred Harris?"*

Blue Hawk nodded. "Yes. And I think perhaps it is a good plan for you to talk to him soon."

Lost in the gathering thought that for a second beat against his mind, the lithe figure on the black only frowned and whistled softly.

CHAPTER XIII

PINK PAPER

O NE VISITOR TO his cellar in a day was an event in the life of Crazy Fred. Two was unprecedented. For that reason his head jerked alert at the sound of boot heels on the cobbles above him. When steps approached his crude doorway, he leaped up nervously.

The agitation of his addled mind was even more when straight into his domicile strode a figure at once familiar and terrorizing. It was the rider he had seen the previous night who stepped from darkness as if by magic created from thin air, who spoke in low soft tones—velvet covering steel.

Crazy Fred backed into the far corner in alarm when the figure stood before him, arms akimbo. But his voice was friendly and Crazy Fred at last moved from his shelter to face The Masked Rider.

To preserve his identity, Morgan had disguised himself before entering Gila. He knew that if he was to draw Fred Harris into conversation, the hood was necessary.

The grim doubts coming to his mind on hearing the surname Crazy Fred claimed for himself had become even more demanding of explanation when Blue Hawk continued his description of the gruesome dark recesses of that cellar.

When Morgan spoke his voice was soothing.

"Last night you asked me to tell you whether Jimmie Weeder's cattle got water. I helped him get them through the fence. That was what you wanted, wasn't it? They got all they wanted to drink." Morgan talked slowly, simply, as one would talk to a child.

Crazy Fred relaxed. He sat on an overturned barrel and for a moment his eyes were downcast. When he looked up a queer smile twisted the mouth half-hidden in his beard. His bright eyes were relieved, happy, as a child's would be.

"I couldn't remember—" he rasped haltingly. "Yes, shore! They were thirsty. I'm glad! I allus did like that Jimmie Weeder."

His face became questioning. "Yo're Th' Masked Rider, ain't you? I heard of you, too. Yo're wanted in lots of places. I wouldn't tell on you, though," he added, confidentially.

The eyes that saw through the twin holes in the black hood were grim, almost cold. Fearful of Crazy Fred's answer, the hooded man hated to ask his next question. But he had to. Something inside him forced him to, just as the demands of his conscience had bade him the night before to stand by the side of the dead John Harris and swear to ferret out the cold-blooded murderer who had downed that white head.

"Understand your name's Harris," he said slowly. "Lots of Harrises around these parts. You any relation to them?"

Crazy Fred eyed the hooded man in surprise. It was moments before he spoke. Finally he bent forward confidentially, his voice low.

"Mister," he said, "yo're th' first man ever axed me that question. Yes, I'm a Harris—an' proud of it. Frederick Colbone Harris, that's me."

He stood up, his matted head cocked to one side. "Mister, did you ever hear of John Harris? Lives in Red Rocks. John Harris o' th' bank there. He's my brother!"

The eyes under the hood narrowed slowly. Through Morgan's mind there raced a hundred quick thoughts that all converged on that one last sentence of Crazy Fred's.

He was John Harris' brother, the uncle of Leona Harris! How many people in Red Rocks knew of this taint that flowed in the veins of the Harrises? Did this—could this have a bearing on John Harris' death?

The masked man pulled his eyes back to the bearded, queer features before him.

"Did John Harris ever come to see you? Would he come if I asked him to now?"

Crazy Fred laughed low, huskily. "That he would, mister! John Harris is th' richest man in this valley. But he's my brother and never acted different. Shore, he dropped in jest last night. With—with that other man—" Memory would not turn the trick.

"Stimson," said the hooded man and wished it couldn't have been.

Crazy Fred's face lit up again. "Yes, he called him Stimson. He said, 'Here, brother,' and was standin' right there where you are now. 'Here, brother, thought I'd pay you a visit passin' through.

Here's a coupla coppers I been saving up to give you.' Laughed sorta. Yuh see, mister, it wasn't coppers a-tall. It was a *five dollar bill!* Look!"

Vainly Crazy Fred searched through the ruins of his overalls. The bill was evidently not to be found. At last he ceased jerking his pockets inside out.

"Musta left it some'ere else." He smiled up at the masked man. "Anyhow, allus doin' that, he is. A dollar here, a dollar there. I allus says, 'Thanks, brother, an' he goes. A fine man, my brother."

"Do you visit him in Red Rocks?"

Crazy Fred shook his head quickly. "Not me. I buy my grub an' leave. I went into th' bank once. A man named Gangling told me I better not again. So I don't. Brother John he comes an' sees me when he wants to; I—" He stopped abruptly, his eyes gleaming with a new, laughing light. "You know much about Red Rocks? Sorta go there when you ain't coverin' up fer somethin'? Do you know John Harris?"

"In a way," said the figure in the dark cape.

Crazy Fred put back his head and laughed high and huskily. "Wall, I got somethin' that'll make yer eyes pop out. Yes, sir; it'd surprise almost anybuddy that seen it! I was thinkin' yesterday I otta show it to someone, long's I got it here."

He turned into the farther corners of the cellar. It was the whisper of moving papers that first brought The Masked Rider's mind alert with a jerk.

"I got it some'ere here," came huskily from the corner. "Nope, can't seem to find it now. Was here last week, sorta. Funny—"

He came back scratching his head. "I put it some'ere's," he said haltingly. "A pink piece of paper, sorta. 'Bout this big, so high, so wide." He measured it with a pair of dirty, long-fingered hands. "Yes, sir, a pink piece of paper."

The hooded eyes were glinting lights of fire. "Paper," the man repeated. "What sort of paper? From whom did you get it?"

The questions seemed to startle Crazy Fred, confuse him only more. The masked man began to curse softly beneath his breath.

"Who'd I get it from? Mebbe from—I don't know!"

In the eyes of Crazy Fred came that look of fright and wonderment that heralded the failing of an addled memory. "I don't know where I got it," he wailed softly. "I had it, that's all. Now I can't find it."

"Did John Harris give it to you."

"Please, mister, I don't know where I got it. It was pink, sorta, that's all I know."

"From Stimson? From Leona Harris? From this Gangling?"

The lithe figure in the dark *serape* shot the questions as fast as his tongue could speak. What if it were the map of which John Harris had spoken? For some unknown reason, had he given this poor brother of his a copy of it—? Or had Stimson in his fatal flight stopped off to leave with Crazy Fred the secret that should reach Leona Harris?

The questions in the hooded man's mind seemed never to be answered. Crazy Fred, hopelessly confused, sank into his chair, his head bowed. "I've forgotten everythin' now," he murmured huskily. "It was a pink slip of paper, so big. It had something on it. I forget what."

"Did it belong to John Harris, to your brother? Would he have wanted you to show it to anyone?"

But Crazy Fred seemed not to hear him. He muttered absently with bated breath. "A pink piece of paper. I remember... I thought I better show it to someone. It had somethin' written on it—I can't remember what. I musta left it some'eres else."

Beneath the hood, the lips set in a tight, grim line. So here was his vital clue to the death of John Harris! Of all the fine places— The man moved forward.

He had stalled off telling the poor, addled bit of humanity that the one guiding stay in his life was gone. John Harris had treated his brother with kindness and charity. The blow of Harris' death was yet to come.

The hooded man gritted his teeth. "I'd hoped that piece of paper had something to do with John Harris. You know, he's dead."

And from the eyes that swept up to his hooded face, he saw that with those words he had dealt as cruel a blow as man could ever mete out to a fellow human.

CHAPTER XIV

HAROLD GANGLING

IT WAS TWELVE o'clock noon and Harold S. Gangling sat at the desk that had been John Harris' in the Cattlemen's Trust. In bygone days the heavily carved piece of furniture had graced the space behind the long barred counter at which Balbeck stood.

Earlier that morning, after Leona Harris had left the bank, Gangling moved the great desk into the Trustees' Room. This, henceforth, would be his domicile. And why not, he considered? He was now the majority stockholder.

From his new desk, Gangling could see the main street of Red Rocks through his office door and the front doors of the bank. That was also as it should be, because quite definitely Harold Gangling had made up his mind that in its forthcoming years Red Rocks was to become more and more a domain entirely his.

Already he owned a controlling interest in the Cattlemen's Trust, and, though it was not generally known about the small town, all or goodly portions of the majority of larger buildings in Red Rock. Moreover, many a ranch outside of town was mortgaged to the hilt by paper held by the Cattlemen's Trust.

The bank was a fine piece of property. John Harris had made it such.

Gangling ran his thumb and forefinger down the lapel seam of his dark gray business coat, a gesture characteristically his own.

There was a hammer of feet on the boardwalk outside the bank. Gangling's dark eyes flicked upward, nervously.

With good reason, for into the fore part of the Cattlemen's Trust burst a big-hatted, long-limbed figure who strode on surging legs directly for the desk behind which Gangling sat.

The new bank president's lips lightened, for he had recognized a thatch of red hair that matched the angry, glaring face of the youth.

Jimmie Weeder didn't herald his approach. He strode into Gangling's office, slammed the door with a truculent crash that rattled windows throughout the building.

Knuckles on the desk, young Weeder's head came within inches of Gangling's long, horsey face.

"*You*, Gangling," he thundered. "I come to talk turkey, if you know what that is! And when I finish, a lot of things Red Rocks don't know will be spread all over this here state. Even if John Harris didn't, *I* know you for the yellow-bellied sidewinder you can be—"

Gangling's eyes rose slowly up the muddy blue shirt front of the young man, stopped finally on his glaring, working face. Gangling's dark eyes changed expression but little. He frowned momentarily as though striving to get the mad drift of the redhead's words.

But when Weeder said "sidewinder," the muscles on Gangling's long jawbone knitted.

"Whoa up," he said softly. "Get hold of yourself, boy."

At the word "boy," Jimmie Weeder colored. For a second he blinked, breathless.

"Whoa up?" he taunted, trying to hold himself in leash. "I'll whoa up—like hell! Yo're president of this bank now, that it? You paid $65,000 for fifty-five per cent of the stock—that makes you able to elect yorself and that water eyed rat outside there whatever you want. Lissen, Gangling, $65,000 wouldn't buy the front steps of this bank when John Harris owned it. I know! Before I move a step outta this office yo're gonna show me two things. One is a bill of sale for that stock, and number two is the stock itself. I'm gonna see them both!"

Gangling heard him out. When Weeder finished he rose in his chair. Something tawny, tigerish shown in his predatory eyes. It seemed to grow, to flame harder.

"You're not going to see a thing, Weeder! No man can talk to me that way and stand there. My deal for this bank was conducted in accordance with the law of this state! Get out!"

The redhead spread his legs apart. Momentarily words would not come from his moving, chapped lips. When they did, they scored the air of the room.

"I'll see you in hell first, you long-legged, horse-faced buzzard! If you did have $65,000 to buy this bank, mebbe it grew outta yore big ears. You never earned it! Yo're gonna show me the bill o' sale, deposit slips an' everything else that went with this sale. You hear me, Gangling?"

Weeder's hand whipped down, and up snapped a blue-barreled, ugly .45.

"Yuh hear—everything! John Harris is dead, an' by golly if I can't prove you ain't got a slick hand taking advantage of it, I'm a loco, ring-tail baboon. *Move!*"

In many years at the bank Gangling had chances to meet up with numerous and queer customers. But the youth who faced him now, wild-eyed, tousle-headed and with threatening gun, was by far the most amusing.

For a moment the hard, cold gleam in Gangling's eyes disappeared and a smile twitched at the corners of his thin-lipped, wide mouth. A second later the gleam was back in his eyes, as they drifted down to the ready .45, then up to the face above it.

"Get out," he sneered. "Get out of my sight and put that cannon away before I take it away from you. I'm practically letting you walk into jail and out again, letting you talk that way to me. But I know you don't mean it." His air was half-patronizing. "I could break you and your father like this"—he gripped his long, slim fingers into a knot before the upturned nose—"if I chose. Perhaps you don't realize that the Cattlemen's Trust has a mortgage on the Closed C, my boy, that has you strung up tight as a kite. It would be well to keep in the good graces of the bank for a few months anyway. In the meantime, I'll condescend to tell you that whatever you wish to see will be exhibited at the Sheriff's Office in a few days. Now, you insolent young puppy, *get out!*"

At that moment the mind of Jimmie Weeder, twirling through a reddened, maddening haze, cleared. He realized where he was. That he had an open gun on the president of the Cattlemen's Trust; and that Harold Gangling said words he could not disregard. Bitterly and silently though he might curse, what Gangling stated was gospel truth.

All at once he knew that he was acting the fool, was saying violent things backed up by not the slightest iota of fact. The gun in his hand was a hideous indictment. For all she loved him, Leona Harris could never condone this most foolhardy act. For the life of him he could not see himself facing her now.

"Get out!" clipped Gangling's voice. "Before I have you thrown out!"

Without a word Jimmie Weeder turned and made his way out of the Cattleman's Trust. But still, rather than regret, there was defiance in his face and gait.

And as he moved down the front steps a voice, like that of doom, broke on his ears. It was Sheriff Beanpole Jackson's.

"Here you, Jimmie Weeder. Wait a minnit. I gotta sorta—sorta sub-*poeena* tuh serve on yuh."

A hand fell on the redhead's shoulders and a voice droned on and on: "Jacob V. Sandell, Plaintiff, versus Paw Weeder, Jimmie Weeder, et al, Defendants. Here y'are, son."

CHAPTER XV

IN A LIBRARY

WHEN HE LEFT the cellar of Crazy Fred, the man in the hood moved purposefully towards the great black stallion, mounted it and spurred to a gallop in the direction of Red Rocks.

Determination that the time had come for him to see Leona Harris as soon as possible urged him on.

Probably never would he forget the tortured face of Crazy Fred when he heard that his benefactor and the man he claimed as his brother was dead. But even then, the mystery of the pink slip of paper that seemed to have paralyzed his mind, could not be solved.

The Masked Rider decided to bide his time. Later, if his plans carried well, he might catch Crazy Fred in a more lucid state of mind.

Stimson, he thought, had been wounded when he rode before John Harris and away into the gloom of the desert. Two previously tough questions were now answered. Stimson was at the scene of the attack. Stimson also had taken part in the encounter.

He traveled rapidly along the bottoms of dry gullies, taking to the upper lands only when the protection of brush or trees made it safe. Clad in the black cloak, he knew he was a potent and inviting target for any man.

Two hours of hard riding brought him in sight of Red Rocks. From the vantage point of a brush-covered hillside, the hooded man surveyed the town.

From Crazy Fred he had gleaned a halting description of John Harris' home. When he saw it in the shimmering distance, well away from the town, he recognized it.

LEONA HARRIS HAD remained in the library after Jimmie Weeder left. Tollito, the squat peon, left for his usual marketing hour in town. The great house was empty, silent. For a long time the only sound in the library was the quick, uneven catches of her breath.

For that reason her terror was tenfold more paralyzing when her head jerked up and an apparition in black, regarding her in silence from the door of the library, was all but burned into her eye-balls.

She leaped to her feet, her slim shape outlined against the black wideness of the great fireplace. A wild, hopeless scream died in her throat. Her eyes flicked this way, that way, for an avenue of possible escape.

For in that second of fright she had recognized the garb of the man framed by the doorway.

"The Masked Rider!" cried her mind.

For a second the two stood there thus regarding each other. The girl saw a pair of booted, slim legs below thin, cowpuncher's hips. Above that, a black flowing cape concealed partially the outlines of a chesty, broad-shouldered torso. The great cape and hood, marked only with eye-holes, reached up to and under the broad brimmed, unornamented black sombrero. Later, when she thought of him, Leona Harris could not recall one revealing feature of his guise that would have marked him without the black *serape*.

The hooded guest saw a girl, tall yet marked with the indelible loveliness of femininity, outlined against the book-bindings. He knew from her expression that uncontrolled terror rode through her mind. Yet purposefully he was silent.

When he spoke, the soft drawl of the range that floated from beneath the hood allayed Leona Harris' fright. Strangely indeed did it contrast with his stern garb, and, too, with the tales of terrorism and bloodshed she had often heard unwarrantedly associated with his name.

The man said: "I gather there's no one else home. That's a help. We can talk."

"Talk!" The girl asked it almost unconsciously. "You—?"

"Powerful uncomfortable dress to do one's visiting in." The voice was half-humorous. "Stands in mighty good stead sometimes, though. If you'll get it out of your mind that I'm here to do you harm or steal something, it'll help, too." He paused. "I was with your father when he died."

"But—? No, I won't scream. Only please don't come closer. You were with him—? Sheriff Jackson said it was an Indian—"

"Perhaps an Indian *brought him in*," said the visitor, smoothly.

"Then you killed him? You—"

The hooded man gritted his teeth and walked towards the girl. She did not scream. In short, clipped sentences he described John Harris' death. The second attack of the knife-thrower—but let the inference sink that the knife had been thrown at himself. And he reported that the trail of Stimson disappeared in the desert.

"When he died," he said, facing her, "your father wanted you to find Stimson. You see, he has the map. If Stimson comes back, like as not you'll find the money safe. If he doesn't...."

Lights appeared in the girl's eyes. "Then the money is safe. I'm glad, for father's sake even more than mine. You see, he worked hard to build up the bank. The money was given him by Gangling for the controlling interest in the Cattlemen's Trust. It's quite a bit. Harold Gangling says Father drew out $65,000 and took it with him. Why he did, we'll probably never know. But if Billy Stimson knows where it is hidden, it's safe."

"That's what I gathered from your father—just before he died. You knew Stimson. Maybe he won't turn double-cross on you. Still"—the hooded man added doubtfully—"why was he running away without your father?"

The girl's eyes clouded. "I don't know," she said. "There must be a good reason. If Billy Stimson knows where the money is, it's safe. Unless"—she paused in painful silence—*"unless he's dead, too!"*

The masked man suddenly understood from the expression on the girl's face what she must have been through within the past twenty-four hours. He realized, too, that, save for Jimmie Weeder, she probably had not a soul to turn to.

Besides her father, it seemed that Bill Stimson had been her only other guiding light. Gangling? Something in her voice, when she mentioned the banker's name, told him he was assuredly not one of them.

Inwardly the masked guest cursed. Somehow he could not bring himself to believe that this girl was related by blood to that pathetic wandering man of Gila. If she did not know of the relationship, no man had a right to tell her! Seeing her in pain and futile suffering, the hooded man swallowed hard. Somehow he and Jimmie Weeder must see her through. It had to be!

The girl turned abruptly. Her voice was now steady, proud.

"Why are *you* doing this—for us?"

The slim hooded shape moved aside. His reply was slow.

"It wouldn't help now—if I told you," he said. "Besides, I doubt you'd believe me. Maybe it's just because I hate to see other people get more than their share of trouble, if I can help it. Maybe I can't see plumb *simpatica* people suffer. Then, too"—his voice was lighter—"I like to meddle in other men's business—particularly if it's crooked."

The girl frowned. "But—?"

"I'd rather ask you questions than answer yours just now," he said. "Lot more comfortable—for me. Have you a silk handkerchief I could borrow? A pink one. Most girls have. It'd be helpful to me—just now."

A sad smile twitched the corners of the girl's mouth. Was this request serious? A pink handkerchief—but surely he couldn't be making fun at this time....

"Are you sure I won't come back with a gun?" she asked as she moved towards the door without answering him.

"I'll take the chance," said the masked man, and when she went out, he thought, "Crazy Fred!" and clenched his teeth.

A moment later she returned with a small square of cloth. For a second it lay in the hooded man's tight-gloved hand, frail, feminine.

"That'll do," he said briefly. "*Gracias*... and *adiós*. I hope your bet on Stimson pans out."

He moved rapidly through the kitchen of the great house and out the back door.

The girl at the library window watched for his shape moving behind the house, for she wondered how it was possible he could have made his approach and entrance unseen.

All she caught was a brief, flashing glimpse of a black shape running light-footed and nearly doubled in the shelter of nearby mesquite. Moments later, farther away, disappearing over the mesa rim, she saw a black horse and rider lining out at a swift gallop towards the west.

When she turned back to the library desk the girl's heavy heart found its burden, though sad, perceptibly lighter.

CHAPTER XVI

THE DESERT SPEAKS

ON HOT AFTERNOONS when the dismal, empty streets of the ghost town of Gila seemed to writhe in heat waves rising straight from the earth, Crazy Fred usually retired to the coolness of the cellar. It was the siesta hour and he slept—as he did this afternoon.

He awoke to the sound of a heavy tread on the decaying steps of his cellar, rose to his elbow on the murky pallet, watching the booted feet descend. For the moment escape was cut off, but the frightened light in his eyes died when he saw the form of The Masked Rider appear.

"*Días*, Fred," said the hooded one. "Dropped in to see how you and the pink paper were getting along. Find it yet?"

Crazy Fred stirred from his bed. His eyes were empty windows that stared at the hooded man. He shook his head "Nope. I forget, now... all about it It was somethin'...."

He stood up. From the musty ancient bedstead issued a long sinuous shape that twined itself off the bed's surface, on to the floor and away. The masked eyes narrowed at the sight of the great diamond-back but the man did not move. "Queer pets," he muttered. "You pull their teeth, Fred?"

The half-witted one shook his head absently. "They never bite me," he mumbled. "Don't have to. I train 'em."

The man in the heavy cape stepped forward. "Thought maybe I could refresh your memory. Does this help?" He removed the great black Stetson, pulled the heavy white silk lining of the hat inside out and held it up to Fred.

"Was the paper this color? You call this pink?"

Crazy Fred raised his eyes, shook his head. "No, mister. It wasn't that color. That ain't pink." But he said it as if he weren't sure of himself.

The hooded eyes were hard, questioning bits of polished steel. A gloved hand held out that fragile bit of cloth brought from the home of John Harris. "Was it this color—pink?"

For a long second, while Crazy Fred stared at the piece of silk, the hooded figure's breath was held. Recognition seemed to come into Crazy Fred's eyes. Then while the man's heart sank the eyes became again vacant, wondering. The bearded face was frightened when Crazy Fred looked up to the slitted hood. "I don't know," the man almost whined. "I don't know what color it was now. I'm not sure. I don't think it was that color—I—I don't think *that's* pink! Is it pink, mister? Tell me. I can't remember!"

The husky voice rose into a pathetic wail.

The Masked Rider clenched his teeth, shoved the handkerchief out of sight.

"Didn't mean to unstring you, *amigo*. We'll remember about that paper yet. But let's forget about it now. Brace up."

He patted the stooped, defeated shoulders, turned and placed a booted foot on the cellar steps. And as he did, muffled by distance, there sounded the long haunting cry of a mountain cat searching for its mate. With a farewell gesture the hooded man was out of the cellar and striding in the direction from which the call had come.

BLUE HAWK'S SORREL pony was caked with sweat and dust. It loped into the deserted street of Gila tired, footsore, and towards the dark hooded figure waiting at a sagging house corner.

When the Indian swung stiffly down from the sorrel's saddle, the hooded man saw many things. In the manner of long-time friends, their greeting was mainly of the eyes. The Masked Rider waited for Blue Hawk to speak the first piece.

As if with a painful duty the Indian's dark eyes lifted.

"*Señor*, he was dead."

Slowly the man in black nodded. "What else?"

"He crossed the lava beds, traveled far into the desert, then turned back. He fell from the saddle twice. The last time he was once again going towards Red Rock, this side of the bad stony ground. He took the pony's tail, *señor*, and let it pull him along way. The pony dragged him into a barranca bottom. There he was, *señor*, dead."

Premonitions already had clutched at the man in the black cape. Yet grimly he held his tongue until Blue Hawk went on.

"He was a brave man, *señor*. The pony was still alive but useless. He must have run it across the lava. I shot it," he paused. "*Señor* Stimson was knifed too!"

"So?" And he bit out the next question eagerly. "Did you search him?"

Blue Hawk's eyes were enigmatic. "*Si, señor*. I search him well. Papers, but no money. You see—a rider was there first!"

"*Someone else?* Who?"

"*Quién sabe?* He rode up the barranca bottom on rocks, then left his pony there. Not one foot print, *señor*, did he leave around the body. When he rode away, he returned by the barranca bottom. It would take five, maybe six days to find the point where he left the barranca. I did not wait, *señor*, because of this."

The Indian reached across the sorrel's saddle, undid an object tied to the saddle strings. It was a sweat stained, bloody sombrero, battered and grimy with dirt of the desert and alkali dust.

"You see why, *señor?*"

The object Blue Hawk exposed to The Masked Rider's grim gaze was not large, yet for a second the hooded man stood in silence, staring. With deft moves the Indian had pulled aside the discolored sweat-band of the sombrero revealing as he did so a bit of paper, a torn corner of what had been a larger piece, between the sweat band and the hat's lining.

"He had the map then!"

"Even so, *señor*," the Indian's words were soft-spoken. "He had the map. This corner remained behind, stuck to the glue of the sweat-band when the map was torn out."

Not for a moment did The Masked Rider doubt that the torn corner of grimy paper that he held up in his fingers had been part of the map. Faint pencil lines still remained on the scrap. And slowly he read the scrawl that ran across its surface:

"*Gila–Red Rocks old road. Take West fork rough two miles....*"

And save for the dim lines that branched into two beneath the word "miles" that was all.

"Do you know what that means?" snapped the hooded man. "He got it—got the map out of Stimson's hat! He must have known it was there even when he knifed John Harris!"

"*Quién sabe?* And this time the killer pulled the knife out and took it with him."

"And then went for the money in the cave!"

Blue Hawk shrugged. "Who knows, *señor?* By a bare chance he might not notice this corner of the map was gone. Perhaps without it, he could not reach the cave."

Hard muscles bulged at the corner of the masked man's jaw.

"By a damn' slim chance!" he snapped angrily. "But if the money is gone, we at least still have a chance of finding who took it. We're going back trail. When we find where Harris was knifed, our hard work starts right from there. Your pony fit to ride—hard?"

The Indian patted the velvety-nosed roan with an easy hand as he smiled slowly. "*Señor El Acedero*—The Sorrel One—he will go where I go, *amigo*. He can run forever!"

CHAPTER XVII

DEATH ON THE TRAIL

N OT FAR OUT of Gila, the man in the black cloak removed his disguise and placed the great cape in its hiding place beneath the saddle of the black stallion. When he remounted and rode again, the youngish angular face of Wayne Morgan was faced to the East and, he hoped, a lucrative destination.

With two pairs of trail-trained eyes on the mountain way, the movements of John Harris and Stimson the night they were attacked become more or less an open book. Keeping well out of sight of beaten trails when they could, Blue Hawk and Morgan rode steadily, backs to the afternoon sun.

They left the lower mesa lands, mounted rapidly into the rises of the Cayugas. Harris and Stimson had ridden a trail little traveled recently. Rains the previous week had left a clean terrain down the mountain-side. In spite of this they lost the trail many times and were forced to retrace their steps.

At last, however, the trail wound up at the bottom of a gravelly gully. Then, almost before they suspected it, Blue Hawk and Morgan were on the scene of the murder.

Casting a hopeful eye over it, Morgan could easily reconstruct much of the killer's movements.

Harris and Stimson had been riding downtrail, Harris evidently leading. A welter of hoof prints, torn gravel, and flattened brush beside the trail told of the panic of their ponies when the attack was made.

Blue Hawk dismounted, examined the whole gully bottom for marks as to where the killer had stood before he delivered the two death-dealing blows.

At last he rose, on the far side of the trail, an object held high. Morgan's rocky jaw clicked when he recognized again the slim, murderous outlines of another stiletto. And this one too was exactly like the long, slim knife he pulled from the *alforja* behind the black's cantle.

It was fantastic, as absurd as the death of the two men was terrible. The killer had struck four times with what might well have been the identical weapon. Once at Harris, at Stimson and at Blue Hawk. Now they had found another, a fourth stiletto, matched to a hairsbreadth by those other knives. It was the sign of the killer once more.

Blue Hawk handed the blade to Morgan. "He stood on that side, *señor*. The first knife—that—missed. Harris' pony reared—here. Next time the man throw his knife it reaches Harris; the next knife Stimson. He throw fast, *señor*, perhaps too fast for the eyes to see."

Morgan nodded grimly. "The first stiletto spelled the end and Harris knew it. He must have jammed the map into Stimson's hand and told him to ride for his life. Then his own pony—went hog-wild."

Blue Hawk clambered cat-like up the gully side from which doubtless the knives had been thrown. When Morgan joined him he bent, picked up a black bandanna at the feet of the motionless Indian.

"Wore a mask," Morgan muttered. "Pulled it off and left it here. That means he knew, positively, his knives had hit true!"

MOMENTS LATER THEY were standing over another mark that was now stamped indelibly in their minds. It was that long-toed, heavy riding boot imprinted solidly in the sandy soil of the gully's lips. There the killer had stood and dealt a death that was a noiseless spurt of white light through the night.

They slid down the gully side to the trail where the black and the sorrel were idling hip-shot in the sun.

But as soon as they reached the trail, the hard hammer of many hoofs sounded beyond a bend in the trail above them.

Instantly Blue Hawk leaped into his saddle with his eyes fastened uptrail.

Wayne Morgan, a slight frown on his face, held his ground, facing the steadily increasing thunder of trotting horses. Suddenly they appeared around the bend and came forward.

"*Madre de Dios,*" snapped Blue Hawk. "Come, *señor*, we can escape them yet!"

But Morgan did not move. His half-squinting eyes examined the seven riders approaching at a fast trot downtrail. Already they had seen him and the Indian; their down-coming ponies' ears shot up in alarm.

What was more surprising was the fact that four of the men who rode at the head of the small phalanx were Sandells.

Morgan's lips were stretched in a tight, hard smile as the horsemen pulled their ponies to a halt, old Jake Sandell well out in the lead, his hard, rat-like eyes scanning both Morgan and the Indian.

"Well," he snapped, "what're you two doin' 'round these parts? This is Bar-H land and we don't hanker to strangers crossin' it at any time." He shifted his head to the men behind him. "Git down boys an' look them ponies over fer familiar brands."

Morgan's pose hadn't changed, but his lowering eyes scanned the faces of Sam, the youngest Sandell, and Louie, who slid off their ponies' backs and stalked out before the group of horsemen.

Behind Old Jake Sandell, Andy, the oldest sat, an old Sharp's rifle now resting across the bows of his saddle. He watched Morgan and the Indian with angry sullen eyes, though he said nothing.

Morgan said: "Unneighborly tactics you use around these parts, stranger. Maybe I won't like your brands any more'n you like mine. Keep your men where they are."

Old Jake Sandell's long mustached face writhed suddenly in grotesque anger. He sneered but did not reply.

Sam Sandell, a lanky, pimply faced youth with already yellowing ragged teeth approached the black near which Morgan stood.

"Tain't packing brands from around here, pop," he said in a drawling, irritating voice. "Guess he ain't stole them after all." He look another step forward.

Morgan's eyes became sullen. "Tell him to stand where he is," he spoke low to Old Jake Sandell. By that time he knew that Blue Hawk had quietly eased the two stilettos they had found and the black bandanna into the roan's saddle bags.

JAKE SANDELL CLENCHED his teeth when Sam and Louie stopped hesitatingly at Morgan's low command. He grunted a low command and instantly the three lolling punchers behind him whipped out three ugly snouted Colts and centered them full on Morgan and the mounted Blue Hawk.

"You talk plumb careless," sneered Jake Sandell. "Lot uh funny things goin' on 'round these parts, an' when I ask questions I like to have them answered straightforward-like."

"You haven't asked me any yet," said Morgan quietly.

Jake Sandell's eyes flashed. "Well, I will!" he croaked. "Go on, Sam. Search 'em an' don't miss their saddle bags either. We got you an Louie covered. If they move a finger we'll blow them plumb to hell an' back. Ain't no saddle-tramp gonna talk back to me!"

Sam and Louie Sandell seemed to stiffen their back bones. They were not ten feet away from Morgan and the black stallion now. They started to step forward and halted again as Wayne Morgan's voice spoke up.

"Maybe you know," he said, "searching people without warrants and the use of deadly weapons is a criminal offense according to the law. To me it means one more thing, highway robbery. If—"

Andy Sandell's low drawl broke out for the first time. His sullen blue eyes shot from Jake Sandell to Morgan and the Indian and he spoke lounging still in the saddle, the rifle across its horn.

"What're you tryin' to do, Paw. Git Sam and Louie murdered! Wait a minnit. You, Frank and you two," he nodded to the armed punchers behind him, "git down and cover those men b'fore they drop Sam and Louie. Git up yer hands, you two."

The rifle came up and centered to a half-dollar's spot on Morgan's chest.

The punchers behind Andy Sandell dropped out of their saddles and a moment later were surrounding both Morgan and Blue Hawk. Then Andy slid his own lanky slow shape to the ground.

He took full charge now.

"Hist 'em," he repeated.

Morgan's eyes were sultry as he complied. A queer tenseness began to tighten in his throat. What would these Sandells say when they started delving in Blue Hawk's *alforjas?*— And when they'd find The Masked Rider's disguise?

He didn't have long to wait. Behind him he heard Sam Sandell rummaging through the roan's saddle bags and a sudden breathless exclamation rip the air.

"Hey, Pop! Here's—here's two knives! They're both th' same too, I'll bet—by Gosh— Yes sir! You know old man Harris was killed with a stiletto. These are jest like the ones Larry Fabry said he was killed with. Hey—!"

Beside Morgan stood two punchers, their guns drawn, fingers on ready triggers. Another one and Louie were holding Blue Hawk. Grimly Morgan clenched his teeth and swore beneath his breath.

Old Jake Sandell's eyes were wide, an exclamation rounding his mouth in a whiskered "O". He popped out of the saddle like an ancient jumping-jack.

"Wait, Sam! Lemme see—! Jumpin' cat-fish if these air—"

But Andy Sandell's harsh voice ripped out above the sudden exclamations. He was standing apart from the group.

"Sam! Leave them knives in that *alforja*. Don't touch a one of them, you dumb galoots. Wait a minnit, I got an idea—" he paused. "If Sheriff Beanpole Jackson ken see where they're sitting thar in them *alforjas* they'll be th' swellest necktie party you never seen. How come you want to spoil it? We'll get Mockerson, LaShay an' everyone we can on the way daown intuh town. You see—" he paused, an open-mouthed sly grin splitting his face, "a lynching-bee. Yes, sir, a lynchin'—"

HE APPROACHED THE group of Sandell men on long-striding legs, the Sharps lolling from his elbow.

Old Jake Sandell guffawed in unholy and mirthful glee. The

surprise of the suddenly found knives was as quickly gone by the fascinating possibilities of Andy Sandell's newest thought.

But on the surprise of that moment Morgan placed the chances for a get-away. With grim lips he had seen Andy Sandell striding forward. In the sudden activity the Sandells had forgotten that he was still armed. The two men guarding him were peering over the black stallion's back at the group gathered around Blue Hawk's roan.

Morgan moved with the sureness and precision of a striking panther.

He hit the puncher on his left a short full-force blow in the solar plexus, wheeling as he did out of reach of the other puncher's gun.

By that time, the polished .45 in his right holster had been whipped out and upward. It exploded with a muffled roar. Like a sodden bag the other cowboy folded, dropped to the rocky earth.

Covered now by the big body of a Sandell stallion from the rest of the Sandell crew, Morgan leaped over the prostrate body, backing away from the shying horse, both guns out and crouching.

The five men surrounding Blue Hawk wheeled with open mouths attracted by the deep groan that had issued from the writhing puncher on the ground. They looked full into the two muzzles of the polished .45s.

Morgan's eyes were sultry, his mouth stretched in a hard tight line.

"Don't move a finger!" he was saying. "You all got guns and they're out. But if a single one doesn't stay where it is now, I start shooting."

Andy Sandell's cold curses cut the air. But the rest of the party were staring at Morgan with unveiled astonishment. Blue Hawk, up on the roan, began to smile his wide understanding grin.

His right hand shifted quickly, brought forth a gun that instantly was glued to the side of Jake Sandell's white-haired head.

"*Si, señor,*" he said with a flash of gleaming white teeth. "An' the first man that dies will be *el padre.* You must understand, *hombrecitos,* you deal with a very sly man. *Madre de Dios,* you did not think that with seven men you will take my friend?"

With a laugh he pulled his moccasined foot out of the stirrup and solemnly kicked one after the other the guns from the hands of the covered Sandells.

CHAPTER XVIII

JIMMIE WEEDER

THE RANCH HOUSE of the Closed C was a rambling, weather-racked building over a range of the wide-strung Cayugas from the Loco Mule. Early in the afternoon Jimmie Weeder rode in between the straggling corrals to the ranch house and Paw Weeder.

Paw Weeder's grim curses rattled the windows when Jimmie handed him Beanpole Jackson's summons. But though he swore eloquently, his heart was nevertheless relieved. He had cut the fence. He was condemned by few cattlemen. It would cost a lot of money and there was the mortgage at the Cattlemen's Trust to be settled up. That, in truth, was a secondary matter— to him. His cattle had gotten water—the main thing. Enough to move them across the Closed C to what was left of the waterhole so many miles away to the south. That he might soon go to jail worried him little.

But Jimmie Weeder shared none of these presents. He wandered out of the ranch house to the ramshackle stable where as a boy he had learned to do his thinking. And of that he had much to do now.

Two things galled him sorely. Billy Stimson had not been found. He must now ride back to town and face Leona. It was the last that hung like a heavy leaden weight on his heart.

Fifteen minutes of solemn consideration on a straw stack behind the stable acted like a bolster to his spirits. Determination in time had come to him. When he arose and walked away, he made straight for the dun pony hitched outside the ranch-house door. Jimmie Weeder was returning to Red Rocks and Leona Harris to make his confession.

It was thus that on his lonesome way back to Red Rocks Jimmie Weeder met Hank LaShay and Whitey Burns jogging slowly toward their spread—the Lazy R—that lay west of the Closed C. Long time neighbors, they hailed the passing figure that sought to avoid them by moving out of their way into a gully bottom.

It was impossible, Jimmie Weeder knew, to escape them. In their air was a pregnant jocularity. He turned the dun pony, pushed it up the gully side to the trail beside them.

Hank LaShay, raw honed and leathery, lolling crosswise in his saddle, drawled a "hello." The other puncher, one of LaShay's hands, eyed Weeder with bated breath. He sensed LaShay's words would be hot in the redhead's ears.

"Down visitin' friends uh mine in th' big town," LaShay drawled. "Powerful hot little village now'days, Jimmie, with the Closed C grabbin' wildcat holts on the Bar-H. How come you folks don't iron out yore troubles over a peaceful afternoon tea, sorta, 'stead uh gettin' the whole countryside rarin' over yore joinin' up with The Masked Rider, th' Jesse Jameses an' whatever border-riders come yer way! Next thing I know th' Closed C will he ridin' intuh my pasture hackin' down my line fence 'cause it's closer tuh drive cattle tuh town that way than down Sand Hill Road."

LaShay's jibe was friendly but the redhead rose not to the occasion. His spirit was too sore. He said: "What's th' news on John Harris? You seen Beanpole Jackson?"

LaShay finished the quirley he was making before he answered. When he did his eyes had lost the air of hurt feelings with which he had gibed the redhead. Now they were brooding, meaningful.

"Figgered you'd want tuh know. Reason I stopped you. Powerful energetic man, that Beanpole person. Seems he sat aroun' all morning sending messages out tuh sheriffs in th' next seventeen counties tuh hold a man named Bill Stimson. Finally, long about noon time, he rares up on his hind legs an' says there's gotta be a posse out *pronto* huntin' fer this Stimson *hombre*. Yes, sir. He done even asked Whitey an' me tuh join up but we begged off to brand some slick ears out Soldier Canyon way."

"Stimson? Then he hasn't showed up yet?"

"He *ain't!*"

With time Jimmie Weeder had come to realize that his first disbelief in the honesty of Billy Stimson was entirely unwarranted. Leona had defended him from the word go. If she did, that satisfied him. Now the act of the Sheriff of Red Rocks scratched his loyalty to the Harris' with angry implications.

"Gangling," he gritted. "That's Gangling's work!"

"Son," said LaShay, "how come you take the words right outta my mouth? I got a stack uh silver dollars long as yer arm that say this *hombre* Ganglin' ain't never had th' $65,000 he's yowlin' 'round town he paid for the Cattlemen's Trust. Not him. Now mixin' that idee in with this Beanpole person's plumb anxiety tuh trail John Harris' murderer 'bout fourteen hours after Harris was killed, it don't seem tuh match up at all with—"

With tight clipped words the redhead cut in. "Gangling's doin' everything he can so mebbe Stimson won't turn up too dang soon fer Gangling's own good. Yes, sir! What Gangling says, Beanpole Jackson does. Mebbe if Stimson don't turn up at all with that $65,000 Gangling will be plumb satisfied! So he tells Sheriff Jackson tuh wait long as possible."

The redhead wheeled his pony. "But even if he does waste

time huntin' fer Stimson, it's the plumb wrong man. I'll tell him. He'll prance around when I get foot inside that Sheriff's office door. *Adiós!*"

LaShay watched the redhead thunder out of sight. "Son," LaShay said to Whitey Burns, "there's a lad as takes an unholy pleasure in bitin' off moren' he kin chew. Couldn't wait fer me tuh tell him Gangling put uh reward uh one thousand dollars gold on Stimson's head hisself. No sir, off he prances tuh corral Beanpole Jackson and Gangling too an' probably accuse them both uh killin' John Harris. Man with uh temper like that's bout as effective as one without no arms ner legs. What d'you think?"

Whitey Burns didn't know. He shook his head doubtfully and kicked his pony off uptrail after LaShay's. "Sometime, old codgers like you, Hank, git surprised," he was saying to himself.

CHAPTER XIX

GANGLING STRIKES BACK

JIMMIE WEEDER PRESSED the dun pony rapidly in the direction of Red Rocks. And as he did, the sun sank lower and lower on the horizon. By the time he had come in sight of the town the long blue shadows of evening were over the land.

Outside of Red Rocks Jimmie paused to take stock. During the ride into town he had had time to turn over carefully his decision to face Beanpole Jackson again. Though LaShay's words had put angry ideas in his head, the longer he rode the less did he believe that facing Beanpole Jackson would help unearth the murderer of John Harris.

Already had he burnt his fingers in his torrid attack on Gangling. The more he thought about it, the less he considered there was a possibility Gangling would have had a hand in the death of John Harris. Gangling and Harris had been friends.

But in spite of this for the life of him Jimmie Weeder could not understand Gangling's rapid rise to power. The man had lived for full fifteen years in Red Rocks and never showed a sign of possessing more than a modicum of *dinero*. $65,000 didn't grow on trees. No, Gangling was smooth. He had control of the bank. But, Jimmie was sure, that had been gained through some hoodwinking of John Harris before his death. It did not matter how. The fact remained that it was doubtful that John Harris would have sold his share of the Cattlemen's Trust stock for a mere $65,000.

Thinking of this the redhead moved carefully into the dark town. From a vantage point well down the Main Street he paused, saw Balbeck turn out the lights of the bank and lock the massive front door.

When Balbeck turned, another figure stepped up onto the boardwalk before the lighted Sheriff's office. It was Gangling. Together the two of them made their way down the street in the direction of Carraway's Chop House and Restaurant. There, evidently, Gangling took his evening meal.

Jimmie Weeder turned his pony towards the back of the bank block, drove in under a low string of pepper trees and hitched the dun to the rear wheel of an abandoned header-bed.

"Now stay there, you string-tailed cayuse," said Jimmie. "Maybe next time yuh see me I'll need you plumb rapid. Don't move."

Many times had he been in the Cattlemen's Trust when John Harris was its president. Jimmie Weeder knew the general plan of the bank, its easiest, least dangerous approach.

With care he hugged the shadows of the sycamores bordering the street, swung over an awry fence behind a grocery store and approached the bank building from its rear. Later, when he thought of it, he was impressed with the ease with which he broke into the inner sanctums of what he had always considered an impregnable fortress. A wooden, panelled door leading out to an incinerator behind the bank yielded to a strong noiseless heave.

A second later Jimmie was inside. On tip-toes he avoided the bulging shadows of heavy furniture, paused and took stock of his surroundings. Gangling, he knew, lived upstairs. The redhead swung through the bank and up a short flight of backstairs that led directly into the main office.

Gangling's apartment was neat, yet unimposing. With enthusiasm Jimmie Weeder went to work. Moments later the entire room had been gone over. Shirts, bed linens, clothing of every kind was scattered over the floor. Suits he pulled down out of their closet and went hurriedly through their pockets. Missing nothing, the redhead did a thorough job of turning the room inside out—and found nothing. There seemed to be no doubt about it, Gangling conducted all of his business downstairs.

The hour was yet early, as Jimmie Weeder hopefully turned his attentions below. Years ago Paw Weeder had invested money from a good calf harvest in bank stock. The folded pieces of stiff legal-looking paper he received for his money, Jimmie knew well. Sixty-five thousand dollars' worth he figured would make a large and bulky package.

If Gangling had that stock, Jimmie Weeder was going to find it out. What he would do with it later was but a dim idea. But if it meant cracking the great safe and ripping out the safe deposit boxes one by one, Jimmie Weeder would do it. How, he was not yet sure.

He turned his attention to the great desk that had been John Harris'.

WHEN GANGLING LAID aside his napkin and faced the watery-blue eyes of Balbeck, he smiled. For the first time that day his dark hard eyes took on a more friendly light.

"Hot, isn't it?" he asked, and wiped his huge, long features with a silk handkerchief.

Balbeck nodded.

Gangling said: "I've had a hard day. I usually enjoy a walk

out along the mesa rim this time o' night. But not today. I'm going to bed early."

Again Balbeck nodded, his watery myopic eyes on the face of his chief.

"I'll walk back to the bank with you," he said.

But Gangling shook his head. "You don't go that way. I wouldn't bother. I'd rather think alone, to tell the truth."

He rose, got his stiff black town-hat from its habitual hook, paid the cashier and walked out. For a long moment Balbeck looked after him.

That his chief was for some reason unduly nervous tonight was obvious. Balbeck didn't blame him for wanting to think. Many things had happened that day. In the first place that wild young puppy of a Weeder—

GANGLING'S APARTMENT WAS connected with the street by a long stairway leading directly up from the boardwalk. But tonight he did not go directly upstairs. He scanned the front of the two-story bank for a minute. Yes, this now was his, or at least 55 per cent of it. With some pride in its locked, secure and stolid appearance he walked around to the side, viewing the strong, honest atmosphere it exuded. The architect John Harris had commissioned to build the bank had done well.

At that moment, he rounded the corner and paused. At first he was not sure of himself. A second later he knew his ears had not deceived him. There were footsteps inside the dark building.

At first his immediate instinct was to call for help, to spread the alarm, apprehend the intruder before he could make further progress. But all the bank's money was locked for the night behind the vault doors he knew to be as impassable as eight inches of cold steel might be. Any ordinary robber should have known that. Robbing the bank in the daytime would be possible—at night, no.

Moreover, his good friend Beanpole Jackson was out of town with a posse in search of Billy Stimson.

These things whipped through Gangling's mind with lightning speed. In courage, of a sort, he was not lacking. A second later he was slinking into the shadows of the bank on noiseless feet, approaching the wide-swung back door through which the man had forced entrance. If he could but see the intruder—

At that moment things went wrong. The man in the bank must have seen his shadow outside the window. For as Gangling's long shape neared the door a dark hurtling figure sprang out through it bent on making its escape. A mad cry formed in Gangling's throat as he unhesitatingly leaped forward, long arms outstretched to catch the shadowy intruder.

The figure stepped aside, shoved out one tight-muscled arm. Off balance, Gangling went to his knees. The figure turned, ran. Gangling wheeled, realizing as he did that his move had been mad. If the man had a gun in his hand—?

Over the tricky ground of the bank's back yard, the man now sprinted. But even as he did there was a sharp hard click, a heavy curse and he was down.

Like a cat Gangling was on his feet. He moved fast, struck with all his weight at the sprawling shadowy form spread-eagled on the ground. For a second their flaying arms beat out for holds. And as they did, the man beneath whipped his body from under Gangling's long shape, rose to one knee.

Gangling shifted his body as best he could. Then something solid struck him behind the ear with a bone-crushing thud. Light sparkled and twirled, gathered momentum and plunged the world about Gangling into absorbing darkness.

But before the blow had been struck, Gangling had seen in the uncertain light of the yard that the man who had broken into his bank was no other than the redheaded Jimmie Weeder.

MOMENTS LATER GANGLING awoke from his daze. Groggily he regained his feet, weaved for a moment, his senses clearing. When they did his reaction was fast.

All his energy concentrated in a dash into the inner sanctums of the bank. What he saw there hardly reassured him. Papers and empty drawers littered the floor. His desk was a welter of legal documents, bank stationery. And over the heap of papers on his desk, as if purposefully adding further injury to insult, an upset bottle of ink dripped a rich mess.

The bank vault, he saw however, was untouched.

Gangling ran for the bank's front doors, threw them open with a resounding crash. Just as he did, far off down the street came a phalanx of eight horsemen and at their head rode a man welcome to Gangling's eyes. It was Sheriff Beanpole Jackson, long and willowy on a roman-nosed, iron-gray mare.

A roar of anger brought Beanpole Jackson at a trot towards the long-legged form waving angry arms on the boardwalk before the Sheriff's Office.

He leaped down, ran to the bank's door at Gangling's snapped command. Behind Jackson a welter of gaping cowboys crowded in through the narrow doors to survey the astounding sight Gangling was pointing out to the goateed constable.

"Robbed!" roared Gangling. "You see this mess. A man broke into the bank ten minutes ago. I fought with him. He knocked me out with his gun butt. Then he got away!"

"Jumping gopher snakes!" Beanpole Jackson's wide mouth was agape. "Lookit that!" he wheeled. "Who was it?"

"Who was it?" grated Gangling. "Yes, I saw him, the thief! Now get out there and do something. Use that posse and bring back that redheaded Weeder kid to me. It was that Jimmie Weeder!"

"Jimmie Weed—!" Jackson's hands went down, shifting the belt-buckle of his gun-belt tighter. "Jimmie Weeder, eh, Mr. Gangling? Well we'll shore do sumthin' about that. I gotta posse, but we jest come in. Following this Stimson. Lost him, by Golly, in the Tule!"

He turned, swelling with an air of injured authority. "Come on, boys. Gotta 'nother job on our hands now seems like. Mr.

Gangling here says Jimmie Weeder broke intuh here an' committed—uh—"

Gangling's close-clipped words took up the sheriff's speech.

"Assault, battery, grand larceny—anything you want to call
it. There's fifteen thousand dollars in five hundred dollar bills
gone out of my desk, Jackson! I want justice done!"

"Fifteen thou—" Beanpole Jackson's goateed face whipped
about. "Stole fifteen thousand dollars? Holy jumpin' gopher
snakes!"

A few minutes later when the rapid thunder of the posse
ponies had died away in the direction Gangling had pointed
out—Gila—he turned to the littered bank. And as he did a
faint enigmatic smile covered his features. Now, he felt, Jimmie
Weeder had embroiled himself in his affairs just once too often.
It would be well to get rid of the boy.

CHAPTER XX

FORTY-EIGHT HOURS

WHEN JIMMIE WEEDER at last put the shadows of Red
Rocks well behind him, he drew up the dun pony and
took stock of the situation. Although his mission had been
fruitless, the fact that he had locked horns physically with the
hated Gangling did him measurable good. Moreover he had
clouted the banker a manly blow on the head. That also, in a
degree, helped lighten his spirits.

His search of the bank had revealed nothing. However, the
fact that he had broken the law worried Jimmie Weeder little.
In the first place he was sure Gangling had attacked him and
had not recognized him in the dark of the bank's rear yard.
Secondly, he had been must careful in covering what tracks
might reveal him as the midnight prowler.

That Gangling was at that moment calling for a posse to

apprehend him for the theft of fifteen thousand dollars was the last thing he could suspect. He had taken nothing from the bank, not even the Weeder bonds, though ideas of what he could have done with them in forcing Gangling's hand still played in his mind.

Now, as he paused on the road to the Closed C, he was more certain than ever that Gangling did not have the bank stocks in his possession. No circumstances of truth backed up this belief. Yet, Jimmie Weeder would have solemnly bet his last dollar on his hunch.

When at last Jimmie Weeder kicked his dun pony in the direction of the Closed C he had decided that his next course of action must be to find Stimson. Already there was a posse on the trail. Led by Jackson it promised nothing. Leading a string of his own Closed C punchers, Jimmie felt he might discover a good deal.

WHEN WAYNE MORGAN and Blue Hawk reached the outskirts of Red Rocks, Morgan stopped in the shelter of sycamores well out of town and sent Blue Hawk in search of Sheriff Jackson. For nearly an hour the black stallion champed its bit nervously in the shadows while Morgan awaited the return of the Indian.

When the Sandells and their clan had been fully disarmed up in the gully, his and the Indian's escape had been quickly and efficiently accomplished. By a simple means of taking the Sandell horses a mile uptrail and leaving them, pursuit was avoided.

One thing bothered Morgan however. They had seen the stilettos and the bandanna. Both Jake Sandell's and Andy Sandell's actions on finding them were hardly convincing. They could very possibly have had a part in Harris' death. Andy had suggested a lynching party immediately. Almost too quickly.

If they were connected with the murder they could quickly warn the guilty man. Even if the Sandells weren't, they had seen the faces of Wayne Morgan and Blue Hawk which made their entry into Red Rocks a dangerous and questionable proposition at any future time.

For that reason Morgan's lips were grim and he waited impatiently for Blue Hawk's return. He had sent the Indian into town to Beanpole Jackson with the stilettos, the bandanna and additional clues to the story of Harris' death. The gully had revealed little else. It now looked as though the law would have to deal with the murder as best it could, and take a long time about it.

When at last Blue Hawk's soft whistle heralded his approach, the grim smile on Morgan's lips relaxed. The sorrel pony joined the great black in the shadows.

"*Señor,*" Blue Hawk's voice was sibilant, "many things have happened since you were here today. Sheriff Jackson is not in town to take these knives. They tell me, *señor,* the sheriff is now riding after Jimmie Weeder!"

"And now what?" Morgan's whistle was low, sharp.

"Diego Gonzales, he cleans the Lariat saloon for *Señor* Tolman. After much talk he finally described what happened. Not long ago he is standing with many men in front the bank. *Señor* Gangling who owns the bank comes out waving his arms. Somebody broke into his bank, the Cattlemen's Trust, says Gonzales, and Gangling nearly caught him. The man ran away. It was Jimmie Weeder. When *Señor* Gangling looks, he finds that fifteen thousand dollars is missing from his desk. Ten minutes later, *Señor* the Sheriff is riding out of town, going to Gila to find him."

"That's the story according to this Gonzales," muttered the grim-lipped Morgan. "But he didn't say that Jimmie Weeder was probably looking for those bonds Gangling claimed he bought. Right?"

"Diego Gonzales is not a man so smart as that, *señor.*"

"No doubt," said the cold voiced man in the shades. "His

story doesn't say either that this Gangling is probably building an airtight frame around Weeder. If Gangling was the only one who saw Weeder, who's there to say whether fifteen thousand dollars were taken out of the desk or whether Jimmie Weeder did the job at all!"

"Such I was thinking as I came back, *señor.* That is best answered by curses, *amigo.* When Gangling speaks, Sheriff Jackson moves fast. That much Diego Gonzales does know."

For minutes the lithe figure on the black stallion was silent. When finally he moved, determination was in his actions. Morgan dismounted, took the flowing black cape and hood from their hiding place beneath the saddle. When he rose to that saddle his shoulders and head were covered.

These movements Blue Hawk watched in silence. The hooded man's voice was like a twinging string when he turned at last to the Indian.

"Better pay this Gangling a visit," he said tersely. "Like as not a good many things'll turn up if I do. If you leave your sorrel hitched some place in town I'll see it—later."

With sombre eyes the Indian watched the great black gallop slowly out of sight towards the shadows and lights of Red Rocks. In the masked man's last words he read many things. The first and most important was that he, Blue Hawk, should be waiting in the Main Street of the town, in case the plans of the man with whom he rode went amiss.

GANGLING WAS NERVOUS. When the sounds of the disappearing posse at last faded into silence, he walked straight to the teller's desk, wrote himself a withdrawal slip on the bank's stationery, dated it as of this very afternoon. Rapidly he opened three large books and in each in turn made an entry that would support his claim that Jimmie Weeder had stolen fifteen thousand dollars.

Moments later he sat at that littered, ink-ruined desk, fingering as he did a tight-rolled bundle of yellow-backs each marked $500. These he had taken from the great vault in the other room.

Balbeck, he told himself, could finish up the entries in the morning. For the present, however, he had drawn from his private account the exact amount he claimed Weeder had stolen. With this money on hand, the framing of the redhead was for all practical purposes complete.

So thinking, he pocketed the money, turned out the light of the bank and mounted the stairs to the ruins of his apartment.

A half hour's steady work and his clothing and personal belongings were back again in their accustomed places. When he had completed this job, Gangling sat on the iron single bed that graced his severely furnished room.

It was just as the springs were creaking under his weight that Harold Gangling received what might well have been the most terror-filled moment in his life.

As if by magical means, the panelled door of his apartment swung open. His head sprang up; his eyes attained the size of doorknobs.

A lithe, hooded figure swung the door behind him with a click, moved with determined steps across the space between him and the windows facing the street, pulled the shades well down.

All this time Gangling had regarded the masked man with twitching unbelieving eyes. The intruder's eyes saw Gangling's own go down, take in the ugly round mouth of the revolver that was centered on the man's forehead as on a bull's-eye.

For a moment, The Masked Rider mentally admired his poise. For all his first paralyzing grip of terror, Gangling said not a word. When at last the outlaw spoke, he knew the man before him had a grip of iron on his will. The hooded man's voice was velvet-covered steel.

"Gangling, we're going to talk short and to the point. You know who I am and I'm not running under a false brand. I've visited bankers before—in this manner. I know who you are. Before I leave I'm going to know a lot more about you."

He saw Gangling shift uneasily, glance briefly around the room for the slightest avenue of escape. The banker looked straight into the masked man's eyes.

"I don't understand you," he said slowly. "I haven't the slightest idea what your purpose might be. If you want—"

"Not money," answered the cold voice. "Facts. If you don't hanker towards answering some of my questions, remember two things. One is that if you yell for help, I'll split you with lead us I would a particularly smelly skunk before I start to shoot my way out of here. The second is—I'll let you guess. If you're smart as I've heard, you'll talk—fast and to the point."

Gangling eyed the intruder, took in every outline of his weird clothing. Something in the flashing dark eyes, visible through the twin holes of his hood, told Gangling that here at last he had met a will stronger and more emotionless than his own. If it was to be a battle of wits, he should think fast and well.

"If John Harris sold you this stock, where's your bill of sale?"

Gangling relaxed, he almost sighed with sudden relief. He took some time before he answered.

THEN HE SAID slowly: "As a matter of fact, if that's all you're after, the answer is simple. There has been some talk about town, in relation to the buying of this portion I own. Tomorrow I am taking the legal data with relation to it to Sheriff Jackson. Then, if it is convenient—"

"It won't be," snapped the man in the hood. "I want to see that bill of sale *tonight*."

Gangling frowned. "It is impossible—" he started.

"Nothing is, if you value your skin," the man in the hood said softly. "Get a move on."

There was no doubt now that the youthful, lithe figure before Gangling was entirely and dangerously in earnest. What he might lose by this encounter Gangling did not know. He might stall indefinitely.

His mind whirled to a halt. In the trouser pockets of his suit there right now reposed a small fortune in yellow-back bills. In fact, fifteen thousand dollars. If this intruder, who was by name a road-agent, laid hold of them Gangling instantly concluded he might just as well have torn them up and cast them to the four winds. For a second the thought of losing fifteen thousand dollars paralyzed him. The demands of the intruder were not impossible to stall off—if maneuvers were clever. Gangling saw dangerous lights in the eyes above him that might well be humored.

He said: "As a matter of fact I have a copy of it in my favorite hiding place. Moreover there are several other papers with it that will assure you—since you doubt it—that the deal was quite legal. If you are thinking of taking them—"

"I'm not," snapped the hooded man. "There'd be other copies."

"Quite right," replied the banker. The hooded man watched the other's movements like a waiting panther as Gangling stood up, went to the drawer of the cheap bureau near his bed. There were several quick clicks as he released a false bottom in the top drawer.

When Gangling turned he held out a small legal envelope.

"You can handle them," said the masked figure.

"As you wish," the banker shrugged. "This," he removed a large white piece of paper from the envelope, "is the bill of sale. Dated as you see, Friday, the sixteenth. Two days, in fact, before John Harris was murdered. This," he removed another bit of paper, "is a copy of my withdrawal slip showing the transference of the money to John Harris' account. These two are all, in fact, that I have a legal right to possess. John Harris' own deposit slips and later his withdrawal slips for the money the day he died are below in the bank. Unfortunately we will have to go below."

The hooded man had eyed each slip as the banker produced it from the envelope. He let Gangling replace them, return the envelope to the false drawer of the bureau before he spoke again.

"Not yet," he said slowly, tersely. "Now, the stock certificates."

Gangling wheeled. "The stocks!" he sneered. "Yes, the stocks themselves. I thought perhaps you would come to them. Find Jimmie Weeder and he will show them to you. They were stolen tonight with fifteen thousand dollars from my desk!"

THE HOODED MAN was silent for a long time. Then he said slowly, "Gangling, you are a horse-nosed liar. Jimmie Weeder couldn't have those stocks. You gave yourself away on that. You forgot. You had your out when you first told Jackson that Weeder had stolen the money. You should have said then that he stole the certificates. Few people will believe you now—and I'm one of the many that won't. Do you mean to say you would have told Jackson a measly fifteen thousand dollars was gone when Weeder had stolen sixty-five thousand dollars' worth of stock above the cash? You're talking to a man, Gangling, not a child!"

The hooded man saw that the mind of the banker before him was working at a furious, frantic rate.

"I found this out later," said Gangling weakly.

The hooded man stepped forward. "Out with it, Gangling. *Where are they?*"

The banker swallowed. His hand, he saw now, had been played with the wrong cards. He swallowed again. "To tell the truth, I haven't got them. You see, I acted not entirely in my own interest in purchasing the controlling stock in this bank. I have a partner, whose name I prefer not to disclose. On receipt of the actual certificate I delivered them into his hands for safe keeping."

"Who is he?"

"You would not know him."

"I don't doubt that, if he is a friend of yours," said the hooded man. "Where is he now?"

Gangling hesitated perceptibly. Then he took the plunge: "In West Branch."

Moments like hours seemed to pass for Gangling before the man in the cape spoke.

"West Branch," said he slowly. "That's a rough day's ride away. Twenty-four hours, Gangling. I came here to see the stock. If you have a share in them and you're not lying, you can get them. I give you forty-eight hours to get them back. Figures don't lie, but the man who made them might. When I see the certificates I'll believe you bought them. Not before!"

"But—" Gangling's response was high-pitched, nervous. "It's impossible, fantastic. I won't be hoodwinked into—"

The drawl of the masked man beat on the ears of the banker with pregnant meaning. "I warn you, Gangling, you get those certificates. In forty-eight hours. If you don't bring them back in that time, the whole town of Red Rocks will be ripped wide open, yowling for your neck! And if I were you, I'd move plumb fast!"

The Masked Rider turned, strode through the door. As he went out, he clicked the outside lock of the apartment which would hold Gangling prisoner a matter of essential minutes. Then he sped noiselessly down the padded stairs, and out through the rear door that had earlier been shattered by the redhead.

He thought of that door as he paused in the shades of a rickety nearby stable, removed the cape and hood and stuffed them inside his dark shirt.

Yes, he was thinking, the impetuous Jimmie Weeder had not only wanted to see those certificates, but get them. In Jimmie's possession they would be a potent argument with which to face Gangling. Now that was not necessary—Gangling was forced to act.

Moments later, in the guise of Wayne Morgan, he walked through the main street of Red Rocks. Blue Hawk, lounging in the shadows of a porticoed store, saw him.

When at last, they were able to meet once more beyond the prying eyes of the town, the Indian joined the rider of the black stallion.

Slowly they trotted in the direction of Gila. And as he went, Morgan thought. He had delivered an ultimatum. If he was a judge of men, Gangling would act fast—in some way. But as Morgan rode, a growing doubt, grew stronger that in the caché John Harris' missing map led to, the bank's stocks and not money would be found.

CHAPTER XXI

DEATH RIDES THE GULLY

WHEN HE REACHED the boardwalk in front of the Cattlemen's Trust, Gangling stopped in the shadows and scrutinized the main street of Red Rocks. The bright flush that had suffused his face gradually died, his lips became straight-lined, predatory.

Decisions came fast then. He clumped up the walk and into the Sheriff's Office.

"Oppie" Leming, a deputy, was there, feet, upon the desk, stubbled chin caressing a wad of Star, the residue from which he deposited solemnly on the cold stove top with a jerk of the head and a splurt of loose lips.

At Gangling's terse greeting, he wheeled in surprise and listened with occasional nods to orders.

When finished Gangling stalked out of the Sheriff's Office and back upstairs to his apartment.

There he sat on the bed and waited with grim lips for the tromp of booted feet on the staircase. Finally, they came.

When Old Jake Sandell and his lean son, Andy, entered the room, quizzical frowns were on their faces. Old Jake's wry face gradually loosened and his rat-like eyes flashed at Gangling's tight, close-clipped sentences. For several moments Jake talked, too, and watched Gangling's face.

Finally Sandell's husky voice look a new note.

"Now lissen, Mister Gangling. You done told me 'twas all right tuh stand my guns at th' Loco Mule. That ain't panned out so damn well. I done told you what we found up in that gully. Harris' death will all be cleared up soon as we git hold uh that sneaking Indian and his runnin' mate. They had them stilettos right on them. Ain't a clearer case in history. Though— though like as not we'll never git th' money often them—"

He let the sentence hang, watching Gangling's face.

The banker's dark, predatory eyes were serious, thoughtful for a passing second. "That situation," he said slowly, as if choosing his words carefully, "is an angle that will be covered by the law. Luckily for you, you were in town and Leming could find you. Incidentally that will give you an idea of the way the law works for me around this town. When I say you'll have all necessary protection, when I say, too, that you have everything— mind you, *everything*—to win, you better take my word for it!

"But disregard that for a moment," he went on. "My life is being threatened by this—this—" he paused, seeking for words to match the contempt that now tinged his tones, "—this abominable monkey, The Masked Rider. Never fear, I am not afraid of him! I merely wish to—to fortify my position, as it were. He has threatened me—quite evidently in the interests of this girl. With her as bait...."

Gangling's voice became less forceful, his words slow, concise. Occasionally Old Jake Sandell swallowed and frowned. For the most part, his son, Andy, eyed Gangling's moving face with sullen, glowering eyes.

At last the long, stooping one said: "One thing, this peon. I think he's called Tollito, the house boy. If he gets away—?"

Gangling's black head shook away the interruption. "If he's in the way for a moment, shoot him! If there's an uproar, as I said, I'll see you're protected. Good Lord, Sandell, who are you to squabble over a job like this? You two stand to win on any count. *You can't afford not to play with me!*"

Dark eyes now flashing with secret gloating, Old Jake Sandell nodded.

"If there's a way," he said, slowly. "We'll find it!"

WITH THE FIRST fingers of dawn streaming in multi-colored glory over the blue-steel ridges of the Cayugas, Jimmie Weeder, his father and five punchers lined out in solitary procession down the rutted wagon road towards Red Rocks.

They trotted slowly, silently. When at last they reached the lower stretches of the mesa, they turned off the beaten track and moved at a slow, easy lope in the direction of the ghost-city Gila.

Jimmie Weeder was now determined that Stimson would be brought back to Red Rocks alive or dead. If it took them ten days to do it, he was prepared. Behind them a lone puncher sat on the ranch bunk house steps, holding the Closed C for their return.

Stimson might be hiding out in Gila to avoid enemies in Red Rocks, of whom the redhead at present knew nothing. If they couldn't find him there, they might find traces of his making after he had left Harris.

With these two lines of reasoning the redhead was to accomplish nothing. For no sooner than had the red tinge of the east strengthened to light, than his search came to a grim and racking termination.

It was coming down a gully thickly lined with pin-oaks and mesquite that the redhead suddenly raised his hand. He had been riding well in advance of the horsemen, far enough ahead to hear the low, sibilant whistle that they did not hear. When Paw Weeder rode up, a wondering question on his lips, the redhead motioned for silence.

Again, almost as if an echo to the first, the whistle sounded.

There was no doubt it had come from human lips, eerie as it seemed to the men gathered now in silence in the gully.

"Someone signalin', mebbe," said Paw Weeder. "I—"

But the redhead gritted his teeth impatiently.

"Sufferin' snakes," said Paw Weeder with equal impatience. "Boy, yo're jumpy as—"

He never finished his sentence. For the plans of the man in the heavy disguising cloak that noiselessly stepped out of the sheltering brush behind the group of riders, had worked perfectly. The reaction of the group had been perfect. Blue Hawk, across the gully, had with his whistle not only halted the riders but turned their unsuspecting backs to the hooded man.

"Powerful unhandy way of getting your attention," said a calm voice behind the Weeders, "but with maybe strangers in your crowd, I figured it'd be a darn sight healthier."

The Weeders and their riders wheeled in their saddles like automatons. Across the gully bottom they saw with startled eyes an apparition that had as if by magic made an appearance. Moreover, in the lineaments of the lithe stranger, they recognized to a man the hooded Nemesis of the Sandells.

Paw Weeder's grin split, his crinkled, lugubrious features almost literally from ear to ear.

"The Rider!" he blurted. "I don't know who you are, stranger, or what your plan in stoppin' us is, but, by golly, I'm shore glad tuh see yuh. Any man that'd do the trick you did for us, is a welcome sight in my eyes. Howdy!"

Several gnarled hands had dropped readily to their guns, but paused over Paw Weeder's words. Moreover, the men now saw, too, that neither of the .45s that glinted light from beneath the black cape was unholstered.

The redhead, however, shared little of his father's joviality. He looked at the man in the cloak with something akin to sullen doubt.

"So yo're back," he spoke up impatiently. "Well, I say I shore gotta thank you, too, fer what you didn't tell me night 'fore last. Mebbe you'll explain now how you happened to know that John Harris wuz dead all the time!" The words were at best a softly padded threat.

"Hush up, boy," cautioned Paw Weeder. How come you don't know when to speak civil to a *hombre* as—"

The man in the cape interrupted him. "Don't blame you, Jimmie. Didn't tell you because it was pleasanter to me for you to find out yourself instead of my telling you. You were ready to bite my hand off as it was. For just giving you friendly advice."

The redhead flushed to the roots of his orange thatch. He grimaced, but even as he did a slow smile began to twirk the angles of his mouth.

"Flyin' off the handle seems tuh be my best act," he said finally. "Excuse me an' howdy," he grinned. "Jest outta curiosity mebbe you'll tell me how you did know. Don't worry, I won't accuse you of killin' Harris. Figger by this time, yore actions plumb embarrass me too. Maybe, mister, you know somethin'—"

The figure in the hood walked steadily towards the horsemen. He motioned with his hand for them to alight.

"Talking with cards as close to my belly as this, doesn't run well in my blood. Besides, Weeder, there's *mucha palabra* we're going to do in the next couple of minutes. I hooked up with you this morning to tell you something mighty unpleasant. Maybe when I finish you'll *sabe* you got some particular fast acting to do, *pronto*."

The punchers with the Weeders eyed the hooded man speculatively. At a signal, however, from Paw Weeder they remained mounted. Slowly the two Weeders swung out of their saddles, walked a few steps with the slim figure in the hood towards the shelter of the pin-oaks near the steep gully wall.

"Sorry I can't talk without this rig," said the masked man. "Found out a long time ago it's powerful unpleasant thing to let sheriffs know too much about my face. Too long on memory, most sheriffs. Maybe it'd interest you to know, Weeder, that Beanpole Jackson's got a posse out right now powerful anxious, it seems, to apprehend a certain redhead. Seems he did powerful wrong by a man named Gangling in Red Rocks. Took fifteen thousand dollars, in fact, out of said Gangling's desk last night. That you?"

"Fifteen thousand dollars. Why, man—"

"Figured you'd likely blow up ready to pop. Why don't you pick out someone more pleasant to euchre out of that much money? Gangling's fit to be tied."

"The rattlesnake! I never took a *centimo* of his. I admit I broke into his bank to see if he had those papers. Then he saw me?"

"According to him, yes." Jimmie Weeder's eyes widened. His lips clenched to a hard, tight line.

"Got a posse out, that it? Try to frame me, will he? I'll give myself up, even if it's just to grab his slimy throat—"

"Whoa up, boy," Paw Weeder cut in. "How come you didn't tell all this to me b'fore we start out on this man-hunt? I don't blame you, son, fer wanting tuh sink a fist in Gangling's long, horse face, but jumpin' cat-fish, boy, don't yuh know we're already plumb up to our noses in trouble? What for must you go committing burglary or whatever it is, jest tuh get even with Gangling! Fifteen thousand dollars? You didn't take that, boy? Now, did you?"

Jimmie Weeder's face colored at the questioning look that shot into the crinkled eyes of his father. Yes, he had done wrong. Not so much by himself as by his father. Holy Gosh, if here wasn't a swell dish of soup—

"Shore not," he snapped. "If I had fifteen thousand dollars of someone else's money I wouldn't be sittin' here waitin' fer Jackson tuh find me. Now would I? This's Gangling's work! By Golly, if I don't hunt up that nanny-goat sheriff an' tell him sumthin' right off, you ken—"

The man in the mask cut in with his soft, even drawl. "That

can wait," he said. "Fact is, I saw Jackson riding out Gila way, so he won't be around these parts come some time. At present maybe you better know that Stimson turned up dead, without the money or the map."

For a second the two Weeders surveyed the masked man with slack-jawed mouths.

From Paw Weeder finally issued a low, understanding whistle. The two men facing him turned. The Masked Rider saw Paw Weeder's eyes flick, as though attracted by some movement above them, up the steep gulley side. Wondering lights in them faded, and suddenly in their stead was quick alarm.

"Look out, Jim! Duck!"

The heads of the two other men swept about. It was no more than a black movement, the downward sweep of a dark-clad arm in the mesquite brush forty feet above them, that they saw.

But as the arm of the hidden man above them was jerked out of sight, a white streak of light sped away from the hand.

Paw Weeder had yelled, then lunged forward. He hit the form of the redhead with his shoulder and elbow, knocking the boy off balance. The man in the hood had moved equally fast. The shot that roared from his revolver screamed over the Weeders' heads and into empty brush.

Paw Weeder seemed to stagger, grasp blindly at the form of his son. He wheeled, face to the two men, fell on one knee, then pitched headlong at the feet of the redhead.

"Paw!"

It was the voice of a mortally stricken wild animal that beat against the ears of the man in the hood.

He saw then that the dart of light had sped true and sure. For, centered in the triangle formed by the throat of Paw Weeder's hickory shirt, there protruded a velvet-covered steel cross. The hilt of another death-dealing stiletto!

And, even as he looked, the hooded man saw Paw Weeder's

eyelids close, contract as in awful pain, then open to show eyes that had in them the glazed, sightless vacancy of death.

The Masked Rider moved. He mounted the gulley-side as effortless and quick as a striking panther. On the rim he paused, hard eyes taking in every movement of the brush, each rustle of the pin-oaks about him.

The killer was gone, leaving death and the empty swish of the soft wind through the leaves. The hooded man bent, searched the ground rapidly for marks of the man on the gully's lip. When he found them, they were again of the long-toed riding boot. His whistle rose, long and sibilant.

Light-footed the masked man ran, his .45 ready. The killer had by his rapid movements left marks that he rapidly translated. He sped down the gully's lip, dodging through the brush and small trees that disguised anything moving before him.

At last the trail of footprints and broken brush before him turned and led into the shelter of a hollow bordering the gully. There he saw the killer had mounted not seconds before him.

His whistle rose shrill and clear. The black stallion, already coming, heard it again and crashed onward through the mesquite to his side.

The hooded figure swung up into the saddle. As he did, from his lips there rose the long, haunting cry of the mountain cat. It was the signal to Blue Hawk.

The black leaped away, into a headlong gallop up and out of the hollow and once again into the brush. Before him, somewhere, the masked man knew the killer was riding the wind. Hidden by undergrowth, his advantage over trailers was tenfold.

Soon the marks of the running pony became harder to follow. Its rider, covering his marks, had forced the pony across an out-jutting ledge of hard rocks and sped onward. For some seconds the hooded man was not sure in which direction they had led off.

Pausing there, he waited for the approaching gallop of Blue

Hawk and the sorrel pony. But, though he listened with trained, sure ears, the man in the hood heard not a sound to break the stillness about him. Again the call of the lonesome mountain cat drifted up and out over the mesa in long, wailing tones.

But, even as before, only silence was its answer.

Blue Hawk had been on the opposite side of the gully when the Weeders stopped, not the side from which the killer had struck. He should have heard the first call. Before that there had been the warning of a shot. Certainly he would have been ready to come then.

Uncertain premonitions dogged the hooded man's mind as he wheeled the black. The trailing of the murderer would now take time. Given respite he would perhaps be able to throw them off the trail entirely. But in the meantime if the masked man went on, behind him he might be leaving Blue Hawk—

The Sandells had seen the killer's stilettos in Blue Hawk's possession. By this time perhaps all Red Rocks, including Beanpole Jackson, might know of it. Had the Sandells or the skulking minions of the law and his posse found the Indian?

It was thus that with a mind heavy now under grim, uneasy doubts the slim figure on the black turned head and pushed at a trot in the direction from which he had come. But as he did a growing conviction came to him that the killer of Paw Weeder and John Harris could be but *one* man!

CHAPTER XXII

COSTIGAN PLAYS A HAND

EARLIER THAT MORNING, about a mile out of Gila, Viego, the gigantic Mexican, had pulled up his gray mare and had watched a rider approaching at an easy lope from the direction of Red Rocks.

The Mexican watched the rider quizzically, a little nervously, since he might well be connected in some way with the arm of the law. However, the desire to talk this morning, to unburden himself of a secret, gave the Mexican added impetus to await the approach of the solitary horseman.

When the pony pulled up from his steady lope, Viego saw with a grin and some relief that the killer, Costigan, dust-stained and hard-eyed, was its rider.

"*Días,*" said the Mexican slowly, observing carefully the face of Costigan.

Costigan nodded tersely. "You goin' Gila-way?"

The big Mex opened his mouth, squinted at Costigan and was about to say something but suddenly thought better of it.

"*Si, señor.* And why?"

Costigan eyed the Mexican coldly. Emphatically he jerked his head in the direction of the ghost-city.

"I'm mebbe gonna need help," he said. "You come along with me. I got plenty *palabra* to make with that loco high-binder down there!"

A meaningful note in Costigan's words made Viego nod and push his pony off after the killer's when the latter sunk home his spurs.

They hammered into the deserted street of Gila across the cobblestones and pulled up with a heavy jerk before the ancient sagging saloon.

Costigan's eyes were smoky as he swung down from the saddle, motioned Viego to follow him and descended into the gloom of the musty cellar.

Crazy Fred, bending over the rumpled deck of cards in the corner, popped erect only when the two riders stood in the middle of his cave.

Something he saw instantly in the sullen eyes of the killer brought quick lines of terror channeling his face.

"What—what d'you want?" he asked with quavering high tones.

Costigan grunted, stepped forward and grasped Crazy Fred by the arm. He ripped the deck from the filthy hands and jammed them in his pocket.

"Just this, you sneaking, filthy pack-rat. I happen to know this Masked Rider's made two trips into this hole since I saw him last. What's he been doin' here? Where'd he go when he left last?"

Crazy Fred's eyes took on a new panic, his mouth fumbled, mouthed at words.

"He—he ain't been here a-tall. Someone's lyin'. What're you gonna do with my cyards?"

Costigan's gloved hands whipped up and slapped—one, two, three—across the terror-carved face before him. Crazy Fred was instantly reduced to a whining, quivering mass.

"Why—why d'you care? What you goin' to do if I tell?" he wailed.

"Kill him, you crawlin' rat." Costigan's head leaned back and his stubbled mouth writhed in mirthless, malignant laughter. "What do you think? He's got $15,000 on his head. Am I going to let that get away?"

Cringing, Crazy Fred pulled his arm away from Costigan's grip. Queerly, Costigan let him go, and watched him with sullen eyes.

With an oily, almost effortless movement, the polished gun in his right holster appeared in his hands.

"Tell me," he said in a low, toneless voice, "where'd he go? What did he talk about when he came here? Do you want me to start thinking of ways to make you talk—?"

Crazy Fred's voice rattled in terror. His eyes shot from Viego, who remained at the mouth of the cave watching the scene with glittering eyes, to the hard-lined face of the killer. Fate, he knew for all his addled senses, had placed an icy finger on his brow. Even if he talked, he might still be killed. If he didn't, Costigan's guns would certainly speak death.

Where the hooded man had last gone, Crazy Fred had not the slightest notion. One thing he did recall…. He shook his head. "I don't know where he went! He—he—"

His mouth stuttered. Costigan ground out an oath, came forward on quick surging legs. His left hand clamped with murderous strength on Crazy Fred's arm. Quaking, the scatter-witted one sank to his knees.

Costigan stooped, squatted beside Crazy Fred, his face not inches from the stubbled, filthy beard.

"What—?" he sneered. "Talk, you dirty rat, or I'll—"

The air of the cave was suddenly rent with a high-pitched, rapid clatter. A quick snap as of wood hitting wood sounded. Viego's eyes widened in surprise.

Costigan leaped backward, momentary astonishment wiping other expressions from his face. And as he came back a long trailing shape followed him as if attached to his belt.

Viego cursed. *"El Diablo!"*

Costigan, now erect, looked down and swore tersely.

There, vicious fangs embedded in the left gun holster at his side, was the tight-skinned, malignant little head of a diamond-back. Its body, a writhing dun tube of muscle, reached to the floor, where the frantic rattle-box pounded the ground.

Costigan's gloved hand coolly descended. His thumb and forefinger gripped the triangular head just at the base of the neck. His fingers squeezed and the fangs loosened.

He lifted the writhing reptile at arm's length. The hollow of the cave was momentarily ripped with thunder as the revolver blew the diamondbacks' head from between his fingers.

Viego sucked in his breath with a whistle.

Crazy Fred stared wide-eyed and silent at the headless body now aimlessly beating the floor.

"Dolly!" he chattered. "You killed her! You—you cold-blood-ed—you—"

Staggering, Crazy Fred was on his feet, his eyes wild, his hands outstretched for Costigan's throat. He lunged.

Costigan stepped back, shot his fist into the hate-contorted face.

Crazy Fred's lunge stopped in mid-air, his body sagged gently in the middle, but he did not lose consciousness.

A second later, Costigan had grappled for his wild, swinging arm, clamped them at his side. He shot his head about, towards the Mexican.

He knows somethin'," he snapped. "Let's take him out of here."

SECONDS LATER COSTIGAN was squatting over the prostrate form of Crazy Fred, back against the rotting boardwalk outside the cave.

The killer's gloved hand was at the supine man's throat, his harsh voice shot rapid questions in the fear-carved face beneath him.

Talk," he said and slapped Crazy Fred a bone-crushing blow alongside the head. "Talk, you loco, cringin' rat. Sic yore rattlers on me, will you! Where'd The Masked Rider go—what'd he want of you?"

To impress his words Costigan rolled Crazy Fred over, whipped his arm around and up his spine in a cruel arm-lock. Crazy Fred cried out.

"Wait—wait! I'll tell you—" The pain in his arm relaxed.

"He was here," quavered the man, weakly. "Yeah, he was, mister. He only wanted to talk to me a little. Ask me if I really was John Harris', the banker's, brother. That's all! An' I told him."

"*Told him what!*" Costigan's tones were like brittle icicles breaking.

Viega, standing above the pair, swore softly beneath his breath.

"I told him 'yes,'" Crazy Fred moaned. "It's true, I am."

For a second Costigan leaned back on his haunches, his eyes lifting to the big Mex's face.

"D'you hear that?" he asked in a low voice. "Harris was killed and they think he left a pot of gold hidden up in the mountains. Also he was here in Gila. If—?" A soft, harsh whistle split his sentence; his eyes left the Mexican's.

For a short second Viego stared at the top of Costigan's haltered hat. He raised his hand as if to stop Costigan, but let it drop. A worried, wondering light, came into his eyes and left them. His hand now moved unconsciously to the rear pocket of his black tight pants. Still he said nothing.

Costigan's voice raised. "Lissen, you!" he snapped. "If y're John Harris' brother, you know something about that gold. That's what The Masked Rider was seein' you about. *Wasn't it. Wasn't it!*"

A gloating note rattled harshly through the air. And in it the supine Crazy Fred recognized the coming end. He cried out with high-pitched, quavering tones that he knew nothing more.

But relentless, strong hands rolled him over, his arm was twisted upward in the crudest of holds once more. Sinews cracked. Crazy Fred screamed in agony.

But, as he did, there was a sharp clatter of horse's hoofs on the ground behind Viego and Costigan. Instantly they wheeled and saw that a rider on a piebald pony had approached unseen and unheard until he was not fifteen feet from them.

CHAPTER XXIII

"DRAW—!"

BOTH THE BIG Mexican and Costigan tightened their muscles, hands drifting down for their guns.

They saw before them a lanky individual, raw-boned, with leathery visage, lolled crosswise on his saddle, ruminating with solemn eyes over the scene before him.

Costigan moved quickly, animal-like, so that he had a clear view of the newcomer. His eyes were shadowy, emotionless.

"Who are you?" he grated slowly.

The figure on the piebald nodded grimly.

"LaShay," he said, taking in every feature of the two men before him. "Hank LaShay, by name, an' Lazy R by brand. An' strange as it seems, I'm not glad to reckanize you, Mister Three-finger Costigan."

Though LaShay's words were lazy, his eyes had hard lights in them that Costigan saw instantly. The Lazy R owner, up on his spread, had heard through quick grapevine sources that Jimmie Weeder was being hunted by a posse headed by Bean-pole Jackson for the theft of fifteen thousand dollars. A friend-ship grown from many years on the same range had made him saddle his pony and lope off in the direction of Gila.

Whatever cases said, Jimmie Weeder was in trouble. If he had stolen the money, that was even acceptable. And Jimmie Weeder needed help. No, LaShay would never back out on a proposition like that. Gila, as it happened, was the place in which LaShay hoped, even as Beanpole Jackson who had passed through there earlier in the morning had hoped, to catch up with the fugitive redhead.

Now, however, a new problem had presented itself. Coming into town, he had spotted the scene going on behind the sagging saloon. As he approached he recognized the face and figure of Costigan from many meetings through the medium of reward posters. He knew Costigan to be a sure and relentless killer. But Crazy Fred's cry had caught LaShay's ears, demanding instant action. Only one look was sufficient to tell him the scatter-witted one was being tortured. For what—?

Costigan shuffled his feet when he heard his name on the

lips of the lolling rider before him. Hate wrote its message instantly across his face. His elbows loosened, let his arms drop.

"I don't like yore face, yore tone uh voice, ner what yo're talking about, LaShay," said the killer slowly.

LaShay smiled humorlessly. "Which matches my sentiments of yours in toto to a T, Mister Costigan," he drawled. "Mebbe we just plumb think alike on that score, but we shore don't on th' subject of that pore critter on th' ground there. How come you don't pick somebody yer own weight!" He raised his voice. "Git up, Fred."

The scatter-witted one lifted himself to his feet and stood ready to run at the slightest provocation.

Costigan's face shifted, shot one glance at Crazy Fred.

"Stay where you are!" he snarled.

Then he turned to LaShay. "Stay out of this." His voice was now toneless. "I don't like nuthin' about you, you —— *Go fer yore gun!*"

LaShay took the insult with a slow twirk of his indulgent mouth.

"Figgered you'd plum rair up an' ask me to draw down," he said slowly. "Ain't surprised me a bit. Funny as it may be, Costigan, I ain't gonna draw. Yer reputation's done awed me. How come I should try to dig my own grave? I got kids tuh support. I only asked one little favorite of you, Costigan. I ain't anxious to give you publicity 'round these parts. In exchange for silence, you leave Crazy Fred be. Business man's proposition."

Costigan's eyes narrowed. He stared at LaShay with cold, merciless eyes, a reptile's.

Unfortunately, LaShay did hot realize the full import of the answer Costigan had just wrung from Crazy Fred. A cave of gold, $65,000, might be at stake for making Crazy Fred talk…. The thought sent a wave of hatred spinning through Costigan's mind. He raised his voice.

"Go to hell!" he blurted. "Why should I make deals with you? *Draw*, I say, LaShay! I'm goin' to kill you shore—"

LaShay's voice was even. "No you ain't—" he started.

But at that second Costigan moved. Fury and insane fires raged in his mind. The thought of that $65,000 cache turned him into a stooping, sultry-eyed animal.

"You won't," he snarled. "You *won't*—*!*"

The gun that suddenly slipped up into his right hand went off with a vicious, ear-splitting report. LaShay's pony shied wildly, leaped aside. And as it did the lanky shape of LaShay on its back, a look of stunned surprise on his face, wheeled and flopped out of the saddle. Square between his eyes a round black hole abruptly spurted blood.

"Madre de Dios, Cos'gan. Why you do that?" snarled the Mexican.

He wheeled his big head to the form of the killer still crouching bent over his smoking gun. Costigan's face still reflected the angry shadows of hatred that had made him pull the trigger.

He walked over to LaShay's prostrate form, kicked the lifeless shell with his boot.

He wheeled to Virgo. "Now—" he started. Then a blank look came over his face.

Viego turned, too. The object of Costigan's gaze was gone. Crazy Fred had disappeared.

"Where'n hell—!" snapped the killer. "Where'd be go? I'll git that crazy rat, choke the life out of him for running away. Come!"

Viego followed the killer as he strode rapidly into the cave below the saloon. But Crazy Fred was not there. For full fifteen minutes they strode along the deserted streets of the town or stamped through the sagging reaches of ancient, rolling buildings. But still Crazy Fred was not to be found.

Finally Viego stopped. *"Madre mia,* Cos'gan, you will nevair find him here. In th' meantime—"

Costigan spoke through clenched teeth. "Somebody'll come and find that dead rat in the street. Anyhow, nobody'll believe Crazy Fred. If he says we killed LaShay—"

Viego's huge mouth parted in a grin. *"We?* An' why 'we,' *señor?"* His laugh was dangerous. "Not mysel', *señor.* I t'ink I go on my own trail from now on. Mebbe," he added half to himself, "that ees *bueno.*"

He wheeled and stepped out of the awry doorway in which they were standing and then turned to Costigan.

"I t'ink our trails part, Mistair Cos'gan. *Adiós!"* he laughed again with a roar that resounded through the deserted streets. "Th' nex' time I see you, Cos'gan, I hope it ees not on th' end of wan beeg rope!"

So saying, the Mexican disappeared. A moment later Costigan, swinging up into the saddle of the Bar-H pony he had appropriated on the Loco Mule, heard the Mexican's gray mare going at a rapid gait in the direction of Red Rocks.

WHEN HE GOT out of sight of Gila, Viego pulled the towering mare up with hard reins and looked behind him. No rider showed on the mesa. The mountainous Mexican's smile at this waned to a frown of puzzlement as he reached in the rear pocket of his tight black pants and pulled out a piece of paper.

Carefully he unfolded it and stared at the writing thereon with the perplexed frown deepening. On the paper were lines which he could understand; but the writing—in English—gave him pause. With Costigan's help the map might have been read. Luckily he had held his tongue.

This map, he knew for sure, was in some way immediately connected with John Harris' death and the $65,000 caché. But the writing, the real key to the map, might as well have been Sanskrit for all the help it gave him.

Up in one corner Viego made out the rude outlines of what

seemed to be a ranch, and a Bar-H indicated its name. With this meager clue, Viego turned his towering mare and moved at a rapid lope westward.

CHAPTER XXIV

BATTLE IN THE BRUSH

COSTIGAN, THE KILLER, rode rapidly out of Gila in the direction of the spiny blue reaches of the Cayugas. The killing of LaShay, he now fully realized, was an unfortunate and dangerous mistake. Both Crazy Fred and Viego had seen him kill the rancher. The word of either was sufficient to string him to the highest limb around Red Rocks.

Grimly Costigan rode. Once in the mountains he would wait for nightfall before returning to Gila. By that time he might be able to catch Crazy Fred alone once more.

Viego was now out of the scene as far as the cachéd money was concerned. But LaShay— As he rode Costigan coldly and bitterly cursed. He had killed a man in cold blood with little or no pretext. The country would soon be blazing beneath his feet. He had to move fast.

An hour later, however, riding up a brush-lined draw that led into the Cayugas, Costigan pulled the Bar-H pony to a halt and cocked his head.

What had first given him pause was a sibilant yet carrying whistle, a signal. Immediately it was followed by another in a higher note.

Costigan frowned. Someone, he knew, was in the draw paralleling his own and was whistling. Curiosity and suspicions urged the killer. He dismounted, tied his pony with forethought to a limb of a *madroña* and mounted the brush-lined draw.

Once above the hillside, Costigan's eyes widened and he cursed through clenched teeth.

There below him in a gully he saw the forms of several punchers and at their head Jimmie Weeder and his father. Near them, in conversation, stood the reason for the surprised whistle that sped between his tight teeth. It was The Masked Rider!

With quick movements the killer slunk behind a huge rock and examined the party below. The masked man was standing well apart from the Weeder gang. Enough to make a perfect pistol shot.

The ideas that suddenly shot through Costigan's mind moved him on rapid yet silent feet down the slope, well out of sight and hearing from below. Fifty yards from where he had spotted the masked man, he dropped to his haunches and slowly drew the .45 in his right holster.

If he killed the masked man, he considered, the next thing would be to get the body. With it only could he collect a reward. But a way to take it from the Weeders and their punchers gave him momentary pause.

But not for long. With lips stretched in a tight, intent line, Costigan lifted the revolver and cuddled it in the crook of his arm. Squinting, he drew the bead up slowly until it centered square between the caped shoulders seventy-five yards below him.

Perhaps it was a movement in the brush that held his finger, perhaps the outlaw's ingrained wariness. Nonetheless Costigan jerked up his head and wheeled his squatting shape.

This, just in time to see from the corner of his eyes a shape that had paused above him, then bent with the agility and suddenness of a striking cougar, and charged at him.

Costigan did not have time to whip up his gun or fire before the charging, half-bent shape of Blue Hawk hit him with all the weight of his lithe body.

Colliding in mid-air, their bodies were thrown apart for a second by the force of the Indian's rush. But no sooner than they had collided, the Indian shifted cat-like and grappled at the revolver in Costigan's hand.

Silent, yet with the fury and intensity of two men who now realized that the right was to the death, they writhed, scrambled and fought.

Blue Hawk was lighter than Costigan but had the advantage of quickness and lean sinewiness. On the other hand Costigan moved and hit with trained precision in a type of combat with which the Indian was little acquainted.

Their whistling breaths came through clenched teeth. Costigan had fallen backward, beneath the Indian, but by sheer weight and strength pulled himself up on his elbow while Blue Hawk clamped grim brown claws on the hand that held the revolver.

For many seconds thus equally tied in combat, both men struggled silently, relentlessly. Neither paid the slightest attention to the incidents which were happening below. Nor had those in the gully time to notice the fray up on the hillside. The blows Costigan could strike were few and glancing. His revolver slipped from his sweating fingers and clanked away into one of the rocky niches nearby.

Once they parted entirely and Costigan made a frantic grab at the remaining gun, only to be knocked down with another quick rush from Blue Hawk.

But soon, it was evident to Costigan, the Indian was weakening under the continuous disadvantage of lesser weight and skill in the arts of scurvy combat. He saved his strength as best he could.

Soon his chance came. The Indian leaped, jerking his body free of Costigan's grappling arms, and hit out twice at the rocky jaw of the killer. Costigan took the blows backing away from the Indian.

When the last blow struck, Costigan ducked in under the Indian's guard, grasped him about the waist and lifted. As he did, he felt the Indian's free hand jerk at the holster at his side. Nevertheless, Costigan grated his teeth and lunged.

The Indian's body made a full arc in the air and landed back down, Costigan on top. For a second Costigan lay there panting, the listless, limp shape of Blue Hawk beneath him. Finally, Costigan sat up and rolled away from the unconscious Indian. He retrieved his gun from the closed brown hand.

The Indian stirred, hawk-nosed face outlined against the rich brown of the earth. Instantly Costigan was on his knees. He lifted the gun, decided suddenly against taking the chance of anyone's hearing the shot.

The Indian moved again. Costigan's left hand shot out, gripped a bulky, jagged rock and raised it shoulder high. Against the leathery tan of his face, his brown, cold eyes glittered with murderous intent. The muscles of his bulky arm tightened—but never acted on their purpose.

The killer's bullet-head shot about at the sound of a voice to his right. He wheeled his body in alarm, clambered to his feet with a lunging, awkward motion.

Fifteen feet away from him, hard hands hanging at his sides from beneath the long black cloak, stood The Masked Rider.

Costigan's voice cursed with a crackling, sobbing sound. The figure before him did not speak and did not move. Yet in its hooded lines Costigan instantly read the crack of doom about his ears. In his right hand he still held the revolver taken from the Indian.

He whipped the gun up without an instant's warning and shot from the hip. But, even as he did, his gun's voice was matched by another which thundered from beneath the black *serape.*

A third shot spoke out. But that, too, was from the man in the hood. It shook the dropping, sagging body of Costigan on its way to the ground. In the brush the limp body of Costigan kicked once or twice and was silent.

Only then did the man in the hood step forward towards the supine Indian. And as he did, a trickle of blood spewed down over the hand that held the smoking revolver, over the gun butt, to drip in big dark globules to the ground.

WHEN BLUE HAWK opened his eyes, he stirred and sat up groggily. Momentary surprise and gratitude shot across his face.

"You, *señor*. You have come back!"

The hooded head nodded.

"Come," the masked man said. "Something has happened to Crazy Fred. I found his pack of cards in this rattler's pocket just now. We'll have to hurry."

"Wait, *señor*," said the Indian, quickly. "You are hurt?"

The man in the mask shook away the question.

"It's nothing. Raked in the forearm, that's all. A bandage will fix it. Come!"

CHAPTER XXV

UP TRAIL

OLD JAKE SANDELL was mounted on his best pony, leading the rest of the horses up the narrow and deserted trail that wound precipitously along a steep canyon side in the Cayugas.

Behind him, in single file, the other horses stumbled and slipped along the treacherous little-used and overgrown trail. On the second pony rode a Bar-H puncher by the name of Willings; on the third, Leona Harris. Immediately behind her, his lanky shape swinging easily to the movements of his sorrel, was Andy Sandell. Another Bar-H puncher brought up the rear of the slow-moving procession.

The girl was dressed in khaki riding breeches and a white open-throated shirt. Her eyes were haggard, flitting through the brush on both sides of the trail for a meager sign of assistance or rescue, just as they had for the past two hours. One sleeve of her while shirt was ripped open to show an ugly, reddening bruise. Her riding breeches were dirty; her wrists tied tightly behind her with a short, cruelly-gripping length of whale-line.

Now and then, over the grunting of the ponies, the leathery creak of saddle gear, she could hear Old Jake Sandell giving orders to puncher Willings behind him.

The trail up which they had turned on first entering the Cayugas was old, never traveled these days. Old Jake Sandell had been wise in choosing it. Chances of meeting strangers were at a minimum. Where her captors were taking her, the girl had not the slightest suspicion. Yet almost instinctively she knew that behind the actions of the Sandells lay the orders of Harold Gangling.

The previous night she had retired early, heart-sick and hopeful that Jimmie Weeder's rash fronting of Gangling would come to nothing. She had not heard of his breaking into the bank.

At four o'clock in the morning a scratching at her door had awakened her. It was Tollito, the houseboy.

"Señorita... señorita!"

She had arisen, opened the door to find Tollito, his wide-eyed and alarmed face staring at her over a flickering candle.

"Señorita, a *caballero* has come just now and woke me. He says Jimmie Weeder has robbed the bank of fifteen thousand dollars and there is a posse with *el alcalde* searching for him. The *caballero* comes from *Señor* Jimmie, who is hiding outside of town waiting to see you. He says you and I come *pronto*—that is his wish!"

Fifteen minutes later, weary and fearful, she had been riding out of town towards the mounting spires of the Cayugas with Tollito on an ancient gray mule behind her. They found the meeting place, but no Jimmie. When Jake Sandell stepped out of the shadows, she had wheeled her pony, sought to flee.

A bullet brought it to its knees. She heard a wild scream, knew that the shadow's squat shape that sank to the ground was Tollito, to rise no more.

Then they had taken her, manacled, off in the direction of the Cayugas.

Often, on their way across the mesa, the band of horsemen she was with had stopped at Jake Sandell's command and withdrawn into the shades of cottonwoods, awaiting the passage of some lone puncher or group of town-bound horsemen. Then her silence was assured by a cold-snouted revolver held by Andy Sandell against her temple, and a dirty hand clamped brutally over her mouth.

The trail became wilder, more rocky as it mounted. The rich brown of earth on the lower stretches changed to red gleaming dirt on either side of the trail. Not once now did Jake Sandell lessen his pace. The sun rose to high noon and passed the zenith. Still they continued forward.

At last descending into a rock-strewn, desolate gully, Old Jake Sandell raised his hand in signal to halt. He turned in the saddle to Andy.

"Reckon we'll wait here. This's where he said he'd be to meet us. Climb down, boys."

Andy helped pull the girl off her mount, let her slide to the hard ground beside the trail. As before she was silent, her eyes brooding, her stubborn chin held firm.

They waited here for nearly an hour. From conversation passed between Andy Sandell and Old Jake she came to the conclusion that the other Sandell boys, Sam and Louie, had been up at the Bar-H at the time of her kidnaping. A message had been sent telling them to meet the rest of the Bar-H clan in this forsaken gully.

At the end of an hour, Andy Sandell suddenly rose, strode up the side of the draw.

When he came back, his dark, hard eyes were flashing. "He's a-comin'," he said briefly.

There was a rattle of horse's hoofs on gravel. Around a huge boulder that hid newcomers approaching from downtrail, trotted a tall *palomina*. And the man on its back was Harold Gangling.

THE GIRL'S LIPS were hard-set as Gangling slid down from the *palomina*, strode towards the squatting group of Sandells and punchers. He was dressed in a black frock coat and gray trousers, both of which were rumpled and dirty with hard riding and trail dust. His dark predatory eyes flashed at her briefly, passed on to the Sandells.

"So you killed the peon," he said bluntly, nervously. "I'd hoped that wouldn't be necessary. The town is in somewhat of an uproar. Never mind, though," he said quickly as Old Jake Sandell's mouth snapped open angrily. "I'll see nothing comes of it. Where's your two other boys?"

"Be here short off," said Jake Sandell. "What's next?"

"The main thing," he snapped, "will be to get this girl well hidden within the next twenty-four hours. At the end of that time, you understand, I am supposed to have an answer for that monkey in the black cape. Well, I shall! I had depended on you two to suggest a hiding place near enough to town for easy communication."

Seated on a nearby rock, Leona Harris looked at the cruel, hard-jawed mouth of Gangling and felt her heart sinking within her. In the hands of this man, whose true nature she was only now beginning to understand, all hope seemed lost. Jimmie, she realized by now, had in truth broken into the bank and was being sought by a posse. Without his help, without—

Her thoughts were interrupted by a rasped word from Andy

Sandell. The elder son rose to his long legs, strode again up the bank.

When he came back his wide mouth was moving rapidly.

"Sam an' Louie air comin'," he snapped. "Got someone with them!"

And with this announcement there swept through Leona Harris a convulsive wave of icy dread that choked down her breath. Suddenly it occurred to her that the Sandells and Gangling, undertaking an enterprise like this—in which one murder had already occurred, that of the peon Tollito—would ordinarily be masked and gruff-toned for concealment of their identities. But they had abducted and murdered without an effort at disguise. Certainly they knew that she would talk—later, when an opportunity came. Knowing that, they let her see and hear everybody. What could they be having in mind? Only one thing, she knew, would silence her. Did they have *that* in mind? Her whole frame shivered. Such craven villainy was to her beyond all human understanding—yet here she was, waiting, waiting for a dark, unknown fate that loomed blacker and bigger before her, with the outlines of a grim death.

CHAPTER XXVI

A SURPRISE PACKAGE

OLD JAKE SANDELL and Gangling rose instantly.
Around the corner of the downtrail rock came a queer procession.

At their head rode the pimply-faced lolling form of young Sam Sandell, then a Bar-H puncher and a huge form wrapped with *reatas*, who, even as he rode, grinned with a big set of pearly teeth that flashed in contrast to his swarthy skin.

The man was astride a towering gray mare, a huge and mountainous man. His hat was gone, his great body with its sickly blue bolero swayed easily, lightly to the scrambling movements of his pony. Behind him rode Louie Sandell, a rifle swaying across his saddle bows.

"Hey, Pop," yelled the leading rider. "Look what we done collected back on th' range. We shore got a surprise this time fer yuh!"

Gangling cursed beneath his breath, strode rapidly towards the now dismounting horsemen.

Sam Sandell turned, looked curiously at Leona Harris, but said nothing.

The banker approached him, looked up at the Mexican Viego and wheeled to the youngest Sandell.

"A desert tramp!" he almost snarled. "Don't you know every move we make is dangerous without bringing more prisoners up here? What have you got him for?"

Sam Sandell's yellow-toothed mouth spread apart angrily.

"None uh yer damn business," he snapped. "You like that answer?"

Old Jake Sandell hastily intervened. "Now—now, Sam. Lay a line on yer tongue, will yer? What you bringing him in fer, boy?"

Louie Sandell, now dismounted, spoke up only to be interrupted by his younger brother.

"Waal," said Sam sullenly, "we'll tell yuh later. First thing you'd like tuh know is we were ridin' down Red Rocks way on th' mountain and shore enough we seen a whole raft uh Weeder Closed C men ridin' uptrail. We done branched off an' watched 'em. They was headin' back fer their spread. Jimmie Weeder was with 'em. They had Paw Weeder strung across a saddle, face down. Dead!"

Old Jake Sandell's mouth sagged agape. "Dead! Paw Weeder *dead?*"

"Shore."

Jake wheeled to Gangling. A slow smile of understanding

was beginning to spread across the banker's lean features. His predatory eyes lighted up, took on new life.

"Dead?" he reiterated. "Well, well. The Closed C owner is dead. How did it happen?"

"Don't know," said Sam. "Only he was shore enough a goner when we seen him. It was a cinch."

Gangling strode back to the circle of Andy and the Bar-H puncher who were squatting near the girl. Looking down, he saw that her eyes were flashing, but were belied by the heavy tremble of her lips. Grimly she clamped her teeth and was silent. Paw Weeder, Jimmie's father, dead, cried her mind. He couldn't be—

Sam Sandell strode up. "Waal, as I wuz going to say—"

"Wait," snapped Gangling, a mounting tone of victory in his voice. "You hear that, Jake Sandell? Weeder is dead. Do you know what that means? The mortgage the Cattlemen's Trust has held on the Closed C was drawn up by John Harris himself. Due to the vicissitudes and dangers of life here in this valley, Harris—"

The ragged-toothed, youngest Sandell cut in again. "John Harris—yeah!" he said. "What I'm goin' tuh say is about him, too. Lissen—"

Gangling's hard eyes flashed at the interruption. Old Jake, intent on Gangling's flashing words, placed a hand on his youngest's shoulder.

"Due to the dangers," Gangling breezed on, "he did not believe in risking the money of his depositors. When he drew up that mortgage he specified that in the event of the death of the mortgagee before the loan was paid off, the mortgage of the Closed C would automatically become a demand note and thus easier to collect from a tied-up estate. In other words, Sandell, that mortgage can be foreclosed on demand at any time after the death of Paw Weeder! Do you understand what that means to you? That range is yours for the asking now! I told you to play in with me—!"

Old Jake Sandell let out a whispered exclamation.

"A demand note, huh? Jumpin' cat-fish, then—"

"But that don't give yuh th' Closed C yet, Paw!" snapped Sam Sandell. "Lissen tuh me, will yuh? I got somethin' that'll pull yer ears out a foot!"

Even Gangling now turned to listen to the youngest Sandell's rasped-out words.

"We wuz comin' down Horse Canyon back there and looked up on th' hillsides and seen this gray mare tied to a stump. We jest happened tuh stroll up tuh see what was happenin', figgerin' we might have a little fun with someone, when shore enough who'd we pop in on but this Spic snorin' away in th' shade of a cottonwood.

"Waal, I recanized right away who it wuz. He wuz up at th' Loco Mule with th' Weeders and Th' Masked Rider that night. When we woke him up, shore enough he was lookin' square intuh the muzzles of about five guns. You shoulda seen his face! Figgerin' we'd still have some more fun we decided tuh bring him up here with us—"

Gangling rapped out an oath. "Why, you blundering idiot. For fun! Don't you understand—"

The Sandell leered. "Shore fer fun. Lookee what we done found in his back pocket!"

Sam reached in his soiled hickory shirt pocket, brought forth a folded piece of grimy paper, quietly opened it and handed it to Gangling. It was John Harris' map.

CHAPTER XXVII

DESOLATION VALLEY

FOR A LONG minute the banker stared at the grimy sheet of paper before him. Finally he turned to Jake Sandell. His voice was high-pitched with victory.

"You see that, Sandell? Justice is served. We have found the killer of John Harris and the map as well. What more can we ask?"

He turned to the mounted Mexican, scanned the grinning huge face with dark, glittering eyes.

"Pull him down, boys," he snapped. "If he has already been to the cave, gotten the money that Harris placed there according to most stories, we'll damn well soon find out!"

Three of the Bar-H men pulled the huge, rope-enfolded shape from the gray mare. The Mexican stood before Gangling, a wide grin twisting his features.

"Dees map," he said in his loud voice. "I have found eet on a dead man. *Madre de Dios,* how could I kill *Señor* Harris, I ask you? I have t'ree witness to prove I was in Gila when dat man was stabbed!"

"You lie, you greasy rat," snarled Gangling. "You killed John Harris and I promise you shall swing for it! Where is the money from the cave?"

The big Mexican swelled out his chest. His black button eyes were flashing. "Mysel' a 'greasy rat' you say? Dees words, *señor,* I will poosh down de t'roat! That money? I do not care whar it ees. *Madre mia,* wit' wan han' I will break yore back, mebbe you, too, *hombrecito!*" He turned to Sam Sandell.

The Sandells chuckled with irritating calmness. Gangling's dark eyes whipped through the faces about him.

"There is only one way to find out the truth," he snarled.

"And if the money is still in the cave, Sandell, our fortunes are made. Why shouldn't we take it? Come. The map indicates Desolation Valley over the ridge. If the money is not there, we'll soon find where it is from this stinking Mexican. Bring the girl, Sandell!"

Within five minutes the whole Sandell clan and their prisoners were mounted and proceeding as fast as possible over the adjoining low range that separated them from the valley shown on the rude map as being the one in which the cave of John Harris' caché was located.

Sore in body, stunned from the happenings of the past few moments, Leona Harris rode between Jake Sandell and the big Mexican. Behind them strung out the remainder of the party.

Her red-rimmed eyes clicked through the farther brush even as before, but with sinking hopes. No one would possibly find them in this most desolate part of the Cayugas. No one would stop them from taking the money, perhaps killing her.

She stared at the broad back of the Mexican before her. And as she did a look of wonderment suddenly sprang into her eyes. Separated by the girl from the following horsemen, the Mexican was laboriously and rapidly working on the bonds that were wrapped about him in a hundred loops and knots.

By the time they had crossed the ridge Viego had one of his wrists partially free and the knots loosened on his other wrist. A glittering light of triumph was already beginning to show in Viego's eyes as Jake Sandell suddenly raised his hand and called a halt.

Without stopping, Gangling trotted up to the head of the riders.

"Yuh see down that." Jake Sandell was pointing. "That's Desolation Valley an' that's what he meant on the map. The map also says something about them two tall oaks down thar on th' north'ard side. Ken you see 'em?"

Gangling squinted and nodded. He pressed spurs to his

palomina and started at a rapid trot downtrail. It was evident that, with the caché almost in sight, his judgment was overcome by his greed and anxiety to get hands on John Harris' cachéd money.

With no pretense at caution now, the other ponies were pushed into a sliding, jarring downhill trot.

THE VALLEY INTO which they descended had not been aptly named. It was neither desolate nor barren. In fact, the brush and trees were thicker here than in any other part of the Cayugas. It was desolate only because it was uninhabited.

Covered by the rapid pace Gangling had set, the giant Mexican worked steadily on the bonds that held him.

Once, descending a steeper part of the trail, Leona's horse shoved itself up close to the gray mare's haunches. Out of the corner of his eyes, Viego saw her face and grinned.

"*Señorita,*" he said quickly. "Eef I get out, you will come with me, eh? *Madre de Dios,* I would not like you to stay with dees murderers!"

A sudden light of hope in the girl's eyes answered his question.

The riders came out on the vestiges of an ancient cattle trail and they wound with it down the valley side. Before them, well apart from the other lower brush, Leona now could pick out the two huge oaks referred to by Sandell. Rising high, they were easy landmarks, almost exactly centered in the middle of the valley.

The ponies slipped and scrambled down the slope and on to the more level brush and tree-covered bottom. But, just as they did, Leona Harris heard Gangling's violent, surprised curse rend the air. Jake Sandell, behind him, pulled his pony up short just as Gangling had. The banker's long arm shot out.

"Look!"

All eyes were turned in the direction his lengthy finger indicated.

In Leona Harris' breast hope bloomed with sudden and tense emotion. Far beyond them, just descending another trail of the valley-side beyond the two sentinel oaks wound a small procession of four men. And at their head a lithe figure, outlined in her memory forever, abruptly pulled his dun pony to a halt. That was Jimmie Weeder and the riders, Closed C punchers.

CHAPTER XXVIII

RESCUE IN THE ROCKS

SIMULTANEOUSLY, IT SEEMED, both groups of riders had seen each other. And, what instantly was more important to Leona was the fact that the two big oaks were almost exactly halfway from each.

Gangling swore again. In an instant the Sandells were out of their saddles, guns unholstered and ready.

"That's Weeder, all right," rasped Jake Sandell. "Now you boys move in close behind them rocks thar, get th' hosses out of sight as quick as you can. If you shoot—make it at young Weeder!"

Gangling wheeled. "How in hell did they learn of this at the same time we did?"

Old Jake turned his hawk-nosed face. "You askin' me?" was all he said.

Still a quarter of a mile away, the Weeder clan wheeled their ponies and took to the protection of a patch of high brush. Almost instantly a rifle spouted a puff of smoke from where they had disappeared. The bullet whined in close to the Sandell puncher named Willings, and ricocheted off a nearby rock. The Sandells ducked to a man.

"They're outnumbered anyway," said Gangling. "I think we're nearer the cave than they are, too. Don't worry, we'll get there first. Just keep your heads, boys—"

"And you keep your bear-trap mouth shut," gritted Sam Sandell. "If I never seen no one do so much talkin' without sayin' anything, it's 'cause you took off all prizes long ago!"

Gangling sputtered with rage at the irritating grin that spread across the Sandell's features. Andy's rifle spoke up. The big Mexican slid down from the mare and strode off into the protection of a patch of tall rocks. Louie and Sam Sandell, still grinning at the angry banker, followed him. The rest of the Sandell crew took to cover.

"They won't stay there," said Jake Sandell. "They're gonna make fer them two oaks fast as they ken. We gotta keep movin', too, 'cause if they get there first, we'll shore never rout them out."

They were interrupted by Andy Sandell's sharp voice. "They're movin' up. I ken see them there in th' brush." He paused. Then, "Hey, look out, will you!"

Immediately from down the valley spoke a rifle. Willings had been staring over a rock. He cursed chokingly, sickeningly, wheeled and crashed back full length on the ground.

The others stood over him momentarily with strained, whitened faces.

"Dead," snapped Sam Sandell. "The damn fool!"

Andy Sandell broke in on them again. "Yuh see, Pop, they're movin' towards them two trees all right. They must know what we're after now. We got more men, though, and if we move over to that bunch of rock there"—he pointed to his right—"we'll have th' advantage of more guns and be able to keep 'em from crossin' that clear space to them trees."

A grim smile broke across Jake Sandell's features. Gangling snapped quick acceptance of the idea.

Sam Sandell, leaning over the jutting rock, suddenly whipped up the rifle Louie had given him, and fired.

He chortled mirthlessly. "There's one of their punchers, by Golly! Now we're even. Only three now. Come on, Andy, let's run for it. We'll git tuh them oaks before they know what's happening!"

But Gangling whipped his lean shape about, stopped them with an upraised hand.

"This way," he said.

With Andy leading, the Sandells and their prisoners backed out of range of the Weeders' guns, circled the brush and look a new position a hundred yards away. Behind they left Sam who kept up a steady stream of rifle shots to cover their movements.

Leona Harris' first hopes began to drag lower and lower. With three men against seven, Jimmie could never hope to reach the caché first. And if he didn't—

In moving, the big Mexican, his bonds still tight around him, brushed rudely against her as they walked. The low words that shot from his mouth made her heart leap within her.

The pony Louie Sandell had ridden was carrying a rifle scabbard. Over it, strapped in the rigging, was a Bar-H branding iron. When he yanked out the rifle, the iron fell with metallic clatter to the rocky ground. Viego's eyes lit up with a smiling and keen light.

The horses were in a little group being held by the remaining Bar-H puncher. The dead man and Sara were behind at the rock, leaving only the three Sandells, Andy, Louie and Jake, and Gangling remaining in the party.

As soon as they reached their new position, Andy and Louie sneaked their rifles between niches in the jutting rocks and began peppering the brush of the valley beyond the oaks.

At Gangling's orders, the Bar-H puncher joined them, leaving the ponies unguarded. This made Viego smile widely. He sidled closer to the girl watching intently the backs of Gangling and Old Jake who now were busy seeking new zones of fire.

While they did, the big one moved his shoulders, writhed his huge arms with a slippery eel-like motion. As if by magic the bonds wrapped about him loosened and dropped away. He moved quickly, snatched at a knife sheathed in an inside pocket of his tight bolero. The knife that appeared brought a look of wonderment in Leona's eyes. It was a stiletto like that which had killed her father!

THE BIG MEXICAN had timed his actions well. At that second Andy Sandell's rifle spoke once more and was silent.

"They've cut for cover!" he yelled. "Let's go now. Run down in th' cover of them rocks near the oaks. We can make it, Pop, while they're not looking."

He scrambled from behind his protecting stone barrier. Old Jake followed him. Both Gangling and Louie Sandell barked an order at the puncher to stay with their prisoners and prepared to run when Andy gave the signal.

"We run too," grated Viego's voice in Leona's ear, and with a single slashing down-motion sliced through the length of whale-line binding her wrists.

With Gangling's and Louie's backs turned to them, a safe dash to the horses seemed like a certainty. Protected then by other rocks they could make their escape.

"Now!" snapped the Mexican. "Come!"

With quick hands Viego grappled for the branding iron that had fallen near Leona. He lifted it, started backing away from the rocks. Leona, crouching, followed him. Andy and Jake Sandell had by now disappeared over the rocks.

But as they went, the Mexican's heavy boot hit a loose stone, crunched it underfoot.

At that second, the puncher who had previously tended the ponies wheeled.

"Hey!" he yelled. "They—"

Instantly Gangling and Louie Sandell shifted their feet and turned. As they did they saw the giant Mexican's arm descend and a knife shoot out from his hand. Like a streak of lightning it cut through the air and stabbed itself hilt-deep in the breast of the puncher who had yelled. The man dropped, dead.

Then, as if she had been jerked by an irresistible force, the girl felt herself lifted almost bodily in the air and pulled backward.

As she was lifted she saw the guns of both Louie Sandell and Gangling flip upward and fire. Behind her sounded a husky, racking cough, the murmur of a groan.

"*Señorita*—run!"

The grip on her arm relaxed, a heavy body stumbled past her and fell to the earth, silent.

But as it did the girl wheeled and ran, stumbling, for the ponies behind her. She heard a rasped oath blurt forth from Louie Sandell and stumbling feet running after her.

A second later, she had swung up into the saddle of one of the shying ponies and yanked its head about.

Turning, she saw Gangling curse and follow the stumbling form of Louie as it approached the pony. She jammed both spurred heels into the pony's haunches. With a snort of terror it reared.

As it did, the diving, hurtling form of Louie Sandell grappled at the bridle and caught it. She saw then that in his headlong approach he had retrieved the branding iron dropped from Viego's lifeless hands.

Gangling had stopped and was watching the scene with a cool and grim smile while the pony reared.

Louie Sandell went with it. He lifted the branding iron, brought it back to strike her. With a cry of alarm, Leona's arms instinctively shot up to protect her head.

At that second a pistol shot sounded off to her right. She saw the form of Louie Sandell, with upraised arm, seem to fold at his middle, loosen the bridle and drop beneath the churning hoofs of the pony.

Her hands dropped, revealing the form of Gangling who

was scrambling in craven terror over the rocks beyond which Jake Sandell and Andy had disappeared. His gray trousered legs vanished from sight.

Wildly she grappled at the reins, prepared to sink her spurs once more into the flanks of the surging pony.

But she did not, for a quick shout stopped her.

Out of the tangle of nearby brush came a stooping, running shape. A smoking gun was in its hand.

"Wait!" the man yelled as he ran. And the girl saw suddenly that the runner's head and shoulders were covered by a flowing black cape and hood that rippled back in the wind as he ran.

"The Masked Rider!" she cried out. *"You!"*

CHAPTER XXIX

CACHÉ!

BY THE TIME the masked man had reached the pony and the girl she had swung herself out of the saddle and was awaiting him.

He did not pause.

"This way," he said quickly. "They can still come back, but I don't think they will."

"Were you with Jimmie? Is he all right?"

For a second be paused. "I wasn't with him," was all he said.

Rapidly he pulled the girl away from the horses up into the shelter of the rocks.

Far beyond them in an open space near the two oaks that lifted their heads above the farther brush, they saw a form running. It was Andy Sandell, alone.

And at that instant a puff of smoke broke out from a nearby rock and was whipped away by wind. The form of Andy Sandell threw back its arms, stumbled and thudded into the earth to lie still.

"One more," said the man in the hood coldly. "That leaves Old Jake and Gangling somewhere between us and Jimmie Weeder."

"And Sam," said the girl quickly. "He was left behind."

"Forever," gritted the man in the hood, tersely, meaningfully.

He mounted the rock, the girl following wonderingly at his heels.

"He's dead, then?" she asked, but he did not answer.

A gloved hand lifted the fringe of the black hood and pointed to the two oaks.

"There's a little cave in some rocks right between those trees," he said. "And that is where the money is. But we can't get there yet. Old Jake Sandell and Gangling are still between us and the Weeders. They should be talking out with their guns any moment now."

The girl turned questioning eyes to him. "How did you know where the cave is?"

The hooded head nodded: "Crazy Fred told me, or rather us. He was with me but I left him behind when I saw you. He should be around here now."

For some seconds the two stood there waiting and watching. No movement showed in the brush beyond them.

Suddenly, however, a long low wail of a coyote ruffled the air of the valley. The masked head jerked up.

"Blue Hawk," he said suddenly. "Jimmie Weeder *is* hurt. But not seriously or the call would have sounded different. That accounts for their silence a time back."

Sudden alarm shot into the girl's eyes. "I'm going over there," she said abruptly. "He's hurt and I—"

A hand on her arm stopped her. "And you'll get shot by Gangling. Remember he still owns the bank."

"Still?"

"Yes. And with you dead, we could hardly have a reason for getting it back for you," the man said without humor. "I'd stay here, if I were you."

The gloved hands rose to the hood. From them issued the long haunting cry of a lonesome and marauding mountain cat.

"Crazy Fred should have been here," the hooded man said, his voice terse. "And I don't like the silence from Old Jake or Gangling. Blue Hawk will meet me out there," he pointed. "We'll come back."

"I'm not afraid," the girl said.

He stepped out from the shelter of the rocks and bending, moved, a flitting tenuous shadow, rapidly in the direction of the two oaks. The girl clenched her fists and watched him disappear.

THE MAN IN the mask stopped a hundred yards away and awaited the sound of soft moccasins through the brush. At last Blue Hawk appeared. Their greeting was terse. Immediately they moved forward together.

When they approached the two sentinel oaks they turned to their right and slunk through brush and low-hanging branches towards the shelter of up-thrown rock between the trees.

At last they saw their goal—a black indentation in the rocks that disappeared into the hollow between two of the greater boulders. The hole was big enough for a man to enter, but when the hooded man stooped and approached the cave, Blue Hawk's hand clamped around his wrist.

"Wait, *señor*. I think—"

The hooded man paused, watched Blue Hawk stoop, smell of the cave mouth before them. Instantly he wheeled and frowned.

"I was afraid, *señor*. We stop here."

The masked man stepped aside while the Indian moved into

the brush and reappeared with a thick bundle in his arms. The sticks, he noticed, were dry as timber, and he nodded shortly, understandingly. Blue Hawk dropped the pile near the cave entrance and applied a lighted match at their base.

Flames suddenly flared up from the stack of brush. Rapidly the Indian grasped each flaming individual piece and flung it into the mouth of the cavern. There was a whining, rustling sound inside. The twisting, sliding sound of tenuous soft bodies on earth.

Then suddenly a clatter broke from the inside of the cavern. A thousand high-pitched wooden rattles sounded. From the mouth of the cave, like sliding brown shadows writhing and twisting in their haste, came a score of diamond-backs. Big ones, small ones, each with its rattle box splitting the air.

Neither Blue Hawk nor the hooded man paused to count or to kill them as the swarm of muscular, hideous bodies crowded out of the cavern. Soon the cave before them was silent.

Then Blue Hawk nodded and stepped to enter.

"They are all gone, *señor*. You see too, *señor*, there are men's footprints here in the mouth. And if I am not mistaken, there is one I know."

The eyes beneath the hood narrowed. For he had seen, too, as the Indian had that at the mouth of the cave was imprinted the long-toed riding boot that marked the "gentleman of the knife."

CHAPTER XXX

AN ADVERTISEMENT

WHEN THE MATCH the masked man brought forth flared inside the cave, both from him and the Indian burst low exclamations.

The cave was neither large nor long. A man could stand within it at virtually full height.

There in the flickering light of the match they saw not two but three bodies. Gangling lay crosswise of the cave, his body twisted in its last terrible agonies from the bites of the snakes. Near his, lay the form of Old Jake Sandell stung to death by a hundred terrible fangs.

But the sight that had clamped grim fingers about the vitals of the two standing men was another shape.

Crazy Fred sat in the corner. His mouth still open, his face a hideous mask of pain-tortured death. And in one hand he held a package covered with brown paper.

The hooded man's voice was low. "He must have come here first, right after I left him at the mouth of the valley. When he said he had 'protected' the cave where he saw Harris hide his bonds in, he meant these snakes. But he never thought they would bite him. Good God, what a death!"

The masked man stepped forward. The air of the cave was dank, putrid with the insistent, terrible odor of the reptiles. He took the package from Crazy Fred's dead hands and pulled it open.

The papers inside brought a low-voiced curse from deep within him. For as he had suspected, the package held not money, but certificates. And each one was printed with information showing that it was representative of one thousand dollars of ownership in the Cattlemen's Trust of Red Rocks.

"He didn't buy Harris' share," snapped the hooded figure. "That controlling interest was never his, every paper he showed me was a forgery! He couldn't get the stocks, so he kidnaped the girl trying to stall me off. With this end—"

"*Si,*" said the Indian, softly. "But, *señor,*" a slow smile ran across the bronzed features, "you have not yet seen this which I have just taken from Crazy Fred's hands."

He held forth a piece of paper, grimy and crumpled, yet still able to show its undeniable color—pink.

"You see, *señor*, he had finally found where he left it."

Slowly the hooded man undid the paper and spread it before him.

It was a poster, an advertising poster, done in a style many years old. One that might have been found on a deserted barn wall or an ancient fence. Across its pink face was reproduced the face and shoulders of a man in a tight, round-necked shirt.

The date was twenty years before and it read:

ATTENTION!

We take great pleasure in presenting tonight the SPEC-TACULAR KNIFE-THROWING ACT supreme. For one thin ten cent piece you can witness the HAIR-RAISING and THRILLING SPECTACLE of an artist throwing KNIVES, AXES, HATCHETS and SWORDS at a HU-MAN FIGURE—and *never touching it!*
HOLCONT'S VARIETY HALL, BISBEE, ARIZONA

And the picture above that old-style wording was that of the man dead at their feet, Harold S. Gangling.

CHAPTER XXXI

WORDS ON A HILLSIDE

L EONA HARRIS SHOOK her head. "Brother?" she asked. "He told you that he was Father's brother?"

The man in the mask nodded. The five figures were on the brush-lined hillside of Desolation Valley. Near the man in the mask stood Blue Hawk. On the ground, his lean lengthy shape outstretched, lay Jimmie Weeder with a bullet wound in his right arm but a wide and reckless grin on his face. A Closed C puncher was just bringing up a hat-full of water ordered by the girl to bathe the flesh wound.

She had stood up, facing the man in the mask with wondering eyes.

"That's what he said," repeated the hooded man. "Claimed he was your father's brother since I first ran into him. Was he?"

The girl smiled slowly. "No. I remember now Father did say something and laughed later about the crazy man of Gila who had told someone, I think it was Harold Gangling, he was father's brother. Evidently his addled mind after a period of time, began to accept Father as one—since Father always had the habit of calling people 'brother.' A habit he brought from the East when a small boy. No one knows exactly who Fred was. Just some poor desert tramp who wandered into Gila and stayed there. How do you think he knew about Father's hiding place?"

The hooded man turned slowly. For some time now the restlessness of his spirit, the desire to be on the move once more with his self-chosen duty accomplished, had shown in his movements.

"We're riding west and we're three days behind on territory covered," he said, "but to make it short, here's how I've mulled it out in what little time I've had. Your father decided he was about through with the banking business and wanted to retire about the time you and Jimmie Weeder wanted to marry. To protect the bank, he decided to sell his interest somewhere out of town and not to Gangling. He must have suspected Gangling and decided to transfer his shares without Gangling's knowledge. The best way to do that was to take them out of the bank where Gangling couldn't see them and carry on the deal in private. Gangling would then not be able to buy up shares of the bank because he didn't know where they were going to be sold. If your father sold them off a share at a time, Gangling couldn't keep up with where they were going. If they had been put on sale, he could have over-bid almost everyone else in Red Rocks.

So your father started out, to go around through the ranches and sell out little by little and keep the bank's control split up among the ranchers.

"Gangling would never know until the stock was sold that the bank's control was in someone else's hands. But he found out about it and made the daring play of killing your father and taking the stock under forged bills of sale. Your father did not have the certificates on him when he died.

"He had hidden them up here and Crazy Fred had seen him. Crazy Fred decided that as long as your father had been so good to him, his reward would be to protect whatever your father had put in the cave. So he planted there a lot of diamond-backs—which he seemed to be collecting. When we returned to Gila this morning, the shocks he had been through had cleared up his mind a lot. He remembered all about the cave, except the rattlesnakes. I sent Blue Hawk for Jimmie Weeder—who was hiding outside his ranch from Beanpole Jackson—and started here with Fred. The first thing I saw was gun smoke and the next thing a Sandell about to brain you."

A slow smile crept across the girl's features as he went on.

"Gangling had set the stage. I warned him, told him to produce the bonds in forty-eight hours. To protect himself he kidnaped you. To get help for that, he had to talk the Sandells into doing it. For their share they would get the Closed C on the Cattlemen's Trust's demand note which he could foreclose on after Paw Weeder's death. But he didn't get that far."

The girl nodded and watched the two men turn and mount their horses that had been idling nearby.

She said with emotion: "After all you've done, you won't let us know who you are or where you are going—"

"Or," added the redhead slowly, "let us thank you. If you come back this way—"

The hooded head shook. "Not us," the masked man said. "We

have a long trail stretching out before us—the Owl Hoot Trail, as they say in Texas—a lonesome one."

He turned his head as if eager to be gone.

"We ride, Hawk?"

Silently the Indian nodded. *"Si, señor.* South?"

"And west," said the hooded one. *"Adiós!"*

With a wave of the hand the hooded man pressed the stout flanks of the black stallion and moved up the steep valley-side. Behind him, clambering cat-like through the brush went *El Acedero*—the sorrel one—with the black-hatted Indian in its saddle.

When the riders reached the valley rim, outlined against the farther blue and ruddy sky, the figures below saw two hands wave in farewell and disappear beyond the horizon.

"He's gone," said the girl as she turned.

"Yes. For good, I'm afraid," said the redhead, stretched on the ground. Then a queer intense light came into his eyes.

"But I'm not!" the last, Weeder said stoutly, his eyes reassuring the girl that still there remained one man who ached for this tragic, tender, beautiful girl to rely upon him.

THE VALLEY
OF CRUCIFIXION

LINCOLN HOFFMAN

DON ATTERO'S CROSS

I T WAS PRECISELY midnight when the eerie cries of a mountain lion shattered the tomb-like silence of Deep Water Valley. They floated on the crisp night air—long-drawn banshee's wails that were ghastly and pregnant with warning. Yet there was nothing unfriendly about them. They rather seemed to beg for a like response from some spot in the valley. But no answer came—immediately.

Silence, intense and oppressive, gripped the moonlit expanse. No living tiling stirred; not a leaf rustled. It was as if the cold hand of death had touched everything capable of sound or motion.

On the top of Mission Ridge, silhouetted against the full moon, a massive wooden cross stood like a guardian sentry watching over the valley, bidding the animal to stop its chilling cries and move on. Then came the answer of another mountain cat.

Still no human eye could have discerned a moving thing. Don Attero—had he stood beside his self-made monument—might have searched the great valley with a spy glass and still failed to discover that all the uncanny cries were born in the throats and mouths of two mounted men who moved like wool-shod ghosts, slowly and always in the thickest shadows of trees, bush, and rook.

Soon the two phantom riders were side by side. Their greetings were whispered, short, but they rang with the sincere

pleasure of men glad to be together again. And in their very greetings was something that told of their being impressed by the awesome valley, by the great wooden cross even now bidding them be on their way—if they valued their lives.

But they sat their horses with that false ease of men whose vigilance never truly relaxes. For a while neither of them spoke nor moved, contenting themselves by studying the silent, silvered scene—especially the wooden cross.

The smaller of the men was first to move and speak. His bronzed, high-cheeked face, long hair, and stately posture marked him as a son of the Rio Grande country. His name was Blue Hawk, a heritage, perhaps, of some Yaqui chief.

"I do not like this place, *señor*," he said blankly. "We ride?"

His companion did not answer, and his very silence, blending with his strange black garb, made him a picture of grim strength—and a doubly unforgettable man. For every inch of him was black, and blended with the high-strung black stallion he sat upon. His Stetson was clean—and black. From beneath its broad, stiff brim flowed a black hood, slotted to see through, long enough to touch his broad shoulders from which hung a great black *mantilla*. His gloves were the finest obtainable anywhere—and black. His high-heeled boots were black and all but buried in the black leather about his stirrups.

"Don Attero's cross, Blue Hawk?" he asked at last, almost reverently.

"*Si, señor.*" He paused as if he struggled against asking a question to which he already knew the answer. "You know the story of the cross, *señor?*"

The hooded head nodded. Not boastfully. Several states would have stopped hunting for The Masked Rider if he did not have the happy faculty of keeping well informed, not only as to where danger lurked, but as to landmarks, history—and the general characters of a given section's inhabitants. And what the famous outlaw once heard he seldom forgot. To that, also, he owed the fact that he was still alive.

"I have heard," he said eventually, "of the cross, but not about what I see there now."

He stared at the gigantic post and the long horizontal beam. Through his mind flashed the story of long dead Don Attero. The Mexican Spaniard was a discredited priest who had settled here and brought in families to found his own kingdom and his own religious sect. Given most fertile land, born a natural leader, he made Deep Water Valley a paradise that knew neither crime nor greed, want nor envy. Here dwelt his chosen people in peace and plenty. He himself had hewn the timbers and erected the colossal cross.

"By this sign I shall always keep you from harm," he had said at the dedication. "Beneath these timbers shall be my grave and they and I shall always be here to rout want and strife—and the curse of heaven on him who brings aught but good to Deep Water Valley."

BUT MAN PROPOSES and God disposes. Don Attero himself died by the gun of one of his followers who sought the throne of Valley King. Crime, greed, want, and envy swept the fertile spot so masterfully that within a half century Attero's sect was unknown. Only the cross remained—above his grave—mutely ridiculing his dreams.

"I have heard," repeated the outlaw in black. "But—"

Blue Hawk sat tensely now. He too stared at the distant symbol of God. "Something is on the cross, *señor!*"

"Something jumps up and down at its base—maybe on Attero's grave. Now I make out a...."

He clipped the sentence. It was a habit with him never to claim or guess, always to be dead certain. In another few minutes he knew!

"Some *hombre's* swung something from each end of the cross beam, Blue Hawk. Never heard tell of any sensible reason to decorate Attero's monument at midnight."

The Indian's face remained blank. "Perhaps a long forgotten member of the Don's party pays his respects, *señor?* Like in my country, once a year—on the day he died—we put flowers on my father's tombstone. Is it not mebbe here the same?"

"Maybe," drawled the outlaw. "But do you climb so high— when it's so hard to do? Now that *hombre* is dragging something closer to the cross."

"*Si!* Heavy, *señor,* no? Look. He throws ropes above. You think mebbe he tries to get that heavy thing up on the cross? Wait, *señor!* Do not go! I have heard that bad luck pursues the man who goes too close to Don Attero's grave. I do not like—"

His mouth closed. For he knew the outlaw had decided—and precious few of his decisions were ever changed, or hasty and smacking of folly that might result in disaster.

The Masked Rider advanced only a few paces. He stopped, melting into the inky blackness beside a great rock. Then quietly and decidedly, he moved on again, never out of cover. His keen eyes were riveted to a spot where the valley walls came close together, and where a river raced swiftly but noiselessly far, far below.

He saw now that what had formerly appeared to be one

immense valley was in reality two; as if some mythical giant had flung down a tremendous dumbbell, removed it and left only two big clefts in the earth with this narrow canyon marking the cross-piece between the balls on each end.

The cross of Don Attero was now directly opposite, mute proof that in time the leader had meant to watch over both valleys, to parcel out the land to newcomers and rule them as he did those families nestled down in the first section.

Blue Hawk pulled up behind the outlaw. "The man's work is finished *señor.* See! He brings a horse from behind those—"

"That's a dog jumping up and down." Shrill, alarmed yelps came hard on The Masked Rider's conclusions. He saw that now the animal had deserted the burdened cross and was yelping and jumping at the rider's mount. Patently the dog objected to the rider's leaving the scene.

For another half minute the phantom in black sat with his mind cleaved in two. Such mysterious things held him in a vise-like grip. But curiosity had led many a wanted man to a six-foot hole.

The Masked Rider turned his stallion. "We ride, Blue Hawk. It's none of our business if some fool finds pleasure in—"

A shot rang out. There came the pitiful yelps of a dog. The outlaw sat stiff as steel. Behind the black hood his mouth was a grim gash; his teeth were so tightly clenched that veins stood out on his temples. Again a six-gun barked. A dark splotch dragging across the ground seemed to rise a few inches, then flatten out. Silence!

Even then the phantom curbed both temper and wonder. A man should not kill a dog, but that alone was not reason enough to rush pell-mell into what might still prove to be a trap. Stranger devices than decorating a cross at midnight and killing a dog had been made to lure outlaws. Yet The Masked Rider began to search out a safe way from the heights to the floor of the valley and up the other side.

BLUE HAWK SENSED this. A slight frown made his face darker. "A man's neck is better than a look at a dead dog, *señor*," he insinuated.

"*Si*. But sometimes a man must get closer to what he sees— if he ever wants to have peace of mind and call himself a man again. And maybe a look at a dead dog won't hurt any—if we keep far enough away."

"The curse of Don Attero is said to be on anybody who comes too close to the grave, *señor*."

The outlaw made no answer. When he moved again, it was toward the cross. And it was upon those hand-hewn timbers that his eyes were riveted. He would satisfy himself as to what those decorations were. It would do no harm to know that one of Don Attero's followers was still alive and paying homage— and killing dogs.

CHAPTER II

GOOD MEN AND BAD

THANKS TO THE mailed fist of Sheriff Lande, Gold Creek had far outstripped cowtowns in any of the bordering counties. No sensible wanted man lingered here. To stay even a few hours was to be impressed with the fact that here was law and order; peace and security, if you wanted it—the calaboose or a quick escort out if you didn't. Here cash and goods were safe, women respected, and men quickly appraised and treated according to assay. Yet Gold Creek could be fooled!

In The Western Sun Saloon where a man could get as drunk as sin if he could handle himself properly when super-cargoed, a middle-aged man in cow clothes leaned heavily on the bar.

His name was Pete Haskell. Tall, thin, his face browned by sun and storm, he was a cattle pioneer; a man who'd fought his way up from a niggardly beginning and was now the unanimously elected guide and counsellor of practically every ranch owner in the county. Men put their troubles into Haskell's hands and he showed them an easy out—until recently.

Haskell's present mood was far from pleasant. No man can see a storm destined to sweep away his life's work come up on the horizon, and feel otherwise. Now he rolled an empty glass between his brown, bony hands and silently cursed because such a storm was brewing and he could do nothing—for himself or any other cattleman.

"No, Tim," he said sourly, without looking at the worried cowman beside him. "I don't know what to do. The hell of it is that they got as much right here as us."

"But this was always free an' open *cattle* range," blasted Tim Callan. "First come—"

"Ain't always first served—nor best served."

Callan scowled, "There ought to be a law—"

"There is a law," said a stern-faced man at the door behind Haskell. "It says that if you own somethin', lock, stock, an' barrel, you can do as you see fit therewith—without consultin' anybody but yoreself."

Haskell and Callan pivoted. Their faces betrayed no animosity toward Sheriff Lande, who approached them as a friend.

Lande was a big, well-fed man of forty-five. The years had not passed him lightly, but he gave the impression of possessing a fount of dormant energy. He stood between the cowmen. The glances he gave them were of understanding and sympathy. At times the law might be distasteful to him, but it was his duty to uphold it—and neither friend nor foe could make him shirk his responsibilities.

"You gents are alarmed over nothin'," he drawled. "I wouldn't howl, 'Wolf!' till there was one in sight."

Haskell scowled. "You've been away three days, Lande. Meanwhile the wolf has moved in. Russ Bartle has advertised land for sale for tobacco raisin' in the north end of Deep Water Valley!"

The sheriff appeared stunned. Then facts routed personal feelings and surprise. "It ain't against the law for him to sell land he owns."

Tim Callan almost exploded. "It ought to be, when farm fences can keep our beef from Deep Water River till after it runs through Alkali Flats an' ain't fit for man or beast. I got half a notion to—"

"I know," cut in Lande. "Half a notion to cut fences, fire buildings, drive these tobacco farmers out—or kill 'em off." He shook his gray head and his hand sought Callan's shoulder. "We're old friends, Tim. I'm hopin' you never get more than half a notion about such doings. Fact is, I wish you wouldn't ever mention 'em again. Because what's been done already in the valley, might be laid at yore door."

Haskell sprang to his friend's defense. "I've told you before that no cattleman had anything to do with any of the fires or killin's in the valley. We aimed to protect our interests legally, *sabe?* That we've done—so far."

"But—"

"I'll blame no one for kickin' over the traces when bread an' butter's taken out o' their mouth. I wouldn't ask any man to sit twiddlin' his thumbs while Bartle brings in' more farmers to squeeze him out o' house an' business."

THE SHERIFF WAS pained. "You ain't advisin' anybody to keep his bread an' house an' business—with the help of a six-gun an' torch?"

"I ain't, till I'm driven to it. Meanwhile I've got another pair of cards to play. Might as well be done now." He turned from the bar reluctantly, read the questions in Lande's eyes and volunteered, "I'm goin' to see Russ Bartle. He must meet me half way."

"If he doesn't?" asked Lande thickly.

Haskell did not answer. He even disliked to think about the aftermath if Russ Bartle failed to see light. He walked slowly down the dark, deserted street like a man bent on a hated errand he knows will be in vain.

A light glowed in a window over the bank. Russ Bartle was running true to form. He was known as a sun-dodger, sleeping most of the hot day and doing business at any ungodly hour.

Haskell knocked; he peered through a glass panel and up a flight of dimly lighted stairs. A man appeared at the landing above. He pulled a lever. Haskell heard the spring bolt slide back. He went in and climbed the steps, knowing he wasn't welcome.

Bartle sat down at his desk in one corner of the miserly furnished room that served as office, kitchen, living-room, and bedroom. He was a sharp-eyed man, forty, turning gray at the temples. Now, sneering at the man who he knew was a bitter enemy, he looked exactly what he was—shrewd, ruthless, a man who would trade his soul for something to deposit in a bank.

"Yes, Haskell!" he gloated. "You've come to see me about my advertisements for land buyers?"

"In a way."

"And you're going to tell me that—"

"That what yo're goin' to do in the valley will bust every cattleman in these parts." Haskell's eyes bored straight into Bartle's. "If yore dad was alive. I wouldn't be here. Two reasons, Russ. He'd be skinned alive before he'd cut up an' fence the north end o' Deep Water Valley."

"The other reason?" smirked Bartle.

"Cattlemen won't take this sittin' down!"

Bartle laughed. "Then they'll have to—standing up." He drummed on a ledger with soft white fingers. "That valley is mine. The law holds that."

"I know. *You* know." Haskell hunched forward in his chair. "Men can be driven to bust laws, Bartle. I've kept several from so doin'—till now. I'm like a dam holdin' back too much water, *sabe?* I'm goin' to get washed aside when yore first tobacco farmer sets hisself up in the north end o' the valley. Then, remember this; me, you, an' all those already in Deep Water will suffer."

Bartle frowned. "I'm not afraid of your threats. Let your damn cattlemen do as they will. For every tobacco man you beef men drive out or kill off, I'll bring in two." A clucking sound issued from his throat. "Your clique burned the drying shed of Mike Chapman. Your clique killed Steve Ransom." He glared at Haskell. "Didn't I bring in four new men? Nothing you fellows can do will make me stop."

"Will you sell us the north end of the valley?" cut in Haskell sharply. "Will you sell every inch north of Don Attero's cross?"

Bartle's mouth stood agape. Figures flashed through his quick brain. "Yes! Why not?" He thumbed the pages of the ledger, ran his finger to the bottom of a long column. "It'll cost you exactly three hundred and fifty thousand dollars—cash."

Haskell gulped. "Twenty times what it's worth—because you've got the whip hand, huh?" He got up from his chair, defeated, bitter, belligerent. "All our ranches an' stock won't fetch that."

"Really?" grinned Bartle. "Why I always thought you lords of all creation were worth millions. You ought to be—if you want to tell all mankind what they can do and what they can not do."

"Listen to me! We can raise mebbe seventy-five thousand cash between us. We'll buy—"

"At my price. My terms. Otherwise you'll have to put up with new neighbors."

HASKELL TRUDGED TO the door. "I've had my say. I'm tellin' you that no tobacco man sets hisself up in the north end o' Deep Water Valley. Now go on with yore damn plans."

He stormed out.

"I will!" shouted Bartle. He turned to his ledger. Behind the first entry on the page there was a red check. He smiled. "Fool! Wonder what he'd have said if I told him that the first of the north end settlers might arrive before he gets home?"

Then Bartle prepared to go out. He knew the imminence of open warfare between cattlemen and tobacco farmers. And he felt happy as a munition manufacturer at a declaration of war. Let 'em fight! Under the smoke screen of battle there would be safety—and profits—for him.

He rode through Gold Creek inwardly laughing at its law and order that caused all criminals to give it wide berth. It would be a long time before any one suspected him.

CHAPTER III

NAILS OF SATAN

THE MASKED RIDER was well aware of the fact that a straight line is the shortest way between two points. For him, it was also the most dangerous. Hence he traveled the more difficult and longer route across the great moonlit valley and up to the brow of Mission Ridge.

Within sight of Don Attero's cross he stopped, slid from his saddle and ground-roped the stallion. He went on afoot, a swift-moving, crouching thing that darted across open silvered spaces and paused in black shadows. Blue Hawk was close behind—another phantom thing streaking through the night.

The dead dog drew their casual glance. The things on Attero's self-made monument froze their blood.

From the ends of the horizontal beam swung bunches of tobacco. Spread-eagled, clumsily spiked, was a youth of not more than nineteen. About his neck hung two stalks of tobacco. If anything was needed to complete the ghastly picture, the moon supplied it; it seemed to center all its brilliance on the victim's agonized face.

At times revulsion paralyzes. Blue Hawk and the outlaw could only look at the fearful thing before them. Neither could speak, but both their hearts pounded at this proof that some human animal roamed these parts unbridled, unchallenged; some fiendish disciple of Satan, unworthy of rope or bullets.

The Masked Rider's determination flamed in the narrowed eyes behind the slits. Only long practiced self-control kept an oath from his lips. He faced the Indian.

"Trail that horse, Blue Hawk. But do nothing—even if you overtake that buzzard."

The Indian was amazed. "I do not give him chance to draw, *señor?* I do not kill him? *Madre de Dios!* Such a one should be even killed from behind!"

"No, Blue Hawk. He must live—for a while."

"It serves some purpose, *señor?* Some good conies of this devil's life? This time you must be mistaken, *señor.*"

"I may be. But something big may be behind this, *sabe?* He shot that kid first. Killed. Why wasn't he satisfied?"

"Mebbe the devil…." The Indian shook his head in defeat. "*Si!* Why wasn't he?"

"We'll try to find out. Trail him. In the morning I'll be in Gold Creek."

The Indian started, not in haste or anxiety, but cautiously like a blue-blooded hound that has a scent he will not lose and quarry he will not harm.

The outlaw moved on in self-condemnation. Why had he wasted so much precious time learning this hideous truth? Even now he might be choking the truth out of the culprit's throat.

He clipped his thoughts. His eyes bulged. He stood like a man who fears for his own sanity. For a few minutes he was as still as the trunk of the towering oak at his back. Then he knew his ears had not been false. He did hear singing!

It came closer. Clearer. The voices were distinctly those of two men and a woman—a young woman, he judged by her notes. Their voices were effervescent with hope and the stuff that dreams are made of.

Easterners, he concluded when he could make out the words of their songs. Natives would sing the solemn songs of the lonely trail, the songs of the puncher riding the edge of the bedded-down herd.

The Masked Rider listened in rapt attention. The rumble of steel-rimmed wheels on stone came to him. The sound told him this was no light buckboard returning with tired merry-makers from some cowtown dance, but a heavy wagon, spring-less and loaded with all it could carry.

HE LOOKED AT the grim cross, considered the hour. Settlers! Probably about to get their first glimpse of the valley. Yes, he remembered now—tales of families come in hopes that Don Attero's peace and plenty was still to be had; tales of disillusioned families going back East or South or North, cynical families glad to get out with fragments of their worldly possessions still intact.

"Coming to hell," gritted the outlaw, "if that cross means anything."

He saw no point in waiting for the wagon to round the bend in the long trail so plain in the moonlight. He mounted, deter-mined to be on his way. But now the woman sang alone—a song so appealing, so full of the peace and contentment she hoped to find here, that it loosened the gloved hands that would turn the stallion about and let them come on unwarned of realities.

Why he looked down into the valley, he did not know. In that startled instant his decision was made. He would—he must—tell these hopefuls now. For below, far to the south, a pillar of flame and smoke had suddenly been born. In a moment he recognized the blazing thing as a tobacco drying shed—and he recalled tales of arson and murder that belied the superficial peace and contentment he had seen in the valley before the flame colored the sky.

Slight side pressure of his stirrups sent the black stallion tearing through the night. He would make that bend before the wagon, run the great risk that always attended his every contact with other human beings, speak his piece and let them elect to heed his warning or drive on. More he could not do.

CHAPTER IV

DREAMS

A ROUND THE BEND in the Mission Ridge trail stood a double teamed wagon piled high with farm tools and household goods. The girl on the seat was worried. The fragile hands that held the reins shook with misgiving. The hopeful song of a moment ago was forgotten. She sat like one who had expected a caress and felt a harsh slap. A lame horse! It loomed like a calamity, a forecast of more bitter disappointments, for they were not yet in sight of Deep Water Valley.

The man beside the girl puffed a cigarette; his hands were clasped over his knees and he was obviously thinking about something pleasant.

Another man was at the head of the left lead horse. He looked like one afraid of finding the worst answer to a bad problem. He lifted the horse's hoof, struggled to get it between his knees and into the moon's rays. Success brought an exclamation of relief, a laugh of thankfulness.

"Told you! Only a stone wedged in beside the frog. I'll have it out in a minute."

The animal jerked its foot free. Chet Maxon jumped aside, escaped an angry lash of the steeled hoof by an inch. Without hesitation or aroused wrath, he tried again to lift the animal's hoof.

"Help him, Clarke," said Ellen sharply to the man beside her.

Clarke Weber scowled. "He can manage alone. Why it's—there you go! He's got the stone out."

The wagon soon moved on. Ellen and her brother dismissed the proof of Clarke's laziness. Nor did they chide him about it. One suffers in silence when the other has made a venture possible. But they did steal side glances at Clarke.

He was a heavy-eyed fellow, sharp-nosed, loose-mouthed. He slouched in the seat staring straight ahead, patiently famished for sight of the promised land. When the wagon was partly around the bend, he snatched at the reins in Chet's hands, stopped the teams and hungrily gazed down into the bit of valley that was visible.

"Paradise," he breathed. "The place to plant an acorn to grow a mighty oak!" He touched Ellen's hand. "A small beginning, fast, steady growth. In time I hope to own all of the valley. Bartle's a fool to sell any of it. With such soil and climate there's a sure fortune in the tobacco that can be raised here."

The girl's eyes were trained ahead—the eyes of a day-dreamer. "Fortune! Who cares? If we find peace and enough to eat, I'll be more than satisfied."

"Same here," said her brother. He looked sadly at Clarke. "Why do you always think about fortunes and a kingdom of your own? Three times you staked everything you had on a try to double your money. When we started for Deep Water you said you were cured, that the simple things of life were enough."

"Ambition runs in the family, I guess," snapped Clarke. "All I expect to do here will be done for Ellen's sake and—well, let's go on. I'm anxious to compare the house with Bartle's description."

A hundred feet of trail went under the wheels. Three faces

changed, three bodies stiffened, and three pairs of wide eyes were on the red sky where sparks shot upward from a blazing pile.

Even as the newcomers stared below, there came the half-muffled barks of a gun. Then, with two surprises still stunning them, they faced the greatest shock of all.

Where he came from or how, no one knew. But sudden as death he was at the head of the team—a man so starkly attired in black that Clarke and the two Maxons blinked unbelievingly.

"The Masked Rider," Clarke squeezed out. He had heard of the black phantom, in a saloon—while Ellen and Chet had struggled to load the wagon. Instantly the most interesting part of the story flashed through his nimble brain; that the outlaw was worth a small fortune, delivered dead or alive.

The hooded apparition walked his mount tensely beside the horses and stopped so close to the trembling girl that he could have touched her fragile hand. "Settlers? Moving into Deep Water Valley?"

The girl shrank from him. "Y-yes."

He looked at her with compassion, her song still in his ears. "Change your mind, ma'am. I know it'll hurt. But if you insist on staying here you'll get hurt even more."

ELLEN WAS IMPRESSED. She had expected commands rasped out while a gun covered her and the two men. She quickly caught the plea, the sincerity of the outlaw's gently spoken words. All her terror vanished.

"Around this bend is Don Attero's cross. A man is nailed to it. That fire below is also a warning that farmers are not wanted here."

"But we couldn't turn back now. We'd lose—"

"Your lives, perhaps, if you stay!"

If the outlaw noticed the sneer on Clarke Weber's face, he gave no sign. Nor did his attitude alter when he must have known that Clarke's hand was sliding beneath a seat blanket and his body was inching forward as if he sought to look around the girl and yet hide behind her.

Tense silence reigned for half a minute. Then sharp and derisively came Clarke's voice.

"Why do you try to frighten us?"

"Frighten you?" The Masked Rider's tone was mild. "If good advice frightens, then God help the three of you—when you're settled down there." He nodded toward the valley.

Clarke sat like a coiled snake. "You'll never nail one of us to Don Attero's cross. You'll never set any of our buildings afire. Because—" He paused. Assured that the phantom expected no worse than cutting words, he rapped out, "Because you've seen your last sunrise!"

Few men could snatch and level a six-gun as fast as Clarke Weber did while he pronounced that sentence of death. But even faster the outlaw's gloved hand flashed out from beneath his black cloak. Gun metal caught the moon's silvered rays. A sliver of flame leaped forth. Lead crunched into a finger of Clarke's hand. He cried out as his weapon slid from limp fingers. Then in utter amazement he wilted with the realization that for failure death must be his portion.

The Masked Rider holstered his smoking Colt. His eyes and voice were still mild when he said, "If you try that stunt again, do it faster, *sabe,* and not when you're looking at me. Another *hombre* might squeeze his trigger *twice.*"

The girl recovered power of speech. "You're sure that—"

"I told you what I know." The Masked Rider backed into the shadow of rock.

There was no sound to tell whether he waited or had gone as silently as he had come.

The trio on the wagon did not move. Suddenly Clarke Weber jumped to the ground and retrieved his gun.

"Damn him!" he growled. "The next time—"

"He might not be as generous as he was a moment ago," interrupted Ellen bitterly. "Why did you draw that gun?"

He was aware of an opening chasm between him and the girl he professed to love. It did not worry him.

"Because he's worth a small fortune—dead or alive," he went on. "And now that I know he's in these parts, I see how we're going to pay Bartle the balance due on our land."

"With the outlaw's body?" demanded Chet savagely. "You'd stoop that low—after he warned us to expect trouble?"

"Warned hell! It wouldn't surprise me if I learned he crucified that man and set that fire. Whether he did or not, I'm paying more attention to getting him than I am to farming."

Chet picked up the reins. The wagon creaked on. Even before it completely turned the bend and stopped near the ghastly cross, the silence of fear and disillusion dropped over it like a clammy blanket.

On Chet's side of the trail stood the cross; on Ellen's side, far below, glowed the embers of the fire. It was as if some mocking son of Satan had prepared fitting welcoming signs so totally discouraging that neither Chet nor Ellen could imagine any one more miserable than they. Nor that greater tragedy even now stalked near those hot ruins below.

CHAPTER V

HAVOC

ALL OF LIFE is not in a cash book. At times men, young and old, are so burdened that their minds reel with countless thoughts, yet money is entirely forgotten.

So it was with Burr Aldman.

Only an hour ago he and his dad had sat at the table and

figured that the contents of the crammed tobacco drying shed would sell for enough to take up the next note due on the farm.

"One thing we ain't figgered, son," the old man had said ominously. "They burned the dryin' shed o' Mike Chapman. They killed Steve Ransom. Tomorrow mornin' we start balin' an' haulin' that tobacco out o' here."

An hour ago! Now Burr Aldman knelt so close to pungent ruins that he could feel the heat of the ashes. And stretched on the ground was his dad—life's blood gushing from a stomach bullet wound; his wrinkled face so distorted by pain that Burr wished death would clip the thread of life that only meant prolonged agony.

"I—I told you, son. It wasn't only Chapman an'—an' Ransom they wanted riddance of. Those beef men ain't stoppin' at—at nothin' till they've run out—every tobacco man in—in the valley."

Burr was twenty-one an hour ago. He was like forty now, bitter as gall, with but one purpose in life—to find the man who tossed that torch into the shed; the man who fired point blank at his unarmed father. Cattleman! Knowing not which one, he heaped his scalding oaths upon the heads of all of them.

"Yes, Dad," he squeezed out. "Beef men. Damn 'em! I'll pay 'em back, coin for coin, till either lead or rope stops me."

"No, son. That ain't the way. You wouldn't get—get far. An'—an' you'd profit none. The thing to do is get out o' this hell-hole. See—see Bartle. He'll help you find somebody to buy the farm. He—he's a good man, son. He'll help you. But get out now. Start as soon as—as your brother Sam gets back."

"You mean pull out tonight, Dad? Let 'em think I'm scared?"

"Tonight, son. 'Member how we planned what we was goin' to do tomorrow? You an' Sam pull out tonight. Promise me you will, Burr."

"All right, Dad. Tonight. Soon as Sam gets back. I—I hate like hell to promise, but—"

No need to say anything more. Pop Aldman's wish when he first sighted Deep Water Valley had been granted. He died in it; stretched on the soil that nature touched with a generous hand.

Burr staggered upright. His weary eyes shifted from corpse to smouldering ash heap. Embers of pleasant dreams. He looked up at Mission Ridge; at Don Attero's cross, that distance made as small as a crucifix a nun wears about her neck. A sneer twisted Burr's mouth. He knew the legend of the Mexican-Spaniard, of cross and grave shielding valley inhabitants from harm.

"Get up, Attero," he cried out in spite of himself. "Get up, look here and see what they've done!"

His teeth clicked together. He spun on his heels, snatching out the six-gun tucked beneath his belt. Then he remembered, swallowed hard and called hopefully, "That you, Sam?"

By the approaching man's stride he knew he was mistaken. The six-gun flung upward. His finger danced on the trigger.

"Keep comin'," he commanded, sensing foe.

A Mexican Indian came into the dying glow of the ruins. At first Burr Aldman knew the grip of suspicion. Memory served him well. The man with the torch and gun was taller, moved like one younger and was not dressed as this stranger. Then too, this weather-tanned face was markedly friendly and sympathetic and the eyes were those of a man who could not lie or deceive unless more than his own life depended upon it.

"I see fire. I come fast. I hear shots. I think mebbe I am of help, *señor*, but—" He looked at the remains of Pop Aldman. "I am too late, no?"

"Yes. Too late."

"Mebbe I can do for you something?"

"No. I'm pullin' out soon's my brother Sam gets back."

"Your brother?" said Blue Hawk. His voice was thick with

pity, for his eyes were on the hoof prints of a horse—fresh prints. They had been once at Don Attero's cross! "Your brother?"

"He went up Mission Ridge. Knows a gal up there."

"Nineteen mebbe? Hair like straw? Blue shirt? Shoes, not boots?"

"That's Sam, all right. You know him?"

THE INDIAN WAS hard-pressed for words. He himself held death in contempt, but he knew that to others the grim reaper—especially when he struck twice in the one night—was vicious and heart-rending. He went closer to Burr.

"*Amigo*, Sam does not come back."

"What?"

"It is true. Sam and this fine old man—they are together, *sabe?*"

Burr winced. "You can't mean that Sam's dead?"

"*Si*. By the hand of a rat." Blue Hawk pointed to the distant cross. "Sam. Like the Saviour on Calvary."

The truth seeped into Burr's mind, ate into his heart like a corroding poison. "That leaves me—on their dead list," he mumbled. "For their sake, I hope they get me quick!"

Blue Hawk comprehended, "You try to find this rat, no?"

"Rats! Not one. All cattlemen, with Pete Haskell the ring leader."

"And you, *amigo?* Alone. You think you fight long? Oh, no. They make of you a candle. Puff! You are finished."

"I don't know who you are or why I should tell you, but this much I'll chance saying—that as they did to my brother and my dad, I'll do to them; in the night, like a sneak thief that hasn't guts enough to work in the open."

The Indian knew a solemn vow when he heard it. "There is much law in this county, *amigo*. In Gold Creek Sheriff Lande is said to—but I see you fear nothing, that you would like to die fighting for what you think is the right. So be it then." He held out a friendly hand. *"Adiós.* Who knows but that you shall not fight alone after all?"

CHAPTER VI

HUNTERS

S HERIFF LANDE ENDED a long vigil, spat a wad of tobacco into the cold stove, and banged down the lid.

"No fool like an ole fool," he said aloud. "What in hell made me think that Tim Callan or Pete Haskell would try an' kill Russ Bartle before dawn? Should've known that plenty smoke means damned little fire."

He strode across the rambling shack that served as home, office, and calaboose, slumping wearily on the bed and kicking off his boots. He peeled off his shirt and pants and started to get under the blankets. He stopped in a ludicrous posture.

Sounded like a rider pulling up. At this hour? Lande snorted and went toward the door in bare feet and underwear. Farm chunk; man in store clothes. A stranger. Now what?

The Sheriff opened the door before the fellow knocked. He lit the oil lamp. "Well, sir?"

"I thought you'd give me a little official information," said Clarke Weber guardedly.

"You wantin' it so bad that you waltz in here at three o'clock in the mornin'?"

"Well, you see that's because—"

"Information about what?"

"Rewards." Clarke's grin was wise and boastful. "I want to know where I stand if I deliver a man worth money in several states; say five thousand here, and ten thousand up north, and fifteen thousand down Texas way. Exactly what would I get?"

Lande's temper was tested. "What in hell do you want to

know that for?" He found the answer himself. "Oh! You figger to try an' deliver this gent where he's worth most—unless everybody pays for the one delivery?"

"Yes. I think it good business to—"

"So do I—to get yore man first. Who is he?"

"I'd rather not say right now. You'll quickly recognize him when he's delivered—probably dead. If this state pays the top price."

For a second Lande's rage blazed in his eyes and he stood not knowing how to handle this obvious Easterner who seemed like a greedy Judas, siding with the law only to get personal profit and determined to wring out the last possible dollar thereof.

Suddenly the officer growled deep in his throat, darted behind Clarke and twisted the key in the lock of the street door. Then he actually sprinted across the shack to throw open the entrance of the barred section that gave a prisoner as much room as a bear in a zoo.

In a lightning-like move he had the visitor by the back of the collar and the seat of the pants. Hustling him into the cage was simplicity itself. Lande banged and locked the door.

"Reckon you'd best rather say right now," he snapped, "Till you do, consider yoreself under arrest—an' without grub or drink. Mebbe you didn't figger that concealin' the whereabouts of any wanted man is as good as workin' in cahoots with him— far as I'm concerned. Good night."

Clarke squirmed under the lash of the second lesson in Western ways. A fine kettle of fish! Name the black outlaw and Lande himself might make a desperate effort to lasso the prize money. Keep silent and he'd stay locked up here. Meanwhile some one else might see the outlaw and so report. Until Lande had blown out the lamp and returned to bed, Clarke was undecided.

"Sheriff," he called in the chilly darkness.

"Yeah?"

"It was—The Masked Rider I referred to."

Silence! Then the sheriff's hilarious laugh all but shook the flimsy building.

"The Masked Rider. An' *you* worryin' about how much you'd collect! Why you locoed squirt if you lifted a finger against that outlaw he'd have you eaten alive—saltless—before you could beg his pardon. Thank me for lookin' you up. I'm savin' yore life. No less."

"But I did see him. I did have a gun on him. I can shoot, but—"

"I know. He can shoot better." Lande swung his feet to the floor. *"Sabe!* He shot yore iron away, huh? That why yore paw is bandaged?"

"Yes. I came upon him just after he'd finished firing a tobacco drying shed—and crucifying a young fellow on Don Attero's cross."

THE SHERIFF SAT reflectively on the edge of his bed. There came the stomping of feet getting into tight boots. "If yo're lyin', mister, plenty skin will be missin' from yore hide shortly after I get back. A posse—"

He swallowed the balance. For outside the door he heard the faint scrape of leather soles on the sandy platform. He darted over, looked out quickly. The street was singularly deserted. All Gold Creek had called it a day—except Russ Bartle. He was betrayed by the light in the window over the bank.

Lande finished dressing. All the things he'd ever heard, all the good things proved about The Masked Rider, passed in mental review. But Lande was sheriff. No outlaw could prowl his territory with immunity.

"Burned a tobacco shed; crucified a young fellow, huh?" he said aloud. His laugh was short and sarcastic. "Mebbe he did. *Mebbe.*"

CHAPTER VII

HELP WANTED

RUSS BARTLE HAD just finished an entry in his books when knuckles rapped on the door below. He went to the landing at the head of the stairs. Promptly he pulled the lever that drew back the spring bolt. A smile spread over his predatory face.

"Howdy, Burr. Glad to see you. Come right in."

The last of the Aldmans walked as if his feet were lead weights. Broken and bitter, he dropped heavily into a chair.

"They—they got us, Mister Bartle. They burned our shed, crop an' all. They—" A lump in his throat almost choked him. Then he rattled out, "They killed Dad an' Sam."

"What?" thundered Bartle. His show of supreme surprise was uncannily genuine, the reward of inherent talents and constant rehearsal. He could write a check and before the ink dried, could appear stunned by his own signature and proclaim to high heaven that it was not of his handicraft. "By God, I'll—you're sure, Burr?"

The lad nodded. "They plugged Dad right before my eyes. He didn't have our only gun on him. When I got in an' out of the house with it, I was too late. The coyote had disappeared."

"You chased after him, of course?"

"No. I should've. But there was a whole year's work goin' up in smoke an' Dad—Dad on his back all twisted in pain."

"Why the devil didn't Sam—"

"Sam'd gone up on Mission Ridge to see Mary Nelson. I didn't know what happened to him till an Indian told me that Sam was—was spiked to Don Attero's cross."

Bartle trembled with fury. "Awful!" he gasped. "The most terrible thing I ever heard of." He put a consoling arm across the lad's shoulders. "I'm sorry, boy. Buck up. I pledge my last dollar, my last breath, to bring these scoundrels to rope. Come. We'll tell Gold Creek's wonderful sheriff about this."

Burr stared at the floor. "That wouldn't help any; help neither Dad, Sam, nor me. Only *you* can help me, Mr. Bartle."

"Yes?"

"Dad made me promise to get out of Deep Water Valley— *when Sam came home*. Sam ain't ever comin', see? So if I stick, I ain't breakin' my promise, am I?"

Bartle was puzzled. He knew better than to press for enlightenment that would come voluntarily. Patience, he told himself.

"You're not breaking your promise, Burr."

"I'll stick. I'll work till I drop behind the plow. I'll pay every cent we owe you, Mr. Bartle. All I'm askin' is time an'—an' a loan for seed an' a new dryin' shed." He looked up into Bartle's blank face. "Will you stake me?"

Russ sat down, silently groping for wise words. "You know I would—if I could. But you see all the money I have is tightly tied up. This very day the bank pressed me for cash. I stalled them off—depending on your poor dad's next payment."

"I—I can't make it."

"I understand, boy. And it puts us both in a hole, so to speak." He was lost in serious thought for a while. Then, still the shark posing as the Good Samaritan, he looked with false pity at the crushed youth. "I know you'd come out on top, Burr—if the cattlemen left you alone. But you'd have to almost work yourself to death. Don't you think it wiser to take your dad's advice?"

"An' clear out?" Burr's eyes were defiant. "I ain't scared. I want to stick. I want to fight fire with fire."

"But they'll lick you. Then I'd lose what is already due me and what I lent you. Even that would be small loss—if I could ever forget that it was through my loan you met—er—death." He shook his head dejectedly. "No. I think the best thing you can do is try and find a buyer for the farm."

BURR GOT UP. "I won't sell—yet. I'll try an' raise a loan at the bank."

"Who'll lend you anything, son? Suppose you put up a new drying shed? On borrowed money. They might burn it down the day after you finish it."

"No they won't!"

Bartle was struck with the lad's positiveness. "You couldn't stop them."

"But I heard about somebody in these parts who might."

"You heard what?"

"That The Masked Rider's in Deep Water Valley. At the cross where Sam—Sam died."

Bartle colored. He knew that the outlaw was always mixing into somebody else's bad troubles, always interested in atrocities, always dealing out bad medicine to the perpetrators. It was impossible for Bartle to hide his concern.

"Who told you that?"

"I was goin' to tell Sheriff Lande about Dad an' Sam. I was at his door. Inside he was talkin' to somebody an'—"

"The Masked Rider," moaned Bartle. In a flash he turned a threat into an advantage. He looked sharply at Burr. "By God, it might have been the outlaw who burned your shed."

"No. It wasn't. Anybody'll tell you that he doesn't do things like that."

"Even the best of outlaws may change! I'll bet he's tired being chased from pillar to post, and that he's thrown in with the beef men in trade for a safe hiding spot on one of their ranches."

"No," insisted Burr. "Can't be. He just ain't made that way. He saw the fire an' Sam. He warned off the new settlers. I'm sure he'll do something about it. And even if he doesn't, news of him bein' here gives me two ideas."

"You'll find that he's working hand in glove with Haskell's crowd."

"That's the first thing I do—find out if he's hired out to beef men. An' I know how to get at the truth." He spoke as though his confidence in The Masked Rider were shaken by Bartle's beliefs.

He started out. Bartle detained him.

"I'll try and find a buyer for your farm. In fact I'll write immediately to a man who might be interested. He'll probably give you two thousand dollars for what's left of the place."

Burr was startled. "Two thousand dollars? With only the shed missin'?"

Bartle nodded. "And I'd take it, son. Quick. Then I'd head back to Kentucky and friends, glad to get away with my life."

"Maybe you would," said Burr, opening the door. "I won't! Somebody's goin' to pay for that shed, the crop—an' Dad an' Sam. Good night." The low figure seemed to have enraged him.

Russ went to his desk, took up a pen and chewed the end of it. Then he wrote in an unsteady hand…

"…the farm in question. To protect my own interests, I have bought the place and shall rebuild a drying shed destroyed by fire. The price of the farm will not be changed. Six thousand dollars gets you this bit of paradise in the world's most fertile valley. Please write me immediately as to when you can come to see for yourself what a bargain this is."

He read the letter over, forgetting Burr, the dead, and the phantom outlaw. Buy Burr out for two thousand; sell to the other party for six thousand. He smiled evilly. Why hadn't his father operated such a scheme? He might have died a millionaire—and left it all to Russ.

"But," Bartle consoled himself, "I haven't done bad. Fifty-five hundred profit on Mike Chapman's place; three thousand on Steve Ransom's—and the ball isn't fairly rolling yet. Wait until I have the north end of the valley to bring 'em in and drive 'em out."

CHAPTER VIII

HASKELL SPEAKS

WHEN EVERYTHING MEN hold dear is at stake, they know no clock or hour. They answer the leader's summons whether it come at high noon or at crack of dawn.

The cold gray of daybreak was in the eastern sky and in that dim light riders converged on the Half Circle S ranch. They came from all points of the compass—grim-faced men who traveled as befits those anxious to hear what is tantamount to a sentence of life or death.

In the modest ranch, Pete Haskell and Tim Callan greeted each new arrival in solemn fashion. Twice Haskell surveyed the room that was now uncomfortably crowded. He stood in the doorway, searching the outdoors with expectant eyes. When two more horses came over the brow of a distant knoll, he breathed a trifle easier.

"Here comes Luke an' Martin. That'll make all hands present an' we can get down to business."

It was not long later when he held up his horny hand for silence. Every ranch owner clamped his tongue and gave attention.

"I been palaverin' with Russ Bartle," began Haskell dryly. "He knows he's got the whip hand an' he aims to make the most of his advantage."

Luke Wallace edged closer to the table over which Haskell spoke. "Did you offer to buy all the north end o' the valley?"

"I did. Russ has been bookkeepin' so damned much that he ain't got much respect for anything less than six figgers crowdin' one behind the other. The price is three hundred an' fifty thousand American dollars. Cash!"

Tim Callan passed around a tray of full glasses. Some of the ranchers seemed to need a stimulant.

"Did you tell him there wasn't that much money in this half the county?" inquired Luke.

"I did—an' should've known enough not to, this bein' an open an' shut case of 'you can't eat yore cake until after you've paid for it.'"

"Did you tell him that no farmer squats in the north end of the valley?"

"I did."

"An' that if one fence went up to keep our cattle away from the water till it was so loaded with alkali that they couldn't drink, that we'd take the law in our own hands an'—"

"I did not. I been hopin, that since last meetin' somebody thought o' something less mangy than ridin' roughshod over farmers."

He paused for suggestions. None came. But on every face he read defiance of the very law he sought so hard to respect and obey.

"We're doin' *something*," barked old Luke. "I've been here too long to be driven out by barbed wire an' worm disturbers. An' since there ain't no help in legal things, then we must try—"

"Force," concluded Haskell. It hurt him to get out the word. *"Gentle* force, men. As fast as fence goes up around sweet water, that fast we rip it down."

Luke snorted. "An' if that silk-glove way doesn't work?"

"We'll cross that bridge when we come to it," said Haskell.

"But might as well pave the road now. If fence bustin' doesn't work, then torches an' six-guns must. Am I right?"

"Mebbe you are. Mebbe."

The door burst open so unexpectedly that Haskell duplicated every rancher's convulsive turn. And like those of his old time friends, his eyes dilated.

For on the threshold stood as awesome a thing as any man

present had ever looked upon; a man so solidly attired in black that he seemed to have popped out of an ink bottle. Statuesquely still, ominously silent, he let his presence sink into every man's mind before he moved a muscle.

Then he took two stiff steps forward and the eyes visible through the black hood fastened themselves on Haskell.

"You're top hand here?"

The veteran beef man had never known fear. He did not make a sudden acquaintance with it. "I am!"

"You've heard of me?"

"Who hasn't?"

"You've heard that the Aldman drying shed in Deep Water Valley was burned during the night?"

"No."

"And that Pop Aldman was shot down in cold blood—when he wasn't packin' a gun?"

"No."

"You've heard that young Sam Aldman was crucified on Don Attero's cross?"

"No."

"Then you know it all now. An' I don't expect you to admit that one of these men obeyed your orders."

HASKELL WAS FIGHTING mad. "I wouldn't admit to a damned lie for any man."

"In time you might admit truth. But I didn't come to argue whether you knew or gave orders. I'm only here to tell you that shortly after the next fire or killin' in Deep Water Valley, you'll finish where Sam Aldman finished—spiked on Don Attero's cross."

The hooded apparition awaited no response. He backed up, a hand behind him groping for the doorway, his eyes on men whom he knew were itching to go for the weapons hanging at their hips. He pivoted, crouched, and ran into the open.

Men snapped alive. Three crowded through the door. Guns blazed. A hail of lead whistled after a jet black horse.

"Got him!" shrilled one marksman as the fleeing horseman swayed in the saddle. "Got him sure as hell."

Haskell rushed out. He saw. "Got him bad, Andy!" He bolted for the corral. "Come on. He won't get far. He can't hug leather very long—not the way he's reelin' in that saddle."

The Half Circle S was never the scene of a wilder race to waiting horses. And yet, as they leaped to saddles, not one man thought of reward money. It was as if each and every one of them was determined on the ride of his life only to avenge the insinuation that beef men were behind the valley outrages.

CHAPTER IX

TWINS

IN THE ARID hills beyond Mission Ridge, where neither cattle nor puncher was wont to stray, Blue Hawk built a camp fire close to the steep side of an arroyo. There was no law against killing the morning chill or cooking a breakfast as only the Indian could. Hence he went about the task openly, without the very caution that might arouse the suspicions of prying eyes.

A hearty meal prepared, he walked aimlessly, to all intents, in a wide circle around the fire. Suddenly he mounted his sorrel and as if bereft of sanity, the cry of a mountain lion came from his skilled lips. He rode off, leaving the breakfast simmer on a pile of hot stones. Drifting on the early morning wind came an answering cat's call.

The Indian rode faster. In town he would on occasion speak to Wayne Morgan as he would to any man who rubbed up an acquaintance. But nowhere, unless it was absolutely unavoidable, would he ever be found in the company of The Masked Rider.

The outlaw knew the fireside was safe. Soon he ate with relish. Who was there to say he had not prepared the meal himself? And who so blessed or mystic that he would recognize in this immaculate, clean-cut man, the famous hooded outlaw? Enrobed in black, no one could mistake him. As Wayne Morgan many men knew him. But no man knew that the names—Morgan and The Masked Rider—were one. Some there were, who did know that the faces were one—and they held death for him—if they chanced to see him first.

He ate leisurely, killed the fire, cleaned and cachéd the kit. Then, hood and *mantilla* stowed away, he rode toward Gold Creek contentedly puffing a cigarette, speculating as to what news there would be from Blue Hawk.

But before he had traveled far, Morgan pulled up tensely. He sat with every sense at rigid attention, trying to convince himself that what he saw was fact and not mirage or imagination.

For on the cold gray skyline, climbing up, crossing the flat top and quickly fleeing down again, a rider traversed a knoll so round it looked like a halved ball. Suddenly as he had heaved into sight, he was gone. Of itself neither spirited horse nor rider meant much. But the black Stetson, the black hood and gloves, the black cloak stretched stiff in the breeze were things so utterly unexpected that Morgan's chin sagged a trifle. It was one of the few occasions upon which he was frank to admit bewilderment—and curiosity he had to fight hard to down.

A bitter grin raised one corner of his mouth. "Riding straighter and a little faster, I'd say I saw myself," he thought. "Worth seeing, too! Means—maybe—that some one's aware I'm here and intends to trade under my brand. I'll hear a lot now about the things The Masked Rider did in Deep Water Valley."

It was nothing new to be held responsible for anything save good that happened whether he was hard by or a thousand miles away.

He nudged the stallion, starting for the knoll, determined that sign should lead him to the lair of the impostor. Two things instantly altered his plans. Far to the north, atop a sharp crowned hill, he saw another rider—unmistakably Blue Hawk. The Indian's wigwagged speech was plain. Briefly it said he had seen something that needed tracking down.

"Twins?" signalled Morgan.

"*Si!*" came the reply, and the Indian dipped out of sight.

Morgan waited, knowing that soon a thunder of hoofs on his right would bring many riders in view. A posse in pursuit of the false Masked Rider, no doubt. As Wayne Morgan, he had little to fear from them.

A score of horsemen poured into the arroyo like charging cavalry. Pete Haskell was in the lead on a mount as white as a fresh snowdrift. His eyes popped when he saw Morgan so still and so placidly smoking. He pulled up. The white reared. Haskell purposely left the saddle like coal down a truck chute. He closed in on Morgan, half suspicious. Over his shoulder went a command to some of the others to keep on in the direction the black phantom had gone. Then he walked a complete circle about Morgan, scrutinizing every inch of man and horse. He disliked to silently confess he saw no signs of bullet wounds.

"A gent in a black hood an' *mantilla* came this way, stranger. You happen to notice?"

Morgan's face was friendly. He looked to the south. Perhaps a lie now and then was the greatest evil he could be accused of.

"Yes," he said quietly. "I saw something black streaking south. Far off. Now that you tell me it was a rider, I feel better. Looked too big to be a horse; too perfectly matched to be horse and rider. I thought it was some strange animal—black *centaur*, maybe, *sabe?*"

"The Masked Rider," clipped Haskell. He spun around the remnants of his followers. "Some of you head south, men. He's not far off an' the earth didn't open up an' swallow him."

MORGAN TOOK A quick liking for the old cattleman, was almost sorry he had to try to lead him away from the impostor. And he admired Haskell for not sending all the men south.

"Masked Rider, did you say?" he asked innocently.

"Yep! An' slick an' fast as always."

"Plaguing you gents?"

"Not yet. But set to—unless he gets a proper steer. You see there's been some rotten things done in Deep Water Valley nearby. He jumps at the conclusion that we cattlemen are responsible. He busts in on our meetin' an' orates that we'll pay for what's been done."

"You being in no wise guilty?"

"Not a damn's worth—yet. An' we aim to get him before he does damage to the wrong parties, *sabe?*"

Morgan's smile was wan. "From what I heard about that outlaw he doesn't stomp until he's sure there's a snake underfoot."

"A man can make a mistake an'—well, we got to push on, stranger. Ride with us? Can't be too many guns on hand if we corner him."

"Sorry," replied Morgan almost sincerely. "I'm a day late making Gold Creek now. I'm bound for a kind of conference. Maybe later I'll be back this way, riding with you gents. *Adiós.*"

Haskell watched Morgan withdraw. He racked his brain in vain to remember a man as strikingly impressive—so clean, so warm, yet so strangely distant and dangerous.

"Gets under a fellow's skin, huh?" he said to old Luke. "Well, let's go north."

And east—the longest way—rode Wayne Morgan, slowly although extremely eager to learn what Blue Hawk had uncovered. Now and then he looked out of the tails of his keen eyes to satisfy himself that he rode alone. Now and then he frankly looked west, wondering how fared the impostor, why he was such, and why he had reached the conclusions voiced by Haskell.

Always an admirer of courage, Morgan already found his

rancid opinion of the false Masked Rider slipping. The fellow was doubtlessly a fool for jumping at conclusions—or Haskell was a shrewd liar—but no man who bucks such a crowd of ranchmen could be termed a coward. And, Morgan knew, courage is most often based on the solid conviction that what a man does is right and just.

"My twin believes that beef men are responsible for what happened last night. Reckon I'm neutral—until I hear from Blue Hawk. Then my chips go with the information."

He pushed on, grim of face and determined to get to the bottom of things, for he felt it his duty to set aright that hideous crucifixion, and that in spite of Gold Creek's reputation, somebody wore a false front in the ruthless pursuit of profit. To unveil that man he solemnly swore, knowing full well the risks he ran and the total absence of any hope of praise or reward.

CHAPTER X

THE WESTERN SUN

IN GOLD CREEK'S most popular saloon Blue Hawk toyed with a drink and watched the door. It was not sheer waste of time, this idleness, for he had already impressed the non-talkative barkeeper with the fact that life is a lonesome affair for a man who hails from below the Rio Grande, and after a while he craves nothing as much as to sit down, play cards, and just talk and talk with any stranger who will volunteer.

Such a man eventually entered the Western Sun. It was Wayne Morgan. He acted as if he had never seen the Indian before. Idle banter flowed between them—comments on the weather, the trail, the town. Inch by inch they moved together, the barkeep glancing in sympathy at Morgan as he would at a man whom he knows is destined to have his ears talked flabby.

"You play with cards, *señor?*" Blue Hawk appeared overjoyed at Morgan's smile and nod. "Good! We sit in far corner, no? At that table not one disturbs us."

Morgan winked at the barkeep. "Might as well listen," he smiled. "Nothing more important to do."

They sat down, the Indian shuffling the cards in high elation—and satisfied that what he said could not be heard by the man behind the bar.

"There is much news, *señor*. All bad." He began to deal. "First, the rat rides water. He knows what he is about. Where he goes, I still do not know. It was like he left the river on wings."

Disappointment never irked Morgan. Like a hound, he knew that lost scents can later be found if one is patient.

"What else?" he asked hopefully.

"I am not yet given up hopes when I see fire in the valley. There are shots. I ride like the wind. Mebbe the sorrel ages, *sabe?* Mebbe I too get old. I find only a dead man, the ashes of a drying shed and a much bitter young *hombre*."

Morgan nodded. "I saw the fire and heard the shots. I was between the devil and deep sea. New settlers were rounding the bend near Attero's cross. I didn't want them to ride into what I expected would be a gun fight. But go on, Blue Hawk. What then?"

"The young one accuses cattlemen, *señor*. By his eyes I know he will fight the whole world alone—because I tell him that it is his brother Sam spiked on the cross."

"He has good reason to suspect beef men?"

"Who knows? I talk with other men—some tobacco, some cattle. It is the old story, *señor;* good for one is bad for the other and each calls the other a dog. But this I *know*—that the rider at the cross was the coyote at the drying shed. By this sign he betrays himself—so far."

"And that black rider?"

"You see him run from cattlemen. He too rides water—but

not like the other. Him I follow, *señor*. To the house near the burned shed."

Morgan's eyes showed comprehension that was not startling. "Starting to fight back at cattlemen—under my brand," he said without animosity.

"Who blames him, *señor?* Death strikes twice at him. Maybe he loses the crop of a year's work. Maybe the farm is lost. He is so young, *señor*, he maybe not think that you are here and proud of your brand—which he will use to frighten beef men to leave these valley farmers in peace. *Quién sabe?*"

Morgan rolled a cigarette, played an ace when the game called for a card of much less value. "No man can use my brand for any reason," he said mildly. "Especially when he acts on anything less than proof that what he's about is true."

The Indian took the pot he had not won. "The young one will not trade long on your brand, *señor*. When I look in window and watch him hide hood and *mantilla,* he bleeds too much. I make to go in house and help him. But a girl comes. She tries hard to stop blood. I think maybe it not good that I be at house twice when bad things happen, *sabe?* So I make camp. All else you know."

"All?"

"*Sí, señor*. I stay in town while places close up for night. I talk with this one and that one. I learn nothing."

"Nothing that points to some one besides beef men behind what happened at the cross?"

"No. But worse may come, *señor*. Men strain at the leash. Cattlemen say no settlers shall enter the north part of Deep Water Valley. One man says they shall."

"And have!"

"Have?" Blue Hawk's face clouded. "Then they shall feel the whip of war."

"This one man you mentioned. Who is he?"

"Russ Bartle. The valley is his heritage from his father—without his father's kind heart. He brings these farmers in, knowing that when they buy they hang their lives on thin threads."

"His reason?"

"None, *señor*. Unless it be to show that he may do as he please with what he owns. He knows that fence will keep cattle from the only water until it runs through Alkali Flats and is useless for cow and horse alike. He holds that to be beef men's bad luck and he swears he will bring in who pleases him and set them down where he alone likes. It is a feud, *señor, sabe?*"

"*Si*—with selfishness on Bartle's part to keep it blazing."

HE BROKE OFF as a group of tired, dusty men entered the saloon. While he and Blue Hawk pretended to be engrossed in their card game, both listened attentively.

The things they heard were easily summed up. An Easterner with a bandaged hand—even now he was in Sheriff Lande's calaboose—had reported seeing The Masked Rider and asked for information that would help him take the outlaw to his greatest profit. The men had combed the valley in vain. The Easterner had been seeing things that did not exist.

Morgan leaned closer to his confederate. "Find out all you can about Russ Bartle. Soon after dusk I'll see the man who wears my hood and *mantilla*. Be there."

The outlaw strolled casually to the street, went to the shed behind the saloon, mounted and started to leave Gold Creek via the rear of its single thoroughfare. There was always the possibility of meeting one who knew him from the distant past; hence the back street and the swift retreat.

Even as he crossed the driveway between two buildings that did not interest him, he glimpsed a farm chunk—and a sour-looking Easterner with a bandaged hand. The latter seemed the worse for wear. He babbled something about one day proving who was a fool and who a wise man.

Morgan caught the threat against himself. It left him cold. He rode on. Men who *blab*, seldom *do*. It was the men who acted before they spoke that held the respect of the outlaw. And yet, when he reached open country, he wondered if the luck of the novice or higher intelligence would help the Easterner make good his boast to deliver The Masked Rider.

CHAPTER XI

FAIR GAME

THE LONG SHADOWS of approaching dusk heralded the end of a tedious day for Wayne Morgan. A rash man would have attempted to accomplish much more than he had. But he was never one to dare fate, always remembering that one bad move meant death—and dead men do nobody any good.

So, as the sun turned the western sky to cloud-streaked crimson, as the myriad colors on the hills faded to somber gray, he had ascertained only two things of which he was previously ignorant—the exact location of both the new arrivals and the ash heap that had been a drying shed. These places were indelibly stamped upon his mind. He knew the best way to them—and the swiftest, safest route away, should unforecast necessity arise.

Hooded and cloaked, he waited until dusk gave way to the thicker shadows of night, with the moon blanketed by as sinister and black a cloud as his own apparel. Then, silently as a falling leaf, he moved on to the Aldman farm—a doubled-over splotch of blackness that might be felt but not seen.

He skirted the ash pile that still gave off warmth, paused a moment beneath a giant tree, then streaked on again and flattened himself against the side of the modest house. Reaching the window where a light shone, he peered in, not yet satisfied that the place was safe to enter.

He saw a girl, young, passably pretty, slender, and tall. Her face, stained with tears, was turned to the bed where lay a lad whose countenance was as white as the sheet tucked under his chin.

An older man stood at the bedside—a man whose clothes showed he was a farmer. It was apparent he had tried to allay the wounded one's pain.

To The Masked Rider night was precious. He flitted around the house to the entrance. Test proved the door to be unlocked. He thrust it open and stood on the threshold with the yellow lamp light full upon him.

The girl cried out in stark terror. The old man gaped like one seeing his first ghost. From the pillow came a half groan, half cry that was at once an expression of hope and fear.

The Masked Rider stepped in and closed the door behind him. "Nothing to fear," he assured them. "I'd have come otherwise if it were possible. You two," he beckoned to the girl and the old man—"stand over there, please. My business concerns your patient only."

They obeyed with misgiving. He went to the bed and behind the black hood there was no response to Burr Aldman's pinched smile.

"You won't wear that hood and cloak again," the outlaw said gently but firmly. "To make sure, we'll burn it. Where will I find it?"

Burr's eyes closed. "I—I thought you'd come to—to help me."

A black-gloved hand rested on the young man's forehead. "What do you call this—my keeping you from running into a second shower of lead?"

"But I—"

"Yes, you tried to throw a scare into men—likely the wrong ones—who don't scare."

"Will you—"

"One thing at a time. Where's that hood and cloak you wore?"

A feeble hand pointed toward the cold fireplace. The outlaw soon held remnants of old dresses crudely cut and pinned. He dropped them on to ashes, touched a match to them. Never did he completely ignore the old man and the quaking girl.

"What made you try such a fool move, kid?"

"I—er—well, Russ Bartle led me to believe that you might have hired out to beef men an' I went there to their meetin' knowin' they'd welcome me if Russ was right."

The outlaw's laugh was short and frigid. "*Sabe.* You didn't think that a man who says what he knows can't be true speaks for a damned good reason?"

"You mean he lied on purpose?" Burr frowned. "Not Mr. Bartle. He's a fine man. He—"

"He'll have a chance to prove he is. I'll ask him to—*pronto.*"

THE OLD MAN stepped forward timidly. "You got no reason to quarrel with Bartle—less'n you are in cahoots with beef men. Bartle's all the boy claims. More. He brought us here, trusted us for tools an' things to build with.

"He's a fine man," agreed The Masked Rider. "I always give everybody the benefit of the doubt, *sabe?* But if he proves to be responsible for what I saw on Don Attero's cross and what I heard happened on this farm last night, then sure enough some other good Samaritan will stake you folks to things—not to be repaid with blood."

Always open-minded, fair, and eager for details that might mean nothing to any one else, the outlaw sank upon the bed and brushed the hair back from Burr's eyes.

"Now tell me what you know, son—everything, from the day you first knew you were going to settle here until the minute you saw me enter that door."

Burr's face changed. Perhaps it was pride that one so famous should visit at his bedside. Perhaps because he could not help but feel that here was a man capable of trumping any crooked ace, a man staking his life on the chance that he could help so insignificant a person as Burr Aldman. At any rate, since the phantom's arrival, Burr glowed as if he had undergone a successful blood transfusion.

Of the four persons in the sick room, not one suspected that outside lurked death. The Masked Rider had no reason to suspect or fear. At dusk Blue Hawk should be on hand. If danger reared its head, the call of a mountain cat would float on the night air.

CHAPTER XII

BAIT

CLARKE WEBER HAD had only ridicule to fear after he was ejected from Gold Creek's calaboose. The wounds of such darts were quickly healed by his egotism. He stalked the cowtown like a scavenger, making every acquaintance he could, promptly discarding one man in favor of another, until he was certain he had tapped every source of information—true or fancied—regarding The Masked Rider.

Shortly before dusk he climaxed his quest with a visit to Russ Bartle who, true to form, was just getting out of bed. The very mention of the phantom outlaw not only quickly rubbed the sleep from his eyes, but also hastened his pulse. On leaving, Weber was convinced of two things—that Bartle was a firm believer in law, order, and pure justice, and also that he was very generous. Otherwise, why should he have cursed the black outlaw; why should he have told Weber that if *he* succeeded in taking The Masked Rider, the balance due on the Maxon-Weber tract would be wiped out as reward?

So Clarke considered he was hunting big game—state rewards and a cancelled mortgage—and he had a head full of data that would help him succeed, the piecing together of which led him to the justifiable conclusion that where atrocity once reared its ugly head, *there,* sooner or later, The Masked Rider might sometimes be seen—pretending an errand of good.

Thus it was that dusk found him patrolling between Don Attero's cross—now its naked self—and the Aldman tobacco farm.

He forked a borrowed pinto that gave promise of being as fleet as The Masked Rider's gallant black stallion. He toted two Colts and in the saddle holster reposed a Winchester. Yet, equipped for running battle or stationary siege, he confessed he lacked something. He couldn't borrow it or buy it, and the longer he patrolled the less he had of it—courage. Until, in the thick of night, he wished there was a genie to appeal to for a chance to shoot the outlaw in the back. And the longer he rode, the slower; as if strangling with fear that once more the hunted man would appear as sudden as lightning flashes.

Centuries it seemed he rode peering into the night, straining eyes and ears. Silence mocked him. He stopped now to mop the cold sweat from his temples, forcing himself to believe the task easy and the reward sufficient. He tensed, head cocked to one side, his heart pounding. The sound was that of a grazing animal.

Guided by the sound he located a sorrel, saddled, bridled, ground-roped. His fingers told him that the saddle skirts were decorated with strange metal studs that spoke of Yaqui kinship and ancient Mexico. The moment Clarke was certain of this, his head buzzed.

"Burr Aldman told me about a visit by a strange Mexican Indian! Why's he prowling so close to the Aldman house afoot?"

He dismounted, nervously led his horse behind a shaft of rock and began to inch toward the house. Fear inspired him to move with super-caution that had him almost going forward on his hands and knees. It seemed hours before he paused. His heart threatened to burst as he looked into a window, through a dark room where the door of the adjoining room was open. Framed in the rectangle of yellow light stood The Masked Rider.

Once in any man's life Lady Luck may smile on him so broadly that his brain is paralyzed by his good fortune. Clarke Weber crouched spellbound. Then as if he feared to shatter a dream, both his hands sagged to the cold butts of his Colts. And snail-like, he began to lift the heavy weapons—to let them drop as a spasm of terror snapped his overwrought nerves.

Behind him sounded the pad of moccasined feet.

Burr Aldman. The strange Mexican. Moccasins! Clarke rallied his reeling senses as the panic of close death clutched him by the throat. All day he'd been asking questions about the far-famed outlaw. Every man he grilled was dead certain the black one was a lone wolf—yet here, thought Clarke, was proof of something else. The Mexican on guard, the phantom inside. Clarke realized both his peril and his good fortune. He was doubtlessly the only man alive who knew the truth—the tie that bound the Indian and the outlaw. Little good it would do him—with the Mexican's footsteps coming closer and closer and closer.

CHILLS RAN DOWN Clarke's spine. No man ever felt more relentlessly squeezed between steam-rollers of fate. Kill The Masked Rider? Simplicity itself. Then die at the hand of the Indian. Unload a gun in the direction whence came those ominous footsteps? Then a repetition of the first lesson that showed the outlaw could move like pronged lightning and shoot straight as an arrow. In the next split second Clarke decided where lay his one chance to sidestep his grave and live to profit by the secret he had learned.

He tried to run silently. Haste and silence would not mix. He caught an angry grunt behind him and broke into reckless flight.

Panting, leg weary, he made his horse, the saddle. He raked the animal with spurs, adding a mouthed command to the sting of rowels. At first he dared hope for no pursuit. The clatter of hoofs behind him burst that bubble. Yet he felt better than he had at that window. Now he had only one man to contend with—and knew where and how that was best done. He dug his heels into his horse without mercy or sense, expecting any moment to hear the bark of a gun, the whistle or caress of a bullet. He knew that only his slight lead, fast horse, and inky night staved off shots. If he could hold out another mile! Three quarters. Half. Here! The same spot he'd noticed when on patrol.

He flung himself from the saddle. Even as he rolled in dust and stones he dragged forth both Colts and scampered up the side of a rock where centuries of storm and erosion had carved many toeholds. Sucking in great draughts of breath, listening to the beat of his own horse's hoofs—it still ran on although riderless—he waited fully decided. The Indian would follow the beaten trail because it made going faster and easier. His horse would almost brush against the toes of Weber's boots, for here the trail ran between rock scarcely spread enough to allow passage of a buckboard. If he couldn't hurl himself upon the Mexican then he would chance bullets—but not aimed to kill.

"He—he's coming," panted Clarke. "If I can get him, I can lure The Masked Rider to a spot where I can pick him off as easily as I would a blind crow."

CHAPTER XIII

CROSS CURRENTS

ON THE SPUR of the moment, when gripped by fear, Russ Bartle had said something that reflection proved nauseous. Until early night he paced his office and cursed himself—for promising to wipe out the Weber-Maxon mortgage if Weber captured The Masked Rider.

"What was wrong with me?" he wanted to know. "The fool might be lucky enough to deliver the goods—and I'll be out four thousand dollars! There must be a way to hedge out of that promise, much as I would like to see the outlaw's riddled corpse."

But how hedge without putting the first blemish on his reputation for being body and soul for the farmers he had imported? Until he was leg-weary and brain-fogged, Bartle paced and planned. Then the way pierced his brain like a bullet—the only way—the perfect way. He hurried to his desk, sat down, and snatched a pencil. Figures drew his guttural laugh.

"By God, that way I can kill three birds with one stone. Get the outlaw before Weber does. Make Chris Pringle damned anxious to sell out. Save myself from any danger of a visit by The Masked Rider."

He worked another few minutes at the desk, then scurried about the large room collecting an assortment of things he piled on a chair beside the door. When he went out, he carried a large tallow candle, a can of oil, and an empty bean tin with the top removed and the bottom punched full of holes. He rode quickly out of town, Deep Water Valley bound.

The black of night was friendly for his mission. He got out of Gold Greek unnoticed. Once in open country with which he was minutely familiar, he lashed and spurred his horse to a furious gallop.

Half an hour brought him to the edge of the valley and from on high he looked down on the buildings of Chris Pringle. Bartle's mind was divided, half noting that only one light showed at the snug house, half given over to recollecting that he had sold the farm to Pringle for six thousand dollars. If he could get the old Kentuckian anxious enough to sell, he might be able to buy the farm back for about three thousand—damage considered. And this very day he had inquiries from a man in Tennessee who sought just such a tobacco farm.

Bartle watched a while. Nothing stirred below. He rode as close as he dared, dismounted, and stealthily advanced with candle, can, and oil. Like a ghoul he made for the long shed, the panels of which had been closed lest frost attack the forest of poles from which hung the year's crop of aromatic, brown leaves.

Bartle bent double and wormed his way to the center of the shed. He knelt, reached above and dragged down a dry stalk. Crumbling the leaves, he made a little nest, soaked it with oil and placed the candle in the center.

A match sputtered. His hand shook. The candle wick smouldered a moment; then, as tallow melted, a spearhead of yellow light was born. To shield such a danger signal from any eyes that might happen to stray into the shed, he carefully set the perforated can over the candle.

Quickly he got up. He sprayed the oil about and dragged down more tobacco stalks. Cautiously he left the doomed building. A mad dash to his horse left him breathless and spent, but he flung himself into the saddle and tore off toward Gold Creek.

If he held to the mad pace, he would be back in his office in about thirty-five minutes. Just so long would it take that candle to burn short enough so that flame would touch the rim of the oil-soaked nest about its base.

Bartle grinned. The Masked Rider might be charged with the fire that nothing could stop. Or perhaps responsibility would be laid to the beef men. Certainly no one would even suspect Russ Bartle. Men can't start fires when they're miles away as flames shoot skyward. Yes, it would all work out very—

Bartle pulled up his horse. A chill shook him. Whence it came he scarcely knew, but the weird cry of a mountain lion turned his blood cold. Again it came in the inky night. Not the ordinary cry of beast calling mate, not the plaintive cry of ordinary prowler protesting against storm or hunger. This cry was surcharged with disappointment and alarm; the cry a mother lion sends forth when she discovers cubs missing from the lair and scents the recent presence of human beings.

Bartle tried to get a grip on himself. After all he was armed. He could punch a hole in a card tossed in the air. Let that yelping beast come near enough! He pushed on, aware now that the eerie cry shifted rapidly; first north, then south, east, and west, until he felt that a whole pack of the obviously enraged animals were in an ever closing circle around him. A circle that hemmed him in so that he felt he could not escape.

Suddenly those cries altered. To Bartle they now sounded like, "Candle! Candle! Thirty-five minutes!" He snatched his lead-tipped quirt and flayed the horse without compunction. Snorting in pain and anger, the animal carried him on at breakneck speed.

AT EIGHT O'CLOCK Russ Bartle slammed his lower door and angrily headed up the street. He reached Sheriff Lande's office with his face distorted by false wrath. Storming in, he found the officer fully clothed, snoring on the bed.

Lande opened his tired eyes at the first rough clutch on his shoulder. He got up with a yawn and an apology for not being able to fork a horse for eighteen hours without going all to pieces.

"And what did you accomplish!" asked Bartle savagely.

"Nothin'—much. Clarke Weber swears he saw The Masked Rider in the valley. Pete Haskell swears the outlaw popped into a cattlemen's meetin'—an' got away weighted down with lead. Both of 'em take an oath they'll never rest till they have a carcass to prove their claims. The hell of it is—"

"That while you're wasting time on the hunt, The Masked Rider pins this to my door with a dagger."

Lande snatched a scrap of paper. He read crudely printed words:

"Pringle is next!"

Bartle expected the angry glare he received. "Well!" he demanded. "You understand?"

"That this is supposed to come from the outlaw? Yeah. Do I believe it? No."

"I was at the landing above the stairs when the door rattled. That was the dagger being driven in. Naturally I looked down. It was the outlaw—black hood, black cloak, black gloves."

"But still not *The* Masked Rider. No man can make me believe that he's suddenly gone loco enough to gallivant around postin' notices, either of what he intends to do, or what he suspects somebody else plans."

Bartle's wrath knew no bounds. "Seems to me that you're always anxious to find an excuse to hedge away from anything that might help farmers in the valley."

"What seems to you doesn't make a damn bit of difference to me. First you bust in here accusin' cattlemen of things that happened at the Chapman an' Ransom farm. You palavered plenty, but none of it was based on more 'n what you *thought*. Now you throw in with everybody who thinks that The Masked Rider is somehow—"

"Working for beef men! And they're set to tackle the Pringle farm next."

Lande struggled in vain to control himself. "Can't you see you don't talk sense, Bartle?" he blasted. "That bein' true, why in hell would they warn you?"

"I don't know. I'm letting the law handle riddles."

"An' if you was wearin' this badge?"

"I'd be pretty anxious and quick—getting out to the Pringle place. I'd take enough men who could hold their tongues. I'd keep a few of them on guard day and night. This warning came from some one who knows the plans of some one else. I consider this a splendid opportunity to learn exactly who's been raising hell in the valley, because sooner or later that party will attack the Pringle place."

"Unless," drawled Lande, "this warnin' is only to draw me an' said pard to the Pringle farm while hell is raised elsewhere."

Bartle went to the door. "You're the law. What you do and

what happens next is your lookout. It was my duty to give you this paper. Certainly I can't do anything about it. Good night."

He stomped out in false anger. Inwardly elated, he felt that Lande would get men together, that he would ride to the valley.

"Fire draws them to the Pringle place. Lande's no fool. He'll post men. And since this outlaw will also be interested in the fire, he'll find himself under guns of the law."

Sure-fire as the trap seemed, happy as he was that it had been successfully set, Bartle was uneasy when he reached home. He confessed that until he looked upon The Masked Rider's corpse, he could never feel entirely safe. And when he was? The planned vicious circle could operate again. Bring settlers in at top prices; drive them out at bottom prices; hide behind a curtain of wrath and keep suspicion pointing at cattlemen.

"Can't fail," he thought. "The outlaw's the one stumbling block and everybody is helping me to get rid of him. Clarke Weber hunts him. Lande will have men on guard. Haskell's sworn to drill him. And I'll see to it that every farmer is posted to watch for him. He can't escape me."

CHAPTER XIV

LOST

THE MASKED RIDER had always considered black night his best friend. Now he cursed it, for had there been moon and stars, he might have found some sign of Blue Hawk.

Once more the ghastly cry of a pained mountain cat came from his lips. There was no response. The outlaw wished that the Indian had not always been so prompt at any rendezvous. But because he always was, his absence now was doubly mysterious and sinister.

Yet there was nothing the hooded man could do in this night of inky darkness. He thought of waiting until the gray of dawn revealed some sign. Even as he so decided, he felt the first big drop of rain strike his Stetson like a pebble. Gripped by a premonition that his bosom friend must be near and in trouble, he also realized that rain would erase his best chance of finding him. The outlaw dejectedly remained in his saddle, admitting that this was one of those rare occasions when he knew not what to do.

A sound snapped him rigidly alert and hopeful. It was well he did not voice the usual signal, for on top of the arroyo rode two men who conversed excitedly. Most of what they said was inaudible. But The Masked Rider caught a few words that cut as deep as a sabre swipe.

"I'd kill him," repeated one of the horsemen. "He needs killin'."

Distance and a clap of thunder made the other's response only a jumble. The outlaw now knew the sting of hopelessness and uncertainty from which he had freed so many people. Kill whom? Blue Hawk? Had the Indian's quest for information been discovered? Had he been marked a spy—and doomed to die? Or was some other innocent marked for slaughter? The Masked Rider was sorely tempted to ride after that pair. But he didn't move.

For again came the *plop, plop, plop* of hoofs in mud. Behind him, these! And though he could see nothing, the outlaw sensed that other riders were going in the same direction as the first pair. Now from the east came more betraying sounds. Seemed like the night became suddenly alive with mysterious horsemen—all heading due south. Where? Why? The hooded one decided—and cautiously followed. Some deviltry was playing havoc. Of that he was absolutely certain.

In torrents of rain that drenched him to the skin, with only his ears to guide him, The Masked Rider rode on until the most unexpected thing brought him up short. He sat sniffing the odor of burning tobacco. A fire in a drying shed? Yes! Straining his eyes he could make out blurred things passing back and forth before the yellow oblong that marked a window beyond which must be a lighted lamp. But the riders did not stop at that hazy group of buildings very long. When they left, no more shadows passed the lighted window.

The outlaw went on again, over a long level stretch, then up to the crown of a valley hill. He saw several lanterns on a farmhouse porch; many horses picketed nearby; riders still arriving, dismounting and quickly entering the house. And as he watched the strange scene, he felt the very air crackling with the presence of death there, death as it lingers over a field marshal's campaign tent when he instructs subordinates with their duties in a coming bloody battle.

Behind the hood, the outlaw's teeth were clenched. Burr Aldman had related how he had burst in upon a conference of cattlemen laying plans for war. About this house below moved only farmers. Had they too been summoned to such a conference? Was open, ruthless war about to be proclaimed?

"Fools!" gritted The Masked Rider. "Fly at each other's throats, turn on blood spigots—because they suspect. And while they kill each other off, somebody else sits back and laughs."

Dropped for the moment, now, the lost and endangered Indian. The welfare of this multitude was vastly more important than the safety of either Blue Hawk or himself.

HE DISMOUNTED. WET cloak clinging fast to him, he streaked toward the farmhouse, scarcely hoping to stave off disaster, yet determined to do his best.

The door stood open, a babble of voices drifted out. The outlaw crossed the porch with the silence of a cat. Inside....

A brown-whiskered man flung the lid off a new wooden box. The lamp suspended from the ceiling threw its yellow rays upon many new Colts and tightly packed boxes of bullets. A young fellow reached for one of the weapons. The old man thrust his hand away; strained silence fell upon the gathering.

"I told you men to come here when the next thing happened in the valley. I said I'd be ready to tell you what we must do—

unless we're content to be burned out an' killed off like we're coyotes. They tried to burn down Chris Pringle's drying shed. This time they didn't do much damage. Reckon we've given the law chance enough to keep peace here. Now we move."

"Haskell!" shouted a man whose hat dripped rain and whose eyes blazed with venom. "The Half Circle S ranch first! That'll teach 'em." He grabbed for one of the Colts.

"Wait!" commanded the old one. "The man who takes one of these, takes a vow that it'll be used only to collect debts owed. It will only be used if necessary to back him up. If a building burns in the valley, these guns will back your claim to the right to burn a ranch building. If there's another killing in the valley, these guns are to collect a life—but only *one for one*. I want no wholesale burning or killing. Those agreeable—and ready to abide by orders—can help themselves."

Men surged toward the table—unarmed men who now itched for the tools of death and justice as they saw it. Then as if some irresistible obstacle had dropped between them and the deadly box, every man stood still and blinked.

In the doorway stood The Masked Rider, as potent a command for silence and attention as any man had ever beheld.

"Shift!" he clipped. "All of you. Away from that box."

His voice was like clanging steel. Men obeyed, some with reluctance. But the young fellow who had first tried to take a gun, stood with his eyes shifting between tempting box and the empty-handed man in black.

"Shift, I said," rapped the outlaw. In a symphony of effortless motion that human eyes were hard put to it to follow, two guns appeared in his hands.

The young fellow blinked, gulped, and backed up. His face was slightly ashen.

"Good sense," complimented the outlaw crisply. "I'm glad. The last thing I want to do is to harm any of you or any cattleman—yet. You"—his eyes singled out the spokesman—"come here. Pick up the box. Don't let a finger get inside, *sabe?*"

The old one moved carefully. He was soon ready for orders.

The Masked Rider looked at no one in particular. "You gents might dig up a gun when I turn my back. All right—as long as you don't try to use it. If you do, you'll need a new leader, *sabe?*"

"An' if we—we don't?" inquired the young fellow. His features betrayed the information that the old man was his dad.

"He'll be back—*pronto,* unharmed. I give you my word. And I'm taking all of yours—ungiven. That for forty-eight hours not one man of you will lift a hand against any cattleman under any alibi or argument. That plain?"

The old man struggled with the heavy box. "We've got a right to protect ourselves. The law does nothing for us and—"

THE OUTLAW SOFTENED but his vigilance did not relax. "The law is sometimes like a mole, *amigo.* The brightest things it can't see. We won't palaver about that. In forty-eight hours you might get information that'll open your eyes—and make you glad that I kept your hands clean of blood."

"But—"

"March. I hope nobody crosses that threshold after we do, *sabe?*"

The old man stepped out. "Feel lots better if I knew whether you were with us or against us."

"I'm with you—you're the ones being burned out, shot, crucified," said The Masked Rider grimly.

When the old man was almost out of sight of the house, the outlaw called a halt. He whistled. There came the slosh of hoofs in mud and the smell of a horse. The animal was all but invisible. Suddenly the old man felt his burden gone, heard retreating plops and saw nothing.

When he reached the house he was smiling. Men stared at him, faces saying they would abide by his command.

"Forty-eight hours," he said happily. "He'll do more than we could—faster, better. Or I don't know a *man* when I buck against one. Meeting adjourned."

CHAPTER XV

PRISONER

CLARKE WEBER DID not have long to crouch like a tightly wound spring on the rock where the trail was narrow. Blue Hawk came, wildly chasing the sounds of the horse that now ran riderless. Clarke steeled himself, leaped like a mountain lion leaps on the back of a fat calf.

The collision sent both of them to the ground in a tangled mass of arms and legs, Blue Hawk fighting with surprised fury—until solid cracks with a gun butt set off shooting stars before his eyes and dropped him in a senseless heap.

Gasping for breath, Weber worked frantically to bind his prisoner's wrists and ankles. Then he stood aside to recover his spent breath.

The Indian stirred, struggled to rise. He lay back when a poised boot and a leveled gun threatened him.

"Why you do this to me?" he demanded angrily, enraged more at himself than at the smirking Easterner. *Dios!* What a fool to let the heat of the chase blind him to this trap. And back there in the Aldman house, The Masked Rider—possibly in danger! "Why you do—"

"Because," laughed Weber, "through you I'm going to get your master."

Blue Hawk trembled with self-condemnation. After years of trial and trouble at last some one knew of his connection with the black phantom. Such knowledge might well prove a death warrant—if this Easterner lived to spread his news. There must be some way to convince him he was in error.

"Master?" he asked plaintively. "*Señor* makes the mistake. I have no master—only God who you cannot—"

"Playing possum, huh? It won't work. You're the lookout man for The Masked Rider."

"The Masked—you mean the famous outlaw, *señor?*" Blue Hawk laughed with feigned hilarity. "He rides alone. He would not suffer me to lick his boots, *señor.* Untie me. Let us call this big mistake finished."

Weber brought the Indian's sorrel. "This big mistake," he mimicked, "will be finished when the outlaw's dead."

"You make the mistake, *señor.* By my mother's honor, I swear—"

Clarke snarled. He stood over the prisoner. He bent slightly. A tense finger danced on the trigger of a gun and the nose of it was trained on Blue Hawk's forehead.

"Don't put a doubt in my mind!" He stooped further. "The truth! Quick! Aren't you in cahoots with him?"

"No, *señor.* I—"

"You lie, damn you! First you called at the Aldman house. Then he came and you were standing guard. Confess it, you fool—and live. If you lie again, I'll kill you—if only to cover up *the big mistake!*"

To Blue Hawk death was insignificant compared with the safety of The Masked Rider. Yet in a flash he knew he must live, at least long enough to warn the outlaw that the Easterner knew of the tie that bound them. He must live—and hope for a chance to down the damage his own carelessness had wrought.

He swallowed hard "*Sí.* I am the servant of The Masked Rider. It is greater honor than even my father dreamed for me."

Clarke's laugh was of vast glee and triumph. He picked up the prisoner, dumped him across the sorrel's saddle, climbed aboard himself and rode off purring with contentment.

Occasionally he paused. At first Blue Hawk wondered why. Then all was plain. Clarke was dropping things the outlaw could not help but see—and follow; a stud from the saddle skirt, the Indian's neckerchief, the Indian's dagger. A trail to certain death.

When Blue Hawk thought his very insides must be ruptured if this cruel ride continued longer, Clarke stopped again. He shifted the prisoner to his shoulder and groped up a flight of creaking stairs that was alive with the mixed odors of tobacco and horses.

The Indian was flung upon the rusty floor. For a moment he thought he was to be left thus and his hopes soared—to be smashed when Clarke lit a lantern, picked up the prisoner, and made short shrift of roping him to a beam that braced the roof.

A PUFF OF Clarke's breath plunged the littered place into darkness so dense it could be felt. "You see!" he gloated. "All I have to do now is wait in the dark. Or maybe at dawn. No matter when he comes, you'll hear the shots."

"*Señor*, you are smart—and very lucky. But you kiss death and do not know it is she, *sabe?* You think this outlaw so big a fool that he walks into your trap as I? No. He comes. Of that you can be sure. But he goes, too, I warn you."

Clark started down the stairs. "You bet he goes—to his grave. Tonight, perhaps. Tomorrow, certainly."

Long before rats again ventured forth in the strangling silence, Blue Hawk was dishearteningly convinced that the Easterner knew how to bind a prisoner. For though he tugged and jerked and sawed at his bonds, the net gain was bleeding wrists and tired, wrenched muscles.

"*Madre de Dios,* help me!" he prayed.

Outside sounded the mournful wail of a dog. The Indian shuddered. His native legends had it that when a dog so wails, death strikes nearby. One thought sustained him. He knew the outlaw would not walk blindly into this infamous trap. He would come—at any risk, once he had reason to believe Blue Hawk here—prepared for trouble. But on such a black night could he see or know that death waited patiently?

FOR AN HOUR Clarke Weber's enthusiasm and day dreams of reward money kept him comfortable. Then, with the thermometer tobogganing and rain changing to sleet, he shivered and looked with envy on the house. The parlor shade was up. He could see the flames of the open fireplace dancing on the walls. Made him feel even colder. Yet he held his precious post, hands numb, teeth chattering.

"If I could watch from in there," he mumbled. "But—"

What a fool he'd been! If there was a light near the north kitchen window, it must dispel the gloomy dark as far as this wagon house door. He could wait inside, crouched near the window. There was but one entrance available to the prisoner's retreat.

He hurried into the house, avoided Ellen and Chet who were seated by the glowing fire. His hopes, he saw, were true. He had scarcely taken off his hat when Ellen stood in the doorway.

"Where've you been all day, Clarke? Did you—why! You're soaked!" She had her first full glimpse of his face and it half frightened her. "What's wrong!"

"Nothing."

She studied him. "Well! At first I thought you were angry at me. Now you resemble a cat that's just eaten the canary. What's so pleasant?"

Chet came and stood beside her. "Bet he's found a gold mine." He laughed to hide his curiosity.

Clarke was in that bad corner of a man who wants to boast and yet fears he'll have to share what he hides, if he does. "I've been out on business that turned out very well," he said curtly.

"In other words it's none of our business," said Ellen with no attempt to conceal her injured feelings. "I thought we were partners—in one business. This farm."

Clarke's anger flared. He whirled from the window. "I'm wondering if that partnership wasn't a mistake. Perhaps we'd better—oh, let it wait until tomorrow. I've something else in mind just now."

"Apparently! It's evidently in the yard. Something that needs close watching," Ellen said sharply. "And as part owners of this place, Chet and I have a right to know. We shall!"

BUT CLARKE REACHED the door first. "You might ruin everything," he barked. "You needn't go out. I'll tell you. I expect a visit from The Masked Rider."

Ellen's face became white. "You tried again to—"

"I've set a trap for him. It can't fail—if I'm ready to shoot him on sight. Now please go. Both of you."

Chet bristled. "You'd shoot an unsuspecting man? You wouldn't give him a chance to defend himself?"

"An outlaw who crucifies men and burns buildings isn't a man. He doesn't rate a chance."

"You fail and he makes us pay for it," interrupted Chet. "I think you've gone the limit, Clarke. In the morning—"

"I'll buy your shares in the place. You can pull out now, if you care to or if you're afraid. But I stand at this window and do as I've planned. Now get out."

Until his sister nudged him, Chet was rooted to the spot. Catching her wink, understanding that she felt capable of accomplishing some good, he turned to leave the room.

"Clarke's right," said Ellen. She hid the effort it was to make the admission. "He is an outlaw. It's fair to take him any way it can be done."

"It is!" insisted Clarke.

"But I don't see why you expect him to come here. You didn't quarrel with him? He didn't ride after you or—"

"He'll be here. For something he needs very badly."

"What?"

Clarke looked at her contemptuously. He did not answer. Why share a priceless secret with any one? Especially one who has always preached against his ambitions, one who proposed to chain him to the bare necessities of life, with which she would be content. Looking at her now, he wondered why he had ever let her get a grip on him. Well, that was all over now. He glanced out of the window. With the reward money he could refund what they had put up to help make the first payment on the farm and the balance would see him fully equipped to grow and grow until he became what Don Attero had been—the master of Deep Water Valley. He began to get impatient; he wished his prey would arrive. So engrossed did he become in the task in hand and the mental picture of the rosy future that he did not hear Ellen bid him good night. He pulled a chair near the window and sat with a Colt in each hand, his eyes riveted on the wagon house door.

CHAPTER XVI

THE HALF CIRCLE S

THE MASKED RIDER cachéd the heavy box of Colts and bullets and spent a few seconds in silent debate. Continue the hopeless hunt for Blue Hawk? Make the most of precious darkness in another effort to uncover the reason and the source of the valley outrages? He cast the die in favor of the latter; not without deepest regrets that the Indian's disappearance could best be looked into and solved in daylight—if ever.

He mounted the stallion, heedless of ice-coated saddle and confident that the sure-footed animal could still carry him swiftly from any danger—or to the Half Circle S ranch and Pete Haskell.

He sacrificed speed for safety, held the spirited animal to a slow trot. Once he pulled up sharp, tensed and listened, believing he had heard something like the distant call of a mountain cat. Only the snap and clink of ice-coated branches rewarded him. He gave the signal cry himself. Nothing stirred. He rode on.

From afar he studied the Half Circle S buildings and corrals. The ranch house alone showed signs of life and there only one room seemed occupied. He rode closer, left his mount. He saw a silver-haired man pick up a green-shaded lamp and begin to climb stairs behind the front door.

A dark window on the floor above soon became bright. The outlaw made out the hazy lines of a front porch whose roof was level with the sill of that window. He ran to the house, used the porch railing, shutters, and rain spout for a ladder and in half a minute was flat on his stomach edging toward what he felt was the ranchman's bedroom. He peered in.

The lamp was on a square table between door and bureau. Haskell was on the edge of the bed drawing off his boots, his back toward the window and the lamp. The outlaw suspected that if the sash was raised slowly, a cold draught would bring the cattleman quickly face about. He had not yet unbuckled holster and weapon.

The very second the bullet-studded belt left Haskell's fingers, the outlaw flung up the sash. He was inside the room as fast as the cowman whirled.

The first appearance of a hooded, cloaked man had surprised the range veteran. The second appearance was almost unbeliev-able. "I thought you stopped lead when—"

"Sit down—not too close to that smoke-piece."

Had it been a command, Haskell would doubtlessly have refused to budge. But the words, while frigid and sharp, seemed to apologize for themselves. Haskell sat.

"Habit of mine to get both sides of any story," said the outlaw quietly.

"About hell raisin' in the valley, you mean!"

"Yes."

"Havin' one side of the story, you know more about it than I do."

"Being kind of range Governor, you ought to be able to answer for all cattlemen in these parts."

"None of us know anything about fires or killin's."

"But you held a war counsel about dawn."

"We did. It was agreed that if tobacco men fence off Deep Water River in the north end of the valley, we'd tear it down—every damned time it went up."

"The valley south of Dan Attero's Cross!"

"That's tobacco. It doesn't hurt us. We want what Russ Bartle's dad always gave us—free and clear route to sweet water. No more; no less."

"Reckon only one law calls for that. The law of common decency. Bartle knows no such law? He won't meet you halfway?"

"Halfway?" Haskell swore. "Won't give an inch. We offered to buy the north end at what it's worth—but not a road agent's prices."

"Then you can't do anything—legally speaking."

"But otherwise we—"

"You can do almost anything—but you won't."

THE RANCHER LOOKED like a cat with its back up and tail fluffed out. "You tell me what we can't do without buckin' the law. Yo're a shinin' example of a law-abidin'—"

"No matter what I am, you'll hold your men in check—for forty-eight hours, *sabe?*"

"And if none of us obey an outlaw?"

"You will obey the guns of farmers! Somebody tried to burn out the Pringle place a while back. If something hadn't happened at a farmer's meeting, your buildings might be ash piles now and if you'd tried to stop 'em, you'd be a corpse."

"I've got eight punchers in the bunk house. They—"

"Then there'd have been nine corpses. Thirty or more men were ready to ride here."

"*You* stopped them?"

"I answer no more questions. You've got your orders. They're for your good. For forty-eight hours you and all cattlemen keep out of that valley, *sabe?* If you don't—"

"You throw in with the farmers. Think that'll keep us scared out?" He laughed, a sour, joyless laugh. "Mebbe it will an' mebbe we'll go there 'specially to get *you*."

Through the open window came the mud-muffled pound of a galloping horse. The outlaw pivoted, shot a glance outdoors. From his position he could glimpse a rider already half out of the saddle. By the wide split skirt he knew it to be a woman even before she cried out Haskell's name.

The old rancher was amazed and alarmed. Tim Callan's daughter! He thrust his head out of the window. "Mary! Up here!"

A dark-haired girl moved into the oblong of light on the ground. "You've got to come, Mr. Haskell! Dad's trying to keep a crowd from riding to the valley. Bartle's brought in two more settlers and there's barbed wire on their wagons."

"Get on home an' tell yore dad I'm comin' *pronto*." He spun from the window, snatched a boot and jammed in his foot. "Thought they'd kick over the traces. I told Bartle as much."

The outlaw sensed disaster. "You can stop those hot-headed fools if you try hard enough."

"Mebbe I can. If not—"

"I will." The Masked Rider slid over the window sill. "There's a forty-eight hour truce on, *sabe?*"

"Not on *you, hombre!*" snapped Haskell. "Looks like yo're dead set against us. That makes you fair game wherever met up with."

Half the rancher's words were waste. The outlaw was well on his way.

CHAPTER XVII

NEWS

RUSS **BARTLE VISIONED** the Chris Pringle drying shed as a long heap of hot ashes. He reasoned that the candle had burned down just as he returned to Gold Creek. Once the fire became noticeable, there was no hope to conquer it.

"By the time Sheriff Lande and his men got there, they could do nothing but wait for the outlaw." He sat at his orderly desk, began to thumb the pages of his ledger. Bad business to trust to memory. Put figures on paper and you'd never cheat your-self—nor calculate too slim a profit. "Let's see! Pringle owes me a thousand dollars, due next Tuesday. He can't sell tobacco ashes. He'll be here tomorrow to plead for time. I'll cry on his shoulder and tell him how sorry I am that I must have the money. Give him sixty days. Diplomatically handled, I ought to be able to convince him that it's best to sell out rather than go deeper into debt for a new shed while he raises another crop. The thing to do—"

He reached for a small file. It contained names and ad-dresses of parties once interested in buying a valley farm. He wrote to several; to the more likely prospects he offered to refund railroad fare if they purchased the Pringle farm. He stood by the window, running the gummed envelope flaps over his moist tongue. In the dimly lighted street he saw something that brought a wise sneer to his face.

He looked closer. Yes, it was Chris Pringle. He was stopping men, speaking to them briefly. Bartle was puzzled—a little delighted when the old farmer cut diagonally across the street, headed straight for Bartle's door.

In a minute the old man climbed the stairs. He looked more

angry than dejected. "You ain't seen Sheriff Lande, Mr. Bartle? I've been a-huntin' him all over town."

Russ was unpleasantly surprised. "He—he isn't on your farm?"

Pringle's shaggy brows raised. "Hell, no. Why would I be here huntin' him?"

"Damn him! I had warning that the next trouble would be at your place. A message was daggered to my door. I gave it to Lande and begged him to protect you. I thought sure he'd take picked men and go at once."

The old man cursed a blue streak. "Ain't seen him or any picked men. You should've known he wouldn't lift a finger to help tobacco men—fearin' he'd catch cowmen. Why in hell didn't you warn *me?*"

Bartle had no defense. The knife of disappointment cut him too deep to allow for any thoughts save all the risk he had run—for nothing. Well, at least he had squeezed Pringle into a tight corner.

"Did the fire do much damage?" he asked with an uncanny display of sympathetic hope.

"It didn't. My boy just happened to go fetch some water. He saw the flame an'—how'd you know it was a fire?"

"Why—why a stranger's spread the news all over town."

"Funny I ain't heard it mentioned," drawled Pringle. "Well, guess I'll get on an' try again to locate our wonderful sheriff."

Bartle's head spun. A good Masked Rider trap ruined; Pringle still in a position to meet that thousand dollar note! And like a chump he had given the old farmer cause for suspicion. Suppose he now scouted around town to see who else knew there had been a fire in his shed? Bartle could change his story a little, but he knew he ought to act even before doubt as to his standing arose. The finger of suspicion must never point his way!

"Lande must be at your place," he insisted. "I'll ride home with you. I'll prove I did all I could to keep you from harm."

He reached into the closet for his coat. His fingers unintentionally touched the cold butt of a gun. It was like some strange drug that fired his imagination. Dark night. Lonely trail. Dead men's suspicions cannot harm; dead men's tongues cannot move! He slipped the weapon into his coat pocket.

Perished now all hopes except to hold his reputation unbesmirched. Later he *must* find another means to rub out that second, personal menace to profit and personal safety—The Masked Rider.

THE LIGHT FROM the north kitchen window of the Weber-Maxon place still burned although it was no longer necessary. For the storm had passed and between rifts in wind-driven clouds a three-quarter moon made the ice-coated wagon shed seem silver-plated.

The ranch house was quiet as a mausoleum—until, in an upper bedroom, Ellen Maxon tiptoed to the door. Behind her Chet frowned and feared. Futile to plead that he be the one to go investigate the wagon house.

"Clarke's asleep," Ellen had said with finality. "I can hear him snoring. But if he awoke and saw a man near the shed door, he'd fire before he was wide awake enough to see that you weren't The Masked Rider. He can't mistake my hair and skirts—not in this moonlight."

She crept down the stairs with less noise than a shifting feather. She had deep-rooted suspicions that ambition again held Clarke in its vise and would make him stoop to anything to serve its ends.

She reached the front door, inched it open, and closed it behind her. In another minute she was safely inside the wagon shed, groping her way up the drafty stairway.

At first the sound of labored breathing frightened her. She hung back, struck a match, cupped her hands about it and tried to guide its light in a sweeping arc about the loft. It dropped in sheer surprise when she saw the Mexican Indian, blood trickling from his bruised wrists.

"Help me, *señorita,*" Blue Hawk pleaded. Her gasp of horror made him feel that she was an ally rather than another foe.

For a moment Ellen hesitated. Then the lantern flared and she sought something to cut stout rope. An ax proved as blunt as it was nicked and rusty, but in time it served its purpose, and with every sawing motion her anger against Clarke rose another notch.

"Why did he—"

"I do not know, *señorita,* why he kidnaps me. Unless it be that he hopes to get gold from my family." What matters a lie—many lies—when they help The Masked Rider? "The dog himself tells me he will pay off farm debts with my family's gold—or leave me here to die of hunger and thirst. Even now he expects my poor father to come with ransom. And I have warned him that mebbe my father also brings a gun!"

As he spoke, Blue Hawk unbound his ankles. He stretched and rubbed his blood into circulation, eyeing the girl, hoping she would believe. She, for her part, was impressed by the naturalness of his manner, the steadiness of his eye. And she was disarmed by the readiness and plausibility of his tale which seemed to jibe with Weber's actions. She hesitated a moment. Then: "He told us he had something here that would lure The Masked Rider."

"It cannot be *me, señorita.* You are Easterner, no? You do not know that the black outlaw is always the lone wolf? You must ask men if that is not true; ask many men—but do not believe the dog who kidnaps me. I can go now, *si?*"

"Yes, but carefully! He is waiting at the kitchen window—with a gun. Understand?"

"*Si!* It is like I have told you; he waits ready to take my father's gold—and then his life, so he may not tell what happened. Mebbe he kill me too. *Quién sabe?*"

He followed Ellen down the stairs, waited for her announcement that all looked safe. Prepared to make the dash of his life, Blue Hawk took time to doff his sombrero.

"One does not forget such a favor as this, *señorita*. *Adiós*. *Madre de Dios* watch over you."

He was gone like a ghost timed to return to the tomb in half a minute.

The girl stood in the wagon shed a moment. She twisted a diamond ring from her finger. "We're through, Clarke; *all* ways."

She went back to the house and found Chet all on edge. Her tale of the prisoner so enraged him that Ellen had difficulty restraining him from going to Clarke and speaking his mind.

"But in the morning we'll have it out," he said fervently. "He leaves this place, or we do! I'd rather be the partner of a coyote. At least then I wouldn't run the risk of a noose tightening around my neck."

"A kidnaper!" Ellen's voice was full of loathing. "And trying to make us believe he expected The Masked Rider when—"

She clipped the sentence. Downstairs the hinges of a door creaked. She flashed to the window. Her hand clutched her throat.

"Clarke!" she said in alarm. "He's going to the wagon shed. He'll find the Mexican gone!"

"Get in bed!" cut in Chet. "Don't answer if he calls. Anything we can do to hold him here gives the Mexican that much more chance to get far away."

He sprinted to his own room. Ellen never undressed faster. She was scarcely beneath the blankets when the lower door banged with a vengeance. Accompanied by oaths, Clarke Weber came pounding up the stairs. In those very steps was maniacal hatred. Ellen waited with bated breath.

CHAPTER XVIII

DEATH STALKS

ON THE VALLEY trail Bartle rode abreast of Chris Pringle, watching the old farmer as if he feared that by some miracle he might become aware that only the absence of a proper spot kept him alive.

In gloomy silence they covered a mile. Suddenly Pringle looked at Bartle. "You think there'll ever be real justice here for tobacco men?"

"I don't doubt it," droned Bartle. "Some day some cattleman will so plainly announce his guilt that even Sheriff Lande must act."

"You ever suspect that maybe it ain't beef men tryin' to run us out?"

"Lord no! Who else—"

"I don't know. It just kinda hit me now. Before Steve Ransom died he said he saw one man run away from his shed. Mike Chapman saw *one*. Burr Aldman saw *one*. Seems like cattle-men—if what I've learned about 'em since coming West is true—'most always ride more than single an' when they make up their minds to do something, they go ahead with a whoop an' holler. To hell with sneakin' around in the dark."

No man ever signed his own death warrant with greater indelibility. All fear and nervousness vanished from Bartle's mind. He glanced at Pringle like a hungry wolf looks at a stray lamb.

"Rather late with those conclusions, Pringle!"

"I guess. Maybe because no man ever thinks real hard till something hits *him*. Then, even if it is part miss, he thinks deep. Reckon I'll ride back to town with you later. Kinda nose around.

Ain't always detectives that dig up bits that fit somebody's door who ain't never been suspected or—"

Bartle held his horse back. His hand dipped into his pocket. Fingers gripped the cold gun butt. Pringle would have died at that precise moment—but the eerie cry of a nearby mountain cat tore at Bartle's nerves.

The respite was short. Bartle's gun boomed. Pringle trembled, slid to one side of the saddle. He clutched the horn to save himself. Death flexed his fingers. He toppled. One foot remained fast in the stirrup until the horse bolted in fright. The farmer lay twisted in the mud and melting sleet of the trail. Then, as if to speed him on his way to eternity, there came again the ghastly cry of a prowling cat. This time, however, the cry was clipped in half. Possibly the sound of the single shot had reached the spot and frightened the animal.

The killer sat his horse as a man does who must be certain he has worked faultlessly and thoroughly. He dismounted, rolled the victim over on his back. Satisfied that Pringle's tongue was forever beyond motion, he turned again to his horse, face frozen in a triumphant leer made doubly hideous by the light of the moon. One foot was ready to hoist him to leather. Then the animal that had plagued him twice tonight, seemed to drop from the sky.

It was Blue Hawk. In his search for The Masked Rider he had inadvertently come upon the sign of the killer once plying his trade at the Aldman farm. He followed, knowing the rat was accompanied by another rider. At a stream he lost the scent for a few minutes and that loss had only been made up after the shot drifted to him. He was glad that the first thing he had done when the girl freed him, was to recover a gun from his sorrel's saddle-pack, and then scent out and retrieve all the things supposed to lure The Masked Rider to death.

"This time, rat, you do not ride water and escape me!" he flared, determined to take a live prisoner that The Masked Rider might wring fact and truth from his mouth.

BARTLE REALIZED HE must spar ingeniously for his life. "You don't think I killed this man?" He stared trembling at the weapon in the Mexican's steady hand—and cursed his own that was in his pocket.

"Him I am not sure about. But the sign of your horse tells me you are the rat of Don Attero's cross; the rat who killed at a burning shed. *Si!* You write your name where you go! It is too bad that only now you know that the toe piece on the front left shoe of your horse is not evenly worn down. You will have that fixed—in hell, mebbe."

"Don't be a damned fool!" exploded Bartle. "We were riding to this man's farm in the valley. I wanted to see how much damage cattlemen had done to his drying shed. Somebody fired at us from behind those bushes in back of you. It was a cow puncher. Turn around and you'll see how easy it is to look through those bushes."

The Indian did not move. "Once tonight I make the big mistake. I do not look behind me, rat! You turn around. Your hands behind your back. I tie you first. I look behind me, *si*— when you are in a safe place and I know who you are."

Bartle took heart. The fellow didn't know him! There was still a chance to save his dreams of easy fortune—and his neck. He obeyed the Indian's commands with a willingness that few innocent men could display.

"Tie and be damned," he stormed "You'll pay for this. I'll have Sheriff Lande hunting you down the minute you discover what a fool you've been."

Blue Hawk was unimpressed. Experience had taught him to believe his eyes in preference to his ears. He took the rope from the sorrel's saddle, advanced on his man wishing he had three hands; two to use for binding, one to hold his gun.

He threw a loop around the prisoner's wrists, marking the obliging and helpful way the fellow held them. Then his opinion changed.

For Bartle turned like a beast at bay, snarling, his fists lashing out in lieu of claws. He flayed the Indian, driving him backward relentlessly, not giving up even when the other's weapon spoke and flame singed his coat sleeve.

Blue Hawk stumbled and fell. Insane fury made Bartle fling himself upon the Indian, pummeling him with one hand while the other sought to snatch away the gun. But as his strength waned, Bartle's common sense returned. The gun in his pocket! Now he could take time to draw it. The Mexican only clung to consciousness by a thread.

But when he was ready to snuff out the second life that threatened his own, Russ Bartle considered all the world suddenly bent on tearing away the mask behind which he hid. On a nearby knoll, so close that a shot must draw them, he saw two horsemen. With the Indian struggling to bring up his gun, Bartle exercised his rattled intelligence as well as circumstances permitted. He threw himself into his saddle and bolted.

Blue Hawk got up shaking cobwebs from his brain. Two things sent him after Bartle in full stride—it would never do to be found near a corpse, and this time the rat must not escape! Even as he urged the sorrel on, the Indian was grimly happy. At least he had met the fiend of Don Attero's cross. That face would live in his memory forever! And since it was that of the man who had killed this old farmer, it must be that of the man behind all the valley atrocities.

CHAPTER XIX

SHOW-DOWN

ELLEN MAXON DID not long have hopes that the man she had loved only a few days ago would consider even an unlocked door of her bedroom a barricade beyond which he must not go.

The knob twisted, wrenched a shiver from Ellen. She wondered how perfectly she feigned sleep as Clarke Weber stamped to the bedside. His breath was audible—fast, bitter snatches.

"Ellen!" he bellowed. The slight flutter of her eyelids enraged him. "Ellen!"

She snapped awake, looked at his fiery face, drew the blanket close about her shoulders.

"Why—"

"Were you in the wagon house loft?"

The denial died at sight of the object on the palm he thrust under her nose. It was a hairpin. Now he stooped, grabbed her shoe, ran a finger over the edge of the sole which was caked with moist mud.

"Yes," she cried "I set him free. And, thank God, you did the same to me when you tried such a contemptible thing. You'll find your ring on the dresser."

His rage shook him. "You little empty-headed—" His teeth clicked off the balance. His fist started for her frightened face. He swung around at the sound of a step behind him.

Chet charged from the doorway.

Clarke tried to drag the Colt from his belt. He succeeded. But in the same heart-beat Chet's knuckles thudded on his ear with the most vicious blow he had ever felt. The room spun. His legs buckled. The floor came up as he felt the weapon tugged out of his fingers.

Chet backed away. His self-control was remarkable. "You can clear out of here, Clarke," he said gladly. "Find another base of operations for your plans to get the outlaw—and kidnaping Mexicans."

"I kidnaped him because—" He swallowed the revelation. One failure can always be amended. Apparently the Indian had lied to gain his freedom. Chet and Ellen didn't know he was The Masked Rider's henchman. It would be well to keep them ignorant. Who knows but what the pinch of poverty might make them less particular as to how they obtained the money that meant relief? Especially when he was through with them—and a thousand-dollar payment due Russ Bartle in the morning.

He picked himself up from the floor, angry yet grinning. "I saw a chance to get some ransom money," he lied smoothly. "I knew you holies would object and so—"

"Please leave. Don't ever let me see you again," Ellen's voice was sharp.

"You'll be anxious to look for me and find me when Bartle calls in the morning for the thousand dollars you haven't got," he jeered. "You'll whine like those mountain cats are whining now."

He went down the stairs with Chet crowding close.

There came an insistent rapping on the door; so hurried and alarmed that both men glanced at each other questioningly before Chet went to answer.

Russ Bartle came in. He attempted to hide jagged nerves behind a weak smile. Only he knew the terrors of the outer night. Pringle butchered. The Mexican. The riders. The cat calls that chilled—and that group of angry ranchers in conference at the valley's edge. So he had sought refuge with the Weber-Maxons. With anxious eyes he watched Clarke put on hat and coat.

"Going to Gold Creek?" he inquired hopefully.

"Yes—permanently. The partnership here is dissolved. There seems an objection to my plans to trap The Masked Rider."

Bartle showed indignation. "That's every man's duty, Chet," he said decidedly. "Nothing should be left undone to get this two-legged coyote who—"

CLARKE WINKED. "IF you're going to town, we can ride together. I have some news that'll interest you."

"I stopped here for two reasons. To see how you liked the place; to fix the front shoes of my horse. He went lame; always does when the shoes wear down. There used to be quite a pile of shoes in your wagon house here. Mind if I try and find a pair?"

"Glad to help you get them on," volunteered Clarke. In the wagon shed they could talk confidentially.

Horse shoes were furthest from Bartle's and Clarke Weber's minds when they reached the wagon house.

"How much will you really give for the outlaw?" blurted Clarke. "I mean, considering it is a hard job to even catch sight of him."

"I offered to cancel the balance due on the farm. Any public spirited citizen would do that to help—"

"The job's worth more. It's dangerous. It's hard." He rubbed his chin, trying to pry into Bartle's mind via his face, trying to learn whether or not it was only public good that urged the landowner to offer a prize. "Would you give ten thousand dollars?"

Bartle seemed struck across the face with a whip. "Ten thousand dollars! Ridiculous!"

"Say no more about it," purred Clarke. He picked up the lantern. "Where did you last see those shoes?"

"In the loft, I believe. There or—you seem real certain you could get the outlaw."

"I am—because I alone know of bait that will draw him. I wouldn't risk my life for less than ten thousand. Perhaps later I'd ask fifteen. The longer a man thinks about risk, the greater it seems, understand?"

"I'll—pay ten." Bartle scowled. "Only because—"

"Because you fear him more than any one else." Clarke smiled wisely. "Five weeks we haggled about the price of this place. Two hundred dollars stood between us. We had to give way. Yet now you're ready to part with ten thousand dollars—for the common good of the county? Bartle, I wasn't born yesterday."

"What're you driving at, Weber? I don't have to offer you anything, you know."

"But you will—to save your own neck. Some things are quite plain to me—now that I'm able to see beyond your surface. Lots of times it takes a total stranger to do that. The Masked Rider could ruin your plans for wealth. Right this minute I can see that the true things I'm saying are hitting you hard. I think—"

"A right smart maverick you are!" Bartle sneered. "Think it'll help me sell land if it gets around that The Masked Rider is burning down the farm houses and spiking the farmers to crosses? Let me get those horse shoes—while you think some more."

Clarke surrendered the lantern. "Get them. But don't you leave this farm until you see me again. I'm going off for a while. I'll be back with proof I can take the outlaw when it pleases me. Then we'll talk about price. And you'll be glad to pay, I swear."

He stepped out into the moonlight. Freezing in grotesque posture, he stared wild-eyed at the corner of another shed. He walked forward uncertainly, peering around its corner while he strove to convince himself it was imagination and not a black splotch that he had seen.

He rode off quickly. Imagination! Why worry about what he thought he had seen when the things that actually were, promised so much? Before many hours had passed he would profit handsomely. Half—if not all—of everything that Bartle owned would be his. Then, but only to safeguard the fortune he meant to get and live to enjoy, he would make strenuous efforts to get The Masked Rider. He coveted ownership of half Bartle's reasons for fearing the Black Caballero.

Clarke whipped his horse into a frantic gallop toward Gold Creek. A man who owns such vast holdings in the valley, and has a stake in all of it, cannot carry all his facts and figures in his head, thought Clarke. He prayed that Bartle's office proved fertile that it yield something upon which he could base his firm conviction that the landowner was not open and above board; something that could be held over his head like Damocles' sword.

CHAPTER XX

REUNION

THERE WERE NO exuberant greetings when their signal cries eventually reunited Blue Hawk and The Masked Rider. Their feelings were beyond gushing sentiment—too deep for expression in mere words. Besides, each had news of vast import; both knew that they must attend to business if the pall of death hanging low was not to fall on tobacco farm and ranch and themselves alike.

The Indian told of his own folly and failure with frankness and regrets. "I should make no more mistakes, *señor,* if the girl was not a partner of the Eastern rat. Mebbe I am dead by now. *Quién sabe?*"

"The Easterner the same man we trail now?"

"*Sí!* I should like for to drop the loop of my rope around his neck and let the sorrel gallop a thousand miles."

"I'd say drag him until there wasn't an inch of his hide or hair left—if it would straighten out the tangle in this valley of crucifixion. It won't."

"So like the killer at the cross, he lives, *señor?*" Blue Hawk shook his head. "*Dios!* Life is full of pities."

"What about that killer whose sign was at the cross? After he spread-eagled the farmer lad?"

The Indian looked sad. "Mebbe he spends all his youth near the valley, *señor.* This I know. He rides strange. East. West. North. South. Like locoed man walks. Now he leaves sign. Now he rides water. Stone. Puff! He is gone like a winged ghost. I do not find his sign again before we meet. Later, mebbe, *señor.*"

"Yes. Later—most likely at the Weber-Maxon farm. Two men in that wagon shed spoke. I could not hear very well, but one voice sounded Eastern. That man we trail. One was Western. We will find out who he is—later."

"But these cowmen, *señor.*"

"You have nothing to fear if they should find you near them. Go. Listen. Watch. If they move on any farm, try and overtake me. I follow the Easterner. If you have to catch up with me, give the cat cry as you ride. If you learn nothing, then watch for me near the Weber-Maxon farm. *Adiós.*"

He left in full pursuit of hoof-beats now only the slightest sound in the night. As he rode, evil thoughts kept abreast of him. Would tobacco and ranch men be at each other's throats before he learned the Easterner's mission and destination? He traveled like the wind, hoping against hope that there was still a chance to rip away the veil of mystery about the fires and killings into which he and Blue Hawk had so accidentally plunged—and which had gripped them in a vise of hatred against the inhuman marauders.

He gave the stallion free rein and with every stride the great black clipped another few inches from the Easterner's lead. Soon there was no room for doubt in The Masked Rider's keen mind.

"He heads for Gold Creek—the longest way." He sent the stallion across a stream in one great splash of spray and water. Short-cut. Why ride four miles if three bring one to the same place? "Gold Creek— He can be picked up there again. His urgent business is either with the sheriff, or Bartle. Nobody else."

PETE HASKELL REACHED the Callan spread in a lather. There, he heard the most alarming news since the first tobacco farmer threw up a long fence in the south end of Deep Water Valley.

"They've kicked over the traces, Pete," the cook told him. "All done, through, waitin' for you to call the play. The hull pack. Tim, he wasn't going with 'em till Luke Wallace said he was scared. Then he joined in. They all ain't more'n three—maybe four miles by now."

Haskell tore away. The die was cast. It was now or never—he must stop them! The fire of youth was in that mad dash of his. The reward was ample. He stopped the crowd at Chinnoc Pass; at its very mouth the main entrance to the valley. And now....

He sat his horse with a gun in his hand, grim determination in his watery blue eyes. "I ain't arguin'. For the last time I'm tellin' you that the man who rides this way an' gets by this pinto does so after he drills me."

Tim Callan was afoot at the pinto's head. "Pete's right. What you gents aim to do helps nobody."

Luke Wallace strode forward. "Why wait for fence to go up? Those new folks fetched reels of it with 'em and barbed wire ain't for clothes' lines. We're ridin' in—unless Pete's found something that'll help us more'n wishin' an' hopin'."

HASKELL KNEW THE futility of prodding his brain. Night after night he lay awake, struggling to find the open sesame to peace—and sweet water. There was none.

"The Masked Rider called at my place a while ago," he bit out, savagely.

"You wouldn't lie to hold us here or make us turn back?" growled Wallace. "He held too much lead to do any visitin' for some time if ever."

"Howsomever, he *came*. Why, I don't know, but he said no cattleman was to enter the valley for forty-eight hours."

"*He* said!" blasted Wallace. He turned to the crowd. "Gents, looks like Baker County's Ranch Owners Association has a new top hand—a mangy outlaw! *He* says we keep out of the valley!"

Haskell shed the ridicule with ease. "I'm willin' to accept a truce for that long. Mebbe he has a stake in the valley. Mebbe he sees clear skies—in forty-eight hours—if all concerned will wait that long."

"Mebbe," snapped a man in the rear. "The chances are—*not*. But I'm agreeable to something else—that don't need any forty-eight hours to prove good or bad."

"Tell it," said Haskell eagerly.

"Pool all the cash we can raise. Fix a fair enough price on all the valley north of Don Attero's cross. Offer Bartle the cash and the balance of the fair price on mortgage."

Haskell's hopes were like a pin-pricked bubble. "He'll laugh an' turn it down."

"Hope so. It can't be a crime to kill such a coyote—and since he's got neither kith nor kin, the State gets the valley and our votes can keep it open and free."

A shout went up from the men. Few propositions were ever accorded the support evidenced by that shout which echoed over the hills and the valley like the battle cry of serfs already tasting victory and freedom.

Only Haskell and Callan kept their mouths closed.

"Well?" demanded Wallace. "You object, Haskell? You'd rather obey the outlaw's orders—an' waste forty-eight hours?"

"It—it'll be murder. I know damned well it will be."

"He'll have a choice—fair price or bullets. Better 'n he deserves, by God!"

"But it ain't fair. It—"

"We know it ain't fair—that one selfish man hold all our bread, our homes, our business, in his dirty paw and laugh when we yell for relief."

Haskell surrendered. Not completely. But he quickly reasoned that none of these angry ranchers would waste time or breath in *appealing*. They'd ask. No more. Their very attitude would rub Bartle the wrong way. His answer was as good as already spoken. But if Haskell himself acted as emissary there might be a chance—slim, indeed—that bloodshed be avoided.

"I ride with you to Bartle's office. Providin' you let me speak to him alone—and kinda let me get away before one of you draw a six-gun. I don't want even a buzzard's blood on my hands or conscience, *sabe?*"

Again a mighty shout echoed in the night. Men flew to saddles and the procession of death was on.

CHAPTER XXI

SNARED

B LUE HAWK, WITHIN earshot of the cowmen's heated debate and sinister decision, crouched in his hiding place until the last of Haskell's men were at a safe distance.

That The Masked Rider would reach Gold Creek first was very plain to the Indian. But would the outlaw be away from that dangerous place before the cattlemen arrived? Would he linger there, blissfully ignorant that death closed in on him while he questioned the Easterner or possibly went to Bartle's place and searched the office? The Indian had a rare faculty of sometimes knowing, untold, what The Masked Rider was about to do.

Blue Hawk was not unduly alarmed—yet. His sorrel was more than a match for the mount of any of Haskell's men, and they, being in no particular hurry, would no doubt stick to the beaten track while Blue Hawk was definitely determined to cut across country and save a mile or more.

HE WAITED, NOT tempted to start too soon, lest the cowmen become aware that they had been overheard. When the retreating sounds of the band died in the distance, the Indian ran towards his sorrel. He saw the sleek animal plain enough in the moonlight, head thrust toward him, ears cocked, eager for the gentle touch of his hand.

But when he gripped the saddle to swing himself up, he saw something not so pleasant.

It was Sheriff Lande.

He was as close to the sorrel on one side as Blue Hawk was on the other. There was no trace of friendliness in his eyes.

"Goin' some place—in a helluva hurry?" Lande's voice was flint hard. "Heard some yellin' clear over to the Pringle place. Reckoned it come from hereabouts."

Blue Hawk could not speak. He suspected other questions would follow an explanation that cowmen had done the shouting.

"Well?" bombarded Lande. "Can't you talk? Don't you *sabe*, I've asked you what happened here?"

"*Si, señor. Sabe*—but nothing happens here. I, too, hear shouts—farther west, mebbe."

Lande did not reply. He walked alertly around the horse, took hold of Blue Hawk's elbow and enticed him to walk about a hundred feet. Then his hand shot out with the index finger stiff as a stove poker—and trained on the jumble of many hoof prints.

"Cowmen, wasn't they?" he snapped. "The truth, *amigo!*"

"I did not see. My eyes they grow weak with age. Riders? *Si.* More I do not know."

Another horseman thundered up. His deputy's badge, his Winchester, marked him as a posseman. "Hell to pay, Sheriff! Jim an' I just stumbled on a corpse. Tobacco farmer sure enough. Drilled through the head—from behind."

Lande glared at the suspect. At the posseman he fired, "Further west, Cal?"

"Yep. Right around that bend, Sheriff. He lays right on the edge o' the trail in the shadow of a rock. Looks like you *did* hear a shot a while ago, huh?"

"Reckoned so. Don't have to reckon that I saw this gent come runnin' from that direction."

"I shoot not from behind!" flared Blue Hawk.

"Take care o' the gent, Cal. At dawn we'll have a look-see at boot prints around the corpse—if any. By that time the boys to relieve us should be on the job."

Boot prints! Blue Hawk knew his would be there. Silence now would not improve his standing. He thought of The Masked Rider in Gold Creek, and of Russ Bartle. Both of them in danger! The condition would never have materialized if he hadn't let the murderer of this farmer escape. Somehow he felt that man to be the explanation of everything sinister that had happened in the valley; that through that man alone could bloody warfare be avoided. He did not know the killer was Russ Bartle, for while he had probed into Bartle's reputation and business, he thought he was still to meet the landowner personally for the first time.

"Hog-tie him an' caché him some place, Sheriff?" asked Cal, dismounting,

"Yeah. Good enough. I'll head back to Pringle's. I sure want to be on hand if The Masked Rider shows up—which I'm beginnin' to doubt."

"Wait, *señor!*" cried Blue Hawk. He had definitely planned—not to be tied up again, but to go on about his *duty*, warning the outlaw, and Bartle. "We build fire. I show you my boot prints by corpse—and the sign of the killer. I will lead you to the rat! *Sí?*"

"So!" exclaimed Lande. "You were there? An' another *hombre?*"

"He killed. I try for to make him prisoner. He tricks me. When I begin to track him down, cowmen come. I afraid they see corpse and me—to think as you, that *I* am the killer."

The sheriff gave the proposition due thought. Not much lost if the Indian did lead them on a wild-goose chase and there was a possibility that he was telling the truth. His consent to being shown was gruff and unbelieving.

Blue Hawk knew what he was about. He led his captors to the gruesome spot, eyeing the sky over his shoulder. Getting darker! Only a thin slice of the rind of the moon was visible over the snow-crowned peaks of Lost Ghost Mountains. Another few minutes and the darkness he craved would fall like an opaque curtain. Then—he prayed—could begin headlong flight to save The Masked Rider.

THE INDIAN QUICKLY kindled a small fire. He knelt close to the rigid corpse. "These are my boots, *señor.*" He reached farther. "These are the killer's. You see difference? I make much bigger sign, no?"

"Yeah," drawled Lande. What difference did it make?

Blue Hawk rose, walked a few yards, dropped again. "The sign of killer's horse, *señor.* You see how toe-piece on shoe makes big dent on *one* end?"

Lande stooped and squinted. To him it was the toe-print of a thousand horses; so ordinary and commonplace that he felt at once that the Indian was trying to make a fool out of him. "Sure," he said hotly. "It's a helluva lot different than all the other toe-prints I looked at. Now let's see you bring us to the *hombre* who forked that cayuse."

"We walk? Ride mebbe better. Killer always goes far, *sabe?*"

"But you couldn't see the sign from yore saddle!" blasted the posseman. He turned to the sheriff. "Wouldn't waste any more time on this yarn o' his, Sheriff."

"I already trail killer to arroyo half-mile south," defended Blue Hawk. "We ride so far, then I walk. But hurry. See how quick darkness comes."

Lande drew a six-gun, covered the Indian as he mounted. "All right. Ride. I'm right anxious to hear how you'll wind up this cock-an'-bull yarn."

The Indian rode in front of the alert pair. Ahead was the

arroyo. There he must face the show-down; he would be expected to dismount and point out sign of the killer he knew was not there! He held the sorrel back as the black mantle of night dropped closer and closer, thicker and thicker; held the sorrel back while he patted its sleek neck as if asking forgiveness for tortures and risks which he meant to put it to. The side of that dry wash was little less perpendicular than a straight wall. It dipped deadly a hundred sheer feet before it touched boulder-strewn bottom. Below would be darkness so dense it might be cleaved. One horse could negotiate that rocky wall, reach bottom without tumbling, break into furious gallop to carry its rider away from lead that must scream after him even though he was practically invisible. That horse was the sorrel. And even now it twitched and quivered beneath Blue Hawk as if to warn him that one rider in ten thousand would make this desperate attempt.

"Watch where yo're goin, *amigo*," counseled Lande. "Yo're damned near Dead Fall arroyo."

The Indian stared tensely ahead. *"Si, señor,* I know. *El Acedero* knows. The sorrel one is not afraid. You?"

He rode on, lips clamped, heart still, thoughts only for the sorrel and the outlaw. Then like a plummet he was out of sight.

Lande's oath was more of admiration than surprise or anger. He flew to the ground, ran forward, peered over the edge, saw nothing, yet emptied his gun at the clanging of hoofs on rocks. His deputy came. The Winchester belched fire. Then only the fading staccato of a galloping sorrel broke the silence.

"Been done before," said Lande. "By another damned lucky gent I couldn't be the third to make it. But we can both try an' head him off."

"At Dillman's, Sheriff! She drops kinda gentle there."

Lande mounted, but in his heart he knew that *El Acedero* could be overtaken by only one horse he could recall—The Masked Rider's great black stallion.

CHAPTER XXII

HOODED DEATH

MEN DEAD SET on a destination and task have no need to hurry. So it was with Clarke Weber, The Masked Rider, and Pete Haskell's men. All of them knew where they were going, knew what they were about to do. All of them were treading the danger trail. No haste, now.

Clarke led the grim parade. He alone did not expect to face Russ Bartle. Like all three factions riding the trail to Gold Creek, he had no reason to suspect that close behind him came other riders. He traveled down the cowtown's mud-puddled street with his face wreathed in a greedy grin that suddenly was wiped away.

The window over the bank showed yellow beneath a partly drawn shade. Clarke stopped short in the center of the street. A sibilant oath escaped his mouth. Light within! Had Bartle left the farm? Damn him! Then he had either pushed a lame horse hard, changed shoes mighty fast—or lied from scratch!

"No difference," growled Clarke, going on. "Even if he's up there I'll make him admit plenty!"

He left his horse at the bank hitching rail. Twice he fisted the door while he peered up the stairway. There was no sign of life above. His mood improved. He walked stealthily around the building, up a drive on the south, across the back, down a drive on the north. He scanned the front of the place. Then he rode to the Western Sun saloon where he sandwiched the horse between punchers' gray and dun animals. Bad business for house-breakers to have their mounts at the door behind which they prowl!

He went up a drive some distance from the bank, then hurried toward his goal. Soft hands and muscles made hard work of getting up on a canopy over the rear door of the bank. Tired and puffing, he reached Bartle's window. The catch annoyed him. But the long thin blade of his pocket knife fitted between sashes and soon the lower sash was up.

He stepped lightly into the large room, quickly pulled the shade lower, then stood wondering which of the books on the orderly desk would yield the most damning information. He picked up the smallest.

It was discouraging. The pages only said that they were kept by a man who had to know where every last penny went. Even postage stamps were listed. Clarke flung the book down with a growl.

He read parts of letters plucked at random from a thick file. A man doesn't brand himself by copies of letters offering to sell land he *does* own. Clarke's castles began to show the cracks of faulty foundations. Had he dreamed all his pleasant dreams to be awakened now and find them only chimeras? Was Bartle on the level after all? He snatched up a ledger and let it fall open haphazardly. A folded blue sheet fell to the floor. He picked that up and spread it out.

A diagram of the entire valley—every farm upon it, some of those in the north end crossed with red crayon. No man need fear for his neck—or The Masked Rider—because he kept such a drawing. Clarke let it flutter from his hands. He glanced at the ledger.

Page ten. Farm Number Thirteen. The page halved by double red lines. Bought from a descendent of *Señor* Don Attero by Louis Augustus Bartle. Price eleven hundred dollars. Sold to Thomas Buckley. Thirteen hundred dollars.

"Legitimate profit!" snarled Clarke, his eyes following the diagonal line drawn almost to the bottom of the page. "Buckley evidently liked the place. Stayed ten years and then—"

His eyes flamed with hope.

Behind Buckley's name, in red ink... "deceased." Bought by

Russ Bartle. Price, including improvements, thirteen hundred dollars. Sold to Steve Ransom. Price fifty-five hundred. Behind Steve's name—"deceased."

Clarke let out a squeal of delight. For then he read that Russ Bartle again bought that same farm and behind the transaction…. "Net profit, twenty-two hundred dollars."

"And—and we've bought that same place from Bartle for fifty-five hundred," he gasped. "By God, I see it now! Bring them in; drive them out or kill them. Buy. Sell. Always at a profit. And—" He glanced at a dozen pages before being convinced that the Ransom place was the only one with a red crayon question mark beneath the last entry. "Does that mean he'll work on us next? Bring us in at fifty-five hundred, drive us out at about three thousand?"

HE SLUMPED INTO a chair at the desk, picking up books and papers, scanning them hurriedly, throwing them aside, until he looked like a dog with so much food in sight that it didn't know which to eat first and bit chunks out of everything.

He got up wet with perspiration, books and papers clutched under his arm, all atremble at Fate's broad smile.

"The Maxons won't hear a word of this! From now on I'm Bartle's partner—until I can get rid of him the way he got rid of people whom he couldn't scare out of Deep Water Valley."

In his eyes blazed the lust for power and wealth that had spurred Bartle on. He thought of the legend of Don Attero. He smiled. He would be the Mexican-Spaniard reincarnated. He turned toward the open window. His visions of the future melted away like lard on a blistering hot stove.

"I'll take those books and papers," said the black-clad terror at the window.

Clarke wilted. "You—" His throat closed up on him.

"Me! One of life's compensations, I guess, that I let you live after our first meeting. I taught you something then. Must I teach you that I seldom ask for anything twice?"

Clark thawed his vocal cords. Only a faint spark of hope was left in him. That spark he strove desperately to fan into flame. There must be a way out! The window? Impossible, for the outlaw was only a foot from the sill. The stairs? There was a lock on the door—but the panel was glass. What man would hesitate in a choice between a fortune and hurling himself through a thin glass sheet?

He backed away from the phantom in black. "There's nothing in the books that will interest you. Bartle sent me to fetch them to—"

"The farm? Then he's the man you spoke with in the wagon shed?"

"He—"

"You threatened him. By those books you must hope to back up that threat. Anyhow, what interests you, interests me, *sabe?* No more palaver! Unload."

Clarke stole another yard nearer the stairs. Tried to get yet closer. The outlaw's command stung his ears. He dared not move another inch. For a second he thought of his gun. One lesson was still a sore brand upon his mind and fifth finger, yet he realized the weapon was his sole hope. A man can't draw when both his hands are full of papers and a heavy book! Clarke rallied his nerves.

"I haven't any objection to you looking at these things—if you'll give them back and let me go."

"You have no objections?" The outlaw's laugh was more a sarcastic snort. "I'm glad. For a while I thought you were considering reaching for your gun and—put the books on that chair. Six-gun on top. Do both kind of careful. Don't let imagination get the best of you again, *sabe?*"

Clarke obeyed. Fright had burned itself out He watched tense strides carry the black cloaked man to the chair. His every nerve and muscle were under rigid control. He stood like a bird poised to take flight, knowing that when he moved it must be with the speed of light. He saw one black-gloved hand seize papers and the other move for the ledger.

"Now! Now!" he told himself.

PETE HASKELL RODE down the street flanked by Luke Wallace and Tim Callan. All three of them saw that Bartle's shade was drawn and that a light glowed within. To Callan and Haskell it gave the effect of candles over a coffin. In their quick trade of glances they showed their disappointment in not finding Bartle out. They knew delay would cool the rancor of the cowmen.

Haskell pulled up his horse. "It was agreed that I speak to Russ alone," he reminded Wallace.

"Yep. I'll ride herd on the boys—but not far from the bank. Get on, Pete. Good luck—for Bartle's sake."

THE RANGE VETERAN went on, eyes lowered and chin down. He knew the aftermath of this night's work—Sheriff Lande's mailed fist of law! It hurt the cowman to think that Lande would move heaven and earth—yes, appeal to the Governor for militia if need be—to get the noose around the right ring leader of this expedition. The hangman's knot looked made-to-order for him. He knew he could not stand up in any court and pass the buck of responsibility to other shoulders, although he was dead set against a killing. To die in silence? Two sons, three daughters in Eastern schools now, left behind to bear the stigma… "Their dad swung for murder."

He eased himself from the saddle at Bartle's door. He raised his hand to knock. The hand dropped. He gaped. Blinked. Eyes up at the landing—where stood what at first seemed an ebony statue. There was one thing that wasn't black—the wisp of smoke curling and fading about the ceiling. There was a gun in the black-gloved hand. Quickly surprise faded and Haskell's eyes recorded other things.

Halfway down the flight, twisted and jammed between

building wall and staircase side, was the body of a man. Papers littered the steps. Even now the black apparition was scooping them up—and at Haskell's elbow stood Luke Wallace demanding to know why the cowman couldn't get in.

Then Wallace saw! His hand swooped on his gun.

"Wait!" commanded Haskell in an angry whisper. "Damned important those papers, or the outlaw wouldn't expose himself that way to get 'em."

"That ain't Bartle on the steps," rasped Wallace. His fingers clawed his gun like an enraged lion claws cage bars. "I begin to see things! This gent in black is in cahoots with Bartle, I'll bet. It's him that's killin' an' burnin' in the valley, *for* Bartle, damn him. Then we're blamed!"

"I wouldn't jump at conclusions," counselled Haskell.

"Ain't he killed a man to save Bartle's papers? Ain't he—"

"Quiet! He's goin' upstairs now. Let's see what happens."

"See hell! *Stop it.*" Wallace whirled, ran to the other ranchers. His orders came like the buzz of a rip saw. "Ring the building. A pair of you stand guard at each trail out o' town. The Masked Rider's in Bartle's office."

"An' Bartle?" asked a startled cowman before any one moved.

"Hell knows—an' makes no difference! Move!"

CHAPTER XXIII

WINGS OF SAFETY

IT WAS A seventh sense that warned the black phantom of the closing jaws of a trap. For even as he hurriedly glanced at the ledger of the landowner, he heard the familiar voice of Pete Haskell. That he met the menace with dispatch was best credited to ability born of long experience so doing. Split seconds were precious, he knew. As Luke Wallace ripped out his hushed orders, the outlaw went over the sill of the window.

Sounds of scuffling feet drifted down the drive as The Masked Rider clutched the edge of the bank door canopy, swung himself into space and dropped to the ground. Bent almost double, looking like a great black rolling ball rather than a running man, he was unsighted when he disappeared behind an open-faced stable where bank patrons were accustomed to stall their horses.

Two ranchers came out of the driveway. The outlaw's stirrups did not squeak as he put his weight upon the one, then found the other. He turned the stallion quietly, watching the two ranchers. Guns in hand, they stood looking at Bartle's open window. They backed away as if they meant to give the intruder time to come out, stand on the canopy to taste of their lead.

The Masked Rider sat like patient death in a sick room. His pulse was normal, nerves steady, eyes calm and clear. For a moment he pictured the four ways out of Gold Creek for any man who *must* ride hard. He realized that death lurked at all of them. No genie or guardian angel told him to turn to the north exit. He knew cowmen. Given a clue as to his whereabouts, or a hint that one of their number had sighted him, they would all rush to be in at the kill. The north exit from town was nearest the bank. The guards there would be first away from their posts; first to reach the bank building if the alarm spread—and for the outlaw, *north* would be the shortest gauntlet to ride to safety. If he could escape the bullets of this pair now within stone's throw of him, he had an even chance to get out of town alive.

A rancher whirled about to face the stalls. To the other he whispered, "Somebody sneeze back there?"

"Thought I heard—"

His gun flew up. It cracked. Once. Twice. Again. His partner hurled four shots at a streaking black thing that looked fantastically like an immense black sail flying wild in a gale. Only four flashing black legs pronounced it at least part horse, and the whole wraithlike object disappeared behind another rear street building as suddenly as it had come from behind the stable of the bank.

A cry went up in the street. From the north rushed two ranchers afoot, guns ready, headed for the bank.

In a drive three buildings from Bartle's office, The Masked Rider touched his stallion gently with his heels. "North. Fast," he said, as if the animal would understand.

Gold Creek hummed behind him. Out of the tails of his eyes he saw men joining the eddy at the bank door. He was glad when the town lights were blotted out by distance and no threatening thud of hoofs sounded behind him.

LUKE WALLACE, WHO by agreement had superseded Pete Haskell as guiding hand of the ranchers, was equal to the occasion when guns behind the bank barked their obvious alarm and warning. He had expected the black phantom to attempt to leave by any route—save the front door. Yet from that exit, Wallace had not stirred.

With the first shot still ringing in his ears, Wallace stabbed the glass panel with his Colt; he stabbed it again and brought the jagged upper half down in a clinking shower. He rushed in, up the stairs, climbed over the twisted body and reached the landing prepared to kill or be killed for the cause he considered right.

That the room should be empty was beyond understanding—for a second. Then he ran to the open window, thrust out his head. His chin dropped. No black shrouded corpse on the ground? He glared at a white-haired man who was cramming bullets into empty chambers.

"So much practice nickin' two bit pieces on the wing an' you can't hit a coyote crawlin' out a window, Silver?"

The berated man looked up. "Said coyote moves quicker than

lead flies—an' he don't come out o' windows. Probably out long before you finished shoutin' how we was to take him. Probably be in Arizona before you make up yore mind what's next an' where it's at."

Wallace turned with a snort.

Pete Haskell was supervising the removal of the body from the stairs. "He's got an inch o' rope left yet, Wallace," announced Haskell thickly. "Sent Buck Andrews for some spirits. Might help this Easterner hold on an' tell us what happened here."

The liquor came. Haskell managed to work some of it down Clarke Weber's twitching throat. It had little effect. Clarke's lips quivered. So did his eyelids. Haskell tried more of the stimulant.

"B-Bartle," gasped Clarke. "The old—Steve Ransom farm. M-Masked Rider—"

"Yeah?" encouraged Haskell. "Outlaw goin' to the Ransom place?"

"To—to meet Bartle and—and show—"

"Papers? Books?"

"Y-yes. There's three—you—you got to get. Bartle. Outlaw. And—and a—" He never got as far as "Mexican Indian."

Haskell got up from his knees. He handed the partly filled glass to Wallace. "The gent has gone dry, Luke. In two ways. He'll do no more drinkin' or talkin'."

"What'd he say? I couldn't make out his whisper."

"Masked Rider gone to show those papers an' books to Bartle—at the old Ransom place."

"Provin' what I told you before—Masked Rider an' Bartle workin' hand in glove an' us cattlemen shoulderin' the blame. Well,—" He started down the stairs. "I'll wager both legs against a horned toad that if the outlaw goes to Ransom's ole place, it won't ever be hard to find him thereafter—'cause I'll put his name on the gravemarker myself."

Ranchers crowded around Wallace in the street. The news

was all the same and all bad. No one had seen the black phantom.

"All you men go to the valley," ordered Wallace. "Roust out every farmer. Bring 'em to Steve Ransom's old place. We're throwin' out a ring of guns that a polecat couldn't get through, *sabe?* With Bartle an' the outlaw on tree limbs, where we'll prove they belong, there'll be no more fence in Deep Water Valley."

The men scattered. Haskell and Tim Callan came down the stairs and stood beside Wallace.

"Reckon we ought to get Sheriff Lande, Wallace?" asked Haskell. "What's done at Ransom's would then be strictly legal, *sabe?*"

Wallace laughed sarcastically. "Yo're sure a sticker for law! There ain't anything more legal than a buzzard on a limb and proof of guilt in yore hands."

He strode off.

THE MASKED RIDER did not long head north, nor did he suddenly swerve east and enter the north end of the valley. His only reason was that that was what would be expected of him by any pursuers—of whom he had neither sight nor sound. It was his policy always to try and fathom out the other fellow's expectations and then do the opposite.

So it was that he did swerve east but expected to enter the valley at such a spot that promised a straight cut to the Weber-Maxon farm. But two miles out of Gold Creek he checked the stallion abruptly. Behind him, so faint that only his ears might have heard, came the cry of a mountain cat. He answered with a distinct knowledge that all was well in the valley. That information was in Blue Hawk's cry, as well as a suggestion they meet and talk. The outlaw waited.

Blue Hawk came, looked at the hooded one with harsh eyes. "I see what you do in town, *señor.* Bad! One day you try to fool too many men. Then?"

"*Si?* Then? Or maybe *pronto?*" He slid the black cloak aside to reveal Bartle's ledger. The ragged hole in the one cover was bored by a bullet that the thick book had stopped before penetration. "I expected no cowmen."

"I am delayed, *señor*. Not long. I am accused of murder done by the rat we seek."

"Sheriff?"

"*Sí*. He waits with posse at Pringle farm."

"But how did you get away?"

Blue Hawk touched the sorrel's neck. "We just ride, *señor*. But we must not go into valley again. Mebbe tomorrow. Not—"

"Tonight. *Now*. To the new Easterner's farm. Bartle's there. At dawn peace is on the valley again, and tonight the curse of Don Attero is on a crucifier. All men will know that it was he who killed and burned—for which he pays and in paying leaves the way open for cowmen to buy a legal route to sweet water."

Blue Hawk had always left the deeper thinking and planning to the outlaw. Legal things were beyond his scope. Now he could not have comprehended if he so desired. For all he heard was that The Masked Rider would enter the valley *now*.

"No, *señor!*" he implored. "Not now. Not by Easterner's farm. Pringle place is too near, *sabe?* Sheriff waits there. I do not know how many possemen are with him. You cannot—"

"Bartle might not wait. Besides, if Lande expects me at the Pringle place, why should he—well, let's hope he waits there. I ride, Blue Hawk. Follow behind. Cowmen in Gold Creek may pick up my sign and trail me. You figure time and distance. I want ten minutes in the Maxon house, *sabe?* Your job is to delay anybody who trails me now, for ten minutes."

"*Sabe, señor*. I do it without danger—if trailers are cowmen. Then?"

"Our job here is finished. We ride. We meet south of the valley. You will hear my call. *Adiós*."

"But, *señor!* The Easterner who knows we ride together? Never can we be safe again if one man lives who knows that—"

"His tongue is stiff, Blue Hawk. He made the same mistake twice. Sometimes one cannot shoot at a finger."

The outlaw's shoulders shrugged. He knew he could rely on Blue Hawk to follow his bidding. The Mexican Indian might disagree with his plan, but it was not for him to question.

The outlaw's knees pressed the stallion and like a black phantom he vanished into the darkness of the night.

CHAPTER XXIV

RINGED GUNS

RUSS BARTLE TASTED of hard work and quickly shied. Damned sight easier to make ledger entries than to change horse shoes. He did succeed in getting off those that branded him, buried them under the dirt floor of the wagon shed and gave no thanks to the unknown Mexican whom he cursed the harder because he was unknown.

But to continue his physical tortures? To put on new shoes of which he had located dozens that would serve in the pinch? Bartle mopped the perspiration from his torrid face. He went to the farmhouse to hire Chet Maxon to finish the job.

"Why didn't Clarke help you?" demanded Chet. "You two acted like old friends."

"He was in a hurry. He's gone to town. I'll give you five dollars for your trouble."

"I don't want your money. I'd put four shoes on for you—if I felt different about you."

"I did nothing to turn you against me, did I? Why—"

"You fell right in with Clarke. And I naturally don't like a man who purrs with one of his type. You also seemed to think I ought to go gunning for The Masked Rider. Outlaw, I'll grant you. Worse men have lived in the shelter of the law, pulling wool over other people's eyes. That is if all I've heard is true."

Bartle's heart began to gallop. Suspicion nicked him. Suddenly he wondered if—like himself—Chet Maxon hid behind a false front. Did he and Clarke have an understanding? Were they both possessed of information that could have his neck stretched? Were they going to bleed him first for all the money they could get—and then consign him to the hangman's noose?

"All you heard about what?" he asked nervously.

"The Masked Rider. The good things he'd done. Some men would never have met up with man-sized justice if he hadn't served it. I think he'll do as good a job here."

The landowner did not speak. He paced the kitchen anxiously for a while. His presence puzzled Chet; it annoyed him as much as it did Ellen, who was finishing the mixing of dough for tomorrow's bread. One way to get rid of the unwelcome guest! Put the shoes on his horse.

In a short while Chet returned to the house, "Done," he announced. "Ready to ride now."

Bartle shed the hint. He couldn't hide conglomerate fears any longer. With less real estate to his credit and less cash in a bank where it could not be touched until morning, he might have rushed out to his horse, ridden away and never ventured near Gold Creek again. But anchored wealth, greed, were stronger than stark terror. He paced faster now, looking out of the window, listening for the arrival of the man he feared as much as he feared the phantom in black and the Maxons.

"Why don't you go?" asked Ellen bluntly. "I thought you just wanted to have your horse's shoes changed."

"I decided to wait for Clarke."

Ellen's brows arched. "He said he was going to town permanently." She stepped into Bartle's path. "What have you two planned? Certainly there's something wrong with you. You act—"

"Clarke has to come back," snapped Bartle. "He's bringing me something."

"Something that can be used to squeeze money out of somebody?" insinuated Chet. "Ellen's right. There's some kind of a dirty deal on—and it won't be settled here. Get out."

The landowner did not move. The delay seemed part defiance, part fear.

"They are up to something!" cried Ellen. "If it happens here, we'll be held partly responsible, Chet! I'm going for the sheriff."

She was out of the parlor door in spite of both men's protest.

For half a minute Bartle stood paralyzed. Clarke soon due! Suppose the girl arrived with Sheriff Lande while he and Clarke debated! Lande would be intensely interested in knowing why tightfisted Bartle was willing to pay so much for The Masked Rider's delivery. Already Bartle condemned all his reasons as unconvincing. He glared at Chet.

"Stop her! If she rides away from this farm, I'll—"

He snatched his gun.

"You've convicted yourself, Bartle!" charged Chet. As if it didn't matter whether he reached it or not, he walked toward the table in the center of the room. The six-gun he had wrenched out of Clarke Weber's hand was in that drawer.

BARTLE FLUNG THE door open as a horse flashed by—his horse, for Ellen had not had time to saddle up if she could have accomplished the task. He leveled his gun leisurely, calmed his twitching nerves. He must not miss! His trigger finger tensed.

"Don't!" blared Chet.

Bartle wheeled. Instantly he fired. Chet floundered backward. Before he toppled he did get out two bullets. They kicked white puffs from the plaster wall over the landowner's shoulder.

All composure routed now, Bartle holstered his gun and dashed for the barn. No amount of real estate, nor millions in a bank could have held him in the house another minute. All he asked of life now was a swift horse—and he had his fearful doubts about getting it, long before he reached for the sliding bolt on the barn door.

A great black shadow fell on the door as he tugged at it. A cry came from his dry lips. He tried to turn around. Like a hangman's hood, a sombre *mantilla* settled over his head as if he were a bull in a ring and some toreador taunted him.

A muscular arm bent around his neck, held him half stifled while another hand snatched away his gun. Suddenly as it had fallen upon him, the black cloak was pulled away. Though he turned face about in convulsive terror, the same cloth was tight about The Masked Rider's lithe body. Only Bartle's own gun, nose poking out from the *mantilla's* joint, broke the symphony in black.

"Back into the house," commanded the outlaw. "Move! Surprise me none to find you've drilled another unarmed man. I know I heard three shots a while back."

"It was fair fight," protested Bartle. "He fired—"

"So will I, if you don't start for that house!"

Bartle walked. He stopped, hope reborn. "The girl's gone to fetch Sheriff Lande! You're risking your life here!"

"No compliment that you're worried about my health. Lande might come—if you're not a liar. But I suspect there'll be very little for him to do after I leave. Get going."

They were soon inside. The bleeding man on the floor made the outlaw's eyes slots of venom. "Fair fight," he squeezed between his teeth. "Born Westerner who cut his teeth on the butt of an old Colt. Easterner maybe feeling his first six-gun. Fair fight!"

"He—"

"Yes, he still breathes." The Masked Rider prodded Bartle with the gun. "Bring him out of that sleep. Quick! I want a witness to what I'm going to say."

Bartle gazed around the kitchen. The best remedy his tottering brain registered was the water bucket. He started for it, hands trembling, knees weak.

"That chest in the wall!" snapped the outlaw. "Believe in that sign. It says 'Medicine.'"

The landowner swung the small door absent-mindedly. Why didn't Clarke come? Or the sheriff? Why didn't somebody come? He twisted the glass stopper from three bottles before he thought he held one partly full of something that might help.

The Masked Rider curbed his anger. Blue Hawk would hold

the cowmen—if they were in pursuit. That the girl who had raced by him in the night was really going to Gold Creek was apparent by the direction in which she rode. Futile ride. The outlaw had Blue Hawk's word that Lande was on guard at the Pringle place. He watched Bartle like a cat watches a mouse.

LUKE WALLACE WAS in the vanguard of the ranchers riding the Valley Trail. Close behind him Pete Haskell and Tim Callan rode in a better frame of mind than they had been for several weeks. Bringing up the rear was a long line of cowmen that grew shorter and shorter as time and distance went by. They were dropping out of the grim caravan in pairs and trios, heading across the valley with their messages of truce and good news, rousing out tobacco men with pleas for cooperation.

"Rather have the punchers from our own spreads," said Callan sourly.

Haskell's grin was the first in weeks. "Luke's got the bit between his teeth. Best let him run himself out o' wind. He'll stop then an' yield to harness. Farmers or punchers, there's enough of us to more than handle anything that pops."

"You think the outlaw deserves what he's sure enough going to get?"

"I do—if he's in cahoots with Bartle an' those books an' papers tell us anything. Otherwise—"

"What's Luke howling about?" Callan spurred ahead.

The three veterans of the range were soon side by side—gaping at the strangest sight any of them ever beheld.

Full in the moonlight beside a towering tree, a Mexican Indian sat upon a sleek sorrel. For all they moved, both might have been mistaken for the work of some insane sculptor who carved, colored, then went his crazy way. But this was no ordinary rider and horse. He appeared armless—because his hands were tied behind his back. There was a gag in his mouth, a noose about his neck and the end of the rope was tied around the trunk of the tree—after it passed over a thick limb.

Haskell was first to realize what would happen if the sorrel was minded to bolt. He went forward cautiously and with one slice of his jack knife he severed the rope close to the tree. In half a minute the Indian was thankfully free.

"*Gracias, señor!* You save my life. I say many prayers for you when—"

"But while I'm alive, tell me what in hell happened."

"I am at rest from hard riding. I wake. I see man who digs. I go by him. Mebbe I am of help, *sabe?* He is very mad. He do to me as you see when first you come. He say first thing I am learning in hell is to mind my own business."

Wallace took charge of the situation. "Who was this *hombre?*" he demanded suspiciously.

The Indian shrugged. "Who knows? I am worth mebbe a fortune when I can say who is behind the black mask and *mantilla.*"

"What I thought!" exclaimed Wallace. "Buried those papers and books! Now we'll find out what was so important an'—where's the caché, *amigo?*"

Blue Hawk pointed west. "Come. I show you. Never can I forget!" A mile would more than suffice, he figured. A man can change his mind about never forgetting. He would be very sorry. Ten minutes The Masked Rider requested. He had much more already.

"It was west, *señor.* Come, I show you."

Haskell did not follow the Indian. "Reckon I'd best ride on to the Maxon place, Luke? The men'll be there with no one to take charge."

"Yeah. You an' Tim go on. I'll fetch this truck *pronto.* Keep everybody clear of the Maxon farm till I arrive. We mustn't scare these buzzards away before we're ready to jump 'em, *sabe?*"

Blue Hawk started away. He did not worry about the pair now galloping on the Maxon place. The Masked Rider had evidently departed before they started for the farm. Sounds to the north! He glanced there. Farmers, ranchers! All headed toward the Maxon place. *"Madre de Dios!"* muttered Blue Hawk. "If the *señor* has not gone away from that place—"

He stopped, looking about him with the gaze of a man who knows he is lost. *"Señor,"* he said to Wallace, "the caché is mebbe more far than I think. I know it is by small aspens. Them I do not see here."

Wallace fumed. He let the Mexican lead him on a short way. He wished he could have been in two places simultaneously. Had he the slightest suspicion about the Indian he would have tried to choke a confession of trickery from the dark-skinned one. But the first glimpse of Blue Hawk was still fresh in mind. That was no prearranged scene. He felt so certain of its genuineness that it never entered his mind to question it.

"Look!" he snapped. "I'll send men to help you. I got to get on to Maxon's."

"Si, señor!" Blue Hawk sighed. He would be glad to get away from the valley—and Don Attero's cross. He wanted once again to ride the lone trail—by the side of his master.

CHAPTER XXV

DEATH'S LAIR

THE MASKED RIDER nudged Bartle's thigh with a boot. Ten minutes he had ordered! Chet gave no sign of coming back to consciousness.

"Get up, Bartle. Pains me to leave the kid that way, but this place isn't the healthiest resort I know of—for me."

The landowner wondered if by some miracle he was to gain a permanent respite. Certainly the outlaw's voice had lost its sting. He got up, stood dry-washing his hands and hoping—until a bullet-plugged ledger slammed on the table. He watched with darting eyes as papers followed the book and his own six-gun served as a paper weight.

The black phantom opened the ledger. His gloved finger was beside…. "Steve Ransom. Deceased." He stared at Bartle. "Well?" he demanded.

"Beef men killed Steve. His wife sold me the place. There's nothing wrong in—"

"Sam Aldman on Don Attero's cross. His dad dead beside their burning shed—drilled though he was unarmed. Beef men?"

"Y-yes. I—I suspected—"

"Bad business, this suspecting. I never do. *Find out, sabe?*" For a few seconds his eyes, fiery through the hood's slots, bored into Bartle's like gimlets. Then with motions smooth and swift, his hands shifted. A horseshoe clanged on the zinc-topped table. He said nothing. His jaws were rigidly set.

"W-what about that?" whined Bartle.

"Yours!"

"No!"

"Yes—and if you hadn't left tools all over the wagon shed floor, if I hadn't heard you speaking about shoes to the other Easterner, I might have gotten in here in time to prevent your drilling that kid."

"That shoe was never—"

"Made to hang on the horizontal beam of Don Attero's cross—like tobacco stalks hung with Sam Aldman? Maybe not. They *will*. With you taking Sam's place!"

Bartle's blood became iced water. His face was as white as the floured loaves Ellen had set near the stove. "You wouldn't crucify an innocent man!" he gasped. "You prove nothing against me. You—"

The figure on the floor stirred. The Masked Rider was on his knees before Chef's effort to sit up resulted in failure.

"Easy, boy," counseled the outlaw. "Plenty help coming *pronto*—for you. All I've got time to do is help you to that couch in the next room. Then I've got to vamoose—with your company. Looks like we've got to finish our pow-wow—at Don Attero's cross. Not all of it will be tongue waggin', by God!"

With the air of a black cloaked arm steadying him from behind, Chet managed to get up. He knew why he was alive, why the *coup de grâce* had not been administered. "Thanks," he said to the outlaw. "You'd better ride, now. Ellen's bringing Sheriff Lande."

"I'll be many miles from here before she discovers that Lande isn't in Gold Creek. That he's—"

Another man would have left the wounded to shift for himself. But at the first sound of an approaching horse, the black outlaw reached out, dragged over a chair, dropped Chet into it. There were no eyes keen enough to say where or when one motion ended and the next began. It was done too smoothly, too swift—for facing suddenly were *two* menaces. For Bartle had seen his golden opportunity and he knew there would never be another.

In that second when the voices outside were heard and that next heart-beat when both the outlaw's hands were occupied, he swooped upon his gun that lay unguarded on the pile of papers. Here was Lady Luck's broadest smile—for him. Kill the outlaw. Finish Chet. What Sheriff could doubt that he had served the law well—killing an outlaw a moment after Chet had died in the same attempt! Bartle felt that even Ellen would believe. He would make it plain to her that The Masked Rider had come to retaliate for Clarke's efforts to trap him.

MEN DO NOT speak when success, fortune, life itself depends on a few ticks of a clock. Bartle grabbed the weapon. It came away from the ledger booming and blazing. Twice it blared its message of death. Two holes showed in the outlaw's wide spread cloak. Then from the folded edges of that sombre black cloth leaped one finger of flame. The landowner pitched forward on his face.

Before Bartle's head thudded on the floor, The Masked Rider had moved decisively—once to puff out the lamp, again to drop the heavy bar across the kitchen door, again to tear through a dark parlor and barricade that last entrance. Walking back to the kitchen with two Colts ready, he caught the disturbing sounds of many horsemen entering the farmyard.

"You should've gone," wheezed Chet in pain. "Now—"

"Yes," agreed the outlaw in a calm whisper. "Reckon you're right. *Now.* It had to be some time. Glad I got him first—and that I'll have my boots on."

He waited, his nerves serene, although in gun smoke and darkness he felt death coming toward him with its clammy hand outstretched to tap his shoulder.

SHERIFF LANDE AND two of his men had been drawn by the shot that chewed into Chet Maxon's chest; the shot they had heard just as another of their men hailed them and escorted forth a girl who had been saved from a futile ride to Gold Creek when she stumbled upon him.

On the verge of bursting into the house, Lande had seen Luke Wallace and many ranchers moving down upon the Maxon farm. He withdrew from the house, hearing three shots within.

"You three men stand guard. Hell knows what's happened in there. Don't let Bartle out."

Angrily he went to meet the cowmen. Ellen Maxon rode beside him, sobs and fears racking her.

"Bartle here?" asked Luke Wallace.

"Yes," volunteered Ellen. "He—"

"Masked Rider?"

Lande stiffened. "By gee, then I did see a black Stetson just a second before the light went out."

For Ellen, the news was the last straw. The three shots heard as she and the sheriff approached the house still rang in her ears. Bolstered first by thoughts that Chet could take care of himself, now she went suddenly to pieces. She recalled one demonstration of the black outlaw's speed and skill. Surrounded by grim-faced men who appeared capable of doing anything except save her brother's life, she gave way to hysterics.

"Guess we've clinched that the outlaw an' Bartle are in cahoots," snapped Wallace. "Anyhow both of 'em are here an'—"

"So am I," cut in Lande, grasping Wallace's unspoken ideas that the death of the pair was the one thing now desired. "I aim to take 'em alive—if possible, *sabe?*"

"If not?"

"I'm askin' 'em to come out peacefully an' empty-handed. Refusing, we'll surround the house—an' drive 'em out with a lead shower."

Ellen gasped. "You can't open fire on that house. My brother's in there. There's still a chance—that—that—"

Lande tried to comfort her. It was vain. "None of us could get near the house, miss. Ain't nothin' we can do except—"

"Let me go in. I want to know what's happened to Chet. I'll—I'll—" She gripped Lande's arm. Fear and hurt were gone from her eyes. Now they were hard, cold, although still swimming in tears. "Let me go in alone. Perhaps I can hold their attention and give you men time to—"

"You mean trick the outlaw?" sneered Wallace. "Or Bartle? No, ma'am. Such coyotes ain't trickable, *sabe?*"

Ellen had no reply. But suddenly she turned and ran toward the house. With every determined stride her anger mounted, until, when she reached the cellar steps, she was resolved that no matter what else she accomplished, no matter what she found, she would deliver Bartle and the outlaw to the law, for she felt that these ranchers must have ample reason to say that they were in cahoots—equally responsible for what had happened in the valley—and in the house!

Wallace saw a new obstacle to his hopes that a bullet-riddled house and two corpses would forever clear up the mysteries of the valley atrocities—and always give cattle a clear route to sweet water. He cupped his hands about his mouth and shouted:

"Five minutes, ma'am! Then you an' yore brother have to be in the cellar out of the way o' lead, *sabe?* Come seventy hells, neither the outlaw nor Bartle get out of that house alive."

He looked over his men, glad of the great number of farmers armed with shotguns and rifles. Looked like his scouts had missed few farms.

Lande took charge of the miniature army. He began to toll off men and order them to stations, until, when finished, he had the house so surrounded that Wallace's promise was fulfilled—it did seem impossible for even a polecat to get away unriddled.

THE MASKED RIDER was aware of the impenetrable ring around the house. It did not quail him. Never had he expected that his end would be different from any other outlaw's. The law would win. It might as well take the jackpot now. Yet he was not the man to smile and bid death tag him, to sit and wait for the law to claim its own. When it moved to take him he would do his best to side-step it. Courage lifted his spirits. He would get out of this house ringed by death! He hoped to do it without harming any man with whom he had no quarrel. How, he did not know.

The knob of the cellar door that opened into the kitchen twisted slowly. Few things went unseen by the outlaw. He looked at the door.

"It's not locked, ma'am," he called smoothly.

Ellen entered timidly. All she spared the outlaw was a fleeting glance. Then she ran to her bleeding brother with a choked cry.

His chest wound made her whirl, loathing eyes upon the hooded man. "You beast! And once I said you were generous! Thank God that tonight marks your finish. I hope you—"

Chet gripped her hand. "You don't understand, Ellen. *Bartle* was too fast for me. I'd be dead now, I'm sure, if The Masked Rider hadn't come."

The girl's mouth stood agape. "You didn't—"

"No ma'am, *I* didn't. Bartle obliged. I only told him how to keep your brother from bleeding to death. His dad ruined a fine doctor when he made Russ a—a farm dealer, shall we say?"

Ellen's eyes avoided him. "And I helped to get you into this—this corner. I brought Sheriff Lande and all his men."

The outlaw's laugh was cold and bitter. "Why regret, ma'am? It takes only one bullet to kill a man—sometimes. Haskell and those ranchers and farmers could supply that one—and you didn't bring them. The honors are mine."

She heard very little of his talk. "What can we do? How can we—"

"Help me?" The outlaw pointed to the ledger, the papers, the horseshoe. "Give those to Sheriff Lande—later. They say that Bartle was the man behind the things that happened here. The dead do not deny—nor do they sell land to be fenced where it shouldn't be. Bartle has no kin. The state gets his holdings. The state will auction off the north end of the valley, and knowing cattlemen as I do, I think Pete Haskell will see that his crowd buys. So peace comes again to Deep Water Valley—as Don Attero wanted."

"But *you*. Here! And outside—"

The booming voice of Luke Wallace rang out.

"Time, ma'am! We're set for business."

The outlaw picked Chet up as if he were a stripling. "Business to that *hombre* means lead, ma'am. You and your brother will be safe in the cellar."

He was soon up again from the musty basement. *"Adiós,"* he called. He closed the door and bolted it on a stifled sob that came from below.

CHAPTER XXVII

RETREAT

S HERIFF LANDE WAS born without a trace of cowardice and he had not deteriorated with age. Yet he allowed no more than a few inches of himself to show beyond the tree trunk.

"Both o' you *hombres* got exactly two minutes to come out o' that house, reachin' for the moon. Failin', we'll come an' get you."

He drew a six-gun and a thick, battered watch. Holding it at nose-end he watched the second hand jerk twice around the smaller dial. The house was weirdly silent; the doors were still closed tight, the windows still dark. Lande had no liking for six-gun justice even when it was compulsory. But without hesitation he set himself to fire the signal shot that would send men closing in on the house with blazing weapons. His trigger-finger came halfway back. It went dead. His eyes threatened to pop from their sockets.

On his left, between barn and hen coop, streaked a horseman bent double, clad in black, with the wind filling his *mantilla* out stiff as the sail of a yacht.

The sheriff drowned his own warning cry with three shots at the flying phantom that was now darting from hen coop to drying shed.

Wallace saw the fleeting thing. He yelled, fired as a host of guns swung and anxious fingers danced on triggers while rancher and farmer alike waited for the target to show again.

The black splotch shot out from behind the long shed. Six-gun, rifle, shotgun boomed in concert. The black rider almost pitched from his saddle. No man who saw that lurch could think otherwise than that death had had a victim at its finger tips but had let him slip away.

Three hundred feet from the end of the drying shed, the land dipped sharply. Down that incline, racing the grim reaper, flashed the black rider. Guns abruptly ceased spitting fire and lead.

Wallace was first to his horse. "After him!" he bellowed excitedly. He spotted Lande still standing by the tree. "You comin'?"

"Take every man you brought," snapped the Sheriff. "I'm stayin' here. *Bartle* won't get away."

Men eager for the chase crowded around Wallace awaiting his lead. He snorted, swung his horse, spurred away. Sheriff Lande looked after the rushing men strung out behind the old leader. He had seen the black outlaw act as if mortally wounded once before. He suspected that before the last of Wallace's men disappeared down that incline the outlaw would be well on his way to safety.

"How in hell he got out o' that house will sure enough keep me awake many nights. Unless—"

He tensed. His gun came up. For a moment he thought he was seeing what couldn't be. But no! The kitchen door *was* opening. He trained his weapon on it. Was Bartle attempting a dash?

"Sheriff!" called Ellen as if to warn it was she. "Sheriff! Quick!" She threw the door wide open and ran out.

Lande caught the alarm in her voice. So did his men who were stationed on that side of the house. The sheriff was well in the lead of running men ready for anything—except what happened.

A shot rang out. A man yelled. Lande turned abruptly, raced around to the other side of the house where two guns now boomed. He saw nothing.

"The Masked Rider," exclaimed the possemen in chorus.

Lande was speechless. Not for long. He flashed about with an oath. "One of 'em was Bartle, I'll be—"

"Bartle's on the kitchen floor—dead," cried Ellen, "When the outlaw went, I—"

"Which one?" growled Lande.

"The one that Wallace went after. There was only one in the house. He— went out a window when— Good Heavens! Didn't you see that?"

"Yeah!" snorted Lande. "No wonder he slipped out under our noses! Too many men; too damned much palaver and—"

He let it hang and pushed into the house as if he suspected Bartle might arise and also get away.

THE MASKED RIDER raced through the night with teeth clenched against pain. He felt the blood flowing down his arm, into his glove. It went unheeded. More important things held every atom of his attention; the thunder of horsemen galloping far ahead—and the knowledge that they pursued a man who had obviously lured them into this chase only to save him.

"Burr Aldman!" the outlaw told himself. "Who else would have the idea—and the guts?"

He flew on, the great stallion needing no quirt or spur. With Wallace's band in sight, the outlaw turned sharply left, gave his horse free rein and knew, when he doubled back again, that he must be between hunted and hunters. Again he complimented Burr's fortitude. Who else could cling to saddle so long when so badly wounded; who could leave Wallace's hungry band so far behind?

Then ahead, as if he rode down upon his own shadow, The Masked Rider sighted his twin. The stallion seemed to take offense. It made short shrift of closing the gap between genuine and impostor. None too soon! For Burr had shot his bolt. He reeled in the saddle and would have toppled beneath flying hoofs had not the outlaw's arm flashed out to pick him out of leather like a train takes mail on the fly. Before The Masked Rider could check the stallion's headlong flight he knew that *three* rode the one gallant horse. Death was also in his arms.

He quickly sought out a niche between high shafts of rock. Dismounting, he propped Burr up, stood guard and watched

Wallace's men thunder by in a muddy shower. Then he knelt beside the moaning youth, a lump of bitterness in his throat going down hard when he realized how short the span of Burr's life. He took off a glove and gripped the kid's quivering hand.

"Thanks, boy. I know of only one other who'd have done as much for me—and he's a man."

Burr's lips stretched in a smile. "A beef man came an'—an' asked if—if anybody from our farm would join up to—to help get Bartle—an' you. I guess he didn't know I—I was the last Aldman. But I knew—when he told me that everything would be all right in the valley forever. I knew *you'd* fixed it an' I—I wasn't goin' to let 'em drill you without doin' something about it."

"*Sabe,*" gulped the outlaw. "Reckon you didn't figure that some things we do cost too much."

The kid squeezed The Masked Rider's hand. "Ain't costin' me much. I—I been to Doc Seely twice. He—he kinda hinted that the first dose o' lead I got wouldn't ever let me be more than half man. I didn't want to—to live that way. I'd rather be—be...."

The outlaw stood up. Sand trickled from his fingers upon the dead kid's boots. "*Adiós,*" he said in a reverent whisper. More would not come.

He walked into the moonlight with slow and heavy steps. Then he suddenly shook off the feeling of bereavement for close and clear came the cry of a mountain lion. He answered speedily.

"The farm girl, *señor!* She comes. See? On ridge."

"No harm. You ride. I'll wait. If she hadn't called Lande and all but two of his men to the kitchen door, I don't think she'd have had to ride far to see me."

"*Sí.* I go."

The outlaw was prepared for the manner in which the girl approached him. He knew that his sinister hood and cloak no longer held any terrors for her. "Yes, ma'am?"

"I couldn't let you ride off without thanking you and asking if you wouldn't like to—to stay with Chet and me."

His short laugh was alive with the bitterness, the loneliness of the outlaw trail. "You know the answer, ma'am. Impossible."

"But every one says that without the—the hood and the cloak, you're unknown. You'd trust *us,* wouldn't you?"

"Yes, you and your brother. But some day, someone that may have known me when—"

"When you weren't what you are? The good you've done must over-balance the past. The law—"

"Never forgets—the things it once chalks up against a man." He held out his gloved hand. *"Adiós,* ma'am. I'm riding. Some day I reckon I *will* settle down. Rope or lead will probably give me no choice about doing that. Until then—" He swung himself into the saddle, looked off into the night. "Until then—*quién sabe?"* He was off.

Not even a sob could make him look back. As though they were one, black horse and rider melted in the night.

JAY J. KALEZ

S OME THIRTY-THREE YEARS ago, old Doc Richter pulled
his team of bays up in front of our house, tossed the reins
to my dad and did a sprint for our front porch. An hour or so
later Doc's job was finished, dad was wearing a grin as wide as
a corral gate and the male population of Spokane County had
been increased by one. That's the start of everything as far as I
am concerned.

I grew up near the town of Spokane, Washington, remember
when curbstones started to take the place of barb-wire fences
and when names like Harry Tracy and Frank Merrill were used
to scare us kids into coming home at dark in place of the bogey
man.

So passed a lot of years, then filled with seeming hardships
as a youngster upon my dad's ranch; now transformed to trea-
sured memories as a cooped-up city dweller. Then came the
War.

As for schooling, I've not much to brag about, so the less
said the better. Enough that my ambition leaned toward some
day stepping into old Doc Richter's shoes, so, in the spring of
1917, I turned all my worldly possessions into cash and started
for Seattle to enter the State University for my pre-medical
course. Here coincidence gave me my boot out into the world.
Out on the range the war was still just camp talk, but in Seattle, sight of thousands of men in uniform made me realize it

was real. Also sight of my first sea-going vessel made me realize a lot more. I enlisted in the Navy.

I was in the service from the spring of 1917 until the fall of 1919. During that time I was transferred to a radio school and gained a radio electrician's rating. As such I served on a freighter, a destroyer, a mine sweeper and last upon a transport. I made a number of trips to France, and as New York was our home port I even began to feel at home there.

Returning home after the War I found that my dad's ranch had fallen to the lure of irrigation ditches and acre tracts. A month and I was back in Seattle signing on as a commercial radio operator. For three years I took in the world, making every port worthy of mention from Singapore to Sydney. Finally I returned to the United States and started taking in the home scenery. Down in a little town in Wyoming I met the one girl. I was married in 1925 and returned to Spokane.

Things weren't going so well for me financially when one day I chanced to read of a contest offering cash prizes for war experiences. I wrote a personal war incident, won a prize and took the writing fever. I've had it ever since.

I've had a hundred or more stories published in darn near as many magazines, and hope I can keep on making the editors think my stuff has a cash value. They're a great bunch of fellows, those editors. They give a fellow his living and write you letters as if you're doing them a favor by allowing them the privilege of continuing.

Guess that's about all, readers. Suppose I've had a few exciting things happen in my meandering, but out in this country it's not considered good form to talk about what happened to yourself.

There are always too many other people within pointing distance who could open up with a tale that would make yours sound like a nursery rime.

JAY J. KALEZ

WHEN PEOPLE COME into the office with little bundles of manuscripts under their arms and pale looks on their faces and tell us they are authors, we always ask them a question: "Where have you been? What did you do before you took to pen-pushing?" We ask them that because we have a theory. We believe that no chap, no matter how clever, can turn out a yarn with real guts unless he knows what he is writing about.

We've tried out our pet belief—and it works. So, when the author has lived a simple, homey life, we show him to the door, tell him to quit writing adventure stories and try articles on bringing up children or growing gladiolus. We don't want his stories about bold, bad men. And, when he thinks about it, he realizes he doesn't really like to write them.

But… when a gent comes in with tan browning his face, and windburn sharpening his lean features… and when he opens with: "Once, when I was in Bangkok…" or: "That time I got throwed by a blind bucker…." Well, guess the answer.

We have a lot of those boys turning out tales for *Action Stories*. And when they write you can jolly well know you're getting the real stuff. Take Jay J. Kalez—you've read his yarns. Want to see why they are so good?

Here's what Mr. Kalez told us of himself:

A cattle ranch up in the panhandle of Idaho was my stamping grounds for about my first eighteen years of claimed existence. Education, I haven't much to brag about, although through the kindheartedness of railroad men that allowed me to hitch my cayuse under the station platform and hook freights the thirty miles to and back from town each day, I managed to get through high-school.

Two years ridin' for a stake and in the spring of 1917 I came in off the spring roundup and again hopped the old freight for Seattle and a try at the university. There I saw my first ship and incidentally learned there was a war on.

I enlisted in the navy, was shipped to the Harvard radio school and six weeks later was at sea on a mine sweeper bound for France. Saw service on transports and destroyers through the war and later submarine service in Panama.

An injury at sea in 1920 finished my navy cruise and after being patched up I again went to sea as a commercial operator. Saw most of the world the next four years as a tramp operator on every kind of packet from cattle boat out of Rio to blue ribbon world cruise on so-called floating palaces.

Coming home on a visit in 1926 I signed up with an outfit bringing a herd of blooded stock up from Wyoming, just to see if I'd forgotten critter nursing. Then it happened. I met the only girl out there in Wyoming and she didn't happen to be sea going. We came to Spokane, Washington, I got a job on a newspaper and started writing for a living. One thing led to another and here I am still pounding a typewriter.

JAY J. KALEZ.

www.ingramcontent.com/pod-product-compliance
Lightning Source LLC
Chambersburg PA
CBHW070804030726
47504CB00003B/690